THE GOOD SOLDIER

FORD MADOX FORD was born Ford Hermann Hueffer in London in 1873. His father, Dr Francis Hueffer, was an immigrant German writer, and music critic of *The Times*, and his maternal grandfather was the Pre-Raphaelite painter Ford Madox Brown. Born and bred an artist, Ford published his first book at the age of 17, under the name Ford Madox Hueffer. In 1919, after serving three and a half years in the British Army during the Great War, Ford dropped out of the London literary scene and changed his name to Ford Madox Ford; soon he moved to his beloved France. In all he produced some eighty volumes of fiction, poetry, reminiscence, biography, history, essays, travel writing, and literary and art criticism, and over four hundred magazine articles. He was the intimate friend and collaborator of Joseph Conrad, and knew well such contemporaries as H. G. Wells, D. H. Lawrence, Ezra Pound, James Joyce, and the American poet William Carlos Williams. He was founder and editor of both the *English Review* and the *Transatlantic Review*, but his greatest achievement lay in the novel, particularly in his undisputed modern masterpieces, *The Good Soldier* (1915) and the Tietjens tetralogy *Parade's End* (1924–8).

Ford early married Elsie Martindale and had by her two daughters. Never divorced, he subsequently had lengthy liaisons with three other women who all took his name: the novelist Violet Hunt, and the artists Stella Bowen (by whom he had a daughter) and Janice Biala. Ford died in Deauville, France, in 1939.

THOMAS C. MOSER is Professor of English at Stanford University. He is the author of *Joseph Conrad: Achievement and Decline* (1957) and *The Life in the Fiction of Ford Madox Ford* (1981). He is also the editor of *Wuthering Heights: Text, Sources, Criticism* (1962) and the Norton Critical Edition of *Lord Jim* (1968).

D0047630

THE WORLD'S CLASSICS

FORD MADOX FORD

The Good Soldier
A Tale of Passion

Edited with an Introduction by
THOMAS C. MOSER

Oxford   New York

OXFORD UNIVERSITY PRESS

Oxford University Press, Walton Street, Oxford OX2 6DP

Oxford New York Toronto
Delhi Bombay Calcutta Madras Karachi
Petaling Jaya Singapore Hong Kong Tokyo
Nairobi Dar es Salaam Cape Town
Melbourne Auckland

and associated companies in
Berlin Ibadan

Oxford is a trade mark of Oxford University Press

Introduction, Note on the Text, Select Bibliography,
Chronology, and Explanatory Notes © Thomas C. Moser 1990

First published as a World's Classics paperback 1990
Reprinted 1992

British Library Cataloguing in Publication Data

Ford, Ford Madox, 1873–1939
The good soldier: a tale of passion.
(The world's classics)
I. Title
823'.912 [F]

ISBN 0–19–282581–X

Library of Congress Cataloging in Publication Data

Ford, Ford Madox, 1873–1939.
The good soldier: a tale of passion
Ford Madox Ford: edited with an
introduction by Thomas C. Moser.
p.   cm. — (The World's classics)
Includes bibliographical references.
I. Moser, Thomas C.   II. Title.   III. Series.
PR6011.053G5 1990 823'.912-dc20 89-22810

ISBN 0–19–282581–X

Printed in Great Britain by
BPCC Hazells Ltd
Aylesbury, Bucks.

CONTENTS

Acknowledgements   vi

Introduction   vii

Note on the Text   xxviii

Select Bibliography   xxxvii

A Chronology of Ford Madox Ford   xl

Dedicatory Letter to Stella Ford   I

THE GOOD SOLDIER   7

Explanatory Notes   295

ACKNOWLEDGEMENTS

MANY people helped with this edition. In the matter of printed texts and manuscripts, I wish to thank William McPheron and Michael Ryan of Stanford University Library and James Tyler of Cornell University Library. Again at Stanford, I am grateful, for advice and support, to Albert and Barbara Gelpi, Albert and Maclin Guerard, Meg Minto, and Ruth and Ian Watt. I am also indebted, for useful information, to Maryann De Julio, C. Ruth Sabol, Todd Bender, and Joseph Wiesenfarth.

Special thanks are due to the following: George Brown, for his invaluable help with Latin passages; Mia Manzulli, for her voluntary and arduous work on collating texts and doing the initial research for the Notes; Judith Luna, of the Oxford University Press, for her wise and precise counsel on the whole project. My greatest debt is to my wife, Joyce Penn Moser, who not only did much of the final annotation but was also deeply involved in every aspect of this edition.

INTRODUCTION

MORE than a half-century after Ford's death and three-quarters of a century after the book's publication, *The Good Soldier* remains the most elusive of modern impressionist masterpieces. Indeed, it is more controversial than such notoriously problematic novels as Conrad's *Lord Jim*, James's *The Ambassadors*, Woolf's *The Waves*, and Faulkner's *Absalom, Absalom!* Even its most ardent admirers disagree strongly about basic questions: the subject (idealism, passion, knowledge?), the narrative voice (honest, deluded, dishonest?), the protagonist's character (good soldier, knave, fool?). Graham Greene, a lifelong advocate of *The Good Soldier*, suggests that the source of the novel's mysterious power may lie in Ford's biography: 'A novelist is not a vegetable absorbing nourishment mechanically from soil and air: material is not easily or painlessly gained, and one cannot help wondering what agonies of frustration and error lay behind *The Good Soldier*.'[1]

I

Ford says in his 1927 dedicatory letter to *The Good Soldier* that he wanted to call it 'The Saddest Story'. Indeed, his publisher so advertised it. That discarded title and the actual subtitle, 'A Tale of Passion', are equally applicable to the story of Ford's life. He was of mixed and unusual parentage. Born in London in 1873 and originally named Ford Hermann Hueffer, he was the first child of a scholarly German

[1] Introduction, *The Bodley Head Ford Madox Ford*, 1962, I, 12. The materials on Ford's life and his impressionistic method discussed in this World's Classics introduction are more fully documented in my book *The Life in the Fiction of Ford Madox Ford*, 1981. For further biographical information, see Arthur Mizener, *The Saddest Story: a Biography of Ford Madox Ford*, 1971. Critics named in this Introduction but not footnoted may be located in the Bibliography of this World's Classics edition.

father, Francis Hueffer, music critic for *The Times* and authority on Provençal love poetry, and of a beautiful, artistic mother, Catherine Madox Brown, daughter of the Pre-Raphaelite painter Ford Madox Brown. Ford's father died suddenly of a heart attack in 1889, leaving his family hard up and dashing all hopes of university education for his children. Three years later, to please rich German relatives, Ford joined the Roman Catholic Church in Paris; on the occasion he took the additional names Joseph Leopold. Nevertheless, out of his great love for his maternal grandfather, he published his books, starting when he was 17, under the name Ford H. Madox Hueffer. (He did not become Ford Madox Ford until 1919.)

In 1894 Ford married, in secret and against her family's furious opposition, his childhood sweetheart Elsie Martindale. He was 20; she, 17. Four years later, after reconciliation with the Martindales and the birth of a daughter, Ford had the greatest experience of his literary life: he met Joseph Conrad. The latter was also recently married and a new father; but unlike Ford, he was already a noted novelist. The two instantly became intimate friends and literary collaborators. Ford adored Conrad, elicited from him two excellent memoirs, supplied him with ideas for stories, loaned him money, and generally waited upon his older and much more distinguished friend. The two families saw much of each other. Conrad obviously appreciated Ford's pretty young wife; Jessie Conrad, however, disliked Ford.

Although Ford's marriage was relatively happy for a while, the pattern of his romantic involvements soon revealed itself. About 1903 he fell in love with his wife's sister, Mary Martindale. At some point, their affair was discovered; in 1904 Ford suffered a severe nervous breakdown. It lasted several years, and nervous illnesses recurred throughout his life. Specifically, he suffered from agoraphobia; Ford and others have eloquently described the debilitating terror he felt in the New Forest, on the desolate Salisbury Plain, and in deserted London streets. In early August 1904 (that crucial moment in *The Good Soldier*) Ford went to Germany for four months, taking various cures at Rhineland spas. The year 1905 saw him considerably better, thanks to the critical success of *The Soul of London* and to a second important friendship. The new friend was Arthur Pierson Marwood, a blond, handsome, Tory country gentleman of brilliant mind and ancient Yorkshire lineage. He was also a permanent invalid, married to a strong, capable woman who had been his nurse. (Caroline Marwood presumably contributed something to the character of Leonora Ashburnham.) Marwood quickly became a close friend of Conrad as well; the three men were near neighbours in southern Kent. It was in this period that Ford dedicated to Conrad and Marwood the first and last volumes of his trilogy of historical novels about Henry VIII's wife, Katharine Howard. *The Fifth Queen* and its sequels were Ford's most serious fictions prior to *The Good Soldier*.

In 1908 Ford founded a wonderful literary journal, the *English Review*, with Conrad as a chief contributor and Marwood as both business manager and principal financial backer. Within a year, however, the arrangement had taken a disastrous turn. First, Elsie Hueffer accused Marwood of having made improper sexual overtures to her. Ford chastised Marwood; Conrad sided with Marwood; both friends broke off relations with Ford. Then Ford once again fell in love; he left his wife for a glamorous, rather notorious, but socially well-connected novelist, Violet Hunt. She was nine years his senior and the daughter of a Pre-Raphaelite artist. Ford asked for a divorce, but his wife, although a Protestant, refused out of deference to her devoutly Roman Catholic daughters. Ford next tried to acquire German citizenship and a German divorce by residing temporarily in Germany. Although the scheme failed, Ford apparently told Violet he was a free man and married her in France in 1911. Ford also made up with Marwood and Conrad, who accepted him and Violet as a married couple.

But worse personal disasters soon struck. When a magazine referred to Violet as 'Mrs Ford Madox Hueffer', Elsie Hueffer sued for the sole right to her married name. Violet did not dare testify to her marriage lest Ford be charged with bigamy. Meanwhile, Ford, ill for some time, cowered in France, awaiting the verdict. In February 1913 Elsie won a large judgment in what had become a highly publicized case, and Ford promptly suffered a serious relapse. Concurrently, Marwood, believing that Ford had portrayed him as a vicious libertine in a satirical novel, *The New Humpty-Dumpty* (1912), permanently severed all relations with him. Although Conrad, who again sided with Marwood, did not explicitly break with Ford, he avoided direct communication from March 1913 to March 1915. At this time, precisely that of *The Good Soldier*'s writing and publication, Violet's friend Rebecca West reports that one did not dare mention Marwood's name in Ford's presence and that Ford's relations with Conrad were very strained. Needless to say, all these vicissitudes were hard on Ford's relations with Violet. By the time he began *The Good Soldier*, he was out of love with her and in love with someone else. This time the beloved was Brigit Patmore, beautiful, melancholy, youngish, musical, Irish and unhappily married. Her husband was a grandson of Coventry Patmore, author of that famously titled Victorian poem *The Angel in the House*. Violet's family had long known the Patmores, and Violet had not only taken a maternal interest in Brigit but had introduced her to Ford. When Ford began dictating *The Good Soldier*, perhaps at Violet's Selsey cottage near the sea, his secretary was, of course, Brigit Patmore.

Clearly, when Ford started to compose the tale of passion that became *The Good Soldier*, he was creating out of an intensely lived history of unhappy marriages, agonized love affairs, and troubled male friendships. His first wife was defaming him in the courts; his second was no longer sympathetic to him; his new beloved was married and was soon to reject him. Even worse, neither his great country-gentleman friend nor his great novelist friend loved him any more.

Previously, Ford's writing had served as an escape from the confusions of his personal life. He wrote historical romances of the court of Henry VIII, medieval fantasies, farces, anything to put a wall between himself and the chaotic content of his life. But here, for the first and perhaps only time, he wrote right from the heart of his own suffering. Thus, although Arthur Marwood and Joseph Conrad must have inspired the creations of Edward Ashburnham and John Dowell, those characters also embody many aspects of Ford himself. Think of Dowell, the agoraphobic, feeling in Nauheim a 'sense ... of ... the nakedness that one feels on the sea-shore or in any great open space' (p. 27), or imagining Edward, Nancy, and Florence 'suspended in mid-air ... upon an immense plain' that 'is the hand of God' (p. 82). Again, to varying degrees, and in different ways, Elsie Hueffer, Violet Hunt, and Brigit Patmore must have energized the creations of, respectively, Florence Dowell, Leonora Ashburnham, and Nancy Rufford. In fact both Ford's wives probably inform both fictional wives. And Rebecca West, when asked if Nancy was modelled on Brigit Patmore, assented instantly. Yet she went on to add: '*But nothing like.*' That wise cautionary note is important. However autobiographical a literary work may be, its author remains a maker; and the precise relations between life and art are, like most relations, ultimately unknowable.

Additionally, the 'germ' of *The Good Soldier* long predated Ford's affair with Brigit. In *The Spirit of the People* (1907), the third volume of Ford's lively trilogy of sociological impressionism about England and the English, he tells a fascinating anecdote to illustrate the Englishman's traditional, deplorable suppression of his feelings. Ford had been staying one summer at the house of a married couple—'good people'. Also staying with them was the husband's ward, a young woman. Between the two an attachment had developed. The situation having become impossible, the girl was to be sent around the world with a friend. The husband asked Ford to ride along in the dogcart to the railway station so as to forestall a scene. The two lovers (who of course had never spoken their love) talked 'in ordinary voices' about trivial matters. Their parting was, Ford writes, 'superhuman. . . . P—— never even shook her by the hand . . . it was playing the game to the bitter end. It was, indeed, very much the bitter end, since Miss W—— died at Brindisi on the voyage out, and P—— spent the next three years at various places on the Continent where nerve cures are attempted' (pp. 148–50). This story obviously anticipates Edward and Nancy's painful parting in Dowell's presence and Nancy's trip to Brindisi. The story's early date suggests why Ford could say in his Preface that *The Good Soldier* had been hatching fully a decade and that it was a 'true story'. Like Conrad, Ford seems to have needed to ground his tale in external facts. On the other hand, the allusion to the husband's three-year illness and visits to nerve-cure places makes one wonder whether the memory of this true story of Miss W—— and P—— could have been an unconscious screen for Ford's own love of his sister-in-law and for his mental illness of 1904–6. Finally, the anecdote underlines Ford's abiding interest in the rectitude (and failings) of the English gentleman, a type he saw as no longer wanted, a type he was to idealize in Christopher Tietjens of *Parade's End*.

Ford looked back on *The Good Soldier* as his 'auk's egg', marking the end of an era. It is at least an interesting coincidence that a novel which is a modernist capstone to the Edwardian era should feature a hero who not only is named Edward but acts as an attendant at the coronation of Edward VII. No doubt an important reason for the novel's problematic quality is the fact of its being written during the terrible malaise immediately preceding the Great War. In June 1914, Ford termed England a 'sack full of cats all at each other's throats', torn apart by fears of socialism, suffragism, Irish independence, and German rearmament.

2

Ford also looked back on *The Good Soldier* as the novel into which—after more than twenty years of authorship—he put '*all* that I knew about writing'. He was telling the truth. Most of what Ford learned, especially on the technical side, he learned from working with Conrad. And yet until Ford wrote *The Good Soldier* neither he nor anyone else had really tried to use Conrad's complex method. Ford called the method 'impressionism' and wrote about it brilliantly in his *Henry James* (1913), in several essays composed at the same time as *The Good Soldier*,[2] and in his *Joseph Conrad* (1924). When, in June 1914, Ford publicly accepted the label impressionist and undertook to give 'an account, from the inside, of how Impressionism is reached', he was invoking a word of some authority and a notion of rich, personal relevance (*CW*, p. 34). In the mid-eighteenth century, the skeptical Scottish empiricist philosopher David Hume had said that 'All the perceptions of the human mind resolve themselves into two distinct kinds, which I shall call *Impressions* and *Ideas*.'[3] By the former, Hume meant sense perceptions; and these Walter Pater, critic and admirer of the Pre-Raphaelites, stressed heavily in his celebrated definition of experience, written a few years before Ford's birth:

At first sight experience seems to bury us under a flood of external objects. . . . But when reflexion begins to play upon those objects . . . each object is loosed into a group of impressions—colour, odour, texture—in the mind of the observer. And if we continue to dwell in thought on this world, not of objects in the solidity with which language invests them, but of impressions, unstable, flickering, inconsistent, . . . it contracts still further: the whole scope of observation is dwarfed into the narrow chamber of the individual mind. Experience, already reduced to a group of impressions, is ringed

[2] These, and other interesting pieces, are conveniently collected in *Critical Writings of Ford Madox Ford*, ed. Frank MacShane, 1964 (hereafter cited as *CW*).

[3] *A Treatise on Human Nature*, I. i. 1 (1739). Quoted by Todd Bender, 'Conrad and Literary Impressionism', *Conradiana*, 10. 3 (1978), 220.

round for each one of us by that thick wall of personality through which no real voice has ever pierced on its way to us, or from us to that which we can only conjecture to be without. Every one of those impressions is the impression of the individual in his isolation, each mind keeping as a solitary prisoner its own dream of a world.[4]

This beautiful, frightening picture of the human mind sadly prefigures John Dowell at the end of *The Good Soldier*. He sits, a virtual prisoner in Branshaw House, conjecturing in solitude about the world outside. Pater's notion of experience focuses wholly upon the observing mind, and his emphasis on the 'thick wall of personality' suggests that impressionism leads to a desperate solipsism. Nevertheless, Dowell is not merely a passive receptor; he is writing a book about his experiences, one intended to make an impression on a reader outside himself.

Prior to Conrad, Ford's model novelist in English was Henry James. In his famous essay, 'The Art of Fiction', James, too, invokes the magic word: 'A novel is in its broadest definition a personal, a direct impression of life: that, to begin with, constitutes its value, which is greater or less according to the intensity of the impression.'[5] Conrad's similarly famous essay, the Preface to *The Nigger of the 'Narcissus'*, written just a year before meeting Ford, does not highlight the word 'impression', but does emphasize sense impressions: 'My task which I am trying to achieve is, by the power of the written word, to make you hear, to make you feel—it is, before all, to make you *see*!'[6] Significantly, Conrad here evokes his writing self as potently active and as concerned with his effect upon the reader. But besides these various literary precedents

---

[4] Walter Pater, *Studies in the Renaissance*, 1873, p. 209. This passage comes from the Conclusion, first published in 1868.

[5] Henry James, *Partial Portraits*, 1888, p. 384. 'The Art of Fiction' first appeared in 1884 in *Longman's Magazine*.

[6] Joseph Conrad, *The Nigger of the 'Narcissus'*, 1914, p. x. The Preface was first published in 1897 in the *New Review* at the end of the serial version. It did not appear with the book until a US edition of 1914.

to Fordian impressionism, one cannot ignore the example of contemporary French Impressionist painters. Their aim, like that of James, Conrad, and Ford, was, in the words of Ian Watt, 'to give a pictorial equivalent of the visual sensations of a particular individual at a particular time and place'.[7]

Although Conrad eschewed all labels, Ford cheerfully yoked himself and Conrad under the rubric: 'We accepted without much protest the stigma: "Impressionists" that was thrown at us . . . we saw that Life did not narrate, but made impressions on our brains' (*CW*, p 73). From their concern with the perceiver, Conrad and Ford were inevitably drawn to a fictional point of view restricted to a single consciousness. Indeed, at the very time the men met, Conrad was developing his greatest personal narrator, that philosophical follower of the sea, Captain Marlow. Moreover, when using Marlow to tell not his own story but Lord Jim's, Conrad employs sub-narrators such as the French lieutenant and Gentleman Brown to provide information and supplemental perspectives on Jim's case. Similarly, Ford's John Dowell, as the long-term deceived husband, must rely on the knowledgeable witnesses Edward and Leonora Ashburnham. Further, Conrad's and Ford's narrators, usually not having been physically present at the most crucial scenes, must employ conjecture to dramatize those scenes for the reader. Thus, Dowell says of the episode in the Casino park where Florence overhears Edward expressing his love to Nancy: 'I pieced it together afterwards' (p. 129).

Conrad and Ford draw attention to their narrators by giving us their locales. Marlow sits with four ex-seamen around a mahogany dinner table ('Youth'); Marlow narrates a second tale on the deck of the cruising yawl *Nellie* ('Heart of Darkness') and a third on the verandah of, presumably, a house in the Far East (*Lord Jim*); John Dowell writes at a desk in the Ashburnhams' country house in

---

[7] Ian Watt, *Conrad in the Nineteenth Century*, 1979, p. 170.

Hampshire. A very important difference is that Marlow tells his tales orally, to auditors, who can talk back. The effect is greater verisimilitude and perhaps greater involvement of the reader, who can temporarily identify with the puzzlement or irritation of Marlow's listeners. However, the fact that Dowell is writing rather than speaking his story underlines his isolation. Dowell compensates for the lack of a congenial audience by addressing his reader directly as 'silent listener', by writing in a casual, informal manner ('Well', 'It suddenly occurs to me . . .'), and, in a lovely, early passage, by figuratively converting the reader into an auditor:

So I shall just imagine myself for a fortnight or so at one side of the fireside of a country cottage, with a sympathetic soul opposite me. And I shall go on talking, in a low voice while the sea sounds in the distance and overhead the great black flood of wind polishes the bright stars. From time to time we shall get up and go to the door and look out at the great moon and say:—'Why, it is nearly as bright as in Provence!' (p. 17.)

Further, while Marlow tells most of Jim's story in a single evening, Dowell pointedly informs the reader that he is spending six months writing the bulk of Edward's story. This difference in narrative method has a vital effect on Dowell's telling, as will appear later. On the other hand, *The Good Soldier* follows *Lord Jim* structurally in having a big gap in the narration, the last portions of both tales being written long after the earlier portions were narrated.

Conrad and Ford believed, then, that it was truer to experience, more real, to focus upon a single observer–narrator. They thought, too, that it was truer to the way we acquire knowledge to have their narrators not tell their stories chronologically. In *Joseph Conrad*, Ford writes:

it became very early evident to us that what was the matter with the Novel, and the British novel in particular, was that it went straight forward, whereas in your gradual making acquaintanceship with your fellows you never do go straight forward. You meet an English gentleman at your golf club. He is beefy, full of health, the moral of the boy from an English Public School of the finest type. You discover, gradually, that he is hopelessly neurasthenic, dishonest in matters of small change, but unexpectedly self-sacrificing, a dreadful liar but a most painfully careful student of lepidoptera and, finally, from the public prints, a bigamist ... To get such a man in fiction you could not begin at his beginning and work his life chronologically to the end. You must first get him in with a strong impression, and then work backwards and forwards over his past. (pp. 129–30.)

Thus Conrad has Jim the water-clerk advancing towards us in some Eastern port, his stare like a charging bull's, his manner self-assertive but not aggressive, all this long after Jim's definitive, disastrous leap from the *Patna*. And Ford, after an initial chapter of John Dowell's cryptic, anguished reflections on the appearance and the reality of his relations with his wife and with the Ashburnhams, and a second chapter mostly on Florence and her family, gives to the reader Dowell's first glimpse of Edward. The latter is lounging around the screen into the dining-room of the Hotel Excelsior in Nauheim: 'His face ... in the wonderful English fashion, expressed nothing whatever.... He seemed to perceive no soul in that crowded room; he might have been walking in a jungle. I never came across such a perfect expression before and I never shall again. It was insolence and not insolence; it was modesty and not modesty' (p. 31). How Fordian the passage is! There are the flat contradictions ('insolence and not insolence'), the extremes ('nothing', 'perfect'), and the incongruous image ('walking in a jungle'). And then, after a period of reflecting, while describing Edward's physical features, and a leap forward in time to include an allusion to 'the poor girl' (Nancy), Dowell notes 'two distinct expressions flicker across [Edward's] immobile eyes' (p. 35). Though Dowell cannot fully interpret those expressions until over nine years after he registers them, he gives his final readings immediately to the reader. One look, directed toward the approaching Leonora, expresses pride and satisfaction in his handsome wife; the other, 'a challenging look', expresses confidence that he may just score a goal and is directed toward—Dowell's wife! Thus Ford, in this crucial, strong first impression, renders Edward's amazing self-control, dramatizes his role as half of an apparently perfect county couple, indicates his recurrent, irrepressible impulse to acquire a new lover, and suggests the true nature of his life: both the society he inhabits and his own heart are a 'jungle'.

After this strong introduction, Ford can then work backwards and forwards over Edward's life. More than once Dowell calls our attention to this aspect of his narration: 'I have, I am aware, told this story in a very rambling way so that it may be difficult for anyone to find their path through what may be a sort of maze. I cannot help it ... when one discusses an affair—a long, sad affair—one goes back, one goes forward' (p. 213). Ford, like Conrad, narrates in an unchronological fashion not only because the story will thereby seem 'most real', but also to add meaning. The method permits the author to juxtapose events and images that would otherwise be far separated. 'Impressionism', says Ford, can

give a sense of two, or three, of as many as you will, places, persons, emotions, all going on simultaneously in the emotions of the writer. ... Indeed, I suppose that Impressionism exists to render those queer effects of real life that are like so many views seen through bright glass—through glass so bright that whilst you perceive through it a landscape or a backyard, you are aware that, on its surface, it reflects a face of a person behind you. For the whole of life is really like that; we are almost always in one place with our minds somewhere quite other. (*CW*, pp. 40–1.)

One of Ford's best effects in unchronological narration comes from having Dowell tell the same story twice in order 'to render those superimposed emotions'. A well-known instance is that of Edward's expensive leather travelling cases. The first time Dowell refers to them, it is to underline how perfectly Edward plays his role of the country gentleman. But the second time around, Dowell reveals his later discovery that all those cases were Leonora's doing, thereby underlining Leonora's insensitive management of her husband's life.

Again, in keeping with his idea that life does 'not narrate', Ford says that one remembers an event as 'various unordered pictures'. In accord with impressionism's central concern with sense perceptions, Ford at his best employs a multitude of vivid visual images. Probably the most striking instance of 'unordered pictures' in *The Good Soldier* is Dowell's account of his immediate response to Florence's death.

my recollection of that night is only the sort of pinkish effulgence from the electric-lamps in the hotel lounge. There seemed to bob into my consciousness, like floating globes, the faces of those three [officials]. Now it would be the bearded, monarchical, benevolent head of the grand-duke; then the sharp-featured, brown, cavalry-moustached features of the chief of police; then the globular, polished and high-collared vacuousness that represented Monsieur Schontz, the proprietor of the hotel. (pp. 127–8.)

Those were Dowell's immediate impressions. Later, he would piece together 'what had actually happened', would convert his impressions into ideas, and would at last understand what his 'inner soul . . . had realized long before[,] that Florence was a personality of paper' (p. 142).

In addition to his technical interests in personal narrators, unchronological structuring, and the plentiful use of visual images, Ford, like James and Conrad, is constantly concerned with his impact upon the reader. A personal narrator makes the reader feel he or she is hearing a real story being told. Vivid pictures help the reader to see. And a mixed-up chronology makes the reader work hard, involves the reader deeply in the novel's psychological, moral, and philosophical questions. One can argue that impressionism's devices tend instead to distance the reader and prevent the kind of wholehearted identification with a sympathetic character that omnisciently told fiction promotes. Nevertheless, Ford beautifully explains the kind of reader-involvement he hopes to inspire, in a 1914 essay that uses language reminiscent of *The Good Soldier*:

And the whole of Impressionism comes to this: having realized that the audience to which you will address yourself must have this particular peasant intelligence, or, if you prefer it, this particular and virgin openness of mind, you will then figure to yourself an individual, a silent listener, who shall be to yourself the *homo bonae voluntatis*— man of goodwill. To him, then, you will address your picture, your poem, your prose story, or your argument. You will seek to capture his interest; you will seek to hold his interest. You will do this by methods of surprise, of fatigue, by passages of sweetness in your language, by passages suggesting the sudden and brutal shock of suicide. You will give him passages of dulness, so that your bright effects may seem more bright; you will alternate, you will dwell for a long time upon an intimate point; you will seek to exasperate so that you may the better enchant. You will, in short, employ all the devices of the prostitute. If you are too proud for this you may be the better gentleman or the better lady, but you will be the worse artist. For the artist must always be humble and humble and again humble, since before the greatness of his task he himself is nothing. He must again be outrageous, since the greatness of his task calls for enormous excesses by means of which he may recoup his energies. That is why the artist is, quite rightly, regarded with suspicion by people who desire to live in tranquil and ordered society. (*CW*, pp. 53–4.)

But what, finally, is the purpose of the impressionist's great task? To generalize, no doubt excessively, the quest of impressionism, in keeping with the word's history, is the quest for knowledge. *What Maisie Knew* is Henry James's evocative title for a book Ford especially admired. At the end of *Lord Jim*, Marlow asks: 'Is he satisfied—quite, now, I wonder? We ought to know. He is one of us . . . Who knows?' As many readers have noted, forms of the verb 'to know' occur seven times in the first paragraph alone of *The Good Soldier*. Indeed, as its *Concordance* reveals, forms of 'to know' occur 289 times in the text, far more frequently than any other verb, except, of course, for linking and auxiliary verbs; more frequently even than that work-horse of narrative, 'to say'. Moreover, the telling phrase, 'I don't know', itself appears about fifty times, and other negations of 'know' some forty times more. Additionally, Ford, as has also been observed, frequently emphasizes Dowell's quest for knowledge by having him repeatedly ask questions (some two dozen in the first chapter). One of the finest and most influential essays on the novel, by Samuel Hynes, 'The Epistemology of *The Good Soldier*', is devoted, as its title indicates, largely to the problem of knowledge.

3

But the nature of the knowledge that Dowell discovers or that the reader acquires has been in dispute almost since Ford's death. Early readers of the novel, though they may have found Dowell an irritating combination of weakness and profundity, never doubted his reliability or the novel's tragic tone. But in 1948 Mark Schorer, in a strongly written piece, called the novel a work of 'comic genius' and Dowell's 'a mind not quite in balance'. The novel's opening sentence is an 'absurdity', 'passionate situations are related by a narrator who is himself incapable of passion, sexual and moral alike', and we readers 'are forced to ask "How can we believe *him*? His must be exactly the *wrong* view."' Schorer's essay has been especially influential in the United States where it has long served as the introduction to the novel's only available paperback edition. (Schorer himself later repudiated his essay in conversation, concluding that Dowell speaks for Ford; consequently, for Schorer, the novel is seriously flawed.) The strongest early response to Schorer is Hynes's previously mentioned, 1961 essay. Though granting Dowell's personal limitations, Hynes sees him as sincerely struggling to understand the tragedy, as proving capable of love, and as arriving at a kind of knowledge. Since then, crudely speaking, readers have tended to fall into the pro- and anti-Dowell camps. The former include Arthur Mizener and Ann Barr Snitow; the latter include Frank Kermode and Avrom

Fleishman, with the pro's outnumbering the anti's. Still, readers have doubted not only Dowell's assertion that the newly married Ashburnhams do not know how babies are made, but even that Florence and Edward have an affair. Readers have actually opined that Edward is Nancy's father. Some readers see Dowell as not merely misled and self-deluded but consciously dishonest. One critic proposes that Dowell knows all along that Florence's heart is sound. He just pretends to believe her story so as to trap her on the Continent. Another critic implies (tongue-in-cheek?) that Dowell, as the last person to see both Florence and Edward alive, does in fact do them in!

Perhaps *The Good Soldier* invites such bizarre readings. Even the title-page, read retrospectively, raises perplexing problems. If Edward is properly playing his inherited role of 'good soldier', how can his be a tale of passion (unless passion ultimately means suffering, in the sense of Christ's passion)? And *who* are the 'Beati Immaculati' of the novel's epigraph? Although they should, logically, include Edward the good soldier, some readers believe that these blameless happy ones who walk in the law of the Lord are the conventional Leonora and her new husband Rodney Bayham. Others, who do apply the phrase to Edward and Nancy, read it as bitterly ironic. I myself, remembering that 'Beati' also means 'Blessed' and that Dowell's last loving impulse is to say 'God bless you' to Edward, would apply the phrase to him and Nancy with no irony at all. At the end, those two, according to Dowell, belong among the 'proud, resolute and unusual individuals'; they are 'splendid and tumultuous creatures', who are best off being 'gone from this earth'. Society needs only 'normal' types (p. 274).

Then there is the novel's puzzling first sentence. Why should Dowell call this the saddest story he has ever 'heard'? He is, after all, one of the five principal characters. Yet the sentence suggests he is a total outsider—which is true, in part because of his personal limitations. More to the point, the true story was, after all, told to him; he did hear it, from

Edward and Leonora. Above all, as Paul Armstrong has said, Dowell really hears the whole story only as he writes it out at his desk.

Readers who see the novel as principally comic and Dowell as unreliable can probably never be disabused. All one can say is that no other of Ford's twenty-nine novels employs such a tone and narrator as the anti-Dowellists propose. Moreover, Conrad, on receiving his copy of *The Good Soldier*, singled out for praise its 'tone of fretful melancholy, extremely effective'.[8] Denis Donoghue, in 'Listening to the Saddest Story', says we accept Dowell as storyteller because he is so scrupulous in airing his doubts and correcting his impressions. 'Accepting him does not mean that we think him infallible but that we think him honest: he may still be obtuse, slow to sense the drift of things.' Paul Armstrong's understanding of the novel comes from his conscious choice to believe Dowell. 'My reading of *The Good Soldier* results from my own decision to regard Dowell as a narrator who struggles, with mixed but increasing success, to give a trustworthy account of his history.' Ford would be pleased. His ideal reader is 'the man with the quite virgin mind . . . Such a peasant intelligence will know that this is such a queer world that anything may be possible' (*CW*, pp. 53, 52).

This ideal reader of good will needs constantly to keep clear the complex task that Dowell, the amateur artist, is essaying in this, his first book. First, Dowell is trying to convey his past impressions of the life he led when he was still ignorant of Florence's affairs with Jimmy and Edward. Thus, when Dowell first mentions Florence and Uncle Hurlbird's precipitate departure from Ludlow Manor, the reason given is pressure of uncle's business. That is what Dowell believes until Bagshawe, the owner of the manor, tells him of Florence being caught there emerging from Jimmy's room. Again, on one vital early occasion, the 'Protest scene', when Leonora bursts out hysterically, it comes to Dowell for a terrifying moment that Leonora 'must be ... jealous of Florence and Captain Ashburnham' (p. 54). To his relief, Leonora gets hold of herself and instead blames Florence for demeaning her Irish Catholicism. (Of course, Dowell is probably so afraid of feeling that he does not want to know.)

Second, Dowell has to convey his constantly shifting feelings while he is in the process of telling his story. Thus, he can expatiate on the perfection of the two couples' relationship, calling it a 'minuet', and then instantly replace the image with that of 'a prison full of screaming hysterics' (pp. 10, 11). Third, the longer Dowell writes, the more he understands. Initially, he honestly believes and faithfully records that in all those years of caring for Florence, he rarely let her out of his sight. Later, he realizes that when he comes 'to think of it she was out of my sight most of the time' (p. 103). Even more moving, Dowell, on repeating a story, can importantly change his emphasis in response to deeper understanding. For example, the first time he tells the Protest story, he stresses Leonora's jealousy of Florence; but the second time, he includes Leonora's concern as to the effect on Maisie of Edward's new love, a concern only too well justified in the poor child's heart failure that very afternoon.

However, even if we find Dowell as honest as his limited, sexually tepid temperament permits, and find this a genuinely sad story, we cannot deny the book its comic aspects. Dowell even says, apropos the Hurlbird sisters' argument over disbursing their brother's money: 'It may strike you, silent listener, as being funny ...' (p. 230). Dowell, himself, especially in the early pages, proves an effective comic ironist: 'poor dear Edward was a great reader' (p. 34). Dowell's account of Edward's fling in Monte Carlo is almost pure farce: Edward 'was cured of the idea that he had any duties towards La Dolciquita—feudal or otherwise. But his sentimentalism required of him an attitude of Byronic gloom—as if his court had gone into half-mourning' (p. 191). Dowell can be merciless to himself, too, especially by means of grotesquely comic images. He pictures himself on the night of his elopement as going up and down the rope ladder like a 'tranquil jumping-jack' (p. 98). The simile recalls the comic posthumous role Dowell envisions for himself: running a heavenly elevator, and thus being serviceable in perpetuity. A dead-pan humorist in the tradition of Mark Twain, Dowell sometimes leaves his listener uncertain whether he realizes how funny he is. One thinks in this connection of his tale of La Louve, her complaisant husband, and her troubadour swain Peire Vidal, or of this comment of Dowell's: 'Edward ought, I suppose, to have gone to the Transvaal. It would have done him a great deal of good to get killed' (p. 199). Read retrospectively, these passages clearly convey mixed feelings, as does Dowell's portrait of Maisie Maidan's corpse: 'her little body had fallen forward into the trunk, and it had closed upon her, like the jaws of a gigantic alligator' (p. 88). Those jaws, like the dogs' fangs that so lacerate Vidal, look forward to all the later, very uncomic images of biting, whipping, and flaying that characterize not only the desperate Leonora but even the gentle Nancy.

Conrad and Ford both espoused the technique Ford called *progression d'effet*: 'we agreed that every word ... must carry the story forward and, that as the story progressed, the story must be carried forward faster and faster and with more and more intensity' (*CW*, p. 87). The way Dowell tells his saddest story surely accomplishes this effect. He moves through three triangles: Florence, Edward, and himself; Florence, Edward, and Leonora; Leonora, Nancy, and Edward. The first is the most comic of the three, with Dowell the unknowing victim. The second is much more touching because Edward and Leonora, wrong-headed as they both are, are complexly human and do not intend to harm one another. Leonora, moreover, suffers genuine pain. Florence, on the other hand, moves, in Dowell's narration, from pitiable to vulgar, deceitful, manipulative, evil. 'I may, in what follows, be a little hard on Florence; but you must remember that I have been writing away at this story now for six months and reflecting longer and longer upon these affairs' (p. 214). The third triangle is, as it should be, much the most excruciating of all, with a mounting series of horrors: from Leonora's illness and Edward's drinking, to Nancy's slow awakening to their desperate unhappiness, forward to the final tragedies.

Particularly moving is the way Dowell conveys everyone's vulnerability; Leonora's and Nancy's and Edward's separate bedroom doors all open on to the gallery, 'gaping to receive whom the chances of the black night might bring' (p. 246). Conrad had said in his congratulatory note to Ford that the three 'women are extraordinary—in the laudatory sense'. Indeed, their creation is beyond praise, and they have been successfully portrayed in Granada's 1981 television version. Dowell also effectively shows how these British 'good people' maintain decorum before outsiders. For nearly a fortnight, Dowell has not the faintest notion that Branshaw Telegraph is anything but 'one of the ancient haunts of English peace' (p. 291). Not, that is, until Edward says to him 'in a perfectly calm voice . . . "I am so desperately in love with Nancy Rufford that I am dying of it"' (p. 287). In *Henry James*, Ford says that James's characters can talk about the rain or an opera and that 'those conversations will convey to your mind that the quiet talkers are living in an atmosphere of horror, of bankruptcy, of passion hopeless as the Dies Irae!' (p. 153). The last phrase recalls Dowell's vision of the dead Florence and Edward as 'only poor wretches, creeping over this earth in the shadow of an eternal wrath' (p. 82).

Fine as are Ford's portraits of the women in *The Good Soldier*, his greatest achievement is his rendition of Dowell's enduring, even growing, affection for Edward Ashburnham, the man who cuckolds him, the man whom he calls 'stupid', the man who, despite his devotion to his feudal ideals of the good landlord and faithful soldier, manages increasingly to wreak havoc. Nevertheless, Edward really suffers, as Dowell sees more and more clearly. In his *Hans Holbein* (1905) Ford says that a 'great portrait . . . makes its subject always a great man' because '*every* man is great if viewed from the sympathetic point of view' and 'great art is above all things generous' (pp. 124–6).

The terms in which Dowell expresses his love of Edward have, it is true, inspired some derisive commentary; but they are most enlightening. Despite admitting his vast inferiority to Edward in terms of 'courage', 'virility', and 'physique', Dowell still insists 'that I love him because he was just myself ... I am just as much of a sentimentalist as he was' (p. 291). Dowell in fact so empathizes with Edward that he refuses to interfere with Edward's final decision. Dowell himself acts on the occasion with perfect propriety, maintaining 'English good form' (p. 294). More importantly, Dowell's love of Edward means complete personal identification. What the Fordian lover, and artist, desires above all is to escape solipsism, to break through what Pater calls 'the thick wall of personality'.

[The] things that cause to arise the passion of love ... are like so many objects on the horizon of the landscape that tempt a man to ... explore. He wants to get, as it were, behind those eye-brows ... as if he desired to see the world with the eyes that they overshadow.... [T]he real fierceness of desire ... is the craving for identity with the woman that he loves. He desires to see with the same eyes, to touch with the same sense of touch, to hear with the same ears ... (p. 135.)

Ford says in his *Joseph Conrad* that everything he wrote after meeting Conrad was written with the idea of reading it aloud to him. And, in *Mightier Than the Sword* (1938), he says that, working with Conrad, he tried to evolve for himself 'a vernacular of an extreme quietness that would suggest someone of some refinement talking in a low voice near the ear of someone else he liked a good deal' (p. 278). We must never forget that Dowell is a *writer* composing and recomposing his story, and thinking of himself as telling it to someone he loves. (We recall that Ford did, in fact, dictate the beginning of the novel to the woman he then loved.) Ford very much and very generously has the reader always in mind. He wants every reader to be free to make of Dowell and *The Good Soldier* what he or she, generously, can. Ford says to his reader, as Dowell says more than once to his silent listener: 'I leave it to you.'

NOTE ON THE TEXT

I

THE only two complete manuscripts of *The Good Soldier* are housed at Cornell University Library. The first is some 376 pages of holograph and typescript; the second, which consists of 305 typed pages, is the printer's copy. The portions of the first manuscript which are in holograph were written by three different people: most of Part I (MS pages 2–44 and 47–82) was written by Brigit Patmore; much of Part III (MS pages 141–96, 206–18, and 225–53) appears to have been written by the American Imagist poet H. D. (Hilda Doolittle); the last two chapters, less the first two, typed pages (MS pages 342–76) look to be in the hand of H. D.'s husband, the English Imagist poet Richard Aldington. In *It Was the Nightingale*, Ford pays ironic tribute to H. D. and Aldington: 'When I was dictating the most tragic portion of my most tragic book to an American poetess she fainted several times. One morning she fainted three times. So I had to call in her husband to finish the last pages of the book. He did not faint' (pp. 220–1).

The holograph portions of the manuscript surely represent first drafts; the typed portions may or may not be. (Theoretically, the first draft of the novel could have been wholly handwritten by secretaries, with large swatches ´so completely rewritten that long holograph portions were simply discarded for typed, second-draft pages. The appearance of the manuscript does not, however, suggest this.) In any case, some of Ford's revisions and excisions in the first manuscript are quite interesting.

Not surprisingly, changes occur with greatest frequency in the early pages where Ford is still feeling his way into the book. Some of the changes are relatively minor—the slight but unerring revisions of the highly experienced professional:

Ford eliminates repetitions, makes small clarifications, delicately adjusts tone. More significantly, Ford eliminates an overly explicit page spelling out how one recognizes 'good people', and cancels a tedious passage on Florence's typical conversation topics.

Beyond these revisions are two sets of more substantial changes having to do with Dowell and Edward respectively. In the manuscript, Ford has Dowell emphasize more strongly than in the final version the fact that he is writing a novel and his sense of ineptitude as a neophyte author. Thus, after the first sentence of Part I, Chapter II, in which Dowell says he does not know how best to tell the story, the manuscript continues: 'I have asked novelists about these things, but they don't seem able to tell you much.' Further on, in the same passage, Dowell admits: 'I don't know that I particularly want to write a novel.' At the very end of the chapter, he apologizes: 'But all this is rather wandering round sort of stuff. Only it's the way it comes into my head'; he concludes: 'I don't know how to tell this story.'[1] All these passages are eliminated in the final version.

Most interesting is the evidence from the first manuscript that Ford initially conceived of Edward Ashburnham as a gross libertine, rather than as a 'normal' man. (In a letter of March 1915 to his publisher, printed in *The Ford Madox Ford Reader*, p. 477, Ford calls *The Good Soldier* a serious 'analysis of the polygamous desires that underlie all men'.) Two passages in the holograph version explicitly portray Edward as the father of a number of illegitimate children. The first (coming in the second paragraph, p. 68) tells how Edward desired, unsuccessfully, that all the young women whom he seduced should be well provided for and all the children he fathered be sent to the best schools. A second passage, a few pages

---

[1] Quoted by Charles G. Hoffmann, 'Ford's Manuscript Revisions of *The Good Soldier*', *English Literature in Transition*, 9: 4 (1966), 147. Although I have studied the manuscripts both in the original and in photocopies, all manuscript quotations come from Hoffmann's invaluable article. All page numbers in parentheses are to the present World's Classics edition.

later, says that the Kilsyte case was a boon to Leonora because 'it certainly meant the end of expenditures on bastards and blackmailers'. Ford must have realized, rightly, that giving Edward such a sordid past would have rendered Dowell's subsequent sympathetic portrayal of him impossible. Wisely, Ford excised both passages.

Unsurprisingly, the printer's copy is very close to the book version. However, there is one striking difference between the two manuscripts and the book. On the next to last page of the novel, Dowell says that Edward, upon reading Nancy's telegram, 'looked up to the roof of the stable, as if he were looking to Heaven, and whispered something that I did not catch' (p. 293). But in both manuscripts, Edward, looking up to the roof as if to Heaven, remarks: 'Girl, I will wait for you there'. The revision is perfect. Ford does not merely avoid the emotional let-down of quoting an Ashburnham banality at this terribly painful moment. He also has Dowell, the characteristically bewildered witness, not quite hear the whispered words. Better yet, Ford avoids explicitness, which Conrad says is fatal to art; Ford instead leaves it to the reader to imagine what Edward whispers.

The first four and a half chapters of *The Good Soldier* appeared in the first issue of Wyndham Lewis's magazine *Blast* (20 June 1914). The instalment ends 'To be continued'. But since the next (and last) number of *Blast* did not appear for thirteen months, four months after the novel was published in book form, there was no second instalment. The forty-two page typescript from which the magazine instalment was printed is also at Cornell. It follows the holograph manuscript, incorporating some, but not all, of its revisions. The *Blast* typescript is identical to the first forty-two pages of the printer's copy, but without its corrections. The *Blast* typescript thus antedates the first and predates the second complete manuscript. The *Blast* instalment contains the novel's epigraph but omits the first sentence. It ends with the words: 'But, you understand, there was no objection' (p. 47).

The differences between the magazine version and the

book are minor. (Most are recorded in the *Blast* entry of Harvey's *Bibliography*.) But a couple of changes involving Florence are interesting. Apparently, Ford was initially going to grant the possibility that Florence actually had heart trouble: 'The reason for poor Florence's broken years *may have been in the first instance congenital, but the immediate occasion* was a storm at sea' (p. 8). (The book omits the italicized words.) Ford wisely decided that there must be no ambiguity about Florence's deliberate deception of Dowell and Edward. Again, the *Blast* version has Florence die 'five days before' her uncle, whereas the book rightly changes 'before' to 'after' (p. 24) so as to account clearly for Dowell inheriting the uncle's fortune through Florence.

2

Four editions of *The Good Soldier* appeared in Ford's lifetime: two English and two American. The first English edition was published on 17 March 1915, the first American probably at the same time. The English was reprinted once in 1915. Spot-checking indicates that these editions are identical, except for their title-pages. In a box at the bottom, the first line of the English edition reads: London, John Lane, The Bodley Head; the second line: New York: John Lane Company. The American edition reverses the order. The second American edition, published by Albert and Charles Boni, appeared in April 1927 with an important new dedicatory letter by Ford, dated 9 January 1927. This edition contains a number of revisions of the first editions, revisions which Arthur Mizener believes could be by Ford himself. Finally, a second English edition, the 'Week-End Library' edition, was published by John Lane, The Bodley Head, on 24 February 1928. It contains the dedicatory letter and is printed from new plates, but otherwise follows the first English edition, as do subsequent English editions.

The first English edition is the copy-text for the present edition. The revisions in the second American edition do not

suggest new insights or serious rethinking but simply an
effort to conform to American linguistic usage and to presumed American attitudes. Although these revisions may
well be Ford's, they could as easily be the work of an American copy-editor. One must nevertheless grant that since
Dowell is an American, Ford would want him to write like
an American. So in several instances the second American
edition follows American grammatical convention. In the
first English edition, when Dowell is talking about his impulse to comfort Florence, he writes: 'You cannot, you see,
have acted as nurse to a person for twelve years without
wishing to go on nursing *them*, even though you hate *them*'
(pp. 82–3, my italics). The second American edition gives
'her' both times. On three subsequent occasions, where the
English gives a plural pronoun (in reference to 'anyone',
'each', and 'neither'), the American gives singular forms.

More interestingly, the second American edition alters
English expressions, presumably to make them clearer to an
American reader. Thus, where Dowell, in the first editions,
twice says Florence 'cut out' Edward (pp. 83, 87), the second
American uses the verb 'annex'. (However, the first use of
'cut out' in the first editions, p. 83, is not changed in the
second American, surely an oversight on the part of the
reviser.) Again, where the first English edition says that at
three o'clock in the morning Dowell and Florence 'knocked
up' the minister (p. 98), the second American uses 'woke up'
to avoid the American slang sense of 'knock up' as impreg-
nate.

Finally, the presentation of Dowell's black servant Julius is
revised in the second American edition, presumably in an
attempt—not wholly successful—to provide a more authen-
tically American racial view. Whereas the first editions call
Julius a 'darky' servant (p. 107), the second American and
subsequent editions confusingly call him 'dark'. Again,
perhaps in a misguided attempt to minimize American racial
prejudice, the second American edition markedly changes
this curious statement of the first editions: 'New England had

NOTE ON THE TEXT xxxiii

not yet [in 1901] come to loathe the darkies as it does now [in
1914]' (p. 108). The later, tamer, but still historically strange
American version says 'that New England no longer idealizes
darkies as it did formerly'.

Some tiny differences between the editions are quite
understandable: English 'cheques' (p. 182) and American
'checks'. The English says that Florence and Dowell have
between them 'fifteen thousand a year in English money' (p.
105); the American says seventy-five thousand dollars. Additionally, the American second edition corrects some minor
errors made in the first and not corrected in the English
second edition. On the other hand, the second American in-
troduces a few trivial new errors and misses some made in the
first editions. Finally, the punctuation in the second American edition is somewhat heavier, perhaps conforming to
American publishing house style. Apart from silently correcting the relatively few and obvious errors, this World's
Classics edition follows the first English edition, which most
clearly expresses Ford's intentions at the height of his involvement with the novel.

3

Besides presenting the problem of the most desirable edition,
the text of *The Good Soldier* raises two questions that can affect
interpretation. When, precisely, was the novel written? What
is the reader to make of the numerous factual mistakes and
inconsistencies in Dowell's narration?

The first question takes its importance from the novel's
obsession with the date, 4 August. On that day of the year,
Florence was born, started around the world, lost her virgin-
ity, married Dowell, appropriated Edward, and died.
(Maisie Maidan, too, died on that day, in 1904.) It was, of
course, on 4 August 1914 that Germany marched into
Belgium and plunged England and France into war. Now, if
Ford really began the novel on his fortieth birthday, 17
December 1913 (as he said in 1927), and if he finished it on

28 June 1914 (as he said in 1931), then he finished the novel before the war, and his use of 4 August is just a fantastic Fordian coincidence. Unfortunately, the *Blast* instalment of 20 June does not quite go up to the first mention of 4 August; that would have clinched the case. Although the 4 August date generally appears in the typescript rather than in the holograph portions of the first manuscript, it does appear in the holograph section assigned to H. D. On only one occasion does Ford later insert in the margin a perhaps later reference to 4 August. Arthur Mizener's informed belief is that Ford finished the novel in July 1914. Mizener says that the printer's 'receive' stamp on the manuscript, dated 3 October, is compatible with a July completion date.

Nevertheless, as far as the finishing date is concerned, my impulse is to follow the Ford of 1914 rather than the Ford of 1931 or Arthur Mizener. In his weekly literary essay in *Outlook* magazine of 5 September 1914, Ford says he has written twenty poems and two chapters of a novel 'since this war began'. Interestingly, Richard Aldington remembers taking dictation from Ford on *The Good Soldier* after the war began, and the last two chapters appear to be in his hand. Moreover, some of the wording of the last two chapters echoes poems Ford wrote and published just after the outbreak of hostilities. In short, I believe that Ford did not finish the novel until after the war started. On the other hand, I also believe that he wrote then only the last two chapters and that, therefore, Mizener is right about the 4 August date being an amazing coincidence. The novel must have been conceived and almost completely written before the Great War began and thus cannot be read as Ford's anguished response to it.

Most attentive readers notice that Dowell's narration exhibits mistakes and inconsistencies, mostly having to do with chronology. Many critics have wrestled with the problem.[2] A

---

[2] Most recently, Vincent J. Cheng, 'A Chronology of *The Good Soldier*', *English Language Notes*, 24: 1 (1986), 91–7.

particularly obvious oddity is the time when Dowell finishes the novel. He begins writing his saddest story in late 1913 or early 1914; he works on it for at least six months; then he interrupts the writing for eighteen months to bring Nancy back from Ceylon. In short, Dowell finished writing the book some nine months after John Lane published it! Considerable confusion attends the crucial first meeting of the Dowells and Ashburnhams, their trip to M——, and Maisie Maidan's death. In the manuscript, Ford initially had the Ashburnhams arrive in Nauheim in July 1906; then he changed it to August 1904. Although 4 August 1904, is the date of the Protest incident in M—— and Maisie's death (pp. 78, 91), Dowell also says that the Ashburnhams and Maisie were in Nauheim for a month before her death (pp. 61, 219). Elsewhere, Dowell has Florence's affair with Edward begin in 1903 (p. 105).

Equal confusion attends the period after Florence's death on 4 August 1913. Dowell sets off for the United States a fortnight afterwards (p. 144). His 'short incursion into American business life' takes place 'during part of August and nearly the whole of September' (p. 179); of this time, he spends a week or ten days in Philadelphia attending to his own business and family and the remainder in Waterbury, Conn., with the Hurlbird sisters. Upon receiving the Ashburnham telegrams, he leaves town 'quite abruptly' (p. 231). Yet Leonora and Nancy do not have their all-night conversation in Nancy's bedroom until 12 November (p. 256), and Edward cables Dowell the next morning (p. 266). A fortnight passes between Dowell's arrival and Nancy's departure for India (p. 280). Enough time passes after that for Edward to hunt twice, attend two political meetings, and get the gardener's daughter acquitted of murdering her baby (p. 289), all this before the arrival of Nancy's fatal telegram from Brindisi. Ten days later, surely mid-December at the earliest, Leonora begins to tell Dowell the whole, true story—on a 'windy November evening' (p. 124). And yet, much earlier, before Dowell has even been sent for, when the

house is 'silent in the drooping winter weather', Nancy kisses
Edward 'under the mistletoe' (p. 241)!

The obvious question is: are these 'mistakes' Dowell's or
Ford's? If the former, then they can be taken as signs of
Dowell's general unreliability. My own feeling is that the
inconsistencies are Ford's. The novel's chronology is complicated, and Ford's changes of dates and characters' ages in
the manuscript suggest he had problems with it. Although
Ford had an impressive memory, a love of history, and a
commitment to concrete detail, he was sometimes impatient
and careless with facts. When Ford has Dowell call Corpus
Christi a 'saint's day' (p. 146), the reader can be reasonably
sure that Ford, the Roman Catholic, is deliberately exposing
an error on the part of his Protestant narrator. But Ford was
telling his tale of passion in a new and complicated way. The
reader should view Dowell's chronological variations with
common sense, with attention, and, once again, with generosity.

SELECT BIBLIOGRAPHY

THE first full bibliography of Ford's works is that of Edward Naumburg, jun.: 'A Catalogue of a Ford Madox Ford Collection', *Princeton University Library Chronicle*, 9: 3 (1948), 134–65. The most comprehensive bibliography is David Dow Harvey's richly annotated *Ford Madox Ford (1873–1939): a Bibliography of Works and Criticism* (1962, repr. 1972). It has been supplemented by two secondary source bibliographies: Linda Tamkin's, covering 1962 to 1979; and Rita Malenczyk's, covering 1979 to 1985, both printed in *Antaeus*, 56 (1986). There is a five-volume selected edition of Ford's works, *The Bodley Head Ford Madox Ford: The Good Soldier, Selected Memories, Poems* (1962), *The Fifth Queen* (1962), *Parade's End* (2 vols., 1963), all edited and introduced by Graham Greene; *Memories and Impressions* (1971), selected and introduced by Michael Killigrew. A most useful selection of Ford's criticism is *Critical Writings of Ford Madox Ford*, ed. Frank MacShane (1964). *The Ford Madox Ford Reader*, ed. Sondra J. Stang (1986), is a generous sampling of Ford's works, plus sixty unpublished letters. Some twenty-five books by Ford are now back in print, including his studies of James and Conrad, various travel books, reminiscences, books of literary criticism, fairy-tales, and some of his most interesting historical romances and novels of modern life.

So far as biographical matters are concerned, there is, first of all, the abundance of Ford's romantic reminiscences: *Ancient Lights* (1911), *Thus to Revisit* (1921), *Return to Yesterday* (1931), and *It Was the Nightingale* (1933), plus the disguised autobiography, *No Enemy* (written shortly after the war, but published in 1929). Richard M. Ludwig edited *Letters of Ford Madox Ford* (1965). Brita Lindberg-Seyersted edited *Pound/Ford, the Story of a Literary Friendship: The Correspondence between Ezra Pound and Ford Madox Ford and Their Writings about Each Other* (1982). Conrad's many and illuminating letters to Ford are currently being published in *The Collected Letters of Joseph Conrad*, 8 vols., ed. Frederick R. Karl and Laurence Davies (1983–). Two of Ford's mistresses and one friend wrote book-length memoirs, principally about him: Violet Hunt, *The Flurried Years* (1926; published in the USA as *I Have This to Say*); Stella Bowen, *Drawn from Life* (1941); Douglas Goldring, *South Lodge* (1943). (See also *The Return of the Good Soldier: Ford Madox Ford and Violet Hunt's 1917 Diary*, ed. Robert and Marie Secor, 1983.) Critical biographies of Ford include: Douglas Goldring, *The Last Pre-Raphaelite* (1948; published in the USA as *Trained for Genius*, 1949); Frank MacShane, *The Life and Works of Ford Madox Ford* (1965); Arthur Mizener, *The Saddest Story, a Biography of Ford Madox Ford* (1971); Thomas C. Moser, *The Life in the Fiction of Ford Madox Ford* (1981).

Most interesting critical books on Ford treat *The Good Soldier* successfully and at length. Some do not, but they are also included here for their general interest: Paul B. Armstrong, *The Challenge of Bewilderment: Understanding and Representation in James, Conrad, and Ford* (1987); Raymond Brebach, *Joseph Conrad, Ford Madox Ford, and the Making of 'Romance'* (1985); Richard A. Cassell, *Ford Madox Ford: A Study of His Novels* (1961); Ambrose Gordon, jun., *The Invisible Tent: The War Novels of Ford Madox Ford* (1964); Samuel Hynes, *Edwardian Occasions* (1972); Hugh Kenner, *Gnomon: Essays on Contemporary Literature* (1958); Richard W. Lid, *Ford Madox Ford: The Essence of His Art* (1964); John A. Meixner, *Ford Madox Ford's Novels: A Critical Study* (1962); Carol Ohmann, *Ford Madox Ford: from Apprentice to Craftsman* (1964); Ann Barr Snitow, *Ford Madox Ford and the Voice of Uncertainty* (1984); Sondra J. Strang, *Ford Madox Ford* (1977); Paul L. Wiley, *Novelist of Three Worlds: Ford Madox Ford* (1962). Many serious critical essays have been written on *The Good Soldier*, as well as quite a few on Ford in general and on his impressionism. Some of the best are to be found in the following collections: *Ford Madox Ford: The Critical Heritage*, ed. Frank MacShane (1972); *Ford Madox Ford: Modern Judgements*, ed.

Richard A. Cassell (1972); *The Presence of Ford Madox Ford*, ed. Sondra J. Stang (including Denis Donoghue's essay, 1981); *Critical Essays on Ford Madox Ford*, ed. Richard A. Cassell (including essays by R. P. Blackmur, Samuel Hynes, and Mark Schorer, 1987). Several journals have devoted special issues to Ford: *Modern Fiction Studies*, 9.1 (1963); *Antaeus*, 56, ed. Sondra J. Stang (1986); *Contemporary Literature*, ed. Joseph Wiesenfarth 30.2 (1989). Among more recent, uncollected, essays, the following may be mentioned: David Eggenschwiler, 'Very like a Whale: The Comical-Tragical Illusions of *The Good Soldier*', *Genre*, 12.3 (1979), 401–14; Avrom Fleishman, 'The Genre of *The Good Soldier*: Ford's Comic Mastery', *Studies in the Literary Imagination*, 13.1 (1980), 31–42; Carol Jacobs, 'The (too) Good Soldier: "A Real Story"', *Glyph*, 3 (1978), 32–51; Frank Kermode, 'Novels: Recognition and Deception', *Critical Inquiry*, 1.1 (1974), 103–21; Michael Levenson, 'Character in *The Good Soldier*', *Twentieth Century Literature*, 30.1 (1984), 373–87. Finally, *A Concordance to Ford Madox Ford's 'The Good Soldier'*, by C. Ruth Sabol and Todd K. Bender (1981) is an obviously useful work.

A CHRONOLOGY OF
FORD MADOX FORD

1873   17 December: born Ford Hermann Hueffer, Merton, Surrey (now part of Greater London). Has two siblings: Oliver (1876–1931), novelist and journalist; Juliet (1880–1943), translator of Russian poetry.

1881   Enters modern, co-educational Praetorius School, Folkestone, Kent.

1889   Death of Ford's father, Dr Francis Hueffer, music critic and Provençal scholar. Ford goes to live with his grandfather, Ford Madox Brown, the Pre-Raphaelite painter. Attends University College School, London, for less than a year.

1891   Publishes first book, *The Brown Owl*, a children's fairy-tale, under the name Ford H. Madox Hueffer.

1892   Conversion to Roman Catholicism. Publishes first novel, *The Shifting of the Fire*; *The Feather* (fairy-tale).

1893   Death of grandfather. *The Questions at the Well* (poems).

1894   17 May: marriage to Elsie Martindale. Moves to southern Kent. *The Queen Who Flew* (fairy-tale).

1896   *Ford Madox Brown* (biography).

1897   Birth of daughter Christina.

1898   Meets Joseph Conrad. Later collaborates with him on *The Inheritors* (1901), *Romance* (1903), and *The Nature of a Crime* (1909).

1900   Birth of daughter Katharine. *Poems for Pictures*, *The Cinque Ports* (history).

1901   Moves near Martindale family at Winchelsea, Sussex.

1902   *Rossetti* (art criticism).

1903(?)   Begins affair with sister-in-law, Mary Martindale.

1904   March: beginning of long spell of neurasthenia. August to December: seeks cure in Germany. *The Face of the Night* (poems).

1905   Meets Arthur Marwood, who becomes a close friend. *The Soul of London* (essays), *The Benefactor* (novel), *Hans Holbein* (art criticism).

1906 Daughters received into the Roman Catholic Church. Visits United States with wife. *The Fifth Queen* (historical romance), *The Heart of the Country* (essays), *Christina's Fairy Book* (fairy-tales).

1907 Rents London *pied-à-terre* to further journalistic career. Meets Violet Hunt. *Privy Seal* (historical romance), *From Inland* (poems), *An English Girl* (novel), *The Pre-Raphaelite Brotherhood* (art criticism), *The Spirit of the People* (essays).

1908 Founds the *English Review*. *The Fifth Queen Crowned* (historical romance), *Mr Apollo* (fantasy).

1909 Quarrels with Conrad and Marwood. Leaves wife for Violet Hunt. Later, collaborates with her on *The Desirable Alien* (1913) and *Zeppelin Nights* (1915). Loses editorship of *The English Review*. The '*Half Moon*' (historical romance).

1910 *A Call* (novel), *Songs from London* (poems), *The Portrait* (historical romance).

1911 Loses custody of his children. Reconciled with Conrad and Marwood. 21 October: marriage to Violet Hunt reported in the *Daily Mirror*; Ford's wife sues *Mirror*. *The Simple Life Limited* (satirical novel), *Ancient Lights* (reminiscences), *Ladies Whose Bright Eyes* (historical fantasy), *The Critical Attitude* (criticism).

1912 *High Germany* (poems), *The Panel* (novel), *The New Humpty-Dumpty* (satirical novel).

1913 7 February: damages awarded to Ford's wife in highly publicized *Throne* magazine case. Ford in Bankruptcy Court. Begins brief infatuation with Brigit Patmore. *Mr Fleight* (satirical novel), *The Young Lovell* (historical romance), *Collected Poems*, *Henry James*.

1914 Begins writing war propaganda for Wellington House.

1915 14 August: commissioned Second Lieutenant, The Welch Regiment. *The Good Soldier* (novel), *When Blood is Their Argument* (war propaganda), *Between St Dennis and St George* (war propaganda).

1916 July: sees daughters for the last time, in London. Attached to First Line Transport, 9th Welch Battalion, under fire for ten days, Battle of the Somme. Collapses, sent to Casualty Clearing Station, reassigned to Wales. Late November: back in Rouen, falls ill and is again hospitalized.

1917　15 March: returns to England to serve in training capacity. Meets Stella Bowen.

1918　*On Heaven* (poems).

1919　January: resigns commission. April: moves to Sussex farmhouse. June: joined by Stella Bowen and changes name to Ford Madox Ford.

1920　Birth of daughter Julia.

1921　*A House* (long poem), *Thus to Revisit* (reminiscences).

1922　Moves to France, alternating between Provence and Paris.

1923　December: begins editing the *Transatlantic Review*. *The Marsden Case* (novel), *Mr Bosphorous and the Muses* (pantomime), *Women & Men* (essays, written in 1911).

1924　Begins affair with Jean Rhys. May: makes first of many postwar trips to United States. November: demise of *Transatlantic Review*. *Some Do Not* (novel, first of the Tietjens tetralogy, posthumously called *Parade's End*), *Joseph Conrad* (reminiscences and criticism).

1925　*No More Parades* (second Tietjens novel).

1926　*A Mirror to France* (essays), *A Man Could Stand Up* (third Tietjens novel).

1927　Separation from Stella Bowen. *New Poems*, *New York is Not America* (essays), *New York Essays*.

1928　*Last Post* (fourth Tietjens novel), *A Little Less Than Gods* (historical romance).

1929　*The English Novel* (literary history and criticism), *No Enemy* (fictionalized autobiography, largely written in 1919).

1930　Meets Janice Biala, Polish–American painter. Lives with her until his death.

1931　*When the Wicked Man* (novel), *Return to Yesterday* (reminiscences, 1894–1914).

1933　*The Rash Act* (novel), *It Was the Nightingale* (reminiscences from 1918 to present).

1934　*Henry for Hugh* (novel, sequel to *The Rash Act*).

1935 *Provence* (travel book).

1936 *Vive Le Roy* (novel), *Collected Poems*.

1937 Appointed writer and critic in residence, Olivet College, Michigan. *Great Trade Route* (travel book), *Portraits from Life* (reminiscences and criticism, published in England in 1938 as *Mightier than the Sword*).

1939 26 June: dies in Deauville, France. *The March of Literature* (literary history and criticism).

1988 *A History of Our Own Times* (history of Western Europe, England, and the United States, 1870–95; finished by 1930, as the first of three planned volumes).

DEDICATORY LETTER
TO STELLA FORD*

My dear Stella,

I have always regarded this as my best book—at any rate as the best book of mine of a pre-war period; and between its writing and the appearance of my next novel nearly ten years must have elapsed, so that whatever I may have since written may be regarded as the work of a different man—as the work of *your* man. For it is certain that without the incentive to live that you offered me I should scarcely have survived the war-period and it is more certain still that without your spurring me again to write I should never have written again. And it happens that, by a queer chance, *The Good Soldier* is almost alone amongst my books in being dedicated to no one: Fate must have elected to let it wait the ten years that it waited—for this dedication.

What I am now I owe to you: what I was when I wrote *The Good Soldier* I owed to the concatenation of circumstances of a rather purposeless and wayward life. Until I sat down to write this book—on the 17th December, 1913—I had never attempted to extend myself, to use a phrase of race-horse training. Partly because I had always entertained very fixedly the idea that—whatever may be the case with other writers—I at least should not be able to write a novel by which I should care to stand before reaching the age of forty; partly because I very definitely did not want to come into competition with other writers whose claim or whose need for recognition and what recognitions bring were greater than my own. I had never really tried to put into any novel of mine *all* that I knew about writing. I had written rather desultorily a number of books—a great number—but they had all been in the nature of *pastiches*, of pieces of rather precious writing, or of *tours de force*. But I have always been mad about writing—about the way writing should be done and partly alone, partly with the companionship of Conrad,* I had even at that date made exhaustive studies into how words should be handled and novels constructed.

So, on the day I was forty I sat down to show what I could do—and *The Good Soldier* resulted. I fully intended it to be my last book. I used to think—and I do not know that I do not think the same now—that one book was enough for any man to write, and, at the date when *The Good Soldier* was finished, London at least and possibly the world appeared to be passing under the dominion of writers newer and much more vivid. Those were the passionate days of the literary Cubists, Vorticists, Imagistes* and the rest of the tapageur* and riotous Jeunes* of that young decade. So I regarded myself as the Eel which, having reached the deep sea, brings forth its young and dies—or as the Great Auk* I considered that, having reached my allotted, I had laid my one egg and might as well die. So I took a formal farewell of Literature in the columns of a magazine called the *Thrush**—which also, poor little auk that it was, died of the effort. Then I prepared to stand aside in favour of our good friends—yours and mine—Ezra, Eliot, Wyndham Lewis, H. D.,* and the rest of the clamorous young writers who were then knocking at the door.

But greater clamours beset London and the world which till then had seemed to lie at the proud feet of those conquerors; Cubism, Vorticism, Imagism and the rest never had their fair chance amid the voices of the cannon, and so I have come out of my hole again and beside your strong, delicate and beautiful works have taken heart to lay some work of my own.

The Good Soldier, however, remains my great auk's egg for me as being something of a race that will have no successors and as it was written so long ago I may not seem over-vain if I consider it for a moment or two. No author, I think, is deserving of much censure for vanity if, taking down one of his ten-year-old books, he exclaims: 'Great Heavens, did I write as well as that then?' for the implication always is that one does not any longer write so well and few are so envious as to censure the complacencies of an extinct volcano.

Be that as it may, I was lately forced into the rather close examination of this book, for I had to translate it into French,* that forcing me to give it much closer attention than would be the case in any reading however minute. And I will permit myself to say that I was astounded at the work I must have put into the construction of the book, at the intricate tangle of references and cross-references. Nor is that to be wondered at for, though I wrote it with comparative rapidity, I had it hatching within myself for fully another decade. That was because the story is a true story and because I had it from Edward Ashburnham himself and I could not write it till all the others were dead. So I carried it about with me all those years, thinking about it from time to time.

I had in those days an ambition: that was to do for the English novel what in *Fort Comme la Mort*, Maupassant* had done for the French. One day I had my reward, for I happened to be in a company where a fervent young admirer exclaimed: 'By Jove, *The Good Soldier* is the finest novel in the English language!' whereupon my friend Mr. John Rodker* who has always had a properly tempered admiration for my work remarked in his clear, slow drawl: 'Ah yes. It is, but you have left out a word. It is the finest French novel in the English language!'

With that—which is my tribute to my masters and betters of France—I will leave the book to the reader. But I should like to say a word about the title. This book was originally called by me *The Saddest Story*, but since it did not appear till the darkest days of the war were upon us, Mr. Lane* importuned me with letters and telegrams—I was by that time engaged in other pursuits!—to change the title which he said would at that date render the book unsaleable. One day, when I was on parade, I received a final wire of appeal from Mr. Lane, and the telegraph being reply-paid I seized the reply-form and wrote in hasty irony: 'Dear Lane, Why not

The Good Soldier?' . . . To my horror six months later the book appeared under that title.

I have never ceased to regret it but, since the War, I have received so much evidence that the book has been read under that name that I hesitate to make a change for fear of causing confusion. Had the chance occurred during the War I should not have hesitated to make the change, for I had only two evidences that anyone had ever heard of it. On one occasion I met the adjutant of my regiment just come off leave and looking extremely sick. I said: 'Great Heavens, man, what is the matter with you?' He replied: 'Well, the day before yesterday I got engaged to be married and to-day I have been reading *The Good Soldier*.'

On the other occasion I was on parade again, being examined in drill, on the Guards' Square at Chelsea. And, since I was petrified with nervousness, having to do it before a half-dozen elderly gentlemen with red hatbands, I got my men about as hopelessly boxed as it is possible to do with the gentlemen privates of H.M. Coldstream Guards. Whilst I stood stiffly at attention one of the elderly red hatbands walked close behind my back and said distinctly in my ear, 'Did you say *The Good Soldier*?' So no doubt Mr. Lane was avenged. At any rate I have learned that irony may be a two-edged sword.

You, my dear Stella, will have heard me tell these stories a great many times. But the seas now divide us and I put them in this, your letter, which you will read before you see me in the hope that they may give you some pleasure with the illusion that you are hearing familiar—and very devoted—tones. And so I subscribe myself in all truth and in the hope that you will accept at once the particular dedication of this book and the general dedication of the edition.   Your

F. M. F.

NEW YORK, *January* 9, 1927.

THE
GOOD SOLDIER

A TALE OF PASSION

BY

FORD MADOX HUEFFER

AUTHOR OF "THE FIFTH QUEEN," ETC.

"Beati Immaculati"[*]

LONDON : JOHN LANE, THE BODLEY HEAD
NEW YORK : JOHN LANE COMPANY
MCMXV

THE
GOOD SOLDIER
A TALE OF PASSION

BY

FORD MADOX HUEFFER

AUTHOR OF "THE FIFTH QUEEN," etc.

"Beati Immaculati"

LONDON JOHN LANE THE BODLEY HEAD
NEW YORK: JOHN LANE COMPANY
MCMXV

THE GOOD SOLDIER

I

THIS is the saddest story I have ever heard.
We had known the Ashburnhams for nine
seasons of the town of Nauheim* with an extreme intimacy—or, rather, with an acquaintanceship
as loose and easy and yet as close as a good glove's
with your hand. My wife and I knew Captain and
Mrs. Ashburnham as well as it was possible to know
anybody, and yet, in another sense, we knew nothing
at all about them. This is, I believe, a state of things
only possible with English people of whom, till to-day,
when I sit down to puzzle out what I know of this
sad affair, I knew nothing whatever. Six months ago
I had never been to England, and, certainly, I had
never sounded the depths of an English heart. I had
known the shallows.

I don't mean to say that we were not acquainted
with many English people. Living, as we perforce
lived, in Europe, and being, as we perforce were,
leisured Americans, which is as much as to say that
we were un-American, we were thrown very much
into the society of the nicer English. Paris, you see,
was our home. Somewhere between Nice and Bordighera* provided yearly winter quarters for us, and Nauheim* always received us from July to September. You

will gather from this statement that one of us had, as
the saying is, a "heart," and, from the statement that
my wife is dead, that she was the sufferer.

Captain Ashburnham also had a heart. But, whereas a yearly month or so at Nauheim tuned him up to
exactly the right pitch for the rest of the twelvemonth,
the two months or so were only just enough to keep
poor Florence alive from year to year. The reason for
his heart was, approximately, polo, or too much hard
sportsmanship in his youth. The reason for poor
Florence's broken years was a storm at sea upon our
first crossing to Europe, and the immediate reasons for
our imprisonment in that continent were doctors' orders. They said that even the short Channel crossing
might well kill the poor thing.

When we all first met, Captain Ashburnham, home
on sick leave from an India to which he was never to
return, was thirty-three; Mrs. Ashburnham—Leonora
—was thirty-one. I was thirty-six and poor Florence
thirty. Thus to-day Florence would have been thirty-
nine and Captain Ashburnham forty-two; whereas I
am forty-five and Leonora forty. You will perceive,
therefore, that our friendship has been a young-mid-
dle-aged affair, since we were all of us of quite quiet
dispositions, the Ashburnhams being more particularly
what in England it is the custom to call "quite good
people."

They were descended, as you will probably expect,
from the Ashburnham* who accompanied Charles I to
the scaffold, and, as you must also expect with this
class of English people, you would never have noticed

it. Mrs. Ashburnham was a Powys; Florence was a Hurlbird of Stamford, Connecticut, where, as you know, they are more old-fashioned than even the inhabitants of Cranford,* England, could have been. I myself am a Dowell of Philadelphia, Pa., where, it is historically true, there are more old English families than you would find in any six English counties taken together. I carry about with me, indeed—as if it were the only thing that invisibly anchored me to any spot upon the globe—the title deeds of my farm, which once covered several blocks between Chestnut and Walnut Streets.* These title deeds are of wampum,* the grant of an Indian chief to the first Dowell, who left Farnham in Surrey in company with William Penn.* Florence's people, as is so often the case with the inhabitants of Connecticut, came from the neighbourhood of Fordingbridge,* where the Ashburnhams' place is. From there, at this moment, I am actually writing.

You may well ask why I write. And yet my reasons are quite many. For it is not unusual in human beings who have witnessed the sack of a city or the falling to pieces of a people to desire to set down what they have witnessed for the benefit of unknown heirs or of generations infinitely remote; or, if you please, just to get the sight out of their heads.

Someone has said that the death of a mouse from cancer is the whole sack of Ròme by the Goths, and I swear to you that the breaking up of our little four-square coterie was such another unthinkable event. Supposing that you should come upon us sitting together at one of the little tables in front of the club

house, let us say, at Homburg,* taking tea of an afternoon and watching the miniature golf, you would have
said that, as human affairs go, we were an extraordinarily safe castle. We were, if you will, one of those
tall ships with the white sails upon a blue sea, one
of those things that seem the proudest and the safest
of all the beautiful and safe things that God has
permitted the mind of men to frame. Where better
could one take refuge? Where better?

Permanence? Stability! I can't believe it's gone.
I can't believe that that long, tranquil life, which was
just stepping a minuet, vanished in four crashing days
at the end of nine years and six weeks. Upon my
word, yes, our intimacy was like a minuet, simply
because on every possible occasion and in every possible circumstance we knew where to go, where to sit,
which table we unanimously should choose; and we
could rise and go, all four together, without a signal
from any one of us, always to the music of the Kur
orchestra, always in the temperate sunshine, or, if it
rained, in discreet shelters. No, indeed, it can't be
gone. You can't kill a minuet de la cour. You may
shut up the music-book, close the harpsichord; in the
cupboard and presses the rats may destroy the white
satin favours.* The mob may sack Versailles; the
Trianon* may fall, but surely the minuet—the minuet
itself is dancing itself away into the furthest stars,
even as our minuet of the Hessian* bathing places must
be stepping itself still. Isn't there any heaven where
old beautiful dances, old beautiful intimacies prolong
themselves? Isn't there any Nirvana* pervaded by the

faint thrilling of instruments that have fallen into the dust of wormwood but that yet had frail, tremulous, and everlasting souls?

No, by God, it is false! It wasn't a minuet that we stepped; it was a prison—a prison full of screaming hysterics, tied down so that they might not outsound the rolling of our carriage wheels as we went along the shaded avenues of the Taunus Wald.*

And yet I swear by the sacred name of my creator that it was true. It was true sunshine; the true music; the true plash of the fountains from the mouth of stone dolphins. For, if for me we were four people with the same tastes, with the same desires, acting—or, no, not acting—sitting here and there unanimously, isn't that the truth? If for nine years I have possessed a goodly apple that is rotten at the core and discover its rottenness only in nine years and six months less four days, isn't it true to say that for nine years I possessed a goodly apple? So it may well be with Edward Ashburnham, with Leonora his wife and with poor dear Florence. And, if you come to think of it, isn't it a little odd that the physical rottenness of at least two pillars of our four-square house never presented itself to my mind as a menace to its security? It doesn't so present itself now though the two of them are actually dead. I don't know . . .

I know nothing—nothing in the world—of the hearts of men. I only know that I am alone—horribly alone. No hearthstone will ever again witness, for me, friendly intercourse. No smoking-room will ever be other than peopled with incalculable simulacra amidst smoke wreaths. Yet, in the name of God, what should I know if I don't know the life of the hearth and of the smoking-room, since my whole life has been passed in those places? The warm hearthside!—Well, there was Florence: I believe that for the twelve years her life lasted, after the storm that seemed irretrievably to have weakened her heart—I don't believe that for one minute she was out of my sight, except when she was safely tucked up in bed and I should be downstairs, talking to some good fellow or other in some lounge or smoking-room or taking my final turn with a cigar before going to bed. I don't, you understand, blame Florence. But how can she have known what she knew? How could she have got to know it? To know it so fully. Heavens! There doesn't seem to have been the actual time. It must have been when I was taking my baths, and my Swedish exercises, being manicured. Leading the life I did, of the sedulous, strained nurse, I had to do something to keep myself fit. It must have been then! Yet even that can't have been enough time to get the tremendously long conversations full of worldly wisdom that Leonora has reported to me since their deaths. And is it possible to imagine that during our prescribed walks in Nauheim and the neighbourhood she found time to carry on the protracted negotiations which she did carry on between Edward Ashburnham and his wife? And isn't it incredible that during all that time Edward and Leonora never spoke a word to each other in private? What is one to think of humanity?

For I swear to you that they were the model couple.

He was as devoted as it was possible to be without appearing fatuous. So well set up, with such honest blue eyes, such a touch of stupidity, such a warm goodheartedness! And she—so tall, so splendid in the saddle, so fair! Yes, Leonora was extraordinarily fair and so extraordinarily the real thing that she seemed too good to be true. You don't, I mean, as a rule, get it all so superlatively together. To be the county family,* to look the county family, to be so appropriately and perfectly wealthy; to be so perfect in manner—even just to the saving touch of insolence that seems to be necessary. To have all that and to be all that! No, it was too good to be true. And yet, only this afternoon, talking over the whole matter she said to me:—"Once I tried to have a lover but I was so sick at the heart, so utterly worn out that I had to send him away." That struck me as the most amazing thing I had ever heard. She said "I was actually in a man's arms. Such a nice chap! Such a dear fellow! And I was saying to myself, fiercely, hissing it between my teeth, as they say in novels—and really clenching them together: I was saying to myself: 'Now, I'm in for it and I'll really have a good time for once in my life— for once in my life!' It was in the dark, in a carriage, coming back from a hunt ball. Eleven miles we had to drive! And then suddenly the bitterness of the endless poverty, of the endless acting—it fell on me like a blight, it spoilt everything. Yes, I had to realise that I had been spoilt even for the good time when it came. And I burst out crying and I cried and I cried for the whole eleven miles. Just imagine *me*

crying! And just imagine me making a fool of the
poor dear chap like that. It certainly wasn't playing
the game, was it now?"

I don't know; I don't know; was that last remark
of hers the remark of a harlot, or is it what every decent woman, county family or not county family,
thinks at the bottom of her heart? Or thinks all the
time for the matter of that? Who knows?

Yet, if one doesn't know that at this hour and day,
at this pitch of civilisation to which we have attained,
after all the preachings of all the moralists, and all
the teachings of all the mothers to all the daughters
*in saeculum saeculorum**. . . but perhaps that is what
all mothers teach all daughters, not with lips but with
the eyes, or with heart whispering to heart. And, if
one doesn't know as much as that about the first thing
in the world, what does one know and why is one
here?

I asked Mrs. Ashburnham whether she had told
Florence that and what Florence had said and she answered:—"Florence didn't offer any comment at all.
What could she say? There wasn't anything to be
said. With the grinding poverty we had to put up with
to keep up appearances, and the way the poverty
came about—*you* know what I mean—any woman
would have been justified in taking a lover and presents
too. Florence once said about a very similar position
—she was a little too well-bred, too American, to talk
about mine—that it was a case of perfectly open riding
and the woman could just act on the spur of the moment. She said it in American of course, but that

was the sense of it. I think her actual words were:—
'That it was up to her to take it or leave it . . .'."

I don't want you to think that I am writing Teddy
Ashburnham down a brute. I don't believe he was.
God knows, perhaps all men are like that. For as
I've said what do I know even of the smoking-room?
Fellows come in and tell the most extraordinarily gross
stories—so gross that they will positively give you a
pain. And yet they'd be offended if you suggested
that they weren't the sort of person you could trust
your wife alone with. And very likely they'd be quite
properly offended—that is if you can trust anybody
alone with anybody. But that sort of fellow obviously
takes more delight in listening to or in telling gross
stories—more delight than in anything else in the
world. They'll hunt languidly and dress languidly and
dine languidly and work without enthusiasm and find
it a bore to carry on three minutes' conversation about
anything whatever and yet, when the other sort of
conversation begins, they'll laugh and wake up and
throw themselves about in their chairs. Then, if they
so delight in the narration, how is it possible that
they can be offended—and properly offended at the
suggestion that they might make attempts upon your
wife's honour? Or again: Edward Ashburnham was
the cleanest looking sort of chap;—an excellent magistrate, a first rate soldier, one of the best landlords,
so they said, in Hampshire, England. To the poor
and to hopeless drunkards, as I myself have witnessed,
he was like a painstaking guardian. And he never
told a story that couldn't have gone into the columns

of the *Field* more than once or twice in all the nine years of my knowing him. He didn't even like hearing them; he would fidget and get up and go out to buy a cigar or something of that sort. You would have said that he was just exactly the sort of chap that you could have trusted your wife with. And I trusted mine—and it was madness.

And yet again you have me. If poor Edward was dangerous because of the chastity of his expressions —and they say that that is always the hall-mark of a libertine—what about myself? For I solemnly avow that not only have I never so much as hinted at an impropriety in my conversation in the whole of my days; and more than that, I will vouch for the cleanness of my thoughts and the absolute chastity of my life. At what, then, does it all work out? Is the whole thing a folly and a mockery? Am I no better than a eunuch or is the proper man—the man with the right to existence—a raging stallion forever neighing after his neighbour's womenkind?

I don't know. And there is nothing to guide us. And if everything is so nebulous about a matter so elementary as the morals of sex, what is there to guide us in the more subtle morality of all other personal contacts, associations, and activities? Or are we meant to act on impulse alone? It is all a darkness.

II

I DON'T know how it is best to put this thing down—whether it would be better to try and tell the story from the beginning, as if it were a story; or whether to tell it from this distance of time, as it reached me from the lips of Leonora or from those of Edward himself.

So I shall just imagine myself for a fortnight or so at one side of the fireplace of a country cottage, with a sympathetic soul opposite me. And I shall go on talking, in a low voice while the sea sounds in the distance and overhead the great black flood of wind polishes the bright stars. From time to time we shall get up and go to the door and look out at the great moon and say:—"Why, it is nearly as bright as in Provence!" And then we shall come back to the fireside, with just the touch of a sigh because we are not in that Provence where even the saddest stories are gay. Consider the lamentable history of Peire Vidal.* Two years ago, Florence and I motored from Biarritz to Las Tours, which is in the Black Mountains. In the middle of a tortuous valley there rises up an immense pinnacle and on the pinnacle are four castles—Las Tours, the Towers. And the immense mistral* blew down that valley which was the way from France into Provence so that the silver grey olive leaves appeared like hair flying in the wind, and the tufts of rosemary crept into the iron rocks that they might not be torn up by the roots.

It was, of course, poor dear Florence who wanted to go to Las Tours. You are to imagine that, however much her bright personality came from Stamford, Connecticut, she was yet a graduate of Vassar.* I never could imagine how she did it—the queer, chattery person that she was. With the far-away look in her eyes—which wasn't, however, in the least romantic—I mean that she didn't look as if she were seeing poetic dreams, or looking through you, for she hardly ever did look at you!—holding up one hand as if she wished to silence any objection—or any comment for the matter of that—she would talk. She would talk about William the Silent,* about Gustave the Loquacious,* about Paris frocks, about how the poor dressed in 1337, about Fantin Latour,* about the Paris-Lyons-Mediterranée train-de-luxe, about whether it would be worth while to get off at Tarascon and go across the windswept suspension-bridge, over the Rhone to take another look at Beaucaire.

We never did take another look at Beaucaire, of course—beautiful Beaucaire, with the high, triangular white tower, that looked as thin as a needle and as tall as the Flatiron,* between Fifth and Broadway— Beaucaire with the grey walls on the top of the pinnacle surrounding an acre and a half of blue irises, beneath the tallness of the stone pines. What a beautiful thing the stone pine is! . . .

No, we never did go back anywhere. Not to Heidelberg, not to Hamelin, not to Verona, not to Mont

Majour—not so much as to Carcassonne itself. We talked of it, of course, but I guess Florence got all she wanted out of one look at a place. She had the seeing eye.

I haven't, unfortunately, so that the world is full of places to which I want to return—towns with the blinding white sun upon them; stone pines against the blue of the sky; corners of gables, all carved and painted with stags and scarlet flowers and crowstepped* gables with the little saint at the top; and grey and pink palazzi* and walled towns a mile or so back from the sea, on the Mediterranean, between Leghorn and Naples. Not one of them did we see more than once, so that the whole world for me is like spots of colour in an immense canvas. Perhaps if it weren't so I should have something to catch hold of now.

Is all this digression or isn't it digression? Again I don't know. You, the listener, sit opposite me. But you are so silent. You don't tell me anything. I am, at any rate, trying to get you to see what sort of life it was I led with Florence and what Florence was like. Well, she was bright; and she danced. She seemed to dance over the floors of castles and over seas and over and over the salons of modistes* and over the *plages* of the Riviera—like a gay tremulous beam, reflected from water upon a ceiling. And my function in life was to keep that bright thing in existence. And it was almost as difficult as trying to catch with your hand that dancing reflection. And the task lasted for years.

Florence's aunts used to say that I must be the

laziest man in Philadelphia. They had never been to Philadelphia and they had the New England conscience. You see, the first thing they said to me when I called in on Florence in the little ancient, colonial, wooden house beneath the high, thin-leaved elms—the first question they asked me was not how I did but what did I do. And I did nothing. I suppose I ought to have done something, but I didn't see any call to do it. Why does one do things? I just drifted in and wanted Florence. First I had drifted in on Florence at a Browning tea,* or something of the sort in Fourteenth Street,* which was then still residential. I don't know why I had gone to New York; I don't know why I had gone to the tea. I don't see why Florence should have gone to that sort of spelling bee. It wasn't the place at which, even then, you expected to find a Vassar graduate. I guess Florence wanted to raise the culture of the Stuyvesant crowd*and did it as she might have gone in slumming. Intellectual slumming, that was what it was. She always wanted to leave the world a little more elevated than she found it. Poor dear thing, I have heard her lecture Teddy Ashburnham by the hour on the difference between a Franz Hals* and a Woovermans* and why the Pre-Mycenaic* statues were cubical with knobs on the top. I wonder what he made of it? Perhaps he was thankful.

I know I was. For do you understand my whole attentions, my whole endeavours were to keep poor dear Florence on to topics like the finds at Gnossos* and the mental spirituality of Walter Pater.* I had to keep her at it, you understand, or she might die. For I was solemnly informed that if she became excited over anything or if her emotions were really stirred her little heart might cease to beat. For twelve years I had to watch every word that any person uttered in any conversation and I had to head it off what the English call "things"—off love, poverty, crime, religion and the rest of it. Yes, the first doctor that we had when she was carried off the ship at Havre assured me that this must be done. Good God, are all these fellows monstrous idiots, or is there a freemasonry between all of them from end to end of the earth? . . . That is what makes me think of that fellow Peire Vidal.

Because, of course, his story is culture and I had to head her towards culture and at the same time it's so funny and she hadn't got to laugh, and it's so full of love and she wasn't to think of love. Do you know the story? Las Tours of the Four Castles had for chatelaine* Blanche Somebody-or-other who was called as a term of commendation, La Louve—the She-Wolf. And Peire Vidal the Troubadour* paid his court to La Louve. And she wouldn't have anything to do with him. So, out of compliment to her—the things people do when they're in love!—he dressed himself up in wolfskins and went up into the Black Mountains. And the shepherds of the Montagne Noire and their dogs mistook him for a wolf and he was torn with the fangs and beaten with clubs. So they carried him back to Las Tours and La Louve wasn't at all impressed. They polished him up and her husband remonstrated seriously with her. Vidal was, you see, a great poet and it was not proper to treat a great poet with indifference.

So Peire Vidal declared himself Emperor of Jerusalem or somewhere and the husband had to kneel down and kiss his feet though La Louve wouldn't. And Peire set sail in a rowing boat with four companions to redeem the Holy Sepulchre.* And they struck on a rock somewhere, and, at great expense, the husband had to fit out an expedition to fetch him back. And Peire Vidal fell all over the Lady's bed while the husband, who was a most ferocious warrior, remonstrated some more about the courtesy that is due to great poets. But I suppose La Louve was the more ferocious of the two. Anyhow, that is all that came of it. Isn't that a story?

You haven't an idea of the queer old fashionedness of Florence's aunts—the Misses Hurlbird,* nor yet of her uncle. An extraordinarily lovable man, that Uncle John. Thin, gentle, and with a "heart" that made his life very much what Florence's afterwards became. He didn't reside at Stamford; his home was in Waterbury*where the watches come from. He had a factory there which, in our queer American way, would change its functions almost from year to year. For nine months or so it would manufacture buttons out of bone. Then it would suddenly produce brass buttons for coachmen's liveries. Then it would take a turn at embossed tin lids for candy boxes. The fact is that the poor old gentleman, with his weak and fluttering heart, didn't want his factory to manufacture

anything at all. He wanted to retire. And he did retire when he was seventy. But he was so worried at
having all the street boys in the town point after him
and exclaim:—"There goes the laziest man in Waterbury!" that he tried taking a tour round the world.
And Florence and a young man called Jimmy went
with him. It appears from what Florence told me
that Jimmy's function with Mr. Hurlbird was to avoid
exciting topics for him. He had to keep him, for
instance, out of political discussions. For the poor
old man was a violent Democrat in' days when you
might travel the world over without finding anything
but a Republican.* Anyhow, they went round the
world.

I think an anecdote is about the best way to give you
an idea of what the old gentleman was like. For it is
perhaps important that you should know what the old
gentleman was; he had a great deal of influence in
forming the character of my poor dear wife.

Just before they set out from San Francisco for
the South Seas old Mr. Hurlbird said he must take
something with him to make little presents to people
he met on the voyage. And it struck him that the
things to take for that purpose were oranges—because California is the orange country—and comfortable folding chairs. So he bought I don't know how
many cases of oranges—the great cool California
oranges, and half-a-dozen folding chairs in a special
case that he always kept in his cabin. There must
have been half a cargo of fruit.

For, to every person on board the several steam-

ers that they employed—to every person with whom
he had so much as a nodding acquaintance, he gave an
orange every morning. And they lasted him right
round the girdle of this mighty globe of ours. When
they were at North Cape,* even, he saw on the horizon, poor dear thin man that he was, a lighthouse.
"Hello," says he to himself, "these fellows must be
very lonely. Let's take them some oranges." So he
had a boatload of his fruit out and had himself rowed
to the lighthouse on the horizon. The folding-chairs he
lent to any lady that he came across and liked or who
seemed tired and invalidish on the ship. And so,
guarded against his heart and, having his niece with
him, he went round the world . . .

He wasn't obtrusive about his heart. You wouldn't
have known he had one. He only left it to the physical laboratory at Waterbury for the benefit of science,
since he considered it to be quite an extraordinary
kind of heart. And the joke of the matter was that,
when, at the age of eighty-four, just five days before
poor Florence, he died of bronchitis there was found
to be absolutely nothing the matter with that organ.
It had certainly jumped or squeaked or something
just sufficiently to take in the doctors, but it appears
that that was because of an odd formation of the
lungs. I don't much understand about these matters.

I inherited his money because Florence died five
days after him. I wish I hadn't. It was a great
worry. I had to go out to Waterbury just after Florence's death because the poor dear old fellow had left
a good many charitable bequests and I had to appoint

trustees. I didn't like the idea of their not being properly handled.

Yes, it was a great worry. And just as I had got things roughly settled I received the extraordinary cable from Ashburnham begging me to come back and have a talk with him. And immediately afterwards came one from Leonora saying, "Yes, please do come. You could be so helpful." It was as if he had sent the cable without consulting her and had afterwards told her. Indeed, that was pretty much what had happened, except that he had told the girl and the girl told the wife. I arrived, however, too late to be of any good if I could have been of any good. And then I had my first taste of English life. It was amazing. It was overwhelming. I never shall forget the polished cob that Edward, beside me, drove; the animal's action, its highstepping, its skin that was like satin. And the peace! And the red cheeks! And the beautiful, beautiful old house.

Just near Branshaw Teleragh it was and we descended on it from the high, clear, windswept waste of the New Forest.* I tell you it was amazing to arrive there from Waterbury. And it came into my head —for Teddy Ashburnham, you remember, had cabled to me to "come and have a talk" with him—that it was unbelievable that anything essentially calamitous could happen to that place and those people. I tell you it was the very spirit of peace. And Leonora, beautiful and smiling, with her coils of yellow hair, stood on the top doorstep, with a butler and footman and a maid or so behind her. And she just said:—"So

glad you've come," as if I'd run down to lunch from
a town ten miles away, instead of having come half
the world over at the call of two urgent telegrams.

The girl was out with the hounds, I think.

And that poor devil beside me was in an agony.
Absolute, hopeless, dumb agony such as passes the
mind of man to imagine.

III

I T was a very hot summer, in August, 1904; and
Florence had already been taking the baths for
a month. I don't know how it feels to be a patient at one of those places. I never was a patient
anywhere. I daresay the patients get a home feeling
and some sort of anchorage in the spot. They seem
to like the bath attendants, with their cheerful faces,
their air of authority, their white linen. But, for
myself, to be at Nauheim gave me a sense—what shall
I say?—a sense almost of nakedness—the nakedness
that one feels on the sea-shore or in any great open
space. I had no attachments, no accumulations. In
one's own home it is as if little, innate sympathies draw
one to particular chairs that seem to enfold one in
an embrace, or take one along particular streets that
seem friendly when others may be hostile. And, believe me, that feeling is a very important part of
life. I know it well, that have been for so long a
wanderer upon the face of public resorts. And one
is too polished up. Heaven knows I was never an untidy man. But the feeling that I had when, whilst
poor Florence was taking her morning bath, I stood
upon the carefully swept steps of the Englischer Hof,*
looking at the carefully arranged trees in tubs upon
the carefully arranged gravel whilst carefully arranged
people walked past in carefully calculated gaiety, at

the carefully calculated hour, the tall trees of the public gardens, going up to the right; the reddish stone
of the baths—or were they white half-timber châlets?*
Upon my word I have forgotten, I who was there so
often. That will give you the measure of how much
I was in the landscape. I could find my way blindfolded to the hot rooms,* to the douche*rooms, to the
fountain in the centre of the quadrangle where the
rusty water gushes out. Yes, I could find my way
blindfolded. I know the exact distances. From the
Hotel Regina you took one hundred and eighty-seven
paces, then, turning sharp, lefthanded, four hundred
and twenty took you straight down to the fountain.
From the Englischer Hof, starting on the sidewalk,
it was ninety-seven paces and the same four hundred
and twenty, but turning lefthanded this time.

And now you understand that, having nothing in
the world to do—but nothing whatever! I fell into
the habit of counting my footsteps. I would walk with
Florence to the baths. And, of course, she entertained
me with her conversation. It was, as I have said, wonderful what she could make conversation out of. She
walked very lightly, and her hair was very nicely done,
and she dressed beautifully and very expensively. Of
course she had money of her own, but I shouldn't have
minded. And yet you know I can't remember a single one of her dresses. Or I can remember just one,
a very simple one of blue figured silk—a Chinese
pattern—very full in the skirts and broadening out
over the shoulders. And her hair was copper-col-
oured, and the heels of her shoes were exceedingly

high, so that she tripped upon the points of her toes. And when she came to the door of the bathing place and, when it opened to receive her, she would look back at me with a little coquettish smile, so that her cheek appeared to be caressing her shoulder.

I seem to remember that, with that dress, she wore an immensely broad Leghorn hat*—like the Chapeau de Paille of Rubens,* only very white. The hat would be tied with a lightly knotted scarf of the same stuff as her dress. She knew how to give value to her blue eyes. And round her neck would be some simple pink, coral beads. And her complexion had a perfect clearness, a perfect smoothness . . .

Yes, that is how I most exactly remember her, in that dress, in that hat, looking over her shoulder at me so that the eyes flashed very blue—dark pebble blue . . .

And, what the devil! For whose benefit did she do it? For that of the bath attendant? of the passers-by? I don't know. Anyhow, it can't have been for me, for never, in all the years of her life never on any possible occasion, or in any other place did she so smile to me, mockingly, invitingly. Ah, she was a riddle; but then, all other women are riddles. And it occurs to me that some way back I began a sentence that I have never finished . . . It was about the feeling that I had when I stood on the steps of my hotel every morning before starting out to fetch Florence back from the bath. Natty, precise, well-brushed, conscious of being rather small amongst the long English, the lank Americans, the rotund Germans, and the obese Russian Jewesses, I should stand there, tapping a cigarette on the outside of my case, surveying for a moment the world in the sunlight. But a day was to come when I was never to do it again alone. You can imagine, therefore, what the coming of the Ashburnhams meant for me.

I have forgotten the aspect of many things but I shall never forget the aspect of the dining-room of the Hotel Excelsior on that evening—and on so many other evenings. Whole castles have vanished from my memory, whole cities that I have never visited again, but that white room, festooned with papier-maché fruits and flowers; the tall windows; the many tables; the black screen round the door with three golden cranes flying upward on each panel; the palm-tree in the centre of the room; the swish of the waiter's feet; the cold expensive elegance; the mien of the diners as they came in every evening—their air of earnestness as if they must go through a meal prescribed by the Kur authorities and their air of sobriety as if they must seek not by any means to enjoy their meals—those things I shall not easily forget. And then, one evening, in the twilight, I saw Edward Ashburnham lounge round the screen into the room. The head waiter, a man with a face all grey—in what subterranean nooks or corners do people cultivate those absolutely grey complexions?—went with the timorous patronage of these creatures towards him and held out a grey ear to be whispered into. It was generally a disagreeable ordeal for newcomers but Edward Ashburnham bore it like an Englishman and a gentleman.

I could see his lips form a word of three syllables—remember I had nothing in the world to do but to notice these niceties—and immediately I knew that he must be Edward Ashburnham, Captain, Fourteenth Hussars, of Branshaw House, Branshaw Teleragh. I knew it because every evening just before dinner, whilst I waited in the hall, I used, by the courtesy of Monsieur Schontz, the proprietor, to inspect the little police reports that each guest was expected to sign upon taking a room.

The head waiter piloted him immediately to a vacant table, three away from my own—the table that the Grenfalls of Falls River, N. J., had just vacated. It struck me that that was not a very nice table for the newcomers, since the sunlight, low though it was, shone straight down upon it, and the same idea seemed to come at the same moment into Captain Ashburnham's head. His face hitherto had, in the wonderful English fashion, expressed nothing whatever. Nothing. There was in it neither joy nor despair; neither hope nor fear; neither boredom nor satisfaction. He seemed to perceive no soul in that crowded room; he might have been walking in a jungle. I never came across such a perfect expression before and I never shall again. It was insolence and not insolence; it was modesty and not modesty. His hair was fair, extraordinarily, ordered in a wave, running from the left temple to the right; his face was a light brick-red, perfectly uniform in tint up to the roots of the hair itself; his yellow moustache was as stiff as a toothbrush and I verily believe that he had his black smok-

ing jacket thickened a little over the shoulder-blades
so as to give himself the air of the slightest possible
stoop. It would be like him to do that; that was the
sort of thing he thought about. Martingales,* Chiffney*
bits, boots; where you got the best soap, the best
brandy, the name of the chap who rode a plater* down
the Khyber cliffs; the spreading power of number
three shot before a charge of number four powder
. . . by heavens, I hardly ever heard him talk of
anything else. Not in all the years that I knew him
did I hear him talk of anything but these subjects. Oh,
yes, once he told me that I could buy my special shade
of blue ties cheaper from a firm in Burlington Arcade*
than from my own people in New York. And I have
bought my ties from that firm ever since. Otherwise
I should not remember the name of the Burlington
Arcade. I wonder what it looks like. I have never
seen it. I imagine it to be two immense rows of pillars, like those of the Forum at Rome, with Edward
Ashburnham striding down between them. But it
probably isn't—the least like that. Once also he advised me to buy Caledonian Deferred, since they were
due to rise. And I did buy them and they did rise.
But of how he got the knowledge I haven't the faintest idea. It seemed to drop out of the blue sky.

And that was absolutely all that I knew of him
until a month ago—that and the profusion of his
cases, all of pigskin and stamped with his initials, E.
F. A. There were guncases, and collar cases, and
shirt cases, and letter cases and cases each containing
four bottles of medicine; and hat cases and helmet

cases. It must have needed a whole herd of the Gadarene swine* to make up his outfit. And, if I ever penetrated into his private room it would be to see him standing, with his coat and waistcoat off and the immensely long line of his perfectly elegant trousers from waist to boot heel. And he would have a slightly reflective air and he would be just opening one kind of case and just closing another.

Good God, what did they all see in him; for I swear that was all there was of him, inside and out; though they said he was a good soldier. Yet, Leonora adored him with a passion that was like an agony, and hated him with an agony that was as bitter as the sea. How could he rouse anything like a sentiment, in anybody?

What did he even talk to them about—when they were under four eyes?—Ah, well, suddenly, as if by a flash of inspiration, I know. For all good soldiers are sentimentalists—all good soldiers of that type. Their profession, for one thing is full of the big words, courage, loyalty, honour, constancy. And I have given a wrong impression of Edward Ashburnham if I have made you think that literally never in the course of our nine years of intimacy did he discuss what he would have called "the graver things." Even before his final outburst to me, at times, very late at night, say, he has blurted out something that gave an insight into the sentimental view of the cosmos that was his. He would say how much the society of a good woman could do towards redeeming you, and he would say that constancy was the finest of the virtues. He said it very stiffly, of course, but still as if the statement admitted of no doubt.

Constancy! Isn't that the queer thought? And yet, I must add that poor dear Edward was a great reader —he would pass hours lost in novels of a sentimental type—novels in which typewriter girls married Marquises and governesses Earls. And in his books, as a rule, the course of true love ran as smooth as buttered honey. And he was fond of poetry, of a certain type—and he could even read a perfectly sad love story. I have seen his eyes filled with tears at reading of a hopeless parting. And he loved, with a sentimental yearning, all children, puppies, and the feeble generally . . .

So, you see, he would have plenty to gurgle about to a woman—with that and his sound common sense about martingales and his—still sentimental—experiences as a county magistrate; and with his intense, optimistic belief that the woman he was making love to at the moment was the one he was destined, at last, to be eternally constant to . . . Well, I fancy he could put up a pretty good deal of talk when there was no man around to make him feel shy. And I was quite astonished, during his final burst out to me— at the very end of things, when the poor girl was on her way to that fatal Brindisi and he was trying to persuade himself and me that he had never really cared for her—I was quite astonished to observe how literary and how just his expressions were. He talked like quite a good book—a book not in the least cheaply sentimental. You see, I suppose he regarded me not

so much as a man. I had to be regarded as a woman
or a solicitor. Anyhow, it burst out of him on that
horrible night. And then, next morning, he took me
over to the Assizes*and I saw how, in a perfectly calm
and business-like way he set to work to secure a verdict of not guilty for a poor girl, the daughter of
one of his tenants who had been accused of murdering her baby. He spent two hundred pounds on her
defence . . . Well, that was Edward Ashburnham.

I had forgotten about his eyes. They were as blue
as the sides of a certain type of box of matches. When
you looked at them carefully you saw that they were
perfectly honest, perfectly straightforward, perfectly,
perfectly stupid. But the brick pink of his complexion,
running perfectly level to the brick pink of his inner
eyelids, gave them a curious, sinister expression—like
a mosaic of blue porcelain set in pink china. And that
chap, coming into a room, snapped up the gaze of
every woman in it, as dexterously as a conjurer pockets billiard balls. It was most amazing. You know
the man on the stage who throws up sixteen balls at
once and they all drop into pockets all over his person, on his shoulders, on his heels, on the inner side
of his sleeves; and he stands perfectly still and does
nothing. Well, it was like that. He had rather a
rough, hoarse voice.

And, there he was, standing by the table. I was
looking at him, with my back to the screen. And,
suddenly, I saw two distinct expressions flicker across
his immobile eyes. How the deuce did they do it,
those unflinching blue eyes with the direct gaze? For

the eyes themselves never moved, gazing over my shoulder towards the screen. And the gaze was perfectly level and perfectly direct and perfectly unchanging. I suppose that the lids really must have rounded themselves a little and perhaps the lips moved a little too, as if he should be saying:—"There you are, my dear." At any rate, the expression was that of pride, of satisfaction, of the possessor. I saw him once afterwards, for a moment, gaze upon the sunny fields of Branshaw and say:—"All this is my land!"

And then again, the gaze was perhaps more direct, harder if possible—hardy too. It was a measuring look; a challenging look. Once when we were at Wiesbaden* watching him play in a polo match against the Bonner Hussaren* I saw the same look come into his eyes, balancing the possibilities, looking over the ground. The German Captain, Count Baron Idigon von Lelöffel,* was right up by their goal posts, coming with the ball in an easy canter in that tricky German fashion. The rest of the field were just anywhere. It was only a scratch sort of affair. Ashburnham was quite close to the rails not five yards from us and I heard him saying to himself:—"Might just be done!" And he did it. Goodness! he swung that pony round with all its four legs spread out, like a cat dropping off a roof. . . .

Well, it was just that look that I noticed in his eyes:—"It might," I seem even now to hear him muttering to himself, "just be done."

I looked round over my shoulder and saw, tall, smiling brilliantly and buoyant—Leonora. And, little and fair, and as radiant as the track of sunlight along the sea—my wife.

That poor wretch! to think that he was at that moment in a perfect devil of a fix, and there he was, saying at the back of his mind:—"It might just be done." It was like a chap in the middle of the eruption of a volcano, saying that he might just manage to bolt into the tumult and set fire to a haystack. Madness? Predestination? Who the devil knows?

Mrs. Ashburnham exhibited at that moment more gaiety than I have ever since known her to show. There are certain classes of English people—the nicer ones when they have been to many spas, who seem to make a point of becoming much more than usually animated when they are introduced to my compatriots. I have noticed this often. Of course, they must first have accepted the Americans. But, that once done, they seem to say to themselves: "Hallo, these women are so bright. We aren't going to be outdone in brightness." And for the time being they certainly aren't. But it wears off. So it was with Leonora—at least until she noticed me. She began, Leonora did—and perhaps it was that that gave me the idea of a touch of insolence in her character, for she never afterwards did any one single thing like it—she began by saying in quite a loud voice and from quite a distance:

"Don't stop over by that stuffy old table, Teddy. Come and sit by these nice people!"

And that was an extraordinary thing to say. Quite extraordinary. I couldn't for the life of me refer to total strangers as nice people. But, of course, she was taking a line of her own in which I at any rate—and no one else in the room, for she too had taken the trouble to read through the list of guests—counted any more than so many clean, bull terriers. And she sat down rather brilliantly at a vacant table, beside ours —one that was reserved for the Guggenheimers. And she just sat absolutely deaf to the remonstrances of the head waiter with his face like a grey ram's. That poor chap was doing his steadfast duty too. He knew that the Guggenheimers of Chicago, after they had stayed there a month and had worried the poor life out of him, would give him two dollars fifty and grumble at the tipping system. And he knew that Teddy Ashburnham and his wife would give him no trouble whatever except what the smiles of Leonora might cause in his apparently unimpressionable bosom— though you never can tell what may go on behind even a not quite spotless plastron!*—And every week Edward Ashburnham would give him a solid, sound, golden English sovereign. Yet this stout fellow was intent on saving that table for the Guggenheimers of Chicago. It ended in Florence saying:

"Why shouldn't we all eat out of the same trough —that's a nasty New York saying. But I'm sure we're all nice quiet people and there can be four seats at our table. It's round."

Then came, as it were, an appreciative gurgle from the Captain and I was perfectly aware of a slight hesitation—a quick sharp motion in Mrs. Ashburnham, as if her horse had checked. But she put it at

the fence all right, rising from the seat she had taken
and sitting down opposite me, as it were, all in one
motion.

I never thought that Leonora looked her best in
evening dress. She seemed to get it too clearly cut,
there was no ruffling. She always affected black and
her shoulders were too classical. She seemed to stand
out of her corsage*as a white marble bust might out of
a black Wedgwood vase. I don't know.

I loved Leonora always and, to-day, I would very
cheerfully lay down my life, what is left of it, in her
service. But I am sure I never had the beginnings
of a trace of what is called the sex instinct towards
her. And I suppose—no I am certain that she never
had it towards me. As far as I am concerned I think
it was those white shoulders that did it. I seemed
to feel when I looked at them that, if ever I should
press my lips upon them that they would be slightly
cold—not icily, not without a touch of human heat,
but, as they say of baths, with the chill off. I seemed
to feel chilled at the end of my lips when I looked at
her . . .

No, Leonora always appeared to me at her best in
a blue tailor-made. Then her glorious hair wasn't
deadened by her white shoulders. Certain women's
lines guide your eyes to their necks, their eyelashes,
their lips, their breasts. But Leonora's seemed to conduct your gaze always to her wrist. And the wrist
was at its best in a black or a dog-skin glove and there
was always a gold circlet with a little chain support-
ing a very small golden key to a dispatch box. Per-

haps it was that in which she locked up her heart and her feelings.

Anyhow, she sat down opposite me and then, for the first time, she paid any attention to my existence. She gave me, suddenly, yet deliberately, one long stare. Her eyes too were blue and dark and the eyelids were so arched that they gave you the whole round of the irises. And it was a most remarkable, a most moving glance, as if for a moment a lighthouse had looked at me. I seemed to perceive the swift questions chasing each other through the brain that was behind them. I seemed to hear the brain ask and the eyes answer with all the simpleness of a woman who was a good hand at taking in qualities of a horse—as indeed she was. "Stands well; has plenty of room for his oats behind the girth. Not so much in the way of shoulders," and so on. And so her eyes asked: "Is this man trustworthy in money matters; is he likely to try to play the lover; is he likely to let his women be troublesome? Is he, above all, likely to babble about my affairs?"

And, suddenly, into those cold, slightly defiant, almost defensive china blue orbs, there came a warmth, a tenderness, a friendly recognition . . . oh, it was very charming and very touching—and quite mortifying. It was the look of a mother to her son, of a sister to her brother. It implied trust; it implied the want of any necessity for barriers. By God, she looked at me as if I were an invalid—as any kind woman may look at a poor chap in a bath chair. And, yes, from that day forward she always treated me and not Florence as if I were the invalid. Why, she would run after me with a rug upon chilly days. I suppose, therefore, that her eyes had made a favourable answer. Or, perhaps, it wasn't a favourable answer. And then Florence said: "And so the whole round table is begun." Again Edward Ashburnham gurgled slightly in his throat; but Leonora shivered a little, as if a goose had walked over her grave. And I was passing her the nickel-silver basket of rolls. Avanti! ...

S O began those nine years of uninterrupted tranquillity. They were characterised by an extraordinary want of any communicativeness on
the part of the Ashburnhams to which, we on our part
replied by leaving out quite as extraordinarily, and
nearly as completely, the personal note. Indeed, you
may take it that what characterised our relationship
was an atmosphere of taking everything for granted.
The given proposition was, that we were all "good
people." We took for granted that we all liked beef
underdone but not too underdone; that both men preferred a good liqueur brandy after lunch; that both
women drank a very light Rhine wine qualified with
Fachingen water*—that sort of thing. It was also
taken for granted that we were both sufficiently well
off to afford anything that we could reasonably want
in the way of amusements fitting to our station—that
we could take motor cars and carriages by the day;
that we could give each other dinners and dine our
friends and we could indulge if we liked in economy.
Thus, Florence was in the habit of having the *Daily
Telegraph* sent to her every day from London. She
was always an Anglo-maniac, was Florence; the Paris
edition of the New York *Herald* was always good
enough for me. But when we discovered that the
Ashburnhams' copy of the London paper followed

them from England, Leonora and Florence decided between them to suppress one subscription one year and the other the next. Similarly it was the habit of the Grand Duke* of Nassau Schwerin, who came yearly to the baths, to dine once with about eighteen families of regular Kur guests. In return he would give a dinner to all the eighteen at once. And, since these dinners were rather expensive (you had to take the Grand Duke and a good many of his suite and any members of the diplomatic bodies that might be there) —Florence and Leonora, putting their heads together, didn't see why we shouldn't give the Grand Duke his dinner together. And so we did. I don't suppose the Serenity minded that economy, or even noticed it. At any rate, our joint dinner to the Royal Personage gradually assumed the aspect of a yearly function. Indeed, it grew larger and larger, until it became a sort of closing function for the season, at any rate, as far as we were concerned.

I don't in the least mean to say that we were the sort of persons who aspired to mix "with royalty." We didn't; we hadn't any claims; we were just "good people." But the Grand Duke was a pleasant, affable sort of royalty, like the late King Edward VII, and it was pleasant to hear him talk about the races and, very occasionally, as a bonne bouche,* about his nephew, the Emperor; or to have him pause for a moment in his walk to ask after the progress of our cures or to be benignantly interested in the amount of money we had put on Lelöffel's hunter for the Frankfurt Welter Stakes.

But upon my word, I don't know how we put in our time. How does one put in one's time? How is it possible to have achieved nine years and to have nothing whatever to show for it? Nothing whatever, you understand. Not so much as a bone penholder, carved to resemble a chessman and with a hole in the top through which you could see four views of Nauheim. And, as for experience, as for knowledge of one's fellow beings—nothing either. Upon my word, I couldn't tell you offhand whether the lady who sold the so expensive violets at the bottom of the road that leads to the station, was cheating me or no; I can't say whether the porter who carried our traps* across the station at Leghorn was a thief or no when he said that the regular tariff was a lire a parcel. The instances of honesty that one comes across in this world are just as amazing as the instances of dishonesty. After forty-five years of mixing with one's kind, one ought to have acquired the habit of being able to know something about one's fellow beings. But one doesn't.

I think the modern civilised habit—the modern English habit of taking everyone for granted is a good deal to blame for this. I have observed this matter long enough to know the queer, subtle thing that it is; to know how the faculty, for what it is worth, never lets you down.

Mind, I am not saying that this is not the most desirable type of life in the world; that it is not an almost unreasonably high standard. For it is really nauseating, when you detest it, to have to eat every day several slices of thin, tepid, pink india rubber, and it is disagreeable to have to drink brandy when you would prefer to be cheered up by warm, sweet Kummel.* And it is nasty to have to take a cold bath in the morning when what you want is really a hot one at night. And it stirs a little of the faith of your fathers that is deep down within you to have to have it taken for granted that you are an Episcopalian when really you are an old-fashioned Philadelphia Quaker.

But these things have to be done; it is the cock that the whole of this society owes to Æsculapius.*

And the odd, queer thing is that the whole collection of rules applies to anybody—to the anybodies that you meet in hotels, in railway trains, to a less degree, perhaps, in steamers, but even, in the end, upon steamers. You meet a man or a woman and, from tiny and intimate sounds, from the slightest of movements, you know at once whether you are concerned with good people or with those who won't do. You know, that is to say, whether they will go rigidly through with the whole programme from the underdone beef to the Anglicanism. It won't matter whether they be short or tall; whether the voice squeak like a marionette or rumble like a town bull's; it won't matter whether they are Germans, Austrians, French, Spanish, or even Brazilians—they will be the Germans or Brazilians who take a cold bath every morning and who move, roughly speaking, in diplomatic circles.

But the inconvenient—well, hang it all, I will say it —the damnable nuisance of the whole thing is, that with all the taking for granted, you never really get an inch deeper than the things I have catalogued.

I can give you a rather extraordinary instance of this. I can't remember whether it was in our first year —the first year of us four at Nauheim, because, of course, it would have been the fourth year of Florence and myself—but it must have been in the first or second year. And that gives the measure at once of the extraordinariness of our discussion and of the swiftness with which intimacy had grown up between us. On the one hand we seemed to start out on the expedition so naturally and with so little preparation, that it was as if we must have made many such excursions before; and our intimacy seemed so deep. . . .

Yet the place to which we went was obviously one to which Florence at least would have wanted to take us quite early, so that you would almost think we should have gone there together at the beginning of our intimacy. Florence was singularly expert as a guide to archæological exceptions and there was nothing she liked so much as taking people round ruins and showing you the window from which someone looked down upon the murder of someone else. She only did it once; but she did it quite magnificently. She could find her way, with the sole help of Baedeker, as easily about any old monument as she could about any American city where the blocks are all square and the streets all numbered, so that you can go perfectly easily from Twenty-fourth to Thirtieth.

Now it happens that fifty minutes away from Nauheim, by a good train, is the ancient city of M——,* upon a great pinnacle of basalt, girt with a triple road running sideways up its shoulder like a scarf. And at the top there is a castle—not a square castle like Windsor—but a castle all slate gables and high peaks with gilt weathercocks flashing bravely—the castle of St. Elizabeth of Hungary.* It has the disadvantage of being in Prussia; and it is always disagreeable to go into that country; but it is very old and there are many double-spired churches and it stands up like a pyramid out of the green valley of the Lahn.* I don't suppose the Ashburnhams wanted especially to go there and I didn't especially want to go there myself. But, you understand, there was no objection. It was part of the cure to make an excursion three or four times a week. So that we were all quite unanimous in being grateful to Florence for providing the motive power. Florence, of course, had a motive of her own. She was at that time engaged in educating Captain Ashburnham—oh, of course, quite pour le bon motif!* She used to say to Leonora: "I simply can't understand how you can let him live by your side and be so ignorant!" Leonora herself always struck me as being remarkably well educated. At any rate, she knew beforehand all that Florence had to tell her. Perhaps she got it up out of Baedeker* before Florence was up in the morning. I don't mean to say that you would ever have known that Leonora knew anything, but if Florence started to tell us how Ludwig the Courageous* wanted to have three wives at once—in which he differed from Henry VIII, who wanted them one after the other, and this caused a good deal of trouble—if Florence started to tell us this, Leonora would just nod her head in a way that quite pleasantly rattled my poor wife.

She used to exclaim: "Well, if you knew it, why haven't you told it all already to Captain Ashburnham? I'm sure he finds it interesting!" And Leonora would look reflectively at her husband and say: "I have an idea that it might injure his hand—the hand, you know, used in connection with horses' mouths . . ." And poor Ashburnham would blush and mutter and would say: "That's all right. Don't you bother about me."

I fancy his wife's irony did quite alarm poor Teddy; because one evening he asked me seriously in the smoking-room if I thought that having too much in one's head would really interfere with one's quickness in polo. It struck him, he said, that brainy Johnnies generally were rather muffs*when they got on to four legs. I reassured him as best I could. I told him that he wasn't likely to take in enough to upset his balance. At that time the Captain was quite evidently enjoying being educated by Florence. She used to do it about three or four times a week under the approving eyes of Leonora and myself. It wasn't, you understand, systematic. It came in bursts. It was Florence clearing up one of the dark places of the earth, leaving the world a little lighter than she had found it. She would tell him the story of Hamlet; explain the form of a symphony, humming the first and second subjects to him, and so on; she would explain to him the difference between Arminians and Erastians;* or she would give him a short lecture on the early history of the United States. And it was done in a way well calculated to arrest a young attention. Did you ever read Mrs. Markham?* Well, it was like that . . .

But our excursion to M—— was a much larger, a much more full dress affair. You see, in the archives of the Schloss*in that city there was a document which Florence thought would finally give her the chance to educate the whole lot of us together. It really worried poor Florence that she couldn't, in matters of culture, ever get the better of Leonora. I don't know what Leonora knew or what she didn't know but certainly she was always there whenever Florence brought out any information. And she gave, somehow, the impression of really knowing what poor Florence gave the impression of having only picked up. I can't exactly define it. It was almost something physical. Have you ever seen a retriever dashing in play after a greyhound? You see the two running over a green field, almost side by side, and suddenly the retriever makes a friendly snap at the other. And the greyhound simply isn't there. You haven't observed it quicken its speed or strain a limb; but there it is, just two yards in front of the retriever's outstretched muzzle. So it was with Florence and Leonora in matters of culture.

But on this occasion I knew that something was up. I found Florence some days before, reading books like Ranke's *History of the Popes,* Symonds' *Renaissance,* Motley's *Rise of the Dutch Republic,* and Luther's *Table Talk.**

I must say that, until the astonishment came, I got nothing but pleasure out of the little expedition. I like catching the two-forty; I like the slow, smooth roll of the great big trains—and they are the best trains in the world! I like being drawn through the green country and looking at it through the clear glass of the great windows. Though, of course, the country isn't really green. The sun shines, the earth is blood red and purple and red and green and red. And the oxen in the ploughlands are bright varnished brown and black and blackish purple; and the peasants are dressed in the black and white of magpies; and there are great flocks of magpies too. Or the peasants' dresses in another field where there are little mounds of hay that will be grey-green on the sunny side and purple in the shadows—the peasants' dresses are vermilion with emerald green ribbons and purple skirts and white shirts and black velvet stomachers.* Still, the impression is that you are drawn through brilliant green meadows that run away on each side to the dark purple fir-woods; the basalt pinnacles; the immense forests. And there is meadow-sweet* at the edge of the streams, and cattle. Why, I remember on that afternoon I saw a brown cow hitch its horns under the stomach of a black and white animal and the black and white one was thrown right into the middle of a narrow stream. I burst out laughing. But Florence was imparting information so hard and Leonora was listening so intently that no one noticed me. As for me, I was pleased to be off duty; I was pleased to think that Florence for the moment was indubitably out of mischief—because she was talking about Ludwig the Courageous (I think it was Ludwig the Courageous but I am not an historian) about Ludwig the Courageous of Hessen* who wanted to have three wives at once and patronised Luther—something like that!—I was so relieved to be off duty, because she couldn't possibly be doing anything to excite herself or set her poor heart a-fluttering—that the incident of the cow was a real joy to me. I chuckled over it from time to time for the whole rest of the day. Because it does look very funny, you know, to see a black and white cow land on its back in the middle of a stream. It is so just exactly what one doesn't expect of a cow.

I suppose I ought to have pitied the poor animal; but I just didn't. I was out for enjoyment. And I just enjoyed myself. It is so pleasant to be drawn along in front of the spectacular towns with the peaked castle and the many double spires. In the sunlight gleams come from the city—gleams from the glass of windows; from the gilt signs of apothecaries; from the ensigns of the student corps high up in the mountains; from the helmets of the funny little soldiers moving their stiff little legs in white linen trousers. And it was pleasant to get out in the great big spectacular Prussian station with the hammered bronze ornaments and the paintings of peasants and flowers and cows; and to hear Florence bargain energetically with the driver of an ancient droschka* drawn by two lean horses. Of course, I spoke German much more correctly than Florence, though I never could rid myself quite of the accent of the Pennsylvania Duitsch* of my childhood. Anyhow, we were drawn in a sort of triumph, for five marks without any trinkgeld,* right up to the castle. And we were taken through the museum and saw the firebacks,* the old glass, the old swords and the antique contraptions. And we went up winding corkscrew staircases and through the Rittersaal, the great painted hall where the Reformer* and his friends met for the first time under the protection of the gentleman that had three wives at once and formed an alliance with the gentleman that had six wives, one after the other (I'm not really interested in these facts but they have a bearing on my story). And we went through chapels, and music rooms, right up immensely high in the air to a large old chamber, full of presses, with heavily-shuttered windows all round. And Florence became positively electric. She told the tired, bored custodian what shutters to open; so that the bright sunlight streamed in palpable shafts into the dim old chamber. She explained that this was Luther's bedroom and that just where the sunlight fell had stood his bed. As a matter of fact, I believe that she was wrong and that Luther only stopped, as it were, for lunch, in order to evade pursuit. But, no doubt, it would have been his bedroom if he could have been persuaded to stop the night. And then, in spite of the protest of the custodian, she threw open another shutter and came tripping back to a large glass case.

"And there," she exclaimed with an accent of gaiety, of triumph, and of audacity. She was pointing at a piece of paper, like the half-sheet of a letter with some faint pencil scrawls that might have been a jotting of the amounts we were spending during the day. And I was extremely happy at her gaiety, in her triumph, in her audacity. Captain Ashburnham had his hands upon the glass case. "There it is—the Protest." And then, as we all properly stage-managed our bewilderment, she continued: "Don't you know that is why we were all called Protestants? That is the pencil draft of the Protest*they drew up. You can see the signatures of Martin Luther, and Martin Bucer, and Zwingli,* and Ludwig the Courageous . . ."

I may have got some of the names wrong, but I know that Luther and Bucer were there. And her animation continued and I was glad. She was better and she was out of mischief. She continued, looking up into Captain Ashburnham's eyes: "It's because of that piece of paper that you're honest, sober, industrious, provident, and clean-lived. If it weren't for that piece of paper you'd be like the Irish or the Italians or the Poles, but particularly the Irish . . ."

And she laid one finger upon Captain Ashburnham's wrist.

I was aware of something treacherous, something frightful, something evil in the day. I can't define it and can't find a simile for it. It wasn't as if a snake had looked out of a hole. No, it was as if my heart had missed a beat. It was as if we were going to run and cry out; all four of us in separate directions, averting our heads. In Ashburnham's face I know that there was absolute panic. I was horribly

frightened and then I discovered that the pain in my
left wrist was caused by Leonora's clutching it:

"I can't stand this," she said with a most extraordinary passion; "I must get out of this."

I was horribly frightened. It came to me for a moment, though I hadn't time to think it, that she must
be a madly jealous woman—jealous of Florence and
Captain Ashburnham, of all people in the world! And
it was a panic in which we fled! We went right down
the winding stairs, across the immense Rittersaal to a
little terrace that overlooks the Lahn, the broad valley
and the immense plain into which it opens out.

"Don't you see?" she said, "don't you see what's
going on?" The panic again stopped my heart. I mut-
tered, I stuttered—I don't know how I got the words
out:

"No! What's the matter? Whatever's the matter?"

She looked me straight in the eyes; and for a moment I had the feeling that those two blue discs were
immense, were overwhelming, were like a wall of blue
that shut me off from the rest of the world. I know
it sounds absurd; but that is what it did feel like.

"Don't you see," she said, with a really horrible
bitterness, with a really horrible lamentation in her
voice, "Don't you see that that's the cause of the whole
miserable affair; of the whole sorrow of the world?
And of the eternal damnation of you and me and
them . . ."

I don't remember how she went on; I was too frightened; I was too amazed. I think I was thinking of

running to fetch assistance—a doctor, perhaps, or Captain Ashburnham. Or possibly she needed Florence's tender care, though, of course, it would have been very bad for Florence's heart. But I know that when I came out of it she was saying: "Oh, where are all the bright, happy, innocent beings in the world? Where's happiness? One reads of it in books!"

She ran her hand with a singular clawing motion upwards over her forehead. Her eyes were enormously distended; her face was exactly that of a person looking into the pit of hell and seeing horrors there. And then suddenly she stopped. She was, most amazingly, just Mrs. Ashburnham again. Her face was perfectly clear, sharp and defined; her hair was glorious in its golden coils. Her nostrils twitched with a sort of contempt. She appeared to look with interest at a gypsy caravan that was coming over a little bridge far below us.

"Don't you know," she said, in her clear hard voice, "don't you know that I'm an Irish Catholic?"

V

THOSE words gave me the greatest relief that I have ever had in my life. They told me, I think, almost more than I have ever gathered at any one moment—about myself. I don't think that before that day I had ever wanted anything very much except Florence. I have, of course, had appetites, impatiences . . . Why, sometimes at a table d'hôte, when there would be, say, caviare handed round, I have been absolutely full of impatience for fear that when the dish came to me there should not be a satisfying portion left over by the other guests. I have been exceedingly impatient at missing trains. The Belgian State Railway has a trick of letting the French trains miss their connections at Brussels. That has always infuriated me. I have written about it letters to the *Times* that the *Times* never printed; those that I wrote to the Paris edition of the New York *Herald* were always printed, but they never seemed to satisfy me when I saw them. Well, that was a sort of frenzy with me.

It was a frenzy that now I can hardly realise. I can understand it intellectually. You see, in those days I was interested in people with "hearts." There was Florence, there was Edward Ashburnham—or, perhaps, it was Leonora that I was more interested in. I don't mean in the way of love. But, you see, we were both of the same profession—at any rate as I saw it. And the profession was that of keeping heart patients alive.

You have no idea how engrossing such a profession may become. Just as the blacksmith says: "By hammer and hand all Art doth stand," just as the baker thinks that all the solar system revolves around his morning delivery of rolls; as the postmaster general believes that he alone is the preserver of society —and surely, surely, these delusions are necessary to keep us going—so did I and, as I believed, Leonora, imagine that the whole world ought to be arranged so as to ensure the keeping alive of heart patients. You have no idea how engrossing such a profession may become—how imbecile, in view of that engrossment, appear the ways of princes, of republics, of municipalities. A rough bit of road beneath the motor tyres, a couple of succeeding "thank'ee-marms"* with their quick jolts would be enough to set me grumbling to Leonora against the Prince or the Grand Duke or the Free City*through whose territory we might be passing. I would grumble like a stockbroker whose conversations over the telephone are incommoded by the ringing of bells from a city church. I would talk about mediæval survivals, about the taxes being surely high enough. The point, by the way, about the missing of the connections of the Calais boat trains at Brussels was that the shortest possible sea journey is frequently of great importance to sufferers from the heart. Now, on the Continent, there are two special heart cure places, Nauheim and Spa,* and to reach both of these baths from England if in order to ensure a short sea passage, you come by Calais—you have to make the connection at Brussels. And the Belgian train never waits by so much of the shade of a second for the one coming from Calais or from Paris. And even if the French trains are just on time, you have to run—imagine a heart patient running!—along the unfamiliar ways of the Brussels station and to scramble up the high steps of the moving train. Or, if you miss the connection, you have to wait five or six hours. . . . I used to keep awake whole nights cursing that abuse.

My wife used to run—she never, in whatever else she may have misled me, tried to give me the impression that she was not a gallant soul. But, once in the German Express, she would lean back, with one hand to her side and her eyes closed. Well, she was a good actress. And I would be in hell. In hell, I tell you. For in Florence I had at once a wife and an unattained mistress—that is what it comes to—and in the retaining of her in this world I had my occupation, my career, my ambition. It is not often that these things are united in one body. Leonora was a good actress too. By Jove she was good! I tell you, she would listen to me by the hour, evolving my plans for a shock-proof world. It is true that, at times I used to notice about her face an air of inattention as if she were listening, a mother, to the child at her knee, or as if, precisely, I were myself the patient.

You understand that there was nothing the matter

with Edward Ashburnham's heart—that he had thrown up his commission and had left India and come half the world over in order to follow a woman who had really had a "heart" to Nauheim. That was the sort of sentimental ass he was. For, you understand, too, that they really needed to live in India, to economise, to let the house at Branshaw Teleragh.

Of course, at that date, I had never heard of the Kilsyte case. Ashburnham had, you know, kissed a servant girl in a railway train and it was only the grace of God, the prompt functioning of the communication cord and the ready sympathy of what I believe you call the Hampshire bench, that kept the poor devil out of Winchester Gaol for years and years. I never heard of that case until the final stages of Leonora's revelations . . .

But just think of that poor wretch . . . I, who have surely the right, beg you to think of that poor wretch. Is it possible that such a luckless devil should be so tormented by blind and inscrutable destiny? For there is no other way to think of it. None. I have the right to say it, since for years he was my wife's lover, since he killed her, since he broke up all the pleasantnesses that there were in my life. There is no priest that has the right to tell me that I must not ask pity for him, from you, silent listener beyond the hearthstone, from the world, or from the God who created in him those desires, those madnesses . . .

Of course, I should not hear of the Kilsyte case. I knew none of their friends; they were for me just good people—fortunate people with broad and sunny

acres in a southern county. Just good people! By
Heavens, I sometimes think that it would have been
better for him, poor dear, if the case had been such
a one that I must needs have heard of it—such a one
as maids and couriers and other Kur guests whisper
about for years after, until gradually it dies away in
the pity that there is knocking about here and there in
the world. Supposing he had spent his seven years in
Winchester Gaol or whatever it is that inscrutable
and blind justice allots to you for following your
natural but ill-timed inclinations—there would have arrived a stage when nodding gossips on the Kursaal*
terrace would have said "Poor fellow," thinking of
his ruined career. He would have been the fine soldier with his back now bent . . . Better for him, poor
devil, if his back had been prematurely bent.

Why, it would have been a thousand times better.
. . . For, of course, the Kilsyte case, which came at
the very beginning of his finding Leonora cold and
unsympathetic, gave him a nasty jar. He left servants
alone after that.

It turned him, naturally, all the more loose amongst
women of his own class. Why, Leonora told me that
Mrs. Maidan, the woman he followed from Burma to
Nauheim—assured her he awakened her attention by
swearing that when he kissed the servant in the train
he was driven to it. I daresay he was driven to it,
by the mad passion to find an ultimately satisfying
woman. I daresay he was sincere enough. Heaven
help me, I daresay he was sincere enough in his love
for Mrs. Maidan. She was a nice little thing, a dear

little dark woman with long lashes, of whom Florence grew quite fond. She had a lisp and a happy smile. We saw plenty of her for the first month of our acquaintance, then she died, quite quietly—of heart trouble.

But you know, poor little Mrs. Maidan—she was so gentle, so young. She cannot have been more than twenty-three and she had a boy husband out in Chitral* not more than twenty-four, I believe. Such young things ought to have been left alone. Of course Ashburnham could not leave her alone. I do not believe that he could. Why, even I, at this distance of time am aware that I am a little in love with her memory. I can't help smiling when I think suddenly of her—as you might at the thought of something wrapped carefully away in lavender, in some drawer, in some old house that you have long left. She was so—so submissive. Why, even to me she had the air of being submissive—to me that not the youngest child will ever pay heed to. Yes, this is the saddest story . . .

No, I cannot help wishing that Florence had left her alone—with her playing with adultery. I suppose it was; though she was such a child that one has the impression that she would hardly have known how to spell such a word. No, it was just submissiveness—to the importunities, to the tempestuous forces that pushed that miserable fellow on to ruin. And I do not suppose that Florence really made much difference. If it had not been for her that Ashburnham left his allegiance for Mrs. Maidan, then it would have been some other woman. But still, I do not know. Perhaps the poor young thing would have died—she was bound to die, anyhow, quite soon—but she would have died without having to soak her noonday pillow with tears whilst Florence, below the window talked to Captain Ashburnham about the Constitution of the United States . . . Yes, it would have left a better taste in the mouth if Florence had let her die in peace . . .

Leonora behaved better in a sense. She just boxed Mrs. Maidan's ears—yes, she hit her, in an uncontrollable access of rage, a hard blow on the side of the cheek, in the corridor of the hotel, outside Edward's room. It was that, you know, that accounted for the sudden, odd intimacy that sprang up between Florence and Mrs. Ashburnham.

Because it was, of course, an odd intimacy. If you look at it from the outside nothing could have been more unlikely than that Leonora, who is the proudest creature on God's earth, would have struck up an acquaintanceship with two casual Yankees whom she could not really have regarded as being much more than a carpet beneath her feet. You may ask what she had to be proud of. Well, she was a Powys married to an Ashburnham—I suppose that gave her the right to despise casual Americans as long as she did it unostentatiously. I don't know what anyone has to be proud of. She might have taken pride in her patience, in her keeping her husband out of the bankruptcy court. Perhaps she did.

At any rate that was how Florence got to know

her. She came round a screen at the corner of the hotel corridor and found Leonora with the gold key that hung from her wrist caught in Mrs. Maidan's hair just before dinner. There was not a single word spoken. Little Mrs. Maidan was very pale, with a red mark down her left cheek and the key would not come out of her black hair. It was Florence who had to disentangle it, for Leonora was in such a state that she could not have brought herself to touch Mrs. Maidan without growing sick.

And there was not a word spoken. You see, under those four eyes—her own and Mrs. Maidan's—Leonora could just let herself go as far as to box Mrs. Maidan's ears. But the moment a stranger came along she pulled herself wonderfully up. She was at first silent and then, the moment the key was disengaged by Florence she was in a state to say: "So awkward of me . . . I was just trying to put the comb straight in Mrs. Maidan's hair . . ."

Mrs. Maidan, however, was not a Powys married to an Ashburnham; she was a poor little O'Flaherty whose husband was a boy of country parsonage origin. So there was no mistaking the sob that she let go as she went desolately away along the corridor. But Leonora was still going to play up. She opened the door of Ashburnham's room quite ostentatiously, so that Florence should hear her address Edward in terms of intimacy and liking. "Edward," she called. But there was no Edward there.

You understand that there was no Edward there. It was then, for the only time of her career that Leonora really compromised herself—She exclaimed . . . "How frightful! . . . Poor little Maisie! . . ."

She caught herself up at that, but of course it was too late. It was a queer sort of affair . . .

I want to do Leonora every justice. I love her very dearly for one thing and in this matter, which was certainly the ruin of my small household cockleshell, she certainly tripped up. I do not believe—and Leonora herself does not believe that poor little Maisie Maidan was ever Edward's mistress. Her heart was really so bad that she would have succumbed to anything like an impassioned embrace. That is the plain English of it, and I suppose plain English is best. She was really what the other two, for reasons of their own just pretended to be. Queer, isn't it? Like one of those sinister jokes that Providence plays upon one. Add to this that I do not suppose that Leonora would much have minded, at any other moment, if Mrs. Maidan had been her husband's mistress. It might have been a relief from Edward's sentimental gurglings over the lady and from the lady's submissive acceptance of those sounds. No, she would not have minded.

But, in boxing Mrs. Maidan's ears Leonora was just striking the face of an intolerable universe. For, that afternoon she had had a frightfully painful scene with Edward.

As far as his letters went, she claimed the right to open them when she chose. She arrogated to herself that right because Edward's affairs were in such a frightful state and he lied so about them that she claimed the privilege of having his secrets at her disposal. There was not, indeed, any other way, for the poor fool was too ashamed of his lapses ever to make a clean breast of anything. She had to drag these things out of him.

It must have been a pretty elevating job for her. But that afternoon, Edward being on his bed for the hour and a half prescribed by the Kur authorities, she had opened a letter that she took to come from a Colonel Hervey. They were going to stay with him in Linlithgowshire* for the month of September and she did not know whether the date fixed would be the eleventh or the eighteenth. The address on this letter was, in handwriting, as like Colonel Hervey's as one blade of corn is like another. So she had at the moment no idea of spying on him.

But she certainly was. For she discovered that Edward Ashburnham was paying a blackmailer of whom she had never heard something like three hundred pounds a year . . . It was a devil of a blow; it was like death; for she imagined that by that time she had really got to the bottom of her husband's liabilities. You see, they were pretty heavy. What had really smashed them up had been a perfectly commonplace affair at Monte Carlo—an affair with a cosmopolitan harpy who passed for the mistress of a Russian Grand Duke. She exacted a twenty thousand pound pearl tiara from him as the price of her favours for a week or so. It would have pipped* him a good deal to have found so much, and he was not in the ordinary way a gambler. He might, indeed,

just have found the twenty thousand and the not slight
charges of a week at an hotel with the fair creature.
He must have been worth at that date five hundred
thousand dollars and a little over.

Well, he must needs go to the tables and lose forty
thousand pounds . . . Forty thousand solid pounds,
borrowed from sharks! And even after that he must
—it was an imperative passion—enjoy the favours of
the lady. He got them, of course, when it was a matter of solid bargaining, for far less than twenty thousand, as he might, no doubt have done from the first.
I daresay ten thousand dollars covered the bill.

Anyhow, there was a pretty solid hole in a fortune
of a hundred thousand pounds or so. And Leonora
had to fix things up; he would have run from money
lender to money lender. And that was quite in the
early days of her discovery of his infidelities—if you
like to call them infidelities. And she discovered that
one from public sources. God knows what would
have happened if she had not discovered it from public sources. I suppose he would have concealed it
from her until they were penniless. But she was able,
by the grace of God, to get hold of the actual lenders
of the money, to learn the exact sums that were needed.
And she went off to England.

Yes, she went right off to England to her attorney
and his while he was still in the arms of his Circe—
at Antibes, to which place they had retired. He got
sick of the lady quite quickly, but not before Leonora
had had such lessons in the art of business from her
attorney that she had her plan as clearly drawn up

as was ever that of General Trochu*for keeping the Prussians out of Paris in 1870. It was about as effectual at first, or it seemed so.

That would have been, you know, in 1895, about nine years before the date of which I am talking—the date of Florence's getting her hold over Leonora; for that was what it amounted to . . . Well, Mrs. Ashburnham had simply forced Edward to settle all his property upon her. She could force him to do anything; in his clumsy, good-natured, inarticulate way he was as frightened of her as of the devil. And he admired her enormously, and he was as fond of her as any man could be of any woman. She took advantage of it to treat him as if he had been a person whose estates are being managed by the court of bankruptcy. I suppose it was the best thing for him.

Anyhow, she had no end of a job for the first three years or so. Unexpected liabilities kept on cropping up—and that afflicted fool did not make it any easier. You see, along with the passion of the chase went a frame of mind that made him be extraordinarily ashamed of himself. You may not believe it, but he really had such a sort of respect for the chastity of Leonora's imagination that he hated—he was positively revolted at the thought that she should know that the sort of thing that he did existed in the world. So he would stick out in an agitated way against the accusation of ever having done anything. He wanted to preserve the virginity of his wife's thoughts. He told me that himself during the long talks we had at the last—while the girl was on the way to Brindisi.

So, of course, for those three years or so, Leonora
had many agitations. And it was then that they really
quarrelled.

Yes, they quarrelled bitterly. That seems rather
extravagant. You might have thought that Leonora
would be just calmly loathing and he lachrymosely con-
trite. But that was not it a bit . . . Along with Edward's passions and his shame for them went the
violent conviction of the duties of his station—a conviction that was quite unreasonably expensive. I trust
I have not, in talking of his liabilities, given the impression that poor Edward was a promiscuous libertine. He was not; he was a sentimentalist. The
servant girl in the Kilsyte case had been pretty, but
mournful of appearance. I think that, when he had
kissed her, he had desired rather to comfort her. And,
if she had succumbed to his blandishments I daresay
he would have set her up in a little house in Portsmouth or Winchester and would have been faithful to
her for four or five years. He was quite capable of
that.

No, the only two of his affairs of the heart that
cost him money were that of the Grand Duke's mistress and that which was the subject of the blackmailing letter that Leonora opened. That had been
a quite passionate affair with quite a nice woman. It
had succeeded the one with the Grand Ducal Lady.
The lady was the wife of a brother officer and Leonora had known all about the passion, which had been
quite a real passion and had lasted for several years.
You see, poor Edward's passions were quite logical

in their progression upwards. They began with a servant, went on to a courtesan and then to a quite nice woman, very unsuitably mated. For she had a quite nasty husband who, by means of letters and things, went on blackmailing poor Edward to the tune of three or four hundred a year—with threats of the divorce court. And after this lady came Maisie Maidan, and after poor Maisie only one more affair and then—the real passion of his life. His marriage with Leonora had been arranged by his parents and, though he always admired her immensely, he had hardly ever pretended to be much more than tender to her, though he desperately needed her moral support, too . . .

But his really trying liabilities were mostly in the nature of generosities proper to his station. He was, according to Leonora, always remitting his tenants' rents and giving the tenants to understand that the reductions would be permanent; he was always redeeming drunkards who came before his magisterial bench; he was always trying to put prostitutes into respectable places—and he was a perfect maniac about children. I don't know how many ill-used people he did not pick up and provide with careers—Leonora has told me, but I daresay she exaggerated and the figure seems so preposterous that I will not put it down. All these things, and the continuance of them seemed to him to be his duty—along with impossible subscriptions to hospitals and boy scouts and to provide prizes at cattle shows and anti-vivisection societies . . .

Well, Leonora saw to it that most of these things

were not continued. They could not possibly keep up Branshaw Manor at that rate after the money had gone to the Grand Duke's mistress. She puts the rents back at their old figures; discharged the drunkards from their homes, and sent all the societies notice that they were to expect no more subscriptions. To the children, she was more tender; nearly all of them she supported till the age of apprenticeship or domestic service. You see, she was childless herself.

She was childless herself, and she considered herself to be to blame. She had come of a penniless branch of the Powys family, and they had forced her upon poor dear Edward without making the stipulation that the children should be brought up as Catholics. And that, of course, was spiritual death to Leonora. I have given you a wrong impression if I have not made you see that Leonora was a woman of a strong, cold conscience, like all English Catholics. (I cannot, myself, help disliking this religion; there is always, at the bottom of my mind, in spite of Leonora, the feeling of shuddering at the Scarlet Woman,* that filtered in upon me in the tranquillity of the little old Friends' Meeting House in Arch Street,* Philadelphia.) So I do set down a good deal of Leonora's mismanagement of poor dear Edward's case to the peculiarly English form of her religion. Because, of course, the only thing to have done for Edward would have been to let him sink down until he became a tramp of gentlemanly address, having, maybe, chance love affairs upon the highways. He would have done so much less harm; he would have been much less agonised, too. At any rate, he would have had fewer chances of ruining and of remorse. For Edward was great at remorse.

But Leonora's English Catholic conscience, her rigid principles, her coldness, even her very patience, were, I cannot help thinking, all wrong in this special case. She quite seriously and naïvely imagined that the Church of Rome disapproves of divorce; she quite seriously and naïvely believed that her church could be such a monstrous and imbecile institution as to expect her to take on the impossible job of making Edward Ashburnham a faithful husband. She had, as the English would say, the Nonconformist* temperament. In the United States of North America we call it the New England conscience. For, of course, that frame of mind has been driven in on the English Catholics. The centuries that they have gone through—centuries of blind and malignant oppression, of ostracism from public employment, of being, as it were, a small beleaguered garrison in a hostile country, and therefore having to act with great formality —all these things have combined to perform that conjuring trick. And I suppose that Papists in England are even technically Nonconformists.

Continental Papists are a dirty, jovial and unscrupulous crew. But that, at least, lets them be opportunists. They would have fixed poor dear Edward up all right. (Forgive my writing of these monstrous things in this frivolous manner. If I did not I should break down and cry.) In Milan, say, or in Paris, Leonora would have had her marriage dissolved in six months for two hundred dollars paid in the right quarter. And Edward would have drifted about until he became a tramp of the kind I have suggested. Or he would have married a barmaid who would have made him such frightful scenes in public places and would so have torn out his moustache and left visible signs upon his face that he would have been faithful to her for the rest of his days. That was what he wanted to redeem him. . . .

For, along with his passions and his shames there went the dread of scenes in public places, of outcry, of excited physical violence; of publicity, in short. Yes, the barmaid would have cured him. And it would have been all the better if she drank; he would have been kept busy looking after her.

I know that I am right in this. I know it because of the Kilsyte case. You see, the servant girl that he then kissed was nurse in the family of the Nonconformist head of the county—whatever that post may be called. And that gentleman was so determined to ruin Edward, who was the chairman of the Tory caucus, or whatever it is—that the poor dear sufferer had the very devil of a time. They asked questions about it in the House of Commons; they tried to get the Hampshire magistrates degraded;* they suggested to the War Ministry that Edward was not the proper person to hold the King's commission. Yes, he got it hot and strong.

The result you have heard. He was completely cured of philandering amongst the lower classes. And that seemed a real blessing to Leonora. It did not revolt her so much to be connected—it is a sort of connection—with people like Mrs. Maidan, instead of with a little kitchenmaid.

In a dim sort of way, Leonora was almost contented when she arrived at Nauheim, that evening. . . .

She had got things nearly straight by the long years of scraping in little stations in Chitral and Burma—stations where living is cheap in comparison with the life of a county magnate, and where, moreover, liaisons of one sort or another are normal and inexpensive, too. So that, when Mrs. Maidan came along—and the Maidan affair might have caused trouble out there because of the youth of the husband—Leonora had just resigned herself to coming home. With pushing and scraping and with letting Branshaw Teleragh, and with selling a picture and a relic of Charles I or so, she had got—and, poor dear, she had never had a really decent dress to her back in all those years and years—she had got, as she imagined, her poor dear husband back into much the same financial position as had been his before the mistress of the Grand Duke had happened along. And, of course, Edward himself had helped her a little on the financial side. He was a fellow that many men liked. He was so presentable and quite ready to lend you his cigar puncher—that sort of thing. So, every now and then some financier whom he met about would give him a good, sound, profitable tip. And Leonora was never afraid of a bit of a gamble—English Papists seldom are, I do not know why.

So nearly all her investments turned up trumps,

and Edward was really in fit case to reopen Branshaw Manor and once more to assume his position in the county. Thus Leonora had accepted Maisie Maidan almost with resignation—almost with a sigh of relief. She really liked the poor child—she had to like somebody. And, at any rate, she felt she could trust Maisie—she could trust her not to rook Edward for several thousands a week, for Maisie had refused to accept so much as a trinket ring from him. It is true that Edward gurgled and raved about the girl in a way that she had never yet experienced. But that, too, was almost a relief. I think she would really have welcomed it if he could have come across the love of his life. It would have given her a rest.

And there could not have been anyone better than poor little Mrs. Maidan; she was so ill she could not want to be taken on expensive jaunts. . . . It was Leonora herself who paid Maisie's expenses to Nauheim. She handed over the money to the boy husband, for Maisie would never have allowed it; but the husband was in agonies of fear. Poor devil!

I fancy that, on the voyage from India, Leonora was as happy as ever she had been in her life. Edward was wrapped up, completely, in his girl—he was almost like a father with a child, trotting about with rugs and physic and things, from deck to deck. He behaved, however, with great circumspection, so that nothing leaked through to the other passengers. And Leonora had almost attained to the attitude of a mother towards Mrs. Maidan. So it had looked very well—the benevolent, wealthy couple of good people, acting as saviours to the poor, dark-eyed, dying young thing. And that attitude of Leonara's towards Mrs. Maidan no doubt partly accounted for the smack in the face. She was hitting a naughty child who had been stealing chocolates at an inopportune moment.

It was certainly an inopportune moment. For, with the opening of that blackmailing letter from that injured brother officer, all the old terrors had redescended upon Leonora. Her road had again seemed to stretch out endless: she imagined that there might be hundreds and hundreds of such things that Edward was concealing from her—that they might necessitate more mortgagings, more pawnings of bracelets, more and always more horrors. She had spent an excruciating afternoon. The matter was one of a divorce case, of course, and she wanted to avoid publicity as much as Edward did, so that she saw the necessity of continuing the payments. And she did not so much mind that. They could find three hundred a year. But it was the horror of there being more such obligations.

She had had no conversation with Edward for many years—none that went beyond the mere arrangements for taking trains or engaging servants. But that afternoon she had to let him have it. And he had been just the same as ever. It was like opening a book after a decade to find the words the same. He had the same motives. He had not wished to tell her about the case because he had not wished her to sully her mind with the idea that there was such a thing as a brother officer who could be a blackmailer

—and he had wanted to protect the credit of his old light of love. That lady was certainly not concerned with her husband. And he swore, and swore, and swore, that there was nothing else in the world against him. She did not believe him.

He had done it once too often—and she was wrong for the first time, so that he acted a rather creditable part in the matter. For he went right straight out to the post-office and spent several hours in coding a telegram to his solicitor, bidding that hard-headed man to threaten to take out at once a warrant against the fellow who was on his track. He said afterwards that it was a bit too thick on poor old Leonora to be ballyragged any more. That was really the last of his outstanding accounts, and he was ready to take his personal chance of the divorce court if the blackmailer turned nasty. He would face it out—the publicity, the papers, the whole bally show. Those were his simple words. . . .

He had made, however, the mistake of not telling Leonora where he was going, so that, having seen him go to his room to fetch the code for the telegram, and seeing, two hours later, Maisie Maidan come out of his room, Leonora imagined that the two hours she had spent in silent agony Edward had spent with Maisie Maidan in his arms. That seemed to her to be too much.

As a matter of fact, Maisie's being in Edward's room had been the result, partly of poverty, partly of pride, partly of sheer innocence. She could not, in the first place, afford a maid; she refrained as much as possible from sending the hotel servants on errands, since every penny was of importance to her, and she feared to have to pay high tips at the end of her stay. Edward had lent her one of his fascinating cases containing fifteen different sizes of scissors, and, having seen, from her window, his departure for the post-office, she had taken the opportunity of returning the case. She could not see why she should not, though she felt a certain remorse at the thought that she had kissed the pillows of his bed. That was the way it took her.

But Leonora could see that, without the shadow of a doubt, the incident gave Florence a hold over her. It let Florence into things and Florence was the only created being who had any idea that the Ashburnhams were not just good people with nothing to their tails. She determined at once, not so much to give Florence the privilege of her intimacy—which would have been the payment of a kind of blackmail—as to keep Florence under observation until she could have demonstrated to Florence that she was not in the least jealous of poor Maisie. So that was why she had entered the dining-room arm in arm with my wife, and why she had so markedly planted herself at our table. She never left us, indeed, for a minute that night, except just to run up to Mrs. Maidan's room to beg her pardon and to beg her also to let Edward take her very markedly out into the gardens that night. She said herself, when Mrs. Maidan came rather wistfully down into the lounge where we were all sitting: "Now, Edward, get up and take Maisie to the Casino.

I want Mrs. Dowell to tell me all about the families in Connecticut who came from Fordingbridge." For it had been discovered that Florence came of a line that had actually owned Branshaw Teleragh for two centuries before the Ashburnhams came there. And there she sat with me in that hall, long after Florence had gone to bed, so that I might witness her gay reception of that pair. She could play up.

And that enables me to fix exactly the day of our going to the town of M——. For it was the very day poor Mrs. Maidan died. We found her dead when we got back—pretty awful, that, when you come to figure out what it all means. . . .

At any rate the measure of my relief when Leonora said that she was an Irish Catholic gives you the measure of my affection for that couple. It was an affection so intense that even to this day I cannot think of Edward without sighing. I do not believe that I could have gone on any more without them. I was getting too tired. And I verily believe, too, that if my suspicion that Leonora was jealous of Florence had been the reason she gave for her outburst I should have turned upon Florence with the maddest kind of rage. Jealousy would have been incurable. But Florence's mere silly gibes at the Irish and at the Catholics could be apologised out of existence. And that I appeared to fix up in two minutes or so.

She looked at me for a long time rather fixedly and queerly while I was doing it. And at last I worked myself up to saying:

"Do accept the situation. I confess that I do not

like your religion. But I like you so intensely. I
don't mind saying that I have never had anyone to be
really fond of, and I do not believe that anyone has
ever been fond of me, as I believe you really to be."

"Oh, I'm fond enough of you," she said. "Fond
enough to say that I wish every man was like you.
But there are others to be considered." She was
thinking, as a matter of fact, of poor Maisie. She
picked a little piece of pellitory* out of the breast-high
wall in front of us. She chafed it for a long minute
between her finger and thumb, then she threw it over
the coping.

"Oh, I accept the situation," she said at last, "if
you can."

VI

I REMEMBER laughing at the phrase, "accept
the situation," which she seemed to repeat with
a gravity too intense. I said to her something
like:

"It's hardly as much as that. I mean, that I must
claim the liberty of a free American citizen to think
what I please about your co-religionists. And I suppose that Florence must have liberty to think what
she pleases and to say what politeness allows her to
say."

"She had better," Leonora answered, "not say one
single word against my people or my faith."

It struck me, at the time, that there was an unusual,
an almost threatening, hardness in her voice. It was
almost as if she were trying to convey to Florence,
through me, that she would seriously harm my wife if
Florence went to something that was an extreme.
Yes, I remember thinking at the time that it was
almost as if Leonora were saying, through me, to
Florence:

"You may outrage me as you will; you may take
all that I personally possess, but do not you dare to
say one single thing in view of the situation that that
will set up—against the faith that makes me become
the doormat for your feet."

But obviously, as I saw it, that could not be her
meaning. Good people, be they ever so diverse in

creed, do not threaten each other. So that I read Leonora's words to mean just no more than:

"It would be better if Florence said nothing at all against my co-religionists, because it is a point that I am touchy about."

That was the hint that, accordingly I conveyed to Florence when, shortly afterwards, she and Edward came down from the tower. And I want you to understand that, from that moment until after Edward and the girl and Florence were all dead together I had never the remotest glimpse, not the shadow of a suspicion, that there was anything wrong, as the saying is. For five minutes, then, I entertained the possibility that Leonora might be jealous; but there was never another flicker in that flame-like personality. How in the world should I get it?

For, all that time, I was just a male sick nurse. And what chance had I against those three hardened gamblers, who were all in league to conceal their hands from me? What earthly chance? They were three to one—and they made me happy. Oh, God, they made me so happy that I doubt if even paradise, that shall smooth out all temporal wrongs, shall ever give me the like. And what could they have done better, or what could they have done that could have been worse? I don't know. . . .

I suppose that, during all that time I was a deceived husband and that Leonora was pimping for Edward. That was the cross that she had to take up during her long Calvary of a life. . . .

You ask how it feels to be a deceived husband.

Just Heavens, I do not know. It feels just nothing
at all. It is not Hell, certainly it is not necessarily
Heaven. So I suppose it is the intermediate stage.
What do they call it? Limbo.* No, I feel nothing at
all about that. They are dead; they have gone before
their Judge who, I hope, will open to them the springs
of His compassion. It is not my business to think
about it. It is simply my business to say, as Leonora's
people say: *"Requiem aeternam dona eis, domine, et
lux perpetua luceat per eis. In memoriam aeternam
erit. . . ."** But what were they? The just? The un-
just? God knows! I think that the pair of them were
only poor wretches, creeping over this earth in the
shadow of an eternal wrath. It is very terrible. . . .

It is almost too terrible, the picture of that judgment, as it appears to me sometimes, at nights. It is
probably the suggestion of some picture that I have
seen somewhere. But upon an immense plain, suspended in mid-air, I seem to see three figures, two of
them clasped close in an intense embrace, and one intolerably solitary. It is in black and white, my picture
of that judgment, an etching, perhaps; only I cannot
tell an etching from a photographic reproduction. And
the immense plain is the hand of God, stretching out
for miles and miles, with great spaces above it and below it. And they are in the sight of God, and it is
Florence that is alone. . . .

And, do you know, at the thought of that intense
solitude I feel an overwhelming desire to rush forward
and comfort her. You cannot, you see, have acted as
nurse to a person for twelve years without wishing to

go on nursing them, even though you hate them with the hatred of the adder, and even in the palm of God. But, in the nights, with that vision of judgment before me, I know that I hold myself back. For I hate Florence. I hate Florence with such a hatred that I would not spare her an eternity of loneliness. She need not have done what she did. She was an American, a New Englander. She had not the hot passions of these Europeans. She cut out that poor imbecile of an Edward—and I pray God that he is really at peace, clasped close in the arms of that poor, poor girl! And, no doubt, Maisie Maidan will find her young husband again, and Leonora will burn, clear and serene, a northern light*and one of the archangels of God. And me. . . . Well, perhaps, they will find me an elevator to run. . . . But Florence. . . .

She should not have done it. She should not have done it. It was playing it too low down. She cut out poor dear Edward from sheer vanity; she meddled between him and Leonora from a sheer, imbecile spirit of district visiting. Do you understand that, whilst she was Edward's mistress, she was perpetually trying to reunite him to his wife? She would gabble on to Leonora about forgiveness—treating the subject from the bright, American point of view. And Leonora would treat her like the whore she was. Once she said to Florence in the early morning:

"You come to me straight out of his bed to tell me that that is my proper place. I know it, thank you."

But even that could not stop Florence. She went on saying that it was her ambition to leave this world a little brighter by the passage of her brief life, and how thankfully she would leave Edward, whom she thought she had brought to a right frame of mind, if Leonora would only give him a chance. He needed, she said, tenderness beyond anything.

And Leonora would answer—for she put up with this outrage for years—Leonora, as I understand, would answer something like:

"Yes, you would give him up. And you would go on writing to each other in secret, and committing adultery in hired rooms. I know the pair of you, you know. No. I prefer the situation as it is."

Half the time Florence would ignore Leonora's remarks. She would think they were not quite ladylike. The other half of the time she would try to persuade Leonora that her love for Edward was quite spiritual—on account of her heart. Once she said:

"If you can believe that of Maisie Maidan, as you say you do, why cannot you believe it of me?"

Leonora was, I understand, doing her hair at that time in front of the mirror in her bedroom. And she looked round at Florence, to whom she did not usually vouchsafe a glance—she looked round coolly and calmly, and said:

"Never do you dare to mention Mrs. Maidan's name again. You murdered her. You and I murdered her between us. I am as much a scoundrel as you. I don't like to be reminded of it."

Florence went off at once into a babble of how could she have hurt a person whom she hardly knew, a person whom, with the best intentions, in pursuance of

her efforts to leave the world a little brighter, she had
tried to save from Edward. That was how she figured
it out to herself. She really thought that. . . . So
Leonora said patiently:

"Very well, just put it that I killed her and that it's
a painful subject. One does not like to think that one
had killed someone. Naturally not. I ought never to
have brought her from India."

And that, indeed, is exactly how Leonora looked at
it. It is stated a little baldly, but Leonora was always
a great one for bald statements.

What had happened on the day of our jaunt to the
ancient city of M—— had been this:

Leonora, who had been even then filled with pity
and contrition for the poor child, on returning to our
hotel had gone straight to Mrs. Maidan's room. She
had wanted just to pet her. And she had perceived at
first only, on the clear, round table covered with red
velvet, a letter addressed to her. It ran something like:

"Oh, Mrs. Ashburnham, how could you have done
it? I trusted you so. You never talked to me about
me and Edward, but I trusted you. How could you
buy me from my husband? I have just heard how
you have—in the hall they were talking about it, Edward and the American lady. You paid the money for
me to come here. Oh, how could you? How could
you? I am going straight back to Bunny. . . ."

Bunny was Mrs. Maidan's husband.

And Leonora said that, as she went on reading the
letter, she had, without looking round her, a sense that
that hotel room was cleared, that there were no papers

on the table, that there were no clothes on the hooks, and that there was a strained silence—a silence, she said, as if there were something in the room that drank up such sounds as there were. She had to fight against that feeling, whilst she read the postscript of the letter.

"I did not know you wanted me for an adulteress," the postscript began. The poor child was hardly literate. "It was surely not right of you and I never wanted to be one. And I heard Edward call me a poor little rat to the American lady. He always called me a little rat in private, and I did not mind. But, if he called me it to her, I think he does not love me any more. Oh, Mrs. Ashburnham, you knew the world and I knew nothing. I thought it would be all right if you thought it could, and I thought you would not have brought me if you did not, too. You should not have done it, and we out of the same convent. . . ."

Leonora said that she screamed when she read that.

And then she saw that Maisie's boxes were all packed, and she began a search for Mrs. Maidan herself—all over the hotel. The manager said that Mrs. Maidan paid her bill, and had gone up to the station to ask the Reiseverkehrsbureau* to make her out a plan for her immediate return to Chitral. He imagined that he had seen her come back, but he was not quite certain. No one in the large hotel had bothered his head about the child. And she, wandering solitarily in the hall, had no doubt sat down beside a screen that had Edward and Florence on the other side. I never heard then or after what had passed between that precious couple. I fancy Florence was just about beginning her cutting out of poor dear Edward by addressing to him some words of friendly warning as to the ravages he might be making in the girl's heart. That would be the sort of way she would begin. And Edward would have sentimentally assured her that there was nothing in it; that Maisie was just a poor little rat whose passage to Nauheim his wife had paid out of her own pocket. That would have been enough to do the trick.

For the trick was pretty efficiently done. Leonora, with panic growing and with contrition very large in her heart, visited every one of the public rooms of the hotel—the dining-room, the lounge, the *Schreibzimmer*,* the winter garden. God knows what they wanted with a winter garden in a hotel that is only open from May till October. But there it was. And then Leonora ran—yes, she ran up the stairs—to see if Maisie had not returned to her rooms. She had determined to take that child right away from that hideous place. It seemed to her to be all unspeakable. I do not mean to say that she was not quite cool about it. Leonora was always Leonora. But the cold justice of the thing demanded that she should play the part of mother to this child who had come from the same convent. She figured it out to amount to that. She would leave Edward to Florence—and to me—and she would devote all her time to providing that child with an atmosphere of love until she could be returned to her poor young husband. It was naturally too late.

She had not cared to look round Maisie's rooms at

first. Now, as soon as she came in, she perceived, sticking out beyond the bed, a small pair of feet in high-heeled shoes. Maisie had died in the effort to strap up a great portmanteau. She had died so grotesquely that her little body had fallen forward into the trunk, and it had closed upon her, like the jaws of a gigantic alligator. The key was in her hand. Her dark hair, like the hair of a Japanese, had come down and covered her body and her face.

Leonora lifted her up—she was the merest featherweight—and laid her on the bed with her hair about her. She was smiling, as if she had just scored a goal in a hockey match. You understand she had not committed suicide. Her heart had just stopped. I saw her, with the long lashes on the cheeks, with the smile about the lips, with the flowers all about her. The stem of a white lily rested in her hand so that the spike of flowers was upon her shoulder. She looked like a bride in the sunlight of the mortuary candles that were all about her, and the white coifs of the two nuns that knelt at her feet with the faces hidden might have been two swans that were to bear her away to kissing-kindness land, or wherever it is. Leonora showed her to me. She would not let either of the others see her. She wanted, you know, to spare poor dear Edward's feelings. He never could bear the sight of a corpse. And, since she never gave him an idea that Maisie had written to her, he imagined that the death had been the most natural thing in the world. He soon got over it. Indeed, it was the one affair of his about which he never felt much remorse.

THE GOOD SOLDIER

PART II

I

THE death of Mrs. Maidan occurred on the 4th of August, 1904. And then nothing happened until the 4th of August, 1913. There is the curious coincidence of dates, but I do not know whether that is one of those sinister, as if half-jocular and altogether merciless proceedings on the part of a cruel Providence that we call a coincidence. Because it may just as well have been the superstitious mind of Florence that forced her to certain acts, as if she had been hypnotised. It is, however, certain that the fourth of August always proved a significant date for her. To begin with, she was born on the fourth of August. Then, on that date, in the year 1899, she set out with her uncle for the tour round the world in company with a young man called Jimmy. But that was not merely a coincidence. Her kindly old uncle, with the supposedly damaged heart, was, in his delicate way, offering her, in this trip, a birthday present to celebrate her coming of age. Then, on the fourth of August, 1900, she yielded to an action that certainly coloured her whole life—as well as mine. She had no luck. She was probably offering herself a birthday present that morning. . . .

On the fourth of August, 1901, she married me, and set sail for Europe in a great gale of wind—the gale that affected her heart. And no doubt there, again, she was offering herself a birthday gift—the birthday gift of my miserable life. It occurs to me that I have never told you anything about my marriage. That was like this: I have told you, as I think, that I first met Florence at the Stuyvesants, in Fourteenth Street. And, from that moment, I determined with all the obstinacy of a possibly weak nature, if not to make her mine, at least to marry her. I had no occupation—I had no business affairs. I simply camped down there in Stamford, in a vile hotel, and just passed my days in the house, or on the verandah of the Misses Hurlbird. The Misses Hurlbird, in an odd, obstinate way, did not like my presence. But they were hampered by the national manners of these occasions. Florence had her own sitting-room. She could ask to it whom she liked, and I simply walked into that apartment. I was as timid as you will, but in that matter I was like a chicken that is determined to get across the road in front of an automobile. I would walk into Florence's pretty, little, old-fashioned room, take off my hat, and sit down.

Florence had, of course, several other fellows, too—strapping young New Englanders, who worked during the day in New York and spent only the evenings in the village of their birth. And, in the evenings, they would march in on Florence with almost as much determination as I myself showed. And I am bound to say that they were received with as much disfavour as was my portion—from the Misses Hurlbird. . . .

They were curious old creatures, those two. It was almost as if they were members of an ancient family under some curse—they were so gentlewomanly, so proper, and they sighed so. Sometimes I would see tears in their eyes. I do not know that my courtship of Florence made much progress at first. Perhaps that was because it took place almost entirely during the daytime, on hot afternoons, when the clouds of dust hung like fog, right up as high as the tops of the thin-leaved elms. The night, I believe, is the proper season, for the gentle feats of love, not a Connecticut July afternoon, when any sort of proximity is an almost appalling thought. But, if I never so much as kissed Florence, she let me discover very easily, in the course of a fortnight, her simple wants. And I could supply those wants. . . .

She wanted to marry a gentleman of leisure; she wanted a European establishment. She wanted her husband to have an English accent, an income of fifty thousand dollars a year from real estate and no ambitions to increase that income. And—she faintly hinted —she did not want much physical passion in the affair. Americans, you know, can envisage such unions without blinking.

She gave out this information in floods of bright talk—she would pop a little bit of it into comments over a view of the Rialto,* Venice, and, whilst she was, brightly describing Balmoral Castle, she would say that her ideal husband would be one who could get her received at the British Court. She had spent, it seemed, two months in Great Britain—seven weeks in touring from Stratford to Strathpeffer,* and one as paying guest in an old English family near Ledbury,* an impoverished, but still stately family, called Bags-hawe. They were to have spent two months more in that tranquil bosom, but inopportune events, apparently in her uncle's business, had caused their rather hurried return to Stamford. The young man called Jimmy had remained in Europe to perfect his knowledge of that continent. He certainly did: he was most useful to us afterwards.

But the point that came out—that there was no mistaking—was that Florence was coldly and calmly determined to take no look at any man who could not give her a European settlement. Her glimpse of English home life had effected this. She meant, on her marriage, to have a year in Paris, and then to have her husband buy some real estate in the neighbourhood of Fordingbridge, from which place the Hurlbirds had come in the year 1688. On the strength of that she was going to take her place in the ranks of English county society. That was fixed.

I used to feel mightily elevated when I considered these details, for I could not figure out that, amongst her acquaintance in Stamford there was any fellow that would fill the bill. The most of them were not as wealthy as I, and those that were were not the type to give up the fascinations of Wall Street even for the protracted companionship of Florence. But nothing really happened during the month of July. On the first of August Florence apparently told her aunts that she intended to marry me.

She had not told me so, but there was no doubt about the aunts, for, on that afternoon, Miss Florence

Hurlbird, Senior, stopped me on my way to Florence's sitting-room and took me, agitatedly, into the parlour. It was a singular interview, in that old-fashioned colonial room, with the spindle-legged furniture, the silhouettes, the miniatures, the portrait of General Braddock,* and the smell of lavender. You see, the two poor maiden ladies were in agonies—and they could not say one single thing direct. They would almost wring their hands and ask if I had considered such a thing as different temperaments. I assure you they were almost affectionate, concerned for me even, as if Florence were too bright for my solid and serious virtues.

For they had discovered in me solid and serious virtues. That might have been because I had once dropped the remark that I preferred General Braddock to General Washington. For the Hurlbirds had backed the losing side in the War of Independence, and had been seriously impoverished and quite efficiently oppressed for that reason. The Misses Hurlbird could never forget it.

Nevertheless they shuddered at the thought of a European career for myself and Florence. Each of them really wailed when they heard that that was what I hoped to give their niece. That may have been partly because they regarded Europe as a sink of iniquity, where strange laxities prevailed. They thought the Mother Country as Erastian as any other. And they carried their protests to extraordinary lengths, for them. . . .

They even, almost, said that marriage was a sacrament; but neither Miss Florence nor Miss Emily could quite bring herself to utter the word. And they almost brought themselves to say that Florence's early life had been characterised by flirtations—something of that sort.

I know I ended the interview by saying:

"I don't care. If Florence has robbed a bank I am going to marry her and take her to Europe."

And at that Miss Emily wailed and fainted. But Miss Florence, in spite of the state of her sister, threw herself on my neck and cried out:

"Don't do it, John. Don't do it. You're a good young man," and she added, whilst I was getting out of the room to send Florence to her aunt's rescue:

"We ought to tell you more. But she's our dear sister's child."

Florence, I remember, received me with a chalk-pale face and the exclamation:

"Have those old cats been saying anything against me?" But I assured her that they had not and hurried her into the room of her strangely afflicted relatives. I had really forgotten all about that exclamation of Florence's until this moment. She treated me so very well—with such tact—that, if I ever thought of it afterwards I put it down to her deep affection for me.

And that evening, when I went to fetch her for a buggy-ride, she had disappeared. I did not lose any time. I went into New York and engaged berths on the "Pocahontas,"*that was to sail on the evening of the fourth of the month, and then, returning to Stamford, I tracked out, in the course of the day, that Florence had been driven to Rye Station.* And there I found that she had taken the cars to Waterbury. She had, of course, gone to her uncle's. The old man received me with a stony, husky face. I was not to see Florence; she was ill; she was keeping her room. And, from something that he let drop—an odd biblical phrase that I have forgotten—I gathered that all that family simply did not intend her to marry ever in her life.

I procured at once the name of the nearest minister and a rope ladder—you have no idea how primitively these matters were arranged in those days in the United States. I daresay that may be so still. And, at one o'clock in the morning of the fourth of August I was standing in Florence's bedroom. I was so one-minded in my purpose that it never struck me there was anything improper in being, at one o'clock in the morning, in Florence's bedroom. I just wanted to wake her up. She was not, however, asleep. She expected me, and her relatives had only just left her. She received me with an embrace of a warmth. . . . Well, it was the first time I had ever been embraced by a woman—and it was the last when a woman's embrace has had in it any warmth for me. . . .

I suppose it was my own fault, what followed. At any rate, I was in such a hurry to get the wedding over, and was so afraid of her relatives finding me there, that I must have received her advances with a certain amount of absence of mind. I was out of that room and down the ladder in under half a minute. She kept me waiting at the foot an unconscionable time—it was certainly three in the morning before we knocked up that minister. And I think that that wait was the only sign Florence ever showed of having a conscience as far as I was concerned, unless her lying for some moments in my arms was also a sign of conscience. I fancy that, if I had shown warmth then, she would have acted the proper wife to me, or would have put me back again. But, because I acted like a Philadelphia gentleman, she made me, I suppose, go through with the part of a male nurse. Perhaps she thought that I should not mind.

After that, as I gather, she had not any more re- morse. She was only anxious to carry out her plans. For, just before she came down the ladder, she called me to the top of that grotesque implement that I went up and down like a tranquil jumping-jack. I was per- fectly collected. She said to me with a certain fierce- ness :

"It is determined that we sail at four this after- noon? You are not lying about having taken berths?"

I understood that she would naturally be anxious to get away from the neighbourhood of her apparently insane relatives, so that I readily excused her for thinking that I should be capable of lying about such a thing. I made it, therefore, plain to her that it was my fixed determination to sail by the "Pocahontas." She said then—it was a moonlit morning, and she was whispering in my ear whilst I stood on the ladder. The hills that surround Waterbury showed, extraordi- narily tranquil, around the villa. She said, almost coldly :

"I wanted to know, so as to pack my trunks." And she added: "I may be ill, you know. I guess my heart is a little like Uncle Hurlbird's. It runs in families."

I whispered that the "Pocahontas" was an extraordinarily steady boat. . . .

Now I wonder what had passed through Florence's mind during the two hours that she had kept me waiting at the foot of the ladder. I would give not a little to know. Till then, I fancy she had had no settled plan in her mind. She certainly never mentioned her heart till that time. Perhaps the renewed sight of her Uncle Hurlbird had given her the idea. Certainly her Aunt Emily, who had come over with her to Waterbury, would have rubbed into her, for hours and hours, the idea that any accentuated discussions would kill the old gentleman. That would recall to her mind all the safeguards against excitement with which the poor silly old gentleman had been hedged in during their trip round the world. That, perhaps, put it into her head. Still, I believe there was some remorse on my account, too. Leonora told me that Florence said there was—for Leonora knew all about it, and once went so far as to ask her how she could do a thing so infamous. She excused herself on the score of an overmastering passion. Well, I always say that an overmastering passion is a good excuse for feelings. You cannot help them. And it is a good excuse for straight actions—she might have bolted with the fellow, before or after she married me. And, if they had not enough money to get along with, they might have cut their throats, or sponged on her family, though, of course, Florence wanted such a lot that it would have suited her very badly to have for a husband a clerk in a drygoods store, which was what old Hurlbird would have made of that fellow. He hated him. No, I do not think that there is much excuse for Florence.

God knows. She was a frightened fool, and she was fantastic, and I suppose that, at that time, she really cared for that imbecile. He certainly didn't care for her. Poor thing. . . . At any rate, after I had assured her that the "Pocahontas" was a steady ship, she just said:

"You'll have to look after me in certain ways—like Uncle Hurlbird is looked after. I will tell you how to do it." And then she stepped over the sill, as if she were stepping on board a boat. I suppose she had burnt hers!

I had, no doubt, eye-openers enough. When we reentered the Hurlbird mansion at eight o'clock the Hurlbirds were just exhausted. Florence had a hard, triumphant air. We had got married about four in the morning and had sat about in the woods above the town till then, listening to a mocking-bird imitate an old tom-cat. So I guess Florence had not found getting married to me a very stimulating process. I had not found anything much more inspiring to say than how glad I was, with variations. I think I was too dazed. Well, the Hurlbirds were too dazed to say much. We had breakfast together, and then Florence went to pack her grips and things. Old Hurlbird took the opportunity to read me a full-blooded lecture, in the style of an American oration, as to the perils for young American girlhood lurking in the European jungle. He said that Paris was full of snakes in the grass, of which he had had bitter experience. He concluded, as they always do, poor, dear old things, with the aspiration that all American women should one day be sexless—though that is not the way they put it. . . .

Well, we made the ship all right by one-thirty—and there was a tempest blowing. That helped Florence a good deal. For we were not ten minutes out from Sandy Hook before Florence went down into her cabin and her heart took her. An agitated stewardess came running up to me, and I went running down. I got my directions how to behave to my wife. Most of them came from her, though it was the ship doctor who discreetly suggested to me that I had better refrain from manifestations of affection. I was ready enough.

I was, of course, full of remorse. It occurred to me that her heart was the reason for the Hurlbirds' mysterious desire to keep their youngest and dearest unmarried. Of course, they would be too refined to put the motive into words. They were old stock New Englanders. They would not want to have to suggest that a husband must not kiss the back of his wife's neck. They would not like to suggest that he might, for the matter of that. I wonder, though, how Florence got the doctor to enter the conspiracy—the several doctors.

Of course her heart squeaked a bit—she had the same configuration of the lungs as her Uncle Hurlbird. And, in his company, she must have heard a great deal of heart talk from specialists. Anyhow, she and they tied me pretty well down—and Jimmy, of course, that dreary boy—what in the world did she see in him? He was lugubrious, silent, morose. He had no talent as a painter. He was very sallow and dark, and he never shaved sufficiently. He met us at Havre, and he proceeded to make himself useful for the next two years, during which he lived in our flat in Paris, whether we were there or not. He studied painting at Julien's, or some such place. . . .

That fellow had his hands always in the pockets of his odious, square-shouldered, broad-hipped, American coats, and his dark eyes were always full of ominous appearances. He was, besides, too fat. Why, I was much the better man. . . .

And I daresay Florence would have given me the better. She showed signs of it. I think, perhaps, the enigmatic smile with which she used to look back at me over her shoulder when she went into the bathing place was a sort of invitation. I have mentioned that. It was as if she were saying: "I am going in here. I am going to stand so stripped and white and straight —and you are a man. . . ." Perhaps it was that . . .

No, she cannot have liked that fellow long. He looked like sallow putty. I understand that he had been slim and dark and very graceful at the time of her first disgrace. But, loafing about in Paris, on her pocket money and on the allowance that old Hurl-

bird made him to keep out of the United States, had
given him a stomach like a man of forty, and dyspep-
tic irritation on top of it.

God, how they worked me! It was those two between them who really elaborated the rules. I have
told you something about them—how I had to head
conversations, for all those eleven years off such topics as love, poverty, crime, and so on. But, looking
over what I have written, I see that I have uninten-
tionally misled you when I said that Florence was
never out of my sight. Yet that was the impression
that I really had until just now. When I come to think
of it she was out of my sight most of the time.

You see, that fellow impressed upon me that what
Florence needed most of all were sleep and privacy.
I must never enter her room without knocking, or her
poor little heart might flutter away to its doom. He
said these things with his lugubrious croak, and his
black eyes like a crow's, so that I seemed to see poor
Florence die ten times a day—a little, pale, frail
corpse. Why, I would as soon have thought of enter-
ing her room without her permission as of burgling
a church. I would sooner have committed that crime.
I would certainly have done it if I had thought the
state of her heart demanded the sacrilege. So at ten
o'clock at night the door closed upon Florence, who
had gently, and, as if reluctantly, backed up that fellow's recommendations; and she would wish me good
night as if she were a *cinque cento**Italian lady saying good-bye to her lover. And at ten o'clock of the
next morning there she would come out the door of

her room as fresh as Venus rising from any of the couches that are mentioned in Greek legends.

Her room door was locked because she was nervous about thieves; but an electric contrivance on a cord was understood to be attached to her little wrist. She had only to press a bulb to raise the house. And I was provided with an axe—an axe!—great gods, with which to break down her door in case she ever failed to answer my knock, after I knocked really loud several times. It was pretty well thought out, you see.

What wasn't so well thought out were the ultimate consequences—our being tied to Europe. For that young man rubbed it so well into me that Florence would die if she crossed the Channel—he impressed it so fully on my mind that, when later Florence wanted to go to Fordingbridge, I cut the proposal short—absolutely short, with a curt no. It fixed her and it frightened her. I was even backed up by all the doctors. I seemed to have had endless interviews with doctor after doctor, cool, quiet men, who would ask, in reasonable tones, whether there was any reason for our going to England—any special reason. And since I could not see any special reason, they would give the verdict: "Better not, then." I daresay they were honest enough, as things go. They probably imagined that the mere associations of the steamer might have effects on Florence's nerves. That would be enough, that and a conscientious desire to keep our money on the Continent.

It must have rattled poor Florence pretty considerably, for you see, the main idea—the only main idea of

her heart, that was otherwise cold—was to get to
Fordingbridge and be a county lady in the home of
her ancestors. But Jimmy got her, there: he shut on
her the door of the Channel; even on the fairest day
of blue sky, with the cliffs of England shining like
mother of pearl in full view of Calais, I would not
have let her cross the steamer gangway to save her
life. I tell you it fixed her.

It fixed her beautifully, because she could not announce herself as cured, since that would have put
an end to the locked bedroom arrangements. And,
by the time she was sick of Jimmy—which happened
in the year 1903—she had taken on Edward Ashburnham. Yes, it was a bad fix for her, because Edward
could have taken her to Fordingbridge and, though
he could not give her Branshaw Manor, that home of
her ancestors being settled on his wife, she could at
least have pretty considerably queened it there or
thereabouts, what with our money and the support of
the Asburnhams. Her uncle, as soon as he considered
that she had really settled down with me—and I sent
him only the most glowing accounts of her virtue and
constancy—made over to her a very considerable part
of his fortune for which he had no use. I suppose
that we had, between us, fifteen thousand a year in
English money, though I never quite knew how much
of hers went to Jimmy. At any rate, we could have
shone in Fordingbridge.

I never quite knew, either, how she and Edward
got rid of Jimmy. I fancy that fat and disreputable
raven must have had his six golden front teeth

knocked down his throat by Edward one morning whilst I had gone out to buy some flowers in the Rue de la Paix, leaving Florence and the flat in charge of those two. And serve him very right, is all that I can say. He was a bad sort of blackmailer; I hope Florence does not have his company in the next world.

As God is my Judge, I do not believe that I would have separated those two if I had known that they really and passionately loved each other. I do not know where the public morality of the case comes in, and, of course, no man really knows what he would have done in any given case. But I truly believe that I would have united them, observing ways and means as decent as I could. I believe that I should have given them money to live upon and that I should have consoled myself somehow. At that date I might have found some young thing, like Maisie Maidan, or the poor girl, and I might have had some peace. For peace I never had with Florence, and I hardly believe that I cared for her in the way of love after a year or two of it. She became for me a rare and fragile object, something burdensome, but very frail. Why, it was as if I had been given a thin-shelled pullet's egg to carry on my palm from Equatorial Africa to Hoboken.* Yes, she became for me, as it were, the subject of a bet—the trophy of an athlete's achievement, a parsley crown that is the symbol of his chastity, his soberness, his abstentions, and of his inflexible will. Of intrinsic value as a wife, I think she had none at all for me. I fancy I was not even proud of the way she dressed.

But her passion for Jimmy was not even a passion, and, mad as the suggestion may appear, she was frightened for her life. Yes, she was afraid of me. I will tell you how that happened.

I had, in the old days, a darky servant, called Julius, who valeted me, and waited on me, and loved me, like the crown of his head. Now, when we left Waterbury to go to the "Pocahontas," Florence intrusted to me one very special and very precious leather grip. She told me that her life might depend on that grip, which contained her drugs against heart attacks. And, since I was never much of a hand at carrying things, I intrusted this, in turn, to Julius, who was a grey-haired chap of sixty or so, and very picturesque at that. He made so much impression on Florence that she regarded him as a sort of father, and absolutely refused to let me take him to Paris. He would have inconvenienced her.

Well, Julius was so overcome with grief at being left behind that he must needs go and drop the precious grip. I saw red, I saw purple. I flew at Julius. On the ferry, it was, I filled up one of his eyes; I threatened to strangle him. And, since an unresisting negro can make a deplorable noise and a deplorable spectacle, and, since that was Florence's first adventure in the married state, she got a pretty idea of my character. It affirmed in her the desperate resolve to conceal from me the fact that she was not what she would have called "a pure woman." For that was really the mainspring of her fantastic actions. She was afraid that I should murder her. . . .

So she got up the heart attack, at the earliest possible opportunity, on board the liner. Perhaps she was not so very much to be blamed. You must remember that she was a New Englander, and that New England had not yet come to loathe darkies as it does now. Whereas, if she had come from even so little south as Philadelphia, and had been of an oldish family, she would have seen that for me to kick Julius was not so outrageous an act as for her cousin, Reggie Hurlbird, to say—as I have heard him say to his English butler—that for two cents he would bat him on the pants. Besides, the medicine-grip did not bulk as largely in her eyes as it did in mine, where it was the symbol of the existence of an adored wife of a day. To her it was just a useful lie. . . .

Well, there you have the position, as clear as I can make it—the husband an ignorant fool, the wife a cold sensualist with imbecile fears—for I was such a fool that I should never have known what she was or was not—and the blackmailing lover. And then the other lover came along. . . .

Well, Edward Ashburnham was worth having. Have I conveyed to you the splendid fellow that he was—the fine soldier, the excellent landlord, the extraordinarily kind, careful and industrious magistrate, the upright, honest, fair-dealing, fair-thinking, public character? I suppose I have not conveyed it to you. The truth is, that I never knew it until the poor girl came along—the poor girl who was just as straight, as splendid and as upright as he. I swear she was. I suppose I ought to have known. I suppose that was, really, why I liked him so much—so infinitely much. Come to think of it, I can remember a thousand little acts of kindliness, of thoughtfulness for his inferiors, even on the Continent. Look here, I know of two families of dirty, unpicturesque, Hessian paupers that that fellow, with an infinite patience, rooted up, got their police reports, set on their feet, or exported to my patient land. And he would do it quite inarticulately, set in motion by seeing a child crying in the street. He would wrestle with dictionaries, in that unfamiliar tongue. . . . Well, he could not bear to see a child cry. Perhaps he could not bear to see a woman and not give her the comfort of his physical attractions.

But, although I liked him so intensely, I was rather apt to take these things for granted. They made me feel comfortable with him, good towards him; they made me trust him. But I guess I thought it was part of the character of any English gentleman. Why, one day he got it into his head that the head waiter at the Excelsior had been crying—the fellow with the grey face and grey whiskers. And then he spent the best part of a week, in correspondence and up at the British consul's, in getting the fellow's wife to come back from London and bring back his girl baby. She had bolted with a Swiss scullion. If she had not come inside the week he would have gone to London himself to fetch her. He was like that.

Edward Ashburnham was like that, and I thought it was only the duty of his rank and station. Perhaps that was all that it was—but I pray God to make

me discharge mine as well. And, but for the poor
girl, I daresay that I should never have seen it, however much the feeling might have been over me. She
had for him such enthusiasm that, although even now
I do not understand the technicalities of English life,
I can gather enough. She was with them during the
whole of our last stay at Nauheim.

Nancy Rufford was her name; she was Leonora's
only friend's only child, and Leonora was her guardian, if that is the correct term. She had lived with
the Ashburnhams ever since she had been of the age
of thirteen, when her mother was said to have committed suicide owing to the brutalities of her father.
Yes, it is a cheerful story. . . .

Edward always called her "the girl," and it was very
pretty, the evident affection he had for her and she
for him. And Leonora's feet she would have kissed—
those two were for her the best man and the best
woman on earth—and in heaven. I think that she
had not a thought of evil in her head—the poor
girl. . . .

Well, anyhow, she chanted Edward's praises to me
for the hour together, but, as I have said, I could not
make much of it. It appeared that he had the D. S. O.,
and that his troop loved him beyond the love of men.
You never saw such a troop as his. And he had the
Royal Humane Society's medal with a clasp. That
meant, apparently, that he had twice jumped off the
deck of a troop-ship to rescue what the girl called
"Tommies," who had fallen overboard in the Red Sea
and such places. He had been twice recommended

for the V. C.,* whatever that might mean, and, although owing to some technicalities he had never received that apparently coveted order, he had some special place about his sovereign at the coronation. Or perhaps it was some post in the Beefeaters'. She made him out like a cross between Lohengrin*and the Chevalier Bayard.* Perhaps he was. . . . But he was too silent a fellow to make that side of him really decorative. I remember going to him, at about that time and asking him what the D. S. O. was, and he grunted out:

"It's a sort of a thing they give grocers who've honourably supplied the troops with adulterated coffee in war-time"—something of that sort. He did not quite carry conviction to me, so, in the end I put it directly to Leonora. I asked her fully and squarely—prefacing the question with some remarks, such as those that I have already given you, as to the difficulty one has in really getting to know people when one's intimacy is conducted as an English acquaintanceship—I asked her whether her husband was not really a splendid fellow—along at least the lines of his public functions. She looked at me with a slightly awakened air —with an air that would have been almost startled if Leonora could ever have been startled.

"Didn't you know?" she asked. "If I come to think of it there is not a more splendid fellow in any three counties, pick them where you will—along those lines." And she added, after she had looked at me reflectively for what seemed a long time:

"To do my husband justice there could not be a

better man on the earth. There would not be room
for it—along those lines."

"Well," I said, "then he must really be Lohengrin
and the Cid*in one body. For there are not any other
lines that count."

Again she looked at me for a long time.

"It's your opinion that there are no other lines that
count?" she asked slowly.

"Well," I answered gayly, "you're not going to ac-
cuse him of not being a good husband, or of not being
a good guardian to your ward?"

She spoke then, slowly, like a person who is listening to the sounds in a sea-shell held to her ear—and,
would you believe it?—she told me afterwards that,
at that speech of mine, for the first time she had a
vague inkling of the tragedy that was to follow so
soon—although the girl had lived with them for eight
years or so:

"Oh, I'm not thinking of saying that he is not the
best of husbands, or that he is not very fond of the
girl."

And then I said something like:

"Well, Leonora, a man sees more of these things
than even a wife. And, let me tell you, that in all
the years I've known Edward he has never, in your
absence, paid a moment's attention to any other woman
—not by the quivering of an eyelash. I should have
noticed. And he talks of you as if you were one of
the angels of God."

"Oh," she came up to the scratch, as you could be

sure Leonora would always come up to the scratch, "I am perfectly sure that he always speaks nicely of me."

I daresay she had practice in that sort of scene—people must have been always complimenting her on her husband's fidelity and adoration. For half the world—the whole of the world that knew Edward and Leonora believed that his conviction in the Kilsyte affair had been a miscarriage of justice—a conspiracy of false evidence, got together by Nonconformist adversaries. But think of the fool that I was. . . .

II

LET me think where we were. Oh, yes . . . that conversation took place on the fourth of August, 1913. I remember saying to her that, on that day, exactly nine years before, I had made their acquaintance, so that it had seemed quite appropriate and like a birthday speech to utter my little testimonial to my friend Edward. I could quite confidently say that, though we four had been about together in all sorts of places, for all that length of time, I had not, for my part, one single complaint to make of either of them. And I added, that that was an unusual record for people who had been so much together. You are not to imagine that it was only at Nauheim that we met. That would not have suited Florence.

I find, on looking at my diaries, that on September the fourth, 1904, Edward accompanied Florence and myself to Paris, where we put him up till the twenty-first of that month. He made another short visit to us in December of that year—the first year of our acquaintance. It must have been during this visit that he knocked Mr. Jimmy's teeth down his throat. I daresay Florence had asked him to come over for that purpose. In 1905 he was in Paris three times—once with Leonora, who wanted some frocks. In 1906 we spent the best part of six weeks together at Mentone, and Edward stayed with us in Paris on his way back to London. That was how it went.

The fact was that in Florence the poor wretch had got hold of a Tartar, compared with whom Leonora was a sucking kid. He must have had a hell of a time. Leonora wanted to keep him for—what shall I say—for the good of her church, as it were, to show that Catholic women do not lose their men. Let it go at that, for the moment. I will write more about her motives later, perhaps. But Florence was sticking on to the proprietor of the home of her ancestors. No doubt he was also a very passionate lover. But I am convinced that he was sick of Florence within three years of even interrupted companionship and the life that she led him. . . .

If ever Leonora so much as mentioned in a letter that they had had a woman staying with them—or, if she so much as mentioned a woman's name in a letter to me—off would go a desperate cable in cipher to that poor wretch at Branshaw, commanding him on pain of an instant and horrible disclosure to come over and assure her of his fidelity. I daresay he would have faced it out; I daresay he would have thrown over Florence and taken the risk of exposure. But there he had Leonora to deal with. And Leonora assured him that, if the minutest fragment of the real situation ever got through to my senses, she would wreak upon him the most terrible vengeance that she could think of. And he did not have a very easy job. Florence called for more and more attentions from him as the time went on. She would make him kiss her at any moment of the day; and it was only by his making it plain that a divorced lady could never assume a position in the county of Hampshire that he could prevent her from making a bolt of it with him in her train. Oh, yes, it was a difficult job for him.

For Florence, if you please, gaining in time a more composed view of nature, and overcome by her habits of garrulity, arrived at a frame of mind in which she found it almost necessary to tell me all about it—nothing less than that. She said that her situation was too unbearable with regard to me.

She proposed to tell me all, secure a divorce from me, and go with Edward and settle in California. . . . I do not suppose that she was really serious in this. It would have meant the extinction of all hopes of Branshaw Manor for her. Besides she had got it into her head that Leonora, who was as sound as a roach, was consumptive. She was always begging Leonora, before me, to go and see a doctor. But, none the less, poor Edward seems to have believed in her determination to carry him off. He would not have gone; he cared for his wife too much. But, if Florence had put him at it, that would have meant my getting to know of it, and his incurring Leonora's vengeance. And she could have made it pretty hot for him in ten or a dozen different ways. And she assured me that she would have used every one of them. She was determined to spare my feelings. And she was quite aware that, at that date, the hottest she could have made it for him would have been to refuse, herself, ever to see him again. . . .

Well, I think I have made it pretty clear. Let me come to the fourth of August, 1913, the last day of my absolute ignorance—and, I assure you, of my perfect happiness. For the coming of that dear girl only added to it all.

On that fourth of August I was sitting in the lounge with a rather odious Englishman called Bagshawe, who had arrived that night, too late for dinner. Leonora had just gone to bed and I was waiting for Florence and Edward and the girl to come back from a concert at the Casino. They had not gone there all together. Florence, I remember, had said at first that she would remain with Leonora and me and Edward and the girl had gone off alone. And then Leonora had said to Florence with perfect calmness:

"I wish you would go with those two. I think the girl ought to have the appearance of being chaperoned with Edward in these places. I think the time has come." So Florence, with her light step had slipped out after them. She was all in black for some cousin or other. Americans are particular in those matters.

We had gone on sitting in the lounge till towards ten, when Leonora had gone up to bed. It had been a very hot day, but there it was cool. The man called Bagshawe had been reading the *Times* on the other side of the room, but then he moved over to me with some trifling question as a prelude to suggesting an acquaintance. I fancy he asked me something about the poll-tax on Kur-guests, and whether it could not be sneaked out of. He was that sort of person.

Well, he was an unmistakable man, with a military

figure, rather exaggerated, with bulbous eyes that avoided your own, and a pallid complexion that suggested vices practised in secret, along with an uneasy desire for making acquaintance at whatever cost . . . The filthy toad. . . .

He began by telling me that he came from Ludlow Manor, near Ledbury. The name had a slightly familiar sound, though I could not fix it in my mind. Then he began to talk about a duty on hops, about Californian hops, about Los Angeles, where he had been. He was fencing for a topic with which he might gain my affection.

And then, quite suddenly, in the bright light of the street, I saw Florence running. It was like that—Florence running with a face whiter than paper and her hand on the black stuff over her heart. I tell you, my own heart stood still; I tell you I could not move. She rushed in at the swing doors. She looked round that place of rush chairs, cane tables and newspapers. She saw me and opened her lips. She saw the man who was talking to me. She stuck her hands over her face as if she wished to push her eyes out. And she was not there any more.

I could not move; I could not stir a finger. And then that man said:

"By Jove: Florry Hurlbird." He turned upon me with an oily and uneasy sound meant for a laugh. He was really going to ingratiate himself with me.

"Do you know who that is?" he asked. "The last time I saw that girl she was coming out of the bedroom of a young man called Jimmy at five o'clock in

the morning. In my house at Ledbury. You saw
her recognise me." He was standing on his feet, looking down at me. I don't know what I looked like.
At any rate, he gave a sort of gurgle and then stuttered :

"Oh, I say . . ." Those were the last words I ever
heard of Mr. Bagshawe's. A long time afterwards
I pulled myself out of the lounge and went up to Florence's room. She had not locked the door—for the
first night of our married life. She was lying, quite
respectably arranged, unlike Mrs. Maidan, on her bed.
She had a little phial that rightly should have contained nitrate of amyl, in her right hand. That was
on the fourth of August, 1913.

THE GOOD SOLDIER

PART III

I

THE odd thing is that what sticks out in my recollection of the rest of that evening was Leonora's saying:

"Of course you might marry her," and, when I asked whom, she answered:

"The girl."

Now that is to me a very amazing thing—amazing for the light of possibilities that it casts into the human heart. For I had never had the slightest conscious idea of marrying the girl; I never had the slightest idea even of caring for her. I must have talked in an odd way, as people do who are recovering from an anæsthetic. It is as if one had a dual personality, the one I being entirely unconscious of the other. I had thought nothing; I had said such an extraordinary thing.

I don't know that analysis of my own psychology matters at all to this story. I should say that it didn't or, at any rate, that I had given enough of it. But that odd remark of mine had a strong influence upon what came after. I mean, that Leonora would probably never have spoken to me at all about Florence's relations with Edward if I hadn't said, two hours after my wife's death:

"Now I can marry the girl."

She had, then, taken it for granted that I had been

suffering all that she had been suffering, or, at least, that I had permitted all that she had permitted. So that, a month ago,—about a week after the funeral of poor Edward she could say to me in the most natural way in the world—I had been talking about the duration of my stay at Branshaw—she said with her clear, reflective intonation:

"O stop here for ever and ever if you can." And then she added, "You couldn't be more of a brother to me, or more of a counsellor, or more of a support. You are all the consolation I have in the world. And isn't it odd to think that if your wife hadn't been my husband's mistress, you would probably never have been here at all?"

That was how I got the news—full in the face, like that. I didn't say anything and I don't suppose I felt anything, unless maybe it was with that mysterious and unconscious self that underlies most people. Perhaps one day when I am unconscious or walking in my sleep I may go and spit upon poor Edward's grave. It seems about the most unlikely thing I could do; but there it is.

No, I remember no emotion of any sort, but just the clear feeling that one has from time to time when one hears that some Mrs. So-and-So is *au mieux* with a certain gentleman. It made things plainer, suddenly, to my curiosity. It was as if I thought, at that moment, of a windy November evening, that, when I came to think it over afterwards, a dozen unexplained things would fit themselves into place. But I wasn't thinking things over then. I remember that distinctly.

I was just sitting back, rather stiffly, in a deep arm-chair. That is what I remember. It was twilight.

Branshaw Manor lies in a little hollow with lawns across it and pine-woods on the fringe of the dip. The immense wind, coming from across the forest, roared overhead. But the view from the window was perfectly quiet and grey. Not a thing stirred, except a couple of rabbits on the extreme edge of the lawn. It was Leonora's own little study that we were in and we were waiting for the tea to be brought. I, as I have said, was sitting in the deep chair, Leonora was standing in the window twirling the wooden acorn at the end of the window-blind cord desultorily round and round. She looked across the lawn and said, as far as I can remember:

"Edward has been dead only ten days and yet there are rabbits on the lawn."

I understand that rabbits do a great deal of harm to the short grass in England. And then she turned round to me and said without any adornment at all, for I remember her exact words:

"I think it was stupid of Florence to commit suicide."

I cannot tell you the extraordinary sense of leisure that we two seemed to have at that moment. It wasn't as if we were waiting for a train, it wasn't as if we were waiting for a meal—it was just that there was nothing to wait for. Nothing.

There was an extreme stillness with the remote and intermittent sound of the wind. There was the grey light in that brown, small room. And there appeared to be nothing else in the world.

I knew then that Leonora was about to let me into her full confidence. It was as if—or no, it was the actual fact that—Leonora with an odd English sense of decency had determined to wait until Edward had been in his grave for a full week before she spoke. And with some vague motive of giving her an idea of the extent to which she must permit herself to make confidences, I said slowly—and these words too I remember with exactitude—

"Did Florence commit suicide? I didn't know."

I was just, you understand, trying to let her know that, if she were going to speak she would have to talk about a much wider range of things than she had before thought necessary.

So that that was the first knowledge I had that Florence had committed suicide. It had never entered my head. You may think that I had been singularly lacking in suspiciousness; you may consider me even to have been an imbecile. But consider exactly the position.

In such circumstances of clamour, of outcry, of the crash of many people running together, of the professional reticence of such people as hotel-keepers, the traditional reticence of such "good people" as the Ashburnhams—in such circumstances it is some little material object, always, that catches the eye and that appeals to the imagination. I had no possible guide to the idea of suicide and the sight of the little flask of nitrate of amyl in Florence's hand suggested instantly to my mind the idea of the failure of her heart. Nitrate of amyl, you understand, is the drug that is given to relieve sufferers from angina pectoris.

Seeing Florence, as I had seen her, running with a white face and with one hand held over her heart, and seeing her, as I immediately afterwards saw her, lying upon her bed with the so familiar little brown flask clenched in her fingers, it was natural enough for my mind to frame the idea. As happened now and again, I thought, she had gone out without her remedy and, having felt an attack coming on whilst she was in the gardens, she had run in to get the nitrate in order, as quickly as possible, to obtain relief. And it was equally inevitable my mind should frame the thought that her heart, unable to stand the strain of the running, should have broken in her side. How could I have known that, during all the years of our married life, that little brown flask had contained, not nitrate of amyl, but prussic acid?* It was inconceivable.

Why, not even Edward Ashburnham, who was, after all, more intimate with her than I was, had an inkling of the truth. He just thought that she had dropped dead of heart disease. Indeed, I fancy that the only people who ever knew that Florence had committed suicide were Leonora, the grand-duke, the head of the police and the hotel-keeper. I mention these last three because, my recollection of that night is only the sort of pinkish effulgence from the electric-lamps in the hotel lounge. There seemed to bob into my consciousness, like floating globes, the faces of those three. Now it would be the bearded, monarchical, benevolent head of the grand-duke; then the sharp-featured, brown, cavalry-moustached features of the chief of police; then the globular, polished and high-collared vacuousness that represented Monsieur Schontz, the proprietor of the hotel. At times one head would be there alone, at another the spiked helmet of the official would be close to the healthy baldness of the prince; then M. Schontz's oiled locks would push in between the two. The sovereign's soft, exquisitely trained voice would say, "Ja, ja, ja!" each word dropping out like so many soft pellets of suet; the subdued rasp of the official would come: "Zum Befehl, Durchlaucht,"* like five revolver-shots; the voice of M. Schontz would go on and on under its breath like that of an unclean priest reciting from his breviary*in the corner of a railway-carriage. That was how it presented itself to me.

They seemed to take no notice of me; I don't suppose that I was even addressed by one of them. But, as long as one or the other, or all three of them were there, they stood between me as if, I being the titular possessor of the corpse, had a right to be present at their conferences. Then they all went away and' I was left alone for a long time.

And I thought nothing; absolutely nothing. I had no ideas; I had no strength. I felt no sorrow, no desire for action, no inclination to go upstairs and fall upon the body of my wife. I just saw the pink effulgence, the cane tables, the palms, the globular match-holders, the indented ash-trays. And then Leonora came to me and it appears that I addressed to her that singular remark:

"Now I can marry the girl."

But I have given you absolutely the whole of my recollection of that evening, as it is the whole of my recollection of the succeeding three or four days. I was in a state just simply cataleptic. They put me to bed and I stayed there; they brought me my clothes and I dressed; they led me to an open grave and I stood beside it. If they had taken me to the edge of a river, or if they had flung me beneath a railway train I should have been drowned or mangled in the same spirit. I was the walking dead.

Well, those are my impressions.

What had actually happened had been this. I pieced it together afterwards. You will remember I said that Edward Ashburnham and the girl had gone off, that night, to a concert at the Casino and that Leonora had asked Florence, almost immediately after their departure, to follow them and to perform the office of chaperon. Florence, you may also remember, was all in black, being the mourning that she wore for a deceased cousin, Jean Hurlbird. It was a very black night and the girl was dressed in cream-coloured muslin, that must have glimmered under the tall trees of the dark park like a phosphorescent fish in a cupboard. You couldn't have had a better beacon.

And it appears that Edward Ashburnham led the girl not up the straight allée that leads to the Casino, but in under the dark trees of the park. Edward

Ashburnham told me all this in his final outburst. I
have told you that, upon that occasion, he became
deucedly vocal. I didn't pump him. I hadn't any motive. At that time I didn't in the least connect him
with my wife. But the fellow talked like a cheap
novelist.—Or like a very good novelist for the matter of that, if it's the business of a novelist to make
you see things clearly. And I tell you I see that
thing as clearly as if it were a dream that never left
me. It appears that, not very far from the Casino,
he and the girl sat down in the darkness upon a public bench. The lights from that place of entertain-
ment must have reached them through the tree-
trunks, since, Edward said, he could quite plainly see
the girl's face—that beloved face with the high forehead, the queer mouth, the tortured eye-brows and
the direct eyes. And to Florence, creeping up behind them, they must have presented the appearance
of silhouettes. For I take it that Florence came creeping up behind them over the short grass to a tree
that, as I quite well remember, was immediately behind that public seat. It was a not very difficult feat
for a woman instinct with jealousy. The Casino orchestra was, as Edward remembered to tell me, playing the Rakocsy march* and although it was not loud
enough, at that distance, to drown the voice of Edward Ashburnham it was certainly sufficiently audi-
ble to efface, amongst the noises of the night, the
slight brushings and rustlings that might have been
made by the feet of Florence or by her gown in coming over the short grass. And that miserable woman

must have got it in the face, good and strong. It must have been horrible for her. Horrible! Well, I suppose she deserved all that she got.

Anyhow, there you have the picture, the immensely tall trees, elms most of them, towering and feathering away up into the black mistiness that trees seem to gather about them at night; the silhouettes of those two upon the seat; the beams of light coming from the Casino, the woman all in black peeping with fear behind the tree-trunk. It is melodrama; but I can't help it.

And then, it appears, something happened to Edward Ashburnham. He assured me—and I see no reason for disbelieving him—that until that moment he had had no idea whatever of caring for the girl. He said that he had regarded her exactly as he would have regarded a daughter. He certainly loved her, but with a very deep, very tender and very tranquil love. He had missed her when she went away to her convent-school; he had been glad when she had returned. But of more than that he had been totally unconscious. Had he been conscious of it, he assured me, he would have fled from it as from a thing accursed. He realized that it was the last outrage upon Leonora. But the real point was his entire unconsciousness. He had gone with her into that dark park with no quickening of the pulse, with no desire for the intimacy of solitude. He had gone, intending to talk about polo-ponies and tennis-racquets; about the temperament of the reverend Mother at the convent she had left and about whether her frock for a party when they got home should be white or blue. It hadn't come into his head that they would talk about a single 'thing that they hadn't always talked about; it had not even come into his head that the tabu which extended around her was not inviolable. And then, suddenly, that——

He was very careful to assure me that at that time there was no physical motive about his declaration. It did not appear to him to be a matter of a dark night and a propinquity and so on. No, it was simply of her effect on the moral side of his life that he appears to have talked. He said that he never had the slightest notion to enfold her in his arms or so much as to touch her hand. He swore that he did not touch her hand. He said that they sat, she at one end of the bench, he at the other; he leaning slightly towards her and she looking straight towards the light of the Casino, her face illuminated by the lamps. The expression upon her face he could only describe as "queer."

At another time, indeed, he made it appear that he thought she was glad. It is easy to imagine that she was glad, since at that time she could have had no idea of what was really happening. Frankly, she adored Edward Ashburnham. He was for her, in everything that she said at that time the model of humanity, the hero, the athlete, the father of his county, the law-giver. So that for her, to be suddenly, intimately and overwhelmingly praised must have been a matter for mere gladness, however overwhelming it were. It must have been as if a god had approved her handiwork or a king her loyalty. She just sat still and listened, smiling.

And it seemed to her that all the bitterness of her childhood, the terrors of her tempestuous father, the bewailings of her cruel-tongued mother were suddenly atoned for. She had her recompense at last. Because, of course, if you come to figure it out, a sudden pouring forth of passion by a man whom you regard as a cross between a pastor and a father might, to a woman, have the aspect of mere praise for good conduct. It wouldn't, I mean, appear at all in the light of an attempt to gain possession. The girl, at least, regarded him as firmly anchored to his Leonora. She had not the slightest inkling of any infidelities. He had always spoken to her of his wife in terms of reverence and deep affection. He had given her the idea that he regarded Leonora as absolutely impeccable and as absolutely satisfying. Their union had appeared to her to be one of those blessed things that are spoken of and contemplated with reverence by her church.

So that, when he spoke of her as being the person he cared most for in the world, she naturally thought that he meant to except Leonora and she was just glad. It was like a father saying that he approved of a marriageable daughter . . . And Edward, when he realised what he was doing, curbed his tongue at once. She was just glad and she went on being just glad.

I suppose that that was the most monstrously wicked thing that Edward Ashburnham ever did in his life. And yet I am so near to all these people that I cannot think any of them wicked. It is impossible

of me to think of Edward Ashburnham as anything
but straight, upright and honourable. That, I mean,
is, in spite of everything, my permanent view of him.
I try at times by dwelling on some of the things that
he did to push that image of him away, as you might
try to push aside a large pendulum. But it always
comes back—the memory of his innumerable acts of
kindness, of his efficiency, of his unspiteful tongue.
He was such a fine fellow.

So I feel myself forced to attempt to excuse him
in this as in so many other things. It is, I have no
doubt, a most monstrous thing to attempt to corrupt a
young girl just out of a convent. But I think Edward
had no idea at all of corrupting her. I believe that
he simply loved her. He said that that was the way
of it and I, at least, believe him and I believe too that
she was the only woman he ever really loved. He
said that that was so; and he did enough to prove
it. And Leonora said that it was so and Leonora
knew him to the bottom of his heart.

I have come to be very much of a cynic in these
matters; I mean that it is impossible to believe in the
permanence of man's or woman's love. Or, at any
rate, it is impossible to believe in the permanence
of any early passion. As I see it, at least, with regard to man, a love affair, a love for any definite
woman—is something in the nature of a widening of
the experience. With each new woman that a man is
attracted to there appears to come a broadening of the
outlook, or, if you like, an acquiring of new territory. A turn of the eye-brow, a tone of the voice,

a queer characteristic gesture—all these things, and it is these things that cause to arise the passion of love—all these things are like so many objects on the horizon of the landscape that tempt a man to walk beyond the horizon, to explore. He wants to get, as it were, behind those eye-brows with the peculiar turn, as if he desired to see the world with the eyes that they overshadow. He wants to hear that voice applying itself to every possible proposition, to every possible topic; he wants to see those characteristic gestures against every possible background. Of the question of the sex-instinct I know very little and I do not think that it counts for very much in a really great passion. It can be aroused by such nothings —by an untied shoe-lace, by a glance of the eye in passing—that I think it might be left out of the calculation. I don't mean to say that any great passion can exist without a desire for consummation. That seems to me to be a commonplace and to be therefore a matter needing no comment at all. It is a thing, with all its accidents, that must be taken for granted, as, in a novel, or a biography, you take it for granted that the characters have their meals with some regularity. But the real fierceness of desire, the real heat of a passion long continued and withering up the soul of a man is the craving for identity with the woman that he loves. He desires to see with the same eyes, to touch with the same sense of touch, to hear with the same ears, to lose his identity, to be enveloped, to be supported. For, whatever may be said of the relation of the sexes, there is no man who loves a woman that does not desire to come to her for the renewal of his courage, for the cutting asunder of his difficulties. And that will be the mainspring of his desire for her. We are all so afraid, we are all so alone, we all so need from the outside the assurance of our own worthiness to exist.

So, for a time, if such a passion come to fruition, the man will get what he wants. He will get the moral support, the encouragement, the relief from the sense of loneliness, the assurance of his own worth. But these things pass away; inevitably they pass away as the shadows pass across sun-dials. It is sad, but it is so. The pages of the book will become familiar; the beautiful corner of the road will have been turned too many times. Well, this is the saddest story.

And yet I do believe that for every man there comes at last a woman—or, no, that is the wrong way of formulating it. For every man there comes at last a time of life when the woman who then sets her seal upon his imagination has set her seal for good. He will travel over no more horizons; he will never again set the knapsack over his shoulders; he will retire from those scenes. He will have gone out of the business.

That at any rate was the case with Edward and the poor girl. It was quite literally the case. It was quite literally the case that his passions—for the mistress of the grand-duke, for Mrs. Basil, for little Mrs. Maidan, for Florence, for whom you will—these passions were merely preliminary canters compared to his final race with death for her. I am certain of that. I am not going to be so American as to say that all true love demands some sacrifice. It doesn't. But I think that love will be truer and more permanent in which self-sacrifice has been exacted. And, in the case of the other women, Edward just cut in and cut them out as he did with the polo-ball from under the nose of Count Baron von Lelöffel. I don't mean to say that he didn't wear himself as thin as a lath in the endeavour to capture the other women; but over her he wore himself to rags and tatters and death—in the effort to leave her alone.

And, in speaking to her on that night, he wasn't, I am convinced, committing a baseness. It was as if his passion for her hadn't existed; as if the very words that he spoke, without knowing that he spoke them, created the passion as they went along. Before he spoke, there was nothing; afterwards, it was the integral fact of his life. Well, I must get back to my story.

And my story was concerning itself with Florence—with Florence, who heard those words from behind the tree. That of course is only conjecture, but I think the conjecture is pretty well justified. You have the fact that those two went out, that she followed them almost immediately afterwards through the darkness and, a little later, she came running back to the hotel with that pallid face and the hand clutching her dress over her heart. It can't have been only Bagshawe. Her face was contorted with agony before ever her eyes fell upon me or upon him beside me. But I dare say Bagshawe may have been the determining influence in her suicide. Leonora says that she had that flask, apparently of nitrate of amyl, but actually of prussic acid, for many years and that she was determined to use it if ever I discovered the nature of her relationship with that fellow Jimmy. You see, the mainspring of her nature must have been vanity. There is no reason why it shouldn't have been; I guess it is vanity that makes most of us keep straight, if we do keep straight, in this world.

If it had been merely a matter of Edward's relations with the girl I dare say Florence would have faced it out. She would no doubt have made him scenes, have threatened him, have appealed to his sense of honour, to his promises. But Mr. Bagshawe and the fact that the date was the 4th of August must have been too much for her superstitious mind. You see, she had two things that she wanted. She wanted to be a great lady, installed in Branshaw Teleragh. She wanted also to retain my respect.

She wanted, that is to say, to retain my respect for as long as she lived with me. I suppose, if she had persuaded Edward Ashburnham to bolt with her she would have let the whole thing go with a run. Or perhaps she would have tried to exact from me a new respect for the greatness of her passion on the lines of all for love and the world well lost. That would be just like Florence.

In all matrimonial associations there is, I believe, one constant factor—a desire to deceive the person with whom one lives as to some weak spot in one's character or in one's career. For it is intolerable to live constantly with one human being who perceives

one's small meannesses. It is really death to do so
—that is why so many marriages turn out unhappily.

I, for instance, am a rather greedy man; I have a
taste for good cookery and a watering tooth at the
mere sound of the names of certain comestibles. If
Florence had discovered this secret of mine I should
have found her knowledge of it so unbearable that
I never could have supported all the other privations
of the régime that she extracted from me. I am bound
to say that Florence never discovered this secret.

Certainly she never alluded to it; I dare say she
never took sufficient interest in me.

And the secret weakness of Florence—the weakness
that she could not bear to have me discover was just
that early escapade with the fellow called Jimmy. Let
me, as this is in all probability the last time I shall
mention Florence's name, dwell a little upon the
change that had taken place in her psychology. She
would not, I mean, have minded if I had discovered
that she was the mistress of Edward Ashburnham.
She would rather have liked it. Indeed, the chief
trouble of poor Leonora in those days was to keep
Florence from making, before me, theatrical displays,
on one line or another, of that very fact. She wanted,
in one mood, to come rushing to me, to cast herself
on her knees at my feet and to declaim a carefully
arranged, frightfully emotional, outpouring as to her
passion. That was to show that she was like one of
the great erotic women of whom history tells us. In
another mood she would desire to come to me disdain-
fully and to tell me that I was considerably less than

a man and that what had happened was what must
happen when a real male came along. She wanted to
say that in cool, balanced and sarcastic sentences.
That was when she wished to appear like the heroine
of a French comedy. Because of course she was always play-acting.

But what she didn't want me to know was the fact
of her first escapade with the fellow called Jimmy.
She had arrived at figuring out the sort of low-down
Bowery*tough that that fellow was. Do you know
what it is to shudder, in later life, for some small,
stupid action—usually for some small, quite genuine
piece of emotionalism—of your early life? Well, it
was that sort of shuddering that came over Florence
at the thought that she had surrendered to such a low
fellow. I don't know that she need have shuddered.
It was her footling old uncle's work; he ought never
to have taken those two round the world together and
shut himself up in his cabin for the greater part of
the time. Anyhow, I am convinced that the sight of
Mr. Bagshawe and the thought that Mr. Bagshawe—
for she knew that unpleasant and toad-like personality—the thought that Mr. Bagshawe would almost
certainly reveal to me that he had caught her coming
out of Jimmy's bedroom at five o'clock in the morning on the 4th of August, 1900—that was the determining influence in her suicide. And no doubt the
effect of the date was too much for her superstitious personality. She had been born on the 4th of
August: she had started to go round the world on
the 4th of August; she had become a low fellow's

mistress on the 4th of August. On the same day of the year she had married me; on that 4th she had lost Edward's love and Bagshawe had appeared like a sinister omen—like a grin on the face of Fate. It was the last straw. She ran upstairs, arranged herself decoratively upon her bed—she was a sweetly pretty woman with smooth pink and white cheeks, long hair, the eyelashes falling like a tiny curtain on her cheeks. She drank the little phial of prussic acid and there she lay.—O, extremely charming and clearcut—looking with a puzzled expression at the electriclight bulb that hung from the ceiling, or perhaps through it, to the stars above. Who knows? Anyhow, there was an end of Florence.

You have no idea how quite extraordinarily for me that was the end of Florence. From that day to this I have never given her another thought; I have not bestowed upon her so much as a sigh. Of course, when it has been necessary to talk about her to Leonora or, when for the purpose of these writings I have tried to figure her out, I have thought about her as I might do about a problem in Algebra. But it has always been as a matter for study, not for remembrance. She just went completely out of existence, like yesterday's paper.

I was so deadly tired. And I dare say that my week or ten days of affaissement*—of what was practically catalepsy—was just the repose that my exhausted nature claimed after twelve years of the repression of my instincts, after twelve years of playing the trained poodle. For that was all that I had been. I suppose that it was the shock that did it—the several shocks. But I am unwilling to attribute my feelings at that time to anything so concrete as a shock. It was a feeling so tranquil. It was as if an immensely heavy—an unbearably heavy knapsack, supported upon my shoulders by straps, had fallen off and had left my shoulders themselves that the straps had cut into, numb and without sensation of life. I tell you, I had no regret. What had I to regret? I suppose that my inner soul—my dual personality—had realized long before that Florence was a personality of paper—that she represented a real human being with a heart, with feelings, with sympathies and with emotions only as a bank note represents a certain quantity of gold. I know that that sort of feeling came to the surface in me the moment the man Bagshawe told me that he had seen her coming out of that fellow's bedroom. I thought suddenly that she wasn't real; she was just a mass of talk out of guide-books, of drawings out of fashion-plates. It is even possible that, if that feeling had not possessed me, I should have run up sooner to her room and might have prevented her drinking the prussic acid. But I just couldn't do it; it would have been like chasing a scrap of paper—an occupation ignoble for a grown man.

And, as it began, so that matter has remained. I didn't care whether she had come out of that bedroom or whether she hadn't. It simply didn't interest me. Florence didn't matter.

I suppose you will retort that I was in love with

Nancy Rufford and that my indifference was therefore discreditable. Well, I am not seeking to avoid discredit. I was in love with Nancy Rufford as I am in love with the poor child's memory, quietly and quite tenderly in my American sort of way. I had never thought about it until I heard Leonora state that I might now marry her. But, from that moment until her worse than death, I do not suppose that I much thought about anything else. I don't mean to say that I sighed about her or groaned; I just wanted to marry her as some people want to go to Carcassonne.

Do you understand the feeling—the sort of feeling that you must get certain matters out of the way, smooth out certain fairly negligible complications before you can go to a place that has, during all your life, been a sort of dream city? I didn't attach much importance to my superior years. I was forty-five and she, poor thing, was only just rising twenty-two. But she was older than her years and quieter. She seemed to have an odd quality of sainthood, as if she must inevitably end in a convent with a white coif framing her face. But she had frequently told me that she had no vocation; it just simply wasn't there— the desire to become a nun. Well, I guess that I was a sort of convent myself; it seemed fairly proper that she should make her vows to me.

No, I didn't see any impediment on the score of age. I dare say no man does, and I was pretty confident that, with a little preparation, I could make a young girl happy. I could spoil her as few young girls have ever been spoiled; and I couldn't regard myself as personally repulsive. No man can, or, if he ever comes to do so, that is the end of him. But, as soon as I came out of my catalepsy, I seemed to perceive that my problem—that what I had to do to prepare myself for getting into contact with her, was just to get back into contact with life. I had been kept for twelve years in a rarefied atmosphere; what I then had to do was a little fighting with real life, some wrestling with men of business, some travelling amongst larger cities, something harsh, something masculine. I didn't want to present myself to Nancy Rufford as a sort of an old maid. That was why, just a fortnight after Florence's suicide, I set off for the United States.

II

IMMEDIATELY after Florence's death Leonora began to put the leash upon Nancy Rufford and Edward. She had guessed what had happened under the trees near the Casino. They stayed at Nauheim some three weeks after I went, and Leonora has told me that that was the most deadly time of her existence. It seemed like a long, silent duel with invisible weapons, so she said. And it was rendered all the more difficult by the girl's entire innocence. For Nancy was always trying to go off alone with Edward—as she had been doing all her life, whenever she was home for holidays. She just wanted him to say nice things to her again.

You see, the position was extremely complicated. It was as complicated as it well could be, along delicate lines. There was the complication caused by the fact that Edward and Leonora never spoke to each other except when other people were present. Then, as I have said, their demeanours were quite perfect. There was the complication caused by the girl's entire innocence; there was the further complication that both Edward and Leonora really regarded the girl as their daughter. Or it might be more precise to say that they regarded her as being Leonora's daughter. And Nancy was a queer girl; it is very difficult to describe her to you.

145

She was tall and strikingly thin; she had a tortured mouth, agonised eyes, and a quite extraordinary sense of fun. You might put it that at times she was exceedingly grotesque and at times extraordinarily beautiful. Why, she had the heaviest head of black hair that I have ever come across; I used to wonder how she could bear the weight of it. She was just over twenty-one and at times she seemed as old as the hills, at times not much more than sixteen. At one moment she would be talking of the lives of the saints and at the next she would be tumbling all over the lawn with the St. Bernard puppy. She could ride to hounds like a Mænad*and she could sit for hours perfectly still, steeping handkerchief after handkerchief in vinegar when Leonora had one of her headaches. She was, in short, a miracle of patience who could be almost miraculously impatient. It was no doubt the convent training that effected that. I remember that one of her letters to me, when she was about sixteen, ran something like:

"On Corpus Christi"*—or it may have been some other saint's day, I cannot keep these things in my head—"our school played Roehampton* at Hockey. And, seeing that our side was losing, being three goals to one against us at half-time, we retired into the chapel and prayed for victory. We won by five goals to three." And I remember that she seemed to describe afterwards a sort of saturnalia.* Apparently, when the victorious fifteen, or eleven, came into the refectory for supper, the whole school jumped upon the tables and cheered and broke the chairs on the floor and smashed the crockery—for a given time, until the Reverend Mother rang a hand-bell. That is of course the Catholic tradition—saturnalia that can end in a moment, like the crack of a whip. I don't of course like the tradition, but I am bound to say that it gave Nancy—or at any rate Nancy had, a sense of rectitude that I have never seen surpassed. It was a thing like a knife that looked out of her eyes and that spoke with her voice, just now and then. It positively frightened me. I suppose that I was almost afraid to be in a world where there could be so fine a standard. I remember when she was about fifteen or sixteen on going back to the convent I once gave her a couple of English sovereigns as a tip. She thanked me in a peculiarly heartfelt way, saying that it would come in extremely handy. I asked her why and she explained. There was a rule at the school that the pupils were not to speak when they walked through the garden from the chapel to the refectory. And, since this rule appeared to be idiotic and arbitrary, she broke it on purpose day after day. In the evening the children were all asked if they had committed any faults during the day, and every evening Nancy confessed that she had broken this particular rule. It cost her sixpence a time, that being the fine attached to the offence. Just for the information I asked her why she always confessed, and she answered in these exact words:

"Oh, well, the girls of the Holy Child have always been noted for their truthfulness. It's a beastly bore, but I've got to do it."

I dare say that the miserable nature of her child-hood, coming before the mixture of saturnalia and discipline that was her convent life, added something to her queernesses. Her father was a violent mad-man of a fellow, a major in one of what I believe are called the Highland regiments. He didn't drink, but he had an ungovernable temper, and the first thing that Nancy could remember was seeing her father strike her mother with his clenched fist so that her mother fell over sideways from the breakfast table and lay motionless. The mother was no doubt an irritating woman and the privates of that regiment ap-pear to have been irritating, too, so that the house was a place of outcries and perpetual disturbance. Mrs. Rufford was Leonora's dearest friend and Leonora could be cutting enough at times. But I fancy she was as nothing to Mrs. Rufford. The Major would come in to lunch harassed and already spitting out oaths after an unsatisfactory morning's drilling of his stubborn men beneath a hot sun. And then Mrs. Rufford would make some cutting remark and pan-demonium would break loose. Once, when she had been about twelve, Nancy had tried to intervene between the pair of them. Her father had struck her full upon the forehead a blow so terrible that she had lain unconscious for three days. Nevertheless Nancy seemed to prefer her father to her mother. She re-membered rough kindnesses from him. Once or twice when she had been quite small he had dressed her in a clumsy, impatient but very tender way. It was nearly always impossible to get a servant to stay in the family and, for days at a time, apparently, Mrs. Rufford would be incapable. I fancy she drank. At any rate she had so cutting a tongue that even Nancy was afraid of her—she so made fun of any tenderness, she so sneered at all emotional displays. Nancy must have been a very emotional child. . . .

Then one day, quite suddenly, on her return from a ride at Fort William,* Nancy had been sent, with her governess, who had a white face, right down South to that convent school. She had been expecting to go there in two months' time. Her mother disappeared from her life at that time. A fortnight later Leonora came to the convent and told her that her mother was dead. Perhaps she was. At any rate I never heard until the very end what became of Mrs. Rufford. Leonora never spoke of her.

And then Major Rufford went to India, from which he returned very seldom and only for very short visits; and Nancy lived herself gradually into the life at Branshaw Teleragh. I think that, from that time onwards, she led a very happy life, till the end. There were dogs and horses and old servants and the Forest.* And there were Edward and Leonora, who loved her.

I had known her all the time—I mean that she always came to the Ashburnhams' at Nauheim for the last fortnight of their stay, and I watched her gradually growing. She was very cheerful with me. She always even kissed me, night and morning, until she was about eighteen. And she would skip about and fetch me things and laugh at my tales of life in

Philadelphia. But, beneath her gaiety, I fancy that there lurked some terrors. I remember one day, when she was just eighteen, during one of her father's rare visits to Europe, we were sitting in the gardens, near the iron-stained fountain. Leonora had one of her headaches and we were waiting for Florence and Edward to come from their baths. You have no idea how beautiful Nancy looked that morning.

We were talking about the desirability of taking tickets in lotteries—of the moral side of it, I mean. She was all in white, and so tall and fragile; and she had only just put her hair up, so that the carriage of her neck had that charming touch of youth and of unfamiliarity. Over her throat there played the reflection from a little pool of water, left by a thunderstorm of the night before, and all the rest of her features were in the diffused and luminous shade of her white parasol. Her dark hair just showed beneath her broad, white hat of pierced, chip straw; her throat was very long and leaned forward, and her eyebrows, arching a little as she laughed at some old-fashionedness in my phraseology, had abandoned their tense line. And there was a little colour in her cheeks and light in her deep blue eyes. And to think that that vivid white thing, that saintly and swanlike being—to think that . . . Why, she was like the sail of a ship, so white and so definite in her movements. And to think that she will never . . . Why, she will never do anything again. I can't believe it . . .

Anyhow we were chattering away about the morality of lotteries. And then, suddenly, there came from the arcades behind us the overtones of her father's unmistakable voice; it was as if a modified foghorn had boomed with a reed inside it. I looked round to catch sight of him. A tall, fair, stiffly upright man of fifty, he was walking away with an Italian baron who had had much to do with the Belgian Congo. They must have been talking about the proper treatment of natives, for I heard him say:

"Oh, hang humanity!"

When I looked again at Nancy her eyes were closed and her face was more pallid than her dress, which had at least some pinkish reflections from the gravel. It was dreadful to see her with her eyes closed like that.

"Oh," she exclaimed, and her hand that had appeared to be groping, settled for a moment on my arm. "Never speak of it. Promise never to tell my father of it. It brings back those dreadful dreams . . ." And, when she opened her eyes she looked straight into mine. "The blessed saints," she said, "you would think they would spare you such things. I don't believe all the sinning in the world could make one deserve them."

They say the poor thing was always allowed a light at night, even in her bedroom. . . . And yet, no young girl could more archly and lovingly have played with an adored father. She was always holding him by both coat lapels; cross-questioning him as to how he spent his time; kissing the top of his head. Ah, she was well-bred, if ever anyone was.

The poor, wretched man cringed before her—but

she could not have done more to put him at his ease.
Perhaps she had had lessons in it at her convent. It
was only that peculiar note of his voice, used when he
was overbearing or dogmatic, that could unman her—
and that was only visible when it came unexpectedly.
That was because the bad dreams that the blessed
saints allowed her to have for her sins always seemed
to her to herald themselves by the booming sound of
her father's voice. It was that sound that had always
preceded his entrance for the terrible lunches of her
childhood . . .

I have reported, earlier in this chapter, that Leonora
said, during that remainder of their stay at Nauheim,
after I had left, it had seemed to her that she was
fighting a long duel with unseen weapons against silent adversaries. Nancy, as I have also said, was always trying to go off with Edward alone. That had
been her habit for years. And Leonora found it to
be her duty to stop that. It was very difficult. Nancy
was used to having her own way, and for years she
had been used to going off with Edward, ratting, rab-
biting, catching salmon down at Fordingbridge, dis-
trict-visiting of the sort that Edward indulged in, or
calling on the tenants. And at Nauheim she and Edward had always gone up to the Casino alone in the
evenings—at any rate whenever Florence did not call
for his attendance. It shows the obviously innocent
nature of the regard of those two that even Florence
had never had any idea of jealousy. Leonora had cul-
tivated the habit of going to bed at ten o'clock.

I don't know how she managed it, but, for all the

time they were at Nauheim, she contrived never to let those two be alone together, except in broad daylight, in very crowded places. If a Protestant had done that it would no doubt have awakened a self-consciousness in the girl. But Catholics, who have always reservations and queer spots of secrecy, can manage these things better. And I dare say that two things made this easier—the death of Florence and the fact that Edward was obviously sickening. He appeared, indeed, to be very ill; his shoulders began to be bowed; there were pockets under his eyes; he had extraordinary moments of inattention.

And Leonora describes herself as watching him as a fierce cat watches an unconscious pigeon in a roadway. In that silent watching, again, I think she was a Catholic—of a people that can think thoughts alien to ours and keep them to themselves. And the thoughts passed through her mind; some of them even got through to Edward with never a word spoken. At first she thought that it might be remorse, or grief, for the death of Florence that was oppressing him. But she watched and watched, and uttered apparently random sentences about Florence before the girl, and she perceived that he had no grief and no remorse. He had not any idea that Florence could have committed suicide without writing at least a tirade to him. The absence of that made him certain that it had been heart disease. For Florence had never undeceived him on that point. She thought it made her seem more romantic.

No, Edward had no remorse. He was able to say

to himself that he had treated Florence with gallant attentiveness of the kind that she desired until two hours before her death. Leonora gathered that from the look in his eyes, and from the way he straightened his shoulders over her as she lay in her coffin—from that and a thousand other little things. She would speak suddenly about Florence to the girl and he would not start in the least; he would not even pay attention, but would sit with bloodshot eyes gazing at the tablecloth. He drank a good deal, at that time—a steady soaking of drink every evening till long after they had gone to bed.

For Leonora made the girl go to bed at ten, unreasonable though that seemed to Nancy. She would understand that, whilst they were in a sort of half mourning for Florence, she ought not to be seen at public places, like the Casino; but she could not see why she should not accompany her uncle upon his evening strolls through the park. I don't know what Leonora put up as an excuse—something, I fancy, in the nature of a nightly orison that she made the girl and herself perform for the soul of Florence. And then, one evening, about a fortnight later, when the girl, growing restive at even devotional exercises, clamoured once more to be allowed to go for a walk with Edward, and when Leonora was really at her wits' end Edward himself gave himself into her hands. He was just standing up from dinner and had his face averted.

But he turned his heavy head and his bloodshot eyes upon his wife and looked full at her.

"Doctor von Hauptmann," he said, "has ordered me to go to bed immediately after dinner. My heart's much worse."

He continued to look at Leonora for a long minute —with a sort of heavy contempt. And Leonora understood that, with his speech, he was giving her the excuse that she needed for separating him from the girl, and with his eyes he was reproaching her for thinking that he would try to corrupt Nancy.

He went silently up to his room and sat there for a long time—until the girl was well in bed—reading in the Anglican prayer book. And about half past ten she heard his footsteps pass her door, going outwards. Two and a half hours later they came back, stumbling heavily.

She remained, reflecting upon this position until the last night of their stay at Nauheim. Then she suddenly acted. For, just in the same way, suddenly after dinner, she looked at him and said:

"Teddy, don't you think you could take a night off from your doctor's orders and go with Nancy to the Casino. The poor child has had her visit so spoiled."

He looked at her in turn for a long, balancing minute.

"Why, yes," he said at last. Nancy jumped out of her chair and kissed him.

Those two words, Leonora said, gave her the greatest relief of any two syllables she had ever heard in her life. For she realised that Edward was breaking up, not under the desire for possession, but from the

dogged determination to hold his hand. She could
relax some of her vigilance.

Nevertheless she sat in the darkness behind her
half-closed jalousies*looking over the street and the
night and the trees until, very late, she could hear
Nancy's clear voice coming closer and saying:

"You did look an old guy*with that false nose."

There had been some sort of celebration of a local
holiday up in the Kursaal. And Edward replied with
his sort of sulky good nature:

"As for you, you looked like old Mother Sideacher."*

The girl came swinging along, a silhouette beneath
a gas-lamp; Edward, another, slouched at her side.
They were talking just as they had talked any time
since the girl had been seventeen; with the same tones,
the same joke about an old beggar woman who always amused them at Branshaw. The girl, a little
later, opened Leonora's door whilst she was still kissing Edward on the forehead as she had done every
night.

"We've had a most glorious time," she said. "He's
ever so much better. He raced me for twenty yards
home. Why are you all in the dark?"

Leonora could hear Edward going about in his
room, but, owing to the girl's chatter, she could not
tell whether he went out again or not. And then, very
much later, because she thought that if he were drinking again something must be done to stop it, she
opened for the first time, and very softly, the never-
opened door between their rooms. She wanted to see
if he had gone out again. Edward was kneeling be-

side his bed with his head hidden in the counterpane. His arms, outstretched, held out before him a little image of the blessed virgin—a tawdry, scarlet and Prussian blue affair that the girl had given him on her first return from the convent. His shoulders heaved convulsively three times, and heavy sobs came from him before she could close the door. He was not a Catholic; but that was the way it took him.

Leonora slept for the first time that night with a sleep from which she never once started.

III

A ND then Leonora completely broke down—on
the day that they returned to . Branshaw
Teleragh. It is the infliction of our miserable minds—it is the scourge of atrocious but probably
just destiny that no grief comes by itself. No, any great
grief, though the grief itself may have gone, leaves
in its place a train of horrors, of misery, and despair.
For Leonora was, in herself, relieved. She felt that
she could trust Edward with the girl and she knew
that Nancy could be absolutely trusted. And then,
with the slackening of her vigilance, came the slackening of her entire mind. This is perhaps the most miserable part of the entire story. For it is miserable to
see a clear intelligence waver; and Leonora wavered.

You are to understand that Leonora loved Edward
with a passion that was yet like an agony of hatred.
And she had lived with him for years and years without addressing to him one word of tenderness. I don't
know how she could do it. At the beginning of that
relationship she had been just married off to him.
She had been one of seven daughters in a bare, untidy
Irish manor house to which she had returned from the
convent I have so often spoken of. She had left it
just a year and she was just nineteen. It is impossible
to imagine such inexperience as was hers. You might
almost say that she had never spoken to a man except

a priest. Coming straight from the convent, she had gone in behind the high walls of the manor-house that was almost more cloistral than any convent could have been. There were the seven girls, there was the strained mother, there was the worried father at whom, three times, in the course of that year the tenants took pot-shots from behind a hedge. The women-folk, upon the whole, the tenants respected. Once a week each of the girls, since there were seven of them, took a drive with the mother in the old basketwork chaise* drawn by a very fat, very lumbering pony. They paid occasionally a call, but even these were so rare that, Leonora has assured me, only three times in the year that succeeded her coming home from the convent did she enter another person's house. For the rest of the time the seven sisters ran about in the neglected gardens between the unpruned espaliers.* Or they played lawn-tennis or fives* in an angle of a great wall that surrounded the garden —an angle from which the fruit trees had long died away. They painted in water-colour; they embroidered; they copied verses into albums. Once a week they went to mass; once a week to the confessional accompanied by an old nurse. They were happy since they had known no other life.

It appeared to them a singular extravagance when, one day, a photographer was brought over from the county town and photographed them standing, all seven, in the shadow of an old apple-tree with the grey lichen on the raddled trunk.

But it wasn't an extravagance.

Three weeks before Colonel Powys had written to Colonel Ashburnham:

"I say, Harry, couldn't your Edward marry one of my girls? It would be a god-send to me, for I'm at the end of my tether and, once one girl begins to go off, the rest of them will follow."

He went on to say that all his daughters were tall, upstanding, clean-limbed and absolutely pure, and he reminded Colonel Ashburnham that, they having been married on the same day, though in different churches, since the one was a Catholic and the other an Anglican —they had said to each other, the night before, that, when the time came, one of their sons should marry one of their daughters. Mrs. Ashburnham had been a Powys and remained Mrs. Powys' dearest friend. They had drifted about the world as English soldiers do, seldom meeting, but their women always in correspondence one with another. They wrote about minute things such as the teething of Edward and of the earlier daughters or the best way to repair a Jacob's ladder in a stocking. And, if they met seldom, yet it was often enough to keep each other's personalities fresh in their minds, gradually growing greyer, gradually growing a little stiff in the joints, but always with enough to talk about and with a store of reminiscences. Then, as his girls began to come of an age when they must leave the convent in which they were regularly interned during his years of active service, Colonel Powys retired from the army with the necessity of making a home for them. It happened that the Ashburnhams had never seen any of the Powys girls, though, whenever the four parents met in London, Edward Ashburnham was always of the party. He was at that time twenty-two and, I believe, almost as pure in mind as Leonora herself. It is odd how a boy can have his virgin intelligence untouched in this world.

That was partly due to the careful handling of his mother, partly to the fact that the house to which he went at Winchester had a particularly pure tone and partly to Edward's own peculiar aversion from anything like coarse language or gross stories. At Sandhurst*he had just kept out of the way of that sort of thing. He was keen on soldiering, keen on mathematics, on land-surveying, on politics and, by a queer warp of his mind, on literature. Even when he was twenty-two he would pass hours reading one of Scott's novels or the Chronicles of Froissart.*

Mrs. Ashburnham considered that she was to be congratulated, and almost every week she wrote to Mrs. Powys, dilating upon her satisfaction.

Then, one day, taking a walk down Bond Street with her son, after having been at Lord's,* she noticed Edward suddenly turn his head round to take a second look at a well-dressed girl who had passed them. She wrote about that, too, to Mrs. Powys, and expressed some alarm. It had been, on Edward's part, the merest reflex action. He was so very abstracted at that time owing to the pressure his crammer was putting upon him that he certainly hadn't known what he was doing.

It was this letter of Mrs. Ashburnham's to Mrs. Powys that had caused the letter from Colonel Powys

to Colonel Ashburnham—a letter that was half humorous, half longing. Mrs. Ashburnham caused her
husband to reply, with a letter a little more jocular—
something to the effect that Colonel Powys ought to
give them some idea of the goods that he was market-
ing. That was the cause of the photograph. I have
seen it, the seven girls, all in white dresses, all very
much alike in feature—all, except Leonora, a little
heavy about the chins and a little stupid about the
eyes. I dare say it would have made Leonora, too,
look a little heavy and a little stupid, for it was not a
good photograph. But the black shadow from one
of the branches of the apple-tree cut right across her
face, which is all but invisible.

There followed an extremely harassing time for
Colonel and Mrs. Powys. Mrs. Ashburnham had
written to say that, quite sincerely, nothing would give
greater ease to her maternal anxieties than to have her
son marry one of Mrs. Powys' daughters if only he
showed some inclination to do so. For, she added,
nothing but a love-match was to be thought of in her
Edward's case. But the poor Powys couple had to
run things so very fine that even the bringing together
of the young people was a desperate hazard.

The mere expenditure upon sending one of the girls
over from Ireland to Branshaw was terrifying to
them; and whichever girl they selected might not be
the one to ring Edward's bell. On the other hand, the
expenditure upon mere food and extra sheets for a
visit from the Ashburnhams to them was terrifying,
too. It would mean, mathematically, going short in

so many meals themselves, afterwards. Nevertheless they chanced it, and all the three Ashburnhams came on a visit to the lonely manor-house. They could give Edward some rough shooting, some rough fishing and a whirl of femininity; but I should say the girls made really more impression upon Mrs. Ashburnham than upon Edward himself. They appeared to her to be so clean run and so safe. They were indeed so clean run that, in a faint sort of way, Edward seems to have regarded them rather as boys than as girls. And then, one evening, Mrs. Ashburnham had with her boy one of those conversations that English mothers have with English sons. It seems to have been a criminal sort of proceeding, though I don't know what took place at it. Anyhow, next morning Colonel Ashburnham asked on behalf of his son for the hand of Leonora. This caused some consternation to the Powys couple, since Leonora was the third daughter and Edward ought to have married the eldest. Mrs. Powys, with her rigid sense of the proprieties, almost wished to reject the proposal. But the Colonel, her husband, pointed out that the visit would have cost them sixty pounds, what with the hire of an extra servant, of a horse and car, and with the purchase of beds and bedding and extra tablecloths. There was nothing else for it but the marriage. In that way Edward and Leonora became man and wife.

I don't know that a very minute study of their progress towards complete disunion is necessary. Perhaps it is. But there are many things that I cannot well make out, about which I cannot well question

Leonora, or about which Edward did not tell me. I do not know that there was ever any question of love from Edward to her. He regarded her, certainly, as desirable amongst her sisters. He was obstinate to the extent of saying that if he could not have her he would not have any of them. And no doubt, before the marriage, he made her pretty speeches out of books that he had read. But, as far as he could describe his feelings at all, later, it seems that, calmly and without any quickening of the pulse, he just carried the girl off, there being no opposition. It had, however, been all so long ago that it seemed to him, at the end of his poor life, a dim and misty affair. He had the greatest admiration for Leonora.

He had the very greatest admiration. He admired her for her truthfulness, for her cleanness of mind, and the clean-run-ness of her limbs, for her efficiency, for the fairness of her skin, for the gold of her hair, for her religion, for her sense of duty. It was a satisfaction to take her about with him.

But she had not for him a touch of magnetism. I suppose, really, he did not love her because she was never mournful; what really made him feel good in life was to comfort somebody who would be darkly and mysteriously mournful. That he had never had to do for Leonora. Perhaps, also, she was at first too obedient. I do not mean to say that she was submissive—that she deferred, in her judgments, to his. She did not. But she had been handed over to him, like some patient mediæval virgin; she had been taught all her life that the first duty of a woman is to obey. And there she was.

In her, at least, admiration for his qualities very soon became love of the deepest description. If his pulses never quickened she, so I have been told, became what is called an altered being when he approached her from the other side of a dancing floor. Her eyes followed him about full of trustfulness, of admiration, of gratitude, and of love. He was also, in a great sense, her pastor and guide—and he guided her into what, for a girl straight out of a convent, was almost heaven. I have not the least idea of what an English officer's wife's existence may be like. At any rate there were feasts, and chatterings, and nice men who gave her the right sort of admiration, and nice women who treated her as if she had been a baby. And her confessor approved of her life, and Edward let her give little treats to the girls of the convent she had left, and the Reverend Mother approved of him. There could not have been a happier girl for five or six years.

For it was only at the end of that time that clouds began, as the saying is, to arise. She was then about twenty-three, and her purposeful efficiency made her perhaps have a desire for mastery. She began to perceive that Edward was extravagant in his largesses. His parents died just about that time, and Edward, though they both decided that he should continue his soldiering, gave a great deal of attention to the management of Branshaw through a steward. Aldershot was not very far away, and they spent all his leaves there.

And, suddenly, she seemed to begin to perceive that his generosities were almost fantastic. He subscribed much too much to things connected with his mess, he pensioned off his father's servants, old or new, much too generously. They had a large income, but every now and then they would find themselves hard up. He began to talk of mortgaging a farm or two, though it never actually came to that.

She made tentative efforts at remonstrating with him. Her father, whom she saw now and then, said that Edward was much too generous to his tenants; the wives of his brother officers remonstrated with her in private; his large subscriptions made it difficult for their husbands to keep up with them. Ironically enough, the first real trouble between them came from his desire to build a Roman Catholic chapel at Branshaw. He wanted to do it to honour Leonora, and he proposed to do it very expensively. Leonora did not want it; she could perfectly well drive from Branshaw to the nearest Catholic Church as often as she liked. There were no Roman Catholic tenants and no Roman Catholic servants except her old nurse who could always drive with her. She had as many priests to stay with her as could be needed—and even the priests did not want a gorgeous chapel in that place where it would have merely seemed an invidious instance of ostentation. They were perfectly ready to celebrate mass for Leonora and her nurse, when they stayed at Branshaw, in a cleaned-up outhouse. But Edward was as obstinate as a hog about it.

He was truly grieved at his wife's want of sentiment—at her refusal to receive that amount of public homage from him. She appeared to him to be wanting in imagination—to be cold and hard. I don't exactly know what part her priests played in the tragedy that it all became; I daresay they behaved quite creditably but mistakenly. But then, who would not have been mistaken with Edward? I believe he was even hurt that Leonora's confessor did not make strenuous efforts to convert him. There was a period when he was quite ready to become an emotional Catholic.

I don't know why they did not take him on the hop; but they have queer sorts of wisdoms, those people, and queer sorts of tact. Perhaps they thought that Edward's too early conversion would frighten off other Protestant desirables from marrying Catholic girls. Perhaps they saw deeper into Edward than he saw himself and thought that he would make a not very creditable convert. At any rate they—and Leonora—left him very much alone. It mortified him very considerably. He has told me that if Leonora had then taken his aspirations seriously everything would have been different. But I daresay that was nor ense.

At any rate it was over the question of the chapel that they had their first and really disastrous quarrel. Edward at that time was not well; he supposed himself to be overworked with his regimental affairs—he was managing the mess at the time. And Leonora was not well—she was beginning to fear that their union might be sterile. And then her father came over from Glasmoyle to stay with them.

Those were troublesome times in Ireland, I understand. At any rate Colonel Powys had tenants on the brain—his own tenants having shot at him with shot-guns. And, in conversation with Edward's landsteward, he got it into his head that Edward managed his estates with a mad generosity towards his tenants. I understand also that those years—the nineties—were very bad for farming. Wheat was fetching only a few shillings the hundred; the price of meat was so low that cattle hardly paid for raising; whole English counties were ruined. And Edward allowed his tenants very high rebates.

To do both justice Leonora has since acknowledged that she was in the wrong at that time and that Edward was following out a more far-seeing policy in nursing his really very good tenants over a bad period. It was not as if the whole of his money came from the land; a good deal of it was in rails. But old Colonel Powys had that bee in his bonnet and, if he never directly approached Edward himself on the subject, he preached unceasingly, whenever he had the opportunity, to Leonora. His pet idea was that Edward ought to sack all his own tenants and import a set of farmers from Scotland. That was what they were doing in Essex. He was of opinion that Edward was riding hot-foot to ruin.

That worried Leonora very much—it worried her dreadfully; she lay awake nights; she had an anxious line round her mouth. And that, again, worried Edward. I do not mean to say that Leonora actually spoke to Edward about his tenants—but he got to know that some one, probably her father, had been talking to her about the matter. He got to know it because it was the habit of his steward to look in on them every morning about breakfast time to report any little happenings. And there was a farmer called Mumford who had only paid half his rent for the last three years. One morning the land-steward reported that Mumford would be unable to pay his rent at all that year. Edward reflected for a moment and then he said something like:

"O well, he's an old fellow and his family have been our tenants for over two hundred years. Let him off altogether."

And then Leonora—you must remember that she had reason for being very nervous and unhappy at that time—let out a sound that was very like a groan. It startled Edward, who more than suspected what was passing in her mind—it startled him into a state of anger. He said sharply:

"You wouldn't have me turn out people who've been earning money for us for centuries—people to whom we have responsibilities—and let in a pack of Scotch farmers?"

He looked at her, Leonora said, with what was practically a glance of hatred and then, precipitately, he left the breakfast-table. Leonora knew that it probably made it all the worse that he had been betrayed into a manifestation of anger before a third party. It was the first and last time that he ever was betrayed into such a manifestation of anger. The land-steward, a moderate and well-balanced man whose family also had been with the Ashburnhams for over a century, took it upon himself to explain that he considered Edward was pursuing a perfectly proper course with his tenants. He erred perhaps a little on the side of generosity, but hard times were hard times, and everyone had to feel the pinch, landlord as well as tenants. The great thing was not to let the land get into a poor state of cultivation. Scotch farmers just skinned your fields and let them go down and down. But Edward had a very good set of tenants who did their best for him and for themselves. These arguments at that time carried very little conviction to Leonora. She was nevertheless much concerned by Edward's outburst of anger.

The fact is that Leonora had been practising economies in her department. Two of the under-house-maids had gone and she had not replaced them; she had spent much less that year upon dress. The fare she had provided at the dinners they gave had been much less bountiful and not nearly so costly as had been the case in preceding years, and Edward began to perceive a hardness and determination in his wife's character. He seemed to see a net closing round him —a net in which they would be forced to live like one of the comparatively poor county families of the neighbourhood. And, in the mysterious way in which two people, living together, get to know each other's thoughts without a word spoken, he had known, even

before his outbreak, that Leonora was worrying about
his managing of the estates. This appeared to him to
be intolerable. He had, too, a great feeling of self-
contempt because he had been betrayed into speaking
harshly to Leonora before that land-steward. He imagined that his nerve must be deserting him, and there
can have been few men more miserable than Edward
was at that period.

You see, he was really a very simple soul—very
simple. He imagined that no man can satisfactorily
accomplish his life's work without loyal and whole-
hearted coöperation of the woman he lives with. And
he was beginning to perceive dimly that, whereas his
own traditions were entirely collective, his wife was a
sheer individualist. His own theory—the feudal theory of an over-lord doing his best by his dependents,
the dependents meanwhile doing their best for the
over-lord—this theory was entirely foreign to Leonora's nature. She came of a family of small Irish
landlords—that hostile garrison in a plundered country. And she was thinking unceasingly of the children she wished to have.

I don't know why they never had any children—
not that I really believe that children would have made
any difference. The dissimilarity of Edward and Leonora was too profound. It will give you some idea of
the extraordinary naïveté of Edward Ashburnham
that, at the time of his marriage and for perhaps a
couple of years after, he did not really know how children are produced. Neither did Leonora. I don't
mean to say that this state of things continued, but

there it was. I daresay it had a good deal of influence on their mentalities. At any rate they never had a child. It was the Will of God.

It certainly presented itself to Leonora as being the Will of God—as being a mysterious and awful chastisement of the Almighty. For she had discovered shortly before this period that her parents had not exacted from Edward's family the promise that any children she should bear should be brought up as Catholics. She herself had never talked of the matter with either her father, her mother, or her husband. When at last her father had let drop some words leading her to believe that that was the fact she tried desperately to extort the promise from Edward. She encountered an unexpected obstinacy. Edward was perfectly willing that the girls should be Catholic; the boys must be Anglican. I don't understand the bearings of these things in English society. Indeed, Englishmen seem to me to be a little mad in matters of politics or of religion. In Edward it was particularly queer because he himself was perfectly ready to become a Romanist.* He seemed, however, to contemplate going over to Rome himself and yet letting his boys be educated in the religion of their immediate ancestors. This may appear illogical, but I daresay it is not so illogical as it looks. Edward, that is to say, regarded himself as having his own body and soul at his own disposal. But his loyalty to the traditions of his family would not permit him to bind any future inheritors of his name or beneficiaries by the death of his ancestors. About the girls it did not so much matter. They would know other homes and other circumstances. Besides, it was the usual thing. But the boys must be given the opportunity of choosing—and they must have first of all the Anglican teaching. He was perfectly unshakable about this.

Leonora was in an agony during all this time. You will have to remember she seriously believed that children who might be born to her went in danger, if not absolutely of damnation at any rate of receiving false doctrine. It was an agony more terrible than she could describe. She didn't indeed attempt to describe it, but I could tell from her voice when she said, almost negligently, "I used to lie awake whole nights. It was no good my spiritual advisers trying to console me." I knew from her voice how terrible and how long those nights must have seemed and of how little avail were the consolations of her spiritual advisers. Her spiritual advisers seemed to have taken the matter a little more calmly. They certainly told her that she must not consider herself in any way to have sinned. Nay, they seem even to have exhorted, to have threatened her, with a view to getting her out of what they considered to be a morbid frame of mind. She would just have to make the best of things, to influence the children when they came, not by propaganda, but by personality. And they warned her that she would be committing a sin if she continued to think that she had sinned. Nevertheless, she continued to think that she had sinned.

Leonora could not but be aware that the man whom she loved passionately and whom, nevertheless, she was beginning to try to rule with a rod of iron—that this man was becoming more and more estranged from her. He seemed to regard her as being not only physically and mentally cold, but even as being actually wicked and mean. There were times when he would almost shudder if she spoke to him. And she could not understand how he could consider her wicked or mean. It only seemed to her a sort of madness in him that he should try to take upon his own shoulders the burden of his troop, of his regiment, of his estate and of half of his county. She could not see that in trying to curb what she regarded as megalomania she was doing anything wicked. She was just trying to keep things together for the sake of the children who did not come. And, little by little, the whole of their intercourse became simply one of agonised discussion as to whether Edward should subscribe to this or that institution or should try to reclaim this or that drunkard. She simp'y could not see it.

Into this really terrible position of strain, from which there appeared to be no issue, the Kilsyte case came almost as a relief. It is part of the peculiar irony of things that Edward would certainly never have kissed that nurse-maid if he had not been trying to please Leonora. Nurse-maids do not travel first-class and, that day, Edward travelled in a third-class carriage in order to prove to Leonora that he was capable of economies. I have said that the Kilsyte case came almost as a relief to the strained situation that then existed between them. It gave Leonora an opportunity of backing him up in a whole-hearted and absolutely loyal manner. It gave her the opportunity of behaving to him as he considered a wife should behave to her husband.

You see, Edward found himself in a railway carriage with a quite pretty girl of about nineteen. And the quite pretty girl of about nineteen, with dark hair and red cheeks and blue eyes was quietly weeping. Edward had been sitting in his corner thinking about nothing at all. He had chanced to look at the nurse-maid; two large, pretty tears came out of her eyes and dropped into her lap. He immediately felt that he had got to do something to comfort her. That was his job in life. He was desperately unhappy himself and it seemed to him the most natural thing in the world that they should pool their sorrows. He was quite democratic; the idea of the difference in their station never seems to have occurred to him. He began to talk to her. He discovered that her young man had been seen walking out with Annie of Number 54. He moved over to her side of the carriage. He told her that the report probably wasn't true; that, after all, a young man might take a walk with Annie from Number 54 without its denoting anything very serious. And he assured me that he felt at least quite half-fatherly when he put his arm around her waist and kissed her. The girl, however, had not forgotten the difference of her station.

All her life, by her mother, by other girls, by schoolteachers, by the whole tradition of her class she had been warned against gentlemen. She was being kissed by a gentleman. She screamed, tore herself away; sprang up and pulled a communication cord.

Edward came fairly well out of the affair in the public estimation; but it did him, mentally, a good deal of harm.

IV

I T is very difficult to give an all-round impression
of any man. I wonder how far I have succeeded
with Edward Ashburnham. I dare say I haven't
succeeded at all. It is even very difficult to see how
such things matter. Was it the important point about
poor Edward that he was very well built, carried himself well, was moderate at the table and led a regular
life—that he had, in fact, all the virtues that are usually accounted English? Or have I in the least succeeded in conveying that he was all those things and
had all those virtues? He certainly was them and
had them up to the last months of his life. They
were the things that one would set upon his tombstone. They will, indeed, be set upon his tombstone
by his widow.

And have I, I wonder, given the due impression of
how his life was portioned and his time laid out?
Because, until the very last, the amount of time taken
up by his various passions was relatively small. I
have been forced to write very much about his passions, but you have to consider—I should like to be
able to make you consider—that he rose every morning
at seven, took a cold bath, breakfasted at eight, was
occupied with his regiment from nine until one;
played polo or cricket with the men when it was the
season for cricket, till tea-time. Afterwards he would

occupy himself with the letters from his land-steward
or with the affairs of his mess, till dinner time. He
would dine and pass the evening playing cards, or
playing billiards with Leonora or at social functions
of one kind or another. And the greater part of his
life was taken up by that—by far the greater part
of his life. His love-affairs, until the very end, were
sandwiched in at odd moments or took place during
the social evenings, the dances and dinners. But I
guess I have made it hard for you, O silent listener,
to get that impression. Anyhow, I hope I have not
given you the idea that Edward Ashburnham was a
pathological case. He wasn't. He was just a normal
man and very much of a sentimentalist. I dare say
the quality of his youth, the nature of his mother's
influence, his ignorances, the crammings that he received at the hands of army coaches—I dare say that
all these excellent influences upon his adolescence were
very bad for him. But we all have to put up with
that sort of thing and no doubt it is very bad for all
of us. Nevertheless, the outline of Edward's life
was an outline perfectly normal of the life of a hard-
working, sentimental and efficient professional man.

That question of first impressions has always bothered me a good deal—but quite academically. I mean
that, from time to time I have wondered whether it
were or were not best to trust to one's first impressions in dealing with people. But I never had anybody to deal with except waiters and chambermaids
and the Ashburnhams, with whom I didn't know that
I was having any dealings. And, as far as waiters

and chambermaids were concerned I have generally found that my first impressions were correct enough. If my first idea of a man was that he was civil, obliging, and attentive, he generally seemed to go on being all those things. Once, however, at our Paris flat we had a maid who appeared to be charming and transparently honest. She stole, nevertheless, one of Florence's diamond rings. She did it, however, to save her young man from going to prison. So here, as somebody says somewhere, was a special case.

And, even in my short incursion into American business life—an incursion that lasted during part of August and nearly the whole of September—I found that to rely upon first impressions was the best thing I could do. I found myself automatically docketing and labelling each man as he was introduced to me, by the run of his features and by the first words that he spoke. I can't, however, be regarded as really doing business during the time that I spent in the United States. I was just winding things up. If it hadn't been for my idea of marrying the girl I might possibly have looked for something to do in my own country. For my experiences there were vivid and amusing. It was exactly as if I had come out of a museum into a riotous fancy-dress ball. During my life with Florence I had almost come to forget that there were such things as fashions or occupations or the greed of gain. I had, in fact, forgotten that there was such a thing as a dollar and that a dollar can be extremely desirable if you don't happen to possess one. And I had forgotten too that there was such

a thing as gossip that mattered. In that particular,
Philadelphia was the most amazing place I have ever
been in in my life. I was not in that city for more
than a week or ten days and I didn't there transact
anything much in the way of business, nevertheless
the number of times that I was warned by everybody
against everybody else was simply amazing. A man
I didn't know would come up behind my lounge chair
in the hotel, and, whispering cautiously beside my
ear, would warn me against some other man that I
equally didn't know but who would be standing by
the bar. I don't know what they thought I was there
to do—perhaps to buy out the city's debt or get a
controlling hold of some railway interest. Or, perhaps, they imagined that I wanted to buy a news-
paper, for they were either politicians or reporters,
which, of course, comes to the same thing. As
a matter of fact, my property in Philadelphia was
mostly real estate in the old-fashioned part of the
city and all I wanted to do there was just to satisfy
myself that the houses were in good repair and the
doors kept properly painted. I wanted also to see
my relations, of whom I had a few. These were
mostly professional people and they were mostly
rather hard up because of the big bank failure in
1907*or thereabouts. Still, they were very nice. They
would have been nicer still if they hadn't, all of
them, had what appeared to me to be the mania that
what they called influences were working against
them. At any rate, the impression of that city was
one of old-fashioned rooms, rather English than

American in type in which handsome but care-worn ladies, cousins of my own, talked principally about mysterious movements that were going on against them. I never got to know what it was all about; perhaps they thought I knew or perhaps there weren't any movements at all. It was all very secret and subtle and subterranean. But there was a nice young fellow called Carter who was a sort of second-nephew of mine, twice removed. He was handsome and dark and gentle and tall and modest. I understand also that he was a good cricketer. He was employed by the real-estate agents who collected my rents. It was he, therefore, who took me over my own property and I saw a good deal of him and of a nice girl called Mary, to whom he was engaged. At that time I did, what I certainly shouldn't do now,—I made some careful inquiries as to his character. I discovered from his employers that he was just all that he appeared, honest, industrious, high-spirited, friendly and ready to do anyone a good turn. His relatives, however, as they were mine too—seemed to have something darkly mysterious against him. I imagined that he must have been mixed up in some case of graft or that he had at least betrayed several innocent and trusting maidens. I pushed, however, that particular mystery home and discovered it was only that he was a Democrat. My own people were mostly Republicans. It seemed to make it worse and more darkly mysterious to them that young Carter was what they called a sort of a Vermont Democrat which was the whole ticket and no mistake. But I don't know what it means. Anyhow, I suppose that my money will go to him when I die—I like the recollection of his friendly image and of the nice girl he was engaged to. May Fate deal very kindly with them.

I have said just now that, in my present frame of mind, nothing would ever make me make inquiries as to the character of any man that I liked at first sight. (The little digression as to my Philadelphia experiences was really meant to lead around to this.) For who in this world can give anyone a character? Who in this world knows anything of any other heart—or of his own? I don't mean to say that one cannot form an average estimate of the way a person will behave. But one cannot be certain of the way any man will behave in every case—and until one can do that a "character" is of no use to anyone. That, for instance, was the way with Florence's maid in Paris. We used to trust that girl with blank cheques for the payment of the tradesmen. For quite a time she was so trusted by us. Then, suddenly, she stole a ring. We should not have believed her capable of it; she would not have believed herself capable of it. It was nothing in her character. So, perhaps, it was with Edward Ashburnham.

Or, perhaps, it wasn't. No, I rather think it wasn't. It is difficult to figure out. I have said that the Kilsyte case eased the immediate tension for him and Leonora. It let him see that she was capable of loyalty to him; it gave her her chance to show that she believed in him. She accepted without question his statement that, in kissing the girl he wasn't trying to do more than administer fatherly comfort to a weeping child. And, indeed, his own world—including the magistrates—took that view of the case. Whatever people say, one's world can be perfectly charitable at times . . . But, again, as I have said, it did Edward a great deal of harm.

That, at least, was his view of it. He assured me that, before that case came on and was wrangled about by counsel with all the sorts of dirty-mindedness that counsel in that sort of case can impute, he had not had the least idea that he was capable of being unfaithful to Leonora. But, in the midst of that tumult—he says that it came suddenly into his head whilst he was in the witness box—in the midst of those august ceremonies of the law there came suddenly into his mind the recollection of the softness of the girl's body as he had pressed her to him. And, from that moment, that girl appeared desirable to him—and Leonora completely unattractive.

He began to indulge in day-dreams in which he approached the nurse-maid more tactfully and carried the matter much further. Occasionally he thought of other women in terms of wary courtship—or, perhaps, it would be more exact to say that he thought of them in terms of tactful comforting, ending in absorption. That was his own view of the case. He saw himself as the victim of the law. I don't mean to say that he saw himself as a kind of Dreyfus.* The law, practically, was quite kind to him. It stated that in its view Captain Ashburnham had been misled by an ill-placed desire to comfort a member of the opposite sex and it fined him five shillings for his want of tact, or of knowledge of the world. But Edward maintained that it had put ideas into his head.

I don't believe it, though he certainly did. He was twenty-seven then, and his wife was out of sympathy with him—some crash was inevitable. There was between them a momentary rapprochement; but it could not last. It made it, probably, all the worse that, in that particular matter Leonora had come so very well up to the scratch. For, whilst Edward respected her more and was grateful to her, it made her seem by so much the more cold in other matters that were near his heart—his responsibilities, his career, his tradition. It brought his despair of her up to a point of exasperation—and it rivetted on him the idea that he might find some other woman who would give him the moral support that he needed. He wanted to be looked upon as a sort of Lohengrin.

At that time, he says, he went about deliberately looking for some woman who could help him. He found several—for there were quite a number of ladies in his set who were capable of agreeing with this handsome and fine fellow that the duties of a feudal gentleman were feudal. He would have liked to pass his days talking to one or other of these ladies. But there was always an obstacle—if the lady were married there would be a husband who claimed the greater part of her time and attention. If, on the other hand, it were an unmarried girl he could not see very much of her for fear of compromising her. At that date, you understand, he had

not the least idea of seducing anyone of these ladies.
He wanted only moral support at the hands of some
female, because he found men difficult to talk to
about ideals. Indeed, I do not believe that he had,
at any time, any idea of making any one his mistress.
That sounds queer; but I believe it is quite true as
a statement of character.

It was, I believe, one of Leonora's priests—a man
of the world—who suggested that she should take
him to Monte Carlo. He had the idea that what Edward needed, in order to fit him for the society of
Leonora was a touch of irresponsibility. For Edward,
at that date, had much the aspect of a prig. I mean
that, if he played polo and was an excellent dancer
he did the one for the sake of keeping himself fit
and the other because it was a social duty to show
himself at dances, and, when there, to dance well. He
did nothing for fun except what he considered to
be his work in life. As the priest saw it, this must
for ever estrange him from Leonora—not because
Leonora set much store by the joy of life, but because
she was out of sympathy with Edward's work. On
the other hand, Leonora did like to have a good time,
now and then, and, as the priest saw it, if Edward
could be got to like having a good time now and then
too, there would be a bond of sympathy between
them. It was a good idea, but it worked out wrongly.

It worked out, in fact, in the mistress of the Grand
Duke. In anyone less sentimental than Edward that
would not have mattered. With Edward it was fatal.
For, such was his honourable nature, that for him,

to enjoy a woman's favours, made him feel that she had a bond on him for life. That was the way it worked out in practice. Psychologically it meant that he could not have a mistress without falling violently in love with her. He was a serious person— and in this particular case it was very expensive. The mistress of the Grand Duke—a Spanish dancer of passionate appearance—singled out Edward for her glances at a ball that was held in their common hotel. Edward was tall, handsome, blond and very wealthy as she understood—and Leonora went up to bed early. She did not care for public dances, but she was relieved to see that Edward appeared to be having a good time with several amiable girls. And that was the end of Edward—for the Spanish dancer of passionate appearance wanted one night of him for his beaux yeux. He took her into the dark gardens and, remembering suddenly the girl of the Kilsyte case, he kissed her. He kissed her passionately, violently, with a sudden explosion of the passion that had been bridled all his life—for Leonora was cold, or, at any rate, well behaved. La Dolciquita liked this reversion, and he passed the night in her bed.

When the palpitating creature was at last asleep in his arms he discovered that he was madly, was passionately, was overwhelmingly in love with her. It was a passion that had arisen like fire in dry corn. He could think of nothing else; he could live for nothing else. But La Dolciquita was a reasonable creature without an ounce of passion in her. She wanted a certain satisfaction of her appetites and Edward had appealed to her the night before. Now that was done with and, quite coldly, she said that she wanted money if he was to have any more of her. It was a perfectly reasonable commercial transaction. She did not care two buttons for Edward or for any man and he was asking her to risk a very good situation with a Grand Duke. If Edward could put up sufficient money to serve as a kind of insurance against accident she was ready to like Edward for a time that would be covered, as it were, by the policy. She was getting fifty thousand dollars a year from her Grand Duke; Edward would have to pay a premium of two years' hire for a month of her society. There would not be much risk of the Grand Duke's finding it out and it was not certain that he would give her the keys of the street if he did find out. But there was the risk—a twenty per cent. risk, as she figured it out. She talked to Edward as if she had been a solicitor with an estate to sell—perfectly quietly and perfectly coldly without any inflections in her voice. She did not want to be unkind to him; but she could see no reason for being kind to him. She was a virtuous business woman with a mother and two sisters and her own old age to be provided comfortably for. She did not expect more than a five years' further run. She was twenty-four and, as she said: "We Spanish women are horrors at thirty." Edward swore that he would provide for her for life if she would come to him and leave off talking so horribly; but she only shrugged one shoulder slowly and contemptuously. He tried to convince this woman, who as he saw it, had surrendered to him her virtue, that he regarded it as in any case his duty to provide for her, and to cherish her and even to love her—for life. In return for her sacrifice he would do that. In return, again, for his honourable love she would listen for ever to the accounts of his estate. That was how he figured it out.

She shrugged the same shoulder with the same gesture and held out her left hand with the elbow at her side:

"Enfin, mon ami," she said, "put in this hand the price of that tiara at Forli's or . . ." And she turned her back on him.

Edward went mad; his world stood on its head; the palms in front of the blue sea danced grotesque dances. You see, he believed in the virtue, tenderness and moral support of women. He wanted more than anything to argue with La Dolciquita; to retire with her to an island and point out to her the damnation of her point of view and how salvation can only be found in true love and the feudal system. She had once been his mistress, he reflected, and, by all the moral laws she ought to have gone on being his mistress or at the very least his sympathetic confidante. But her rooms were closed to him; she did not appear in the hotel. Nothing: blank silence. To break that down he had to have twenty thousand pounds. You have heard what happened.

He spent a week of madness; he hungered; his eyes sank in; he shuddered at Leonora's touch. I daresay that nine-tenths of what he took to be his pas-

sion for La Dolciquita was really discomfort at the
thought that he had been unfaithful to Leonora. He
felt uncommonly bad, that is to say—oh, unbearably
bad, and he took it all to be love. Poor devil, he
was incredibly naif. He drank like a fish after Leonora was in bed and he spread himself over the tables, and this went on for about a fortnight. Heaven
knows what would have happened; he would have
thrown away every penny that he possessed.

On the night after he had lost about forty thousand
pounds and whilst the whole hotel was whispering
about it, La Dolciquita walked composedly into his
bedroom. He was too drunk to recognise her, and
she sat in his armchair, knitting and holding smelling
salts to her nose—for he was pretty far gone with
alcoholic poisoning—and, as soon as he was able to
understand her, she said:

"Look here, mon ami, do not go to the tables again.
Take a good sleep now and come and see me this
afternoon."

He slept till the lunch hour. By that time Leonora
had heard the news. A Mrs. Colonel Whelen had
told her. Mrs. Colonel Whelen seems to have been
the only sensible person who was ever connected with
the Ashburnhams. She had argued it out that there
must be a woman of the harpy variety connected
with Edward's incredible behaviour and mien; and
she advised Leonora to go straight off to Town*—
which might have the effect of bringing Edward to
his senses—and to consult her solicitor and her spiritual adviser. She had better go that very morning; it

was no good arguing with a man in Edward's condition.

Edward, indeed, did not know that she had gone. As soon as he woke he went straight to La Dolciquita's room and she stood him his lunch in her own apartments. He fell on her neck and wept, and she put up with it for a time. She was quite a good-natured woman. And, when she had calmed him down with Eau de Melisse,* she said:

"Look here, my friend, how much money have you left? Five thousand dollars? Ten?" For the rumour went that Edward had lost two kings' ransoms a night for fourteen nights and she imagined that he must be near the end of his resources.

The Eau de Melisse had calmed Edward to such an extent that, for the moment, he really had a head on his shoulders. He did nothing more than grunt:

"And then?"

"Why," she answered, "I may just as well have the ten thousand dollars as the tables. I will go with you to Antibes for a week for that sum."

Edward grunted: "Five." She tried to get seven thousand five hundred; but he stuck to his five thousand and the hotel expenses at Antibes. The sedative carried him just as far as that and then he collapsed again. He had to leave for Antibes at three; he could not do without it. He left a note for Leonora saying that he had gone off for a week with the Clinton Morleys, yachting.

He did not enjoy himself very much at Antibes. La Dolciquita could talk of nothing with any enthusiasm except money, and she tired him unceasingly, during every waking hour for presents of the most expensive description. And, at the end of a week, she just quietly kicked him out. He hung about in Antibes for three days. He was cured of the idea that he had any duties towards La Dolciquita—feudal or otherwise. But his sentimentalism required of him an attitude of Byronic gloom—as if his court had gone into half-mourning. Then his appetite suddenly returned, and he remembered Leonora. He found at his hotel at Monte Carlo a telegram from Leonora, despatched from London, saying: "Please return as soon as convenient." He could not understand why Leonora should have abandoned him so precipitately when she only thought that he had gone yachting with the Clinton Morleys. Then he discovered that she had left the hotel before he had written the note. He had a pretty rocky journey back to town; he was frightened out of his life—and Leonora had never seemed so desirable to him.

I CALL this the Saddest Story, rather than "The Ashburnham Tragedy," just because it is so sad, just because there was no current to draw things along to a swift and inevitable end. There is about it none of the elevation that accompanies tragedy; there is about it no nemesis, no destiny. Here were two noble people—for I am convinced that both Edward and Leonora had noble natures—here then, were two noble natures, drifting down life, like fire-ships *afloat on a lagoon and causing miseries, heart-aches, agony of the mind and death. And they themselves steadily deteriorated? And why? For what purpose? To point what lesson? It is all a darkness.

There is not even any villain in the story—for even Major Basil, the husband of the lady who next, and really, comforted the unfortunate Edward—even Major Basil was not a villain in this piece. He was a slack, loose, shiftless sort of fellow—but he did not do anything to Edward. Whilst they were in the same station in Burma he borrowed a good deal of money—though, really, since Major Basil had no particular vices, it was difficult to know why he wanted it. He collected—different types of horses' bits from the earliest times to the present day—but, since he did not prosecute even this occupation with any vigour, he cannot have needed much money for the acquirement, say, of the bit of Genghis Khan's charger—if Genghis Khan had a charger. And when I say that he borrowed a good deal of money from Edward I do not mean to say that he had more than a thousand pounds from him during the five years that the connection lasted. Edward, of course, did not have a great deal of money; Leonora was seeing to that. Still he may have had five hundred pounds a year English, for his menus plaisirs*—for his regimental subscriptions and for keeping his men smart. Leonora hated that; she would have preferred to buy dresses for herself or to have devoted the money to paying off a mortgage. Still, with her sense of justice, she saw that, since she was managing a property bringing in three thousand a year with a view to re-establishing it as a property of five thousand a year, and since the property really, if not legally, belonged to Edward, it was reasonable and just that Edward should get a slice of his own. Of course she had the devil of a job.

I don't know that I have got the financial details exactly right. I am a pretty good head at figures, but my mind, still, sometimes mixes up pounds with dollars and I get a figure wrong. Anyhow, the proposition was something like this: Properly worked and without rebates to the tenants and keeping up schools and things, the Branshaw estate should have brought in about five thousand a year when Edward had it. It brought in actually about four. (I am talking in pounds, not dollars.) Edward's excesses with the

Spanish Lady had reduced its value to about three
—as the maximum figure, without reductions. Leonora wanted to get it back to five.

She was, of course, very young to be faced with
such a proposition—twenty-four is not a very advanced age. So she did things with a youthful vigour that she would, very likely, have made more mer-
ciful, if she had known more about life. She got
Edward remarkably on the hop. He had to face her
in a London hotel, when he crept back from Monte
Carlo with his poor tail between his poor legs. As
far as I can make out, she cut short his first mum-
blings and his first attempts at affectionate speech with
words something like:

"We're on the verge of ruin. Do you intend to
let me pull things together? If not I shall retire to
Hendon on my jointure."* (Hendon represented a convent to which she occasionally went for what is called
a "retreat" in Catholic circles.)

And poor dear Edward knew nothing—absolutely
nothing. He did not know how much money he had,
as he put it, "blued"* at the tables. It might have
been a quarter of a million for all he remembered.
He did not know whether she knew about La Dolciquita or whether she imagined that he had gone off
yachting or had stayed at Monte Carlo. He was just
dumb and he just wanted to get into a hole and not
have to talk. Leonora did not make him talk and she
said nothing herself.

I do not know much about English legal proce-
dure—I cannot, I mean, give technical details of how

they tied him up. But I know that, two days later, without her having said more than I have reported to you, Leonora and her attorney had become the trustees, as I believe it is called, of all Edward's property and there was an end of Edward as the good landlord and father of his people. He went out.

Leonora then had three thousand a year at her disposal. She occupied Edward with getting himself transferred to a part of his regiment that was in Burma—if that is the right way to put it. She herself had an interview, lasting a week or so—with Edward's land-steward. She made him understand that the estate would have to yield up to its last penny. Before they left for India she had let Branshaw for seven years at a thousand a year. She sold two Vandykes and a little silver for eleven thousand pounds and she raised, on mortgage, twenty-nine thousand. That went to Edward's money-lending friends in Monte Carlo. So she had to get the twenty-nine thousand back, for she did not regard the Vandykes and the silver as things she would have to replace. They were just frills to the Ashburnham vanity. Edward cried for two days over the disappearance of his ancestors and then she wished she had not done it; but it did not teach her anything and it lessened such esteem as she had for him. She did not also understand that to let Branshaw affected him with a feeling of physical soiling—that it was almost as bad for him as if a woman belonging to him had become a prostitute. That was how it did affect him; but I daresay she felt just as bad about the Spanish dancer.

So she went at it. They were eight years in India, and during the whole of that time she insisted that they must be self-supporting—they had to live on his Captain's pay, plus the extra allowance for being at the front. She gave him the five hundred a year for Ashburnham frills as she called it to herself—and she considered she was doing him very well.

Indeed, in a way, she did him very well—but it was not his way. She was always buying him expensive things which, as it were, she took off her own back. I have, for instance, spoken of Edward's leather cases. Well, they were not Edward's at all; they were Leonora's manifestations. He liked to be clean, but he preferred, as it were, to be threadbare. She never understood that and all that pigskin was her idea of a reward to him for putting her up to a little speculation by which she made eleven hundred pounds. She did, herself, the threadbare business. When they went up to a place called Simla,* where, as I understand, it is cool in the summer and very social—when they went up to Simla for their healths it was she who had him prancing around, as we should say in the United States, on a thousand dollar horse with the gladdest of glad rags all over him. She herself used to go into "retreat." I believe that was very good for her health and it was also very inexpensive.

It was probably also very good for Edward's health, because he pranced about mostly with Mrs. Basil, who was a nice woman and very, very kind to him. I suppose she was his mistress, but I never heard it from

Edward, of course. I seem to gather that they carried it on in a high romantic fashion, very proper to both of them—or, at any rate, for Edward; she seems to have been a tender and gentle soul who did what he wanted. I do not mean to say that she was without character; that was her job, to do what Edward wanted. So I figured it out that, for those five years, Edward wanted long passages of deep affection kept up in long, long talks and that every now and then they "fell," which would give Edward an opportunity for remorse and an excuse to lend the Major another fifty. I don't think that Mrs. Basil considered it to be "falling"; she just pitied him and loved him.

You see, Leonora and Edward had to talk about something during all those years. You cannot be absolutely dumb when you live with a person unless you are an inhabitant of the North of England or the State of Maine. So Leonora imagined the cheerful device of letting him see the accounts of his estate and discussing them with him. He did not discuss them much; he was trying to behave prettily. But it was old Mr. Mumford—the farmer who did not pay his rent—that threw Edward into Mrs. Basil's arms. Mrs. Basil came upon Edward in the dusk, in the Burmese garden, with all sorts of flowers and things.. And he was cutting up that crop—with his sword, not a walking stick. He was also carrying on and cursing in a way you would not believe.

She ascertained that an old gentleman called Mumford had been ejected from his farm and had been

given a little cottage rent-free, where he lived on ten
shillings a week from a farmers' benevolent society,
supplemented by seven that was being allowed him
by the Ashburnham trustees. Edward had just discovered that fact from the estate accounts. Leonora
had left them in his dressing room and he had begun
to read them before taking off his marching kit. That
was how he came to have a sword. Leonora considered that she had been unusually generous to old
Mr. Mumford in allowing him to inhabit a cottage,
rent-free, and in giving him seven shillings a week.
Anyhow, Mrs. Basil had never seen a man in such a
state as Edward was. She had been passionately in
love with him for quite a time, and he had been longing for her sympathy and admiration with a passion
as deep. That was how they came to speak about
it, in the Burmese garden, under the pale sky, with
sheafs of severed vegetation, misty and odorous in
the night around their feet. I think they behaved
themselves with decorum for quite a time after that,
though Mrs. Basil spent so many hours over the accounts of the Ashburnham estate that she got the
name of every field by heart. Edward had a huge
map of his lands in his harness room and Major Basil
did not seem to mind. I believe that people do not
mind much in lonely stations.

It might have lasted for ever if the Major had not
been made what is called a brevet-colonel during the
shuffling of troops that went on just before the South
African War.* He was sent off somewhere else and,
of course, Mrs. Basil could not stay with Edward.

Edward ought, I suppose, to have gone to the Trans-vaal. It would have done him a great deal of good to get killed. But Leonora would not let him; she had heard awful stories of the extravagance of the hussar regiment in war-time—how they left hundred-bottle cases of champagne at five guineas a bottle, on the veldt* and so on. Besides, she preferred to see how Edward was spending his five hundred a year. I don't mean to say that Edward had any grievance in that. He was never a man of the deeds of heroism sort and it was just as good for him to be sniped at up in the hills on the North Western frontier, as to be shot at by an old gentleman in a top hat at the bottom of some spruit.* Those are more or less his words about it. I believe he quite distinguished himself over there. At any rate, he had his D. S. O. and was made a brevet-major.

Leonora, however, was not in the least keen on his soldiering. She hated also his deeds of heroism. One of their bitterest quarrels came after he had, for the second time, in the Red Sea, jumped overboard from the troop-ship and rescued a private soldier. She stood it the first time and even complimented him. But the Red Sea was awful, that trip, and the private soldiers seemed to develop a suicidal craze. It got on Leonora's nerves; she figured Edward, for the rest of that trip, jumping overboard every ten minutes. And the mere cry of "Man overboard" is a disagreeable, alarming and disturbing thing. The ship gets stopped and there are all sorts of shouts. And Edward would not promise not to do it again, though, fortunately they struck a streak of cooler weather when they were in the Persian Gulf. Leonora had got it into her head that Edward was trying to commit suicide, so I guess it was pretty awful for her when he would not give the promise. Leonora ought never to have been on that troop-ship; but she got there somehow, as an economy.

Major Basil discovered his wife's relation with Edward just before he was sent to his other station. I don't know whether that was a blackmailer's adroitness or just a trick of destiny. He may have known of it all the time or he may not. At any rate, he got hold of, just about then, some letters and things. It cost Edward three hundred pounds immediately. I do not know how it was arranged; I cannot imagine how even a blackmailer can make his demands. I suppose there is some sort of way of saving your face. I figure the Major as disclosing the letters to Edward with furious oaths, then accepting his explanations that the letters were perfectly innocent if the wrong construction were not put upon them. Then the Major would say: "I say, old chap, I'm deuced hard up. Couldn't you lend me three hundred or so?" I fancy that was how it was. And, year by year, after that there would come a letter from the Major, saying that he was deuced hard up and couldn't Edward lend him three hundred or so.

Edward was pretty hard hit when Mrs. Basil had to go away. He really had been very fond of her, and he remained faithful to her memory for quite a long time. And Mrs. Basil had loved him very much and continued to cherish a hope of reunion with him. Three days ago there came a quite proper, but very lamentable letter from her to Leonora, asking to be given particulars as to Edward's death. She had read the advertisement of it in an Indian paper. I think she must have been a very nice woman. . . .

And then the Ashburnhams were moved somewhere up towards a place or a district called Chitral. I am no good at geography of the Indian Empire. By that time they had settled down into a model couple and they never spoke in private to each other. Leonora had given up even showing the accounts of the Ashburnham estate to Edward. He thought that that was because she had piled up such a lot of money that she did not want him to know how she was getting on any more. But, as a matter of fact, after five or six years it had penetrated to her mind that it was painful to Edward to have to look on at the accounts of his estate and have no hand in the management of it. She was trying to do him a kindness. And, up in Chitral, poor dear little Maisie Maidan came along. . . .

That was the most unsettling to Edward of all his affairs. It made him suspect that he was inconstant. The affair with the Dolciquita he had sized up as a short attack of madness like hydrophobia. His relations with Mrs. Basil had not seemed to him to imply moral turpitude of a gross kind. The husband had been complaisant; they had really loved each other; his wife was very cruel to him and had long ceased to be a wife to him. He thought that Mrs. Basil had been his soul-mate, separated from him by an unkind fate—something sentimental of that sort.

But he discovered that, whilst he was still writing long weekly letters to Mrs. Basil, he was beginning to be furiously impatient if he missed seeing Maisie Maidan during the course of the day. He discovered himself watching the doorways with impatience; he discovered that he disliked her boy husband very much for hours at a time. He discovered that he was getting up at unearthly hours in order to have time, later in the morning, to go for a walk with Maisie Maidan. He discovered himself using little slang words that she used and attaching a sentimental value to those words. These, you understand, were discoveries that came so late that he could do nothing but drift. He was losing weight; his eyes were beginning to fall in; he had touches of bad fever. He was, as he described it, pipped.

And, one ghastly hot day, he suddenly heard himself say to Leonora:

"I say, couldn't we take little Mrs. Maidan with us to Europe and drop her at Nauheim."

He hadn't had the least idea of saying that to Leonora. He had merely been standing, looking at an illustrated paper, waiting for dinner. Dinner was twenty minutes late or the Ashburnhams would not have been alone together. No, he hadn't had the least idea of framing that speech. He had just been standing in a silent agony of fear, of longing, of heat, of fever. He was thinking that they were going back to Branshaw in a month and that Maisie Maidan was going to remain behind and die. And then, that had come out.

The punkah* swished in the darkened room; Leonora lay exhausted and motionless in her cane-lounge; neither of them stirred. They were both at that time very ill in indefinite ways.

And then Leonora said:

"Yes. I promised it to Charlie Maidan this afternoon. I have offered to pay her ex's* myself."

Edward just saved himself from saying: "Good God!" You see, he had not the least idea of what Leonora knew—about Maisie, about Mrs. Basil, or even about La Dolciquita. It was a pretty enigmatic situation for him. It struck him that Leonora must be intending to manage his loves as she managed his money affairs and it made her more hateful to him— and more worthy of respect.

Leonora, at any rate, had managed his money to some purpose. She had spoken to him, a week before, for the first time in several years—about money. She had made twenty-two thousand pounds out of the Branshaw land and seven by the letting of Branshaw furnished. By fortunate investments—in which Edward had helped her—she had made another six or seven thousand that might well become more. The mortgages were all paid off so that, except for the departure of the two Vandykes and the silver, they were as well off as they had been before the Dolciquita had acted the locust. It was Leonora's great achievement. She laid the figures before Edward, who maintained an unbroken silence.

"I propose," she said, "that you should resign from the army and that we should go back to Branshaw. We are both too ill to stay here any longer."

Edward said nothing at all.

"This," Leonora continued passionlessly, "is the great day of my life."

Edward said:

"You have managed the job amazingly. You are a wonderful woman." He was thinking that if they went back to Branshaw they would leave Maisie Maidan behind. That thought occupied him exclusively. They must, undoubtedly, return to Branshaw; there could be no doubt that Leonora was too ill to stay in that place. She said:

"You understand that the management of the whole of the expenditure of the income will be in your hands. There will be five thousand a year."

She thought that he cared very much about the expenditure of an income of five thousand a year and that the fact that she had done so much for him would rouse in him some affection for her. But he was thinking exclusively of Maisie Maidan—of Maisie, thousands of miles away from him. He was seeing the mountains between them—blue mountains and the sea and sunlit plains. He said:

"That is very generous of you." And she did not know whether that were praise or a sneer. That had been a week before. And all that week he had passed in an increasing agony at the thought that those mountains, that sea and those sunlit plains would be between him and Maisie Maidan. That thought shook him in the burning nights: the sweat poured from him and he trembled with cold, in the burning noons— at that thought. He had no minute's rest; his bowels turned round and round within him: his tongue was perpetually dry and it seemed to him that the breath between his teeth was like air from a pest-house.*

He gave no thought to Leonora at all; he had sent in his papers.* They were to leave in a month. It seemed to him to be his duty to leave that place and to go away, to support Leonora. He did his duty.

It was horrible, in their relationship at that time, that whatever she did caused him to hate her. He hated her when he found that she proposed to set him up as the Lord of Branshaw again—as a sort of dummy lord, in swaddling clothes. He imagined that she had done this in order to separate him from Maisie Maidan. Hatred hung in all the heavy nights and filled the shadowy corners of the room. So when he heard that she had offered to the Maidan boy to take his wife to Europe with him, automatically he hated her since he hated all that she did. It seemed to him, at that time, that she could never be other than cruel even if, by accident, an act of hers were kind. . . . Yes, it was a horrible situation.

But the cool breezes of the ocean seemed to clear up that hatred as if it had been a curtain. They seemed to give him back admiration for her, and respect. The agreeableness of having money lavishly at command, the fact that it had bought for him the companionship of Maisie Maidan—these things began to make him see that his wife might have been right in the starving and scraping upon which she had insisted. He was at ease; he was even radiantly happy when he carried cups of bouillon for Maisie Maidan along the deck. One night, when he was leaning, beside Leonora, over the ship's side he said suddenly:

"By Jove, you're the finest woman in the world. I wish we could be better friends."

She just turned away, without a word and went to her cabin. Still, she was very much better in health.

* * * * *

And, now, I suppose I must give you Leonora's side of the case. . . .

That is very difficult. For Leonora, if she preserved an unchanged front, changed very frequently her point of view. She had been drilled—in her tradition, in her upbringing—to keep her mouth shut. But there were times, she said, when she was so near yielding to the temptation of speaking that afterwards she shuddered to think of those times. You must postulate that what she desired above all things was to keep a shut mouth to the world, to Edward and to the women that he loved. If she spoke she would despise herself.

From the moment of his unfaithfulness with La Dolciquita she never acted the part of wife to Edward. It was not that she intended to keep herself from him as a principle, for ever. Her spiritual advisers, I believe, forbade that. But she stipulated that he must, in some way, perhaps symbolical, come back to her. She was not very clear as to what she meant; probably she did not know herself. Or perhaps she did.

There were moments when he seemed to be coming back to her; there were moments when she was within a hair of yielding to her physical passion for him. In just the same way, at moments, she almost yielded to the temptation to denounce Mrs. Basil to her husband or Maisie Maidan to hers. She desired then to cause the horrors and pains of public scandals. For, watching Edward more intently and with more straining of ears than that which a cat bestows upon a bird overhead, she was aware of the progress of his passion for each of these ladies. She was aware of it from the way in which his eyes returned to doors and gateways; she knew from his tranquillities when he had received satisfactions.

At times she imagined herself to see more than was warranted. She imagined that Edward was carrying on intrigues with other women—with two at once; with three. For whole periods she imagined him to be a monster of libertinage and she could not see that he could have anything against her. She left him his liberty; she was starving herself to build up his fortunes; she allowed herself none of the joys of femininity—no dresses, no jewels—hardly even any friendships, for fear they should cost money.

And yet, oddly, she could not but be aware that both Mrs. Basil and Maisie Maidan were nice women. The curious, discounting eye which one woman can turn on another did not prevent her seeing that Mrs. Basil was very good to Edward and Mrs. Maidan very good for him. That seemed to her to be a monstrous and incomprehensible working of Fate's. Incomprehensible! Why, she asked herself again and again, did none of the good deeds that she did for her husband ever come through to him, or appear to him as good deeds. By what trick of mania could not he let her be as good to him as Mrs. Basil was? Mrs. Basil was not so extraordinarily dissimilar to herself. She was, it was true, tall, dark, with a soft mournful voice and a great kindness of manner for every created thing, from punkah men to flowers on the trees. But she was not so well read as Leonora, at any rate in learned books. Leonora could not stand novels. But, even with all her differences Mrs. Basil did not appear to Leonora to differ so very much from herself. She was truthful, honest and, for the rest, just a woman. And Leonora had a vague sort of idea that, to a man, all women are the same after three weeks of close intercourse. She thought that the kindness should no longer appeal, the soft and mournful voice no longer thrill, the tall darkness no longer give a man the illusion that he was going into the depths of an unexplored wood. She could not understand how Edward could go on and on maundering* over Mrs. Basil. She could not see why he should continue to write her long letters after their separation. After that, indeed, she had a very bad time.

She had at that period what I will call the "monstrous" theory of Edward. She was always imagining him ogling at every woman that he came across. She did not, that year, go into "retreat" at Simla because she was afraid that he would corrupt her maid in her absence. She imagined him carrying on intrigues with native women or Eurasians. At dances she was in a fever of watchfulness. . . .

She persuaded herself that this was because she had a dread of scandals. Edward might get himself mixed up with a marriageable daughter of some man who would make a row or some husband who would matter. But, really, she acknowledged afterwards to herself, she was hoping that, Mrs. Basil being out of the way, the time might have come when Edward should return to her. All that period she passed in an agony of jealousy and fear—the fear that Edward might really become promiscuous in his habits.

So that, in an odd way, she was glad when Maisie Maidan came along—and she realised that she had not, before, been afraid of husbands and of scandals, since, then, she did her best to keep Maisie's husband unsuspicious. She wished to appear so trustful of Edward that Maidan could not possibly have any suspicions. It was an evil position for her. But Edward was very ill and she wanted to see him smile again. She thought that if he could smile again through her agency he might return, through gratitude and satisfied love—to her. At that time she thought that Edward was a person of light and fleeting passions. And she could understand Edward's passion for Maisie, since Maisie was one of those women to whom other women will allow magnetism.

She was very pretty; she was very young; in spite of her heart she was very gay and light on her feet.

And Leonora was really very fond of Maisie, who was fond enough of Leonora. Leonora, indeed, imagined that she could manage this affair all right. She had no thought of Maisie's being led into adultery; she imagined that if she could take Maisie and Edward to Nauheim, Edward would see enough of her to get tired of her pretty little chatterings, and of the pretty little motions of her hands and feet. And she thought she could trust Edward. For there was not any doubt of Maisie's passion for Edward. She raved about him to Leonora as Leonora had heard girls rave about drawing masters in schools. She was perpetually asking her boy husband why he could not dress, ride, shoot, play polo, or even recite sentimental poems, like their major. And young Maidan had the greatest admiration for Edward and he adored, was bewildered by and entirely trusted his wife. It appeared to him that Edward was devoted to Leonora. And Leonora imagined that when poor Maisie was cured of her heart and Edward had seen enough of her, he would return to her. She had the vague, passionate idea that, when Edward had exhausted a number of other types of women he must turn to her. Why should not her type have its turn in his heart? She imagined that, by now, she understood him better, that she understood better his vanities and that, by making him happier, she could arouse his love.

Florence knocked all that on the head. . . .

THE GOOD SOLDIER

PART IV

I

I HAVE, I am aware, told this story in a very
rambling way so that it may be difficult for
anyone to find their path through what may be
a sort of maze. I cannot help it. I have stuck to my
idea of being in a country cottage with a silent listener, hearing between the gusts of the wind and
amidst the noises of the distant sea, the story as it
comes. And, when one discusses an affair—a long,
sad affair—one goes back, one goes forward. One remembers points that one has forgotten and one explains them all the more minutely since one recognises
that one has forgotten to mention them in their proper
places and that one may have given, by omitting them,
a false impression. I console myself with thinking
that this is a real story and that, after all, real stories
are probably told best in the way a person telling a
story would tell them. They will then seem most
real.

At any rate, I think I have brought my story up to
the date of Maisie Maidan's death. I mean that I
have explained everything that went before it from
the several points of view that were necessary—
from Leonora's, from Edward's and to some extent,
from my own. You have the facts for the trouble of
finding them; you have the points of view as far as
I could ascertain or put them. Let me imagine my-

self back, then, at the day of Maisie's death—or rather at the moment of Florence's dissertation on the Protest, up in the old Castle of the town of M——. Let us consider Leonora's point of view with regard to Florence; Edward's, of course, I cannot give you for Edward naturally never spoke of his affair with my wife. (I may, in what follows, be a little hard on Florence; but you must remember that I have been writing away at this story now for six months and reflecting longer and longer upon these affairs.)

And the longer I think about them the more certain I become that Florence was a contaminating influence—she depressed and deteriorated poor Edward; she deteriorated, hopelessly, the miserable Leonora. There is no doubt that she caused Leonora's character to deteriorate. If there was a fine point about Leonora it was that she was proud and that she was silent. But that pride and that silence broke when she made that extraordinary outburst, in the shadowy room that contained the Protest, and in the little terrace looking over the river. I don't mean to say that she was doing a wrong thing. She was certainly doing right in trying to warn me that Florence was making eyes at her husband. But, if she did the right thing, she was doing it in the wrong way. Perhaps she should have reflected longer; she should have spoken, if she wanted to speak, only after reflection. Or it would have been better if she had acted—if, for instance, she had so chaperoned Florence that private communication between her and Edward became impossible. She should have gone eavesdropping; she should have watched outside bedroom doors. It is odious; but that is the way the job is done. She should have taken Edward away the moment Maisie was dead. No, she acted wrongly. . . .

And yet, poor thing, is it for me to condemn her —and what did it matter in the end? If it had not been Florence, it would have been some other . . . Still, it might have been a better woman than my wife. For Florence was vulgar; Florence was a common flirt who would not, at the last, *lâcher prise;* and Florence was an unstoppable talker. You could not stop her; nothing would stop her. Edward and Leonora were at least proud and reserved people. Pride and reserve are not the only things in life; perhaps they are not even the best things. But, if they happen to be your particular virtues you will go all to pieces if you let them go. And Leonora let them go. She let them go before poor Edward did even. Consider her position when she burst out over the Luther-Protest . . . Consider her agonies . . .

You are to remember that the main passion of her life was to get Edward back; she had never, till that moment, despaired of getting him back. That may seem ignoble; but you have also to remember that her getting him back represented to her not only a victory for herself. It would, as it appeared to her, have been a victory for all wives and a victory for her Church. That was how it presented itself to her. These things are a little inscrutable. I don't know why the getting back of Edward should have represented to her a victory for all wives, for Society and for her Church. Or, maybe, I have a glimmering of it.

She saw life as a perpetual sex-battle between husbands who desire to be unfaithful to their wives, and wives who desire to recapture their husbands in the end. That was her sad and modest view of matrimony. Man, for her, was a sort of brute who must have his divagations, his moments of excess, his nights out, his, let us say, rutting seasons. She had read few novels, so that the idea of a pure and constant love succeeding the sound of wedding bells had never been very much presented to her. She went, numbed and terrified, to the Mother Superior of her childhood's convent with the tale of Edward's infidelities with the Spanish dancer and all that the old nun, who appeared to her to be infinitely wise, mystic and reverend, had done had been to shake her head sadly and to say:

"Men are like that. By the blessing of God it will all come right in the end."

That was what was put before her by her spiritual advisers as her programme in life. Or, at any rate, that was how their teachings came through to her—that was the lesson she told me she had learned of them. I don't know exactly what they taught her. The lot of women was patience and patience and again patience—*ad majorem Dei gloriam**—until upon the appointed day, if God saw fit, she should have her reward. If then, in the end, she should have succeeded in getting Edward back she would have kept her man within the limits that are all that wifehood has to expect. She was even taught that such excesses in men are natural, excusable—as if they had been children.

And the great thing was that there should be no scandal before the congregation. So she had clung to the idea of getting Edward back with a fierce passion that was like an agony. She had looked the other way; she had occupied herself solely with one idea. That was the idea of having Edward appear, when she did get him back, wealthy, glorious as it were, on account of his lands, and upright. She would show, in fact, that in an unfaithful world one Catholic woman had succeeded in retaining the fidelity of her husband. And she thought she had come near her desires.

Her plan with regard to Maisie had appeared to be working admirably. Edward had seemed to be cooling off towards the girl. He did not hunger to pass every minute of the time at Nauheim beside the child's recumbent form; he went out to polo matches; he played auction bridge in the evenings; he was cheerful and bright. She was certain that he was not trying to seduce that poor child; she was beginning to think that he had never tried to do so. He seemed in fact to be dropping back into what he had been for Maisie in the beginning—a kind, attentive, superior officer in the regiment, paying gallant attentions to a bride. They were as open in their little flirtations as the dayspring from on high. And Maisie had not appeared to fret when he went off on excursions with us; she had to lie down for so many hours on her bed every afternoon, and she had not appeared to crave for the attentions of Edward at those times.

And Edward was beginning to make little advances to Leonora. Once or twice, in private—for he often did it before people—he had said: "How nice you look!" or "What a pretty dress!" She had gone with Florence to Frankfurt, where they dress as well as in Paris, and had got herself a gown or two. She could afford it and Florence was an excellent adviser as to dress. She seemed to have got hold of the clue to the riddle.

Yes, Leonora seemed to have got hold of the clue to the riddle. She imagined herself to have been in the wrong to some extent in the past. She should not have kept Edward on such a tight rein with regard to money. She thought she was on the right tack in letting him—as she had done only with fear and irresolution—have again the control of his income. He came even a step towards her and acknowledged, spontaneously, that she had been right in husbanding, for all those years, their resources. He said to her one day:

"You've done right, old girl. There's nothing I like so much as to have a little to chuck away. And I can do it, thanks to you."

That was really, she said, the happiest moment of her life. And he, seeming to realise it, had ventured to pat her on the shoulder. He had, ostensibly, come in to borrow a safety pin of her.

And the occasion of her boxing Maisie's ears, had, after it was over, rivetted in her mind the idea that there was no intrigue between Edward and Mrs. Maidan. She imagined that, from henceforward, all that she had to do was to keep him well supplied with money and his mind amused with pretty girls. She was convinced that he was coming back to her. For that month she no longer repelled his timid advances that never went very far. For he certainly made timid advances. He patted her on the shoulder; he whispered into her ear little jokes about the odd figures that they saw up at the Casino. It was not much to make a little joke—but the whispering of it was a precious intimacy. . . .

And then—smash—it all went. It went to pieces at the moment when Florence laid her hand upon Edward's wrist, as it lay on the glass sheltering the manuscript of the Protest, up in the high tower with the shutters where the sunlight here and there streamed in. Or, rather, it went when she noticed the look in Edward's eyes as he gazed back into Florence's. She knew that look.

She had known—since the first moment of their meeting, since the moment of our all sitting down to dinner together—that Florence was making eyes at Edward. But she had seen so many women make eyes at Edward—hundreds and hundreds of women, in railway trains, in hotels, aboard liners, at street corners. And she had arrived at thinking that Edward took little stock in women that made eyes at him. She had formed what was, at that time, a fairly correct estimate of the methods of, the reasons for, Edward's loves. She was certain that hitherto they had consisted of the short passion for the Dolciquita, the real sort of love for Mrs. Basil, and what she deemed the pretty courtship of Maisie Maidan. Besides she despised Florence so haughtily that she could not imagine Edward's being attracted by her. And she and Maisie were a sort of bulwark round him.

She wanted, besides, to keep her eyes on Florence —for Florence knew that she had boxed Maisie's ears. And Leonora so desperately desired that her union with Edward should appear to be flawless. But all that went . . .

With the answering gaze of Edward into Florence's blue and uplifted eyes, she knew that it had all gone. She knew that that gaze meant that those two had had long conversations of an intimate kind—about their likes and dislikes, about their natures, about their views of marriage. She knew what it meant that she, when we all four walked out together, had always been with me ten yards ahead of Florence and Edward. She did not imagine that it had gone further than talks about their likes and dislikes, about their natures or about marriage as an institution. But, having watched Edward all her life, she knew that that laying on of hands, that answering of gaze with gaze, meant that the thing was unavoidable. Edward was such a serious person.

She knew that any attempt on her part to separate those two would be to rivet on Edward an irrevocable passion; that, as I have before told you, it was a trick of Edward's nature to believe that the seducing of a woman gave her an irrevocable hold over him for life. And that touching of hands, she knew, would give that woman an irrevocable claim—to be seduced.

And she so despised Florence that she would have preferred it to be a parlour-maid. There are very decent
parlour-maids.

And, suddenly, there came into her mind the conviction that Maisie Maidan had a real passion for
Edward; that this would break her heart—and that,
she, Leonora, would be responsible for that. She
went, for the moment, mad. She clutched me by the
wrist; she dragged me down those stairs and across
that whispering Rittersaal with the high painted pillars, the high painted chimney piece. I guess she
did not go mad enough.

She ought to have said:

"Your wife is a harlot who is going to be my husband's mistress . . ." That might have done the
trick. But, even in her madness she was afraid to
go as far as that. She was afraid that, if she did,
Edward and Florence would make a bolt of it and
that, if they did that she would lose forever all chance
of getting him back in the end. She acted very badly
to me.

Well, she was a tortured soul who put her Church
before the interests of a Philadelphia Quaker. That
is all right—I daresay the Church of Rome is the
more important of the two.

A week after Maisie Maidan's death she was aware
that Florence had become Edward's mistress. She
waited outside Florence's door and met Edward as he
came away. She said nothing and he only grunted.
But I guess he had a bad time.

Yes, the mental deterioration that Florence worked

in Leonora was extraordinary; it smashed up her whole life and all her chances. It made her, in the first place, hopeless—for she could not see how, after that, Edward could return to her—after a vulgar intrigue with a vulgar woman. His affair with Mrs. Basil, which was now all that she had to bring, in her heart, against him, she could not find it in her to call an intrigue. It was a love affair—a pure enough thing in its way. But this seemed to her to be a horror—a wantonness, all the more detestable to her, because she so detested Florence. And Florence talked . . .

That was what was terrible, because Florence forced Leonora herself to abandon her high reserve—Florence and the situation. It appears that Florence was in two minds whether to confess to me or to Leonora. Confess she had to. And she pitched at last on Leonora, because if it had been me she would have had to confess a great deal more. Or, at least, I might have guessed a great deal more, about her "heart," and about Jimmy. So she went to Leonora one day and began hinting and hinting. And she enraged Leonora to such an extent that at last Leonora said:

"You want to tell me that you are Edward's mistress. You can be. I have no use for him."

That was really a calamity for Leonora, because, once started, there was no stopping the talking. She tried to stop—but it was not to be done. She found it necessary to send Edward messages through Florence; for she would not speak to him. She had to give him, for instance, to understand that if I ever came to know of his intrigue she would ruin him beyond repair. And it complicated matters a good deal that Edward, at about this time, was really a little in love with her. He thought that he had treated her so badly; that she was so fine. She was so mournful that he longed to comfort her, and he thought himself such a blackguard that there was nothing he would not have done to make amends. And Florence communicated these items of information to Leonora.

I don't in the least blame Leonora for her coarseness to Florence; it must have done Florence a world of good. But I do blame her for giving way to what was in the end a desire for communicativeness. You see that business cut her off from her Church. She did not want to confess what she was doing because she was afraid that her spiritual advisers would blame her for deceiving me. I rather imagine that she would have preferred damnation to breaking my heart. That is what it works out at. She need not have troubled.

But, having no priests to talk to she had to talk to someone and, as Florence insisted on talking to her, she talked back, in short, explosive sentences, like one of the damned. Precisely like one of the damned. Well, if a pretty period in hell on this earth can spare her any period of pain in Eternity—where there are not any periods—I guess Leonora will escape Hell fire.

Her conversations with Florence would be like this. Florence would happen in on her, whilst she was doing her wonderful hair, with a proposition from

Edward, who seems about that time to have conceived
the naïve idea that he might become a polygamist. I
daresay it was Florence who put it into his head. Anyhow, I am not responsible for the oddities of the human psychology. But it certainly appears that, at
about that date Edward cared more for Leonora than
he had ever done before—or, at any rate, for a long
time. And, if Leonora had been a person to play
cards and if she had played her cards well, and if she
had had no sense of shame and so on, she might then
have shared Edward with Florence until the time came
for jerking that poor cuckoo out of the nest.

Well, Florence would come to Leonora with some
such proposition. I do not mean to say that she put
it baldly, like that. She stood out that she was not
Edward's mistress until Leonora said that she had seen
Edward coming out of her room at an advanced hour
of the night. That checked Florence a bit; but she
fell back upon her "heart" and stuck out that she
had merely been conversing with Edward in order
to bring him to a better frame of mind. Florence
had, of course, to stick to that story; for even Florence would not have had the face to implore Leonora
to grant her favours to Edward if she had admitted
that she was Edward's mistress. That could not be
done. At the same time Florence had such a pressing
desire to talk about something. There would have
been nothing else to talk about but a rapprochement
between that estranged pair. So Florence would go
on babbling and Leonora would go on brushing her

hair. And then Leonora would say suddenly something like:

"I should think myself defiled if Edward touched me now that he has touched you."

That would discourage Florence a bit; but after a week or so, on another morning she would have another try.

And, even in other things Leonora deteriorated. She had promised Edward to leave the spending of his own income in his own hands. And she had fully meant to do that. I daresay she would have done it too; though, no doubt, she would have spied upon his banking account in secret. She was not a Roman Catholic for nothing. But she took so serious a view of Edward's unfaithfulness to the memory of poor little Maisie that she could not trust him any more at all.

So, when she got back to Branshaw she started, after less than a month, to worry him about the minutest items of his expenditure. She allowed him to draw his own cheques, but there was hardly a cheque that she did not scrutinise—except for a private account of about five hundred a year which, tacitly, she allowed him to keep for expenditure on his mistress or mistresses. He had to have his jaunts to Paris; he had to send expensive cables in cipher to Florence about twice a week. But she worried him about his expenditure on wines, on fruit trees, on harness, on gates, on the account at his blacksmith's for work done to a new patent army stirrup that he was trying to invent. She could not see why he should bother to invent a new army stirrup and she was really enraged when, after the invention was mature, he made a present to the War Office of the designs and the patent rights. It was a remarkably good stirrup.

I have told you, I think, that Edward spent a great deal of time, and about two hundred pounds for law-fees on getting a poor girl, the daughter of one of his gardeners, acquitted of a charge of murdering her baby. That was positively the last act of Edward's life. It came at a time when Nancy Rufford was on her way to India; when the most horrible gloom was over the household; when Edward, himself, was in an agony and behaving as prettily as he knew how. Yet even then Leonora made him a terrible scene about this expenditure of time and trouble. She sort of had the vague idea that what had passed with the girl and the rest of it ought to have taught Edward a lesson—the lesson of economy. She threatened to take his banking account away from him again. I guess that made him cut his throat. He might have stuck it out otherwise—but the thought that he had lost his Nancy and that, in addition, there was nothing left for him but a dreary, dreary succession of days in which he could be of no public service . . . Well, it finished him.

It was during those years that Leonora tried to get up a love affair of her own with a fellow called Bayham—a decent sort of fellow. A really nice man. But the affair was no sort of success. I have told you about it already. . . .

II

WELL, that about brings me up to the date of my receiving, in Waterbury, the laconic cable from Edward to the effect that he wanted me to go to Branshaw and have a chat. I was pretty busy at the time and I was half minded to send him a reply cable to the effect that I would start in a fortnight. But I was having a long interview with old Mr. Hurlbird's attorneys and immediately afterwards I had to have a long interview with the Misses Hurlbird, so I delayed cabling.

I had expected to find the Misses Hurlbird excessively old—in the nineties or thereabouts. The time had passed so slowly that I had the impression that it must have been thirty years since I had been in the United States. It was only twelve years. Actually Miss Hurlbird was just sixty-one and Miss Florence Hurlbird fifty-nine and they were both, mentally and physically, as vigorous as could be desired. They were, indeed, more vigorous, mentally, than suited my purpose, which was to get away from the United States as quickly as I could. The Hurlbirds were an exceedingly united family—exceedingly united except on one set of points. Each of the three of them had a separate doctor, whom they trusted implicitly—and each had a separate attorney. And each of them distrusted the other's doctor and the other's attorney.

227

And, naturally, the doctors and the attorneys warned one all the time—against each other. You cannot imagine how complicated it all became for me. Of course I had an attorney of my own—recommended to me by young Carter, my Philadelphia nephew.

I do not mean to say that there was any unpleasantness of a grasping kind. The problem was quite another one—a moral dilemma. You see, old Mr. Hurlbird had left all his property to Florence with the mere request that she would have erected to him in the city of Waterbury, Ill., a memorial that should take the form of some sort of institution for the relief of sufferers from the heart. Florence's money had all come to me—and with it old Mr. Hurlbird's. He had died just five days before Florence.

Well, I was quite ready to spend a round million dollars on the relief of sufferers from the heart. The old gentleman had left about a million and a half; Florence had been worth about eight hundred thousand—and as I figured it out, I should cut up at about a million myself. Anyhow, there was ample money. But I naturally wanted to consult the wishes of his surviving relatives and then the trouble really began. You see, it had been discovered that Mr. Hurlbird had had nothing whatever the matter with his heart. His lungs had been a little affected all through his life and he had died of bronchitis.

It struck Miss Florence Hurlbird that, since her brother had died of lungs and not of heart, his money ought to go to lung patients. That, she considered, was what her brother would have wished. On the other hand, by a kink, that I could not at the time understand, Miss Hurlbird insisted that I ought to keep the money all to myself. She said that she did not wish for any monuments to the Hurlbird family.

At the time I thought that that was because of a New England dislike for necrological ostentation. But I can figure out now, when I remember certain insistent and continued questions that she put to me, about Edward Ashburnham, that there was another idea in her mind. And Leonora has told me that, on Florence's dressing-table, beside her dead body there had lain a letter to Miss Hurlbird—a letter which Leonora posted without telling me. I don't know how Florence had time to write to her aunt; but I can quite understand that she would not like to go out of the world without making some comments. So I guess Florence had told Miss Hurlbird a good bit about Edward Ashburnham in a few scrawled words —and that that was why the old lady did not wish the name of Hurlbird perpetuated. Perhaps also she thought that I had earned the Hurlbird money.

It meant a pretty tidy lot of discussing, what with the doctors warning each other about the bad effects of discussions, on the health of the old ladies, and warning me covertly against each other, and saying that old Mr. Hurlbird might have died of heart, after all, in spite of the diagnosis of *his* doctor. And the solicitors all had separate methods of arranging about how the money should be invested and entrusted and bound.

Personally, I wanted to invest the money so that

the interest could be used for the relief of sufferers
from the heart. If old Mr. Hurlbird had not died
of any defects in that organ he had considered that
it was defective. Moreover, Florence had certainly
died of her heart, as I saw it. And when Miss Florence Hurlbird stood out that the money ought to go
to chest sufferers I was brought to thinking that there
ought to be a chest institution too, and I advanced
the sum that I was ready to provide to a million and
a half of dollars. That would have given seven hundred and fifty thousand to each class of invalid. I
did not want money at all badly. All I wanted it for
was to be able to give Nancy Rufford a good time. I
did not know much about housekeeping expenses in
England where, I presumed, she would wish to live.
I knew that her needs at that time were limited to
good chocolates, and a good horse or two and simple,
pretty frocks. Probably she would want more than
that later on. But even if I gave a million and a half
dollars to these institutions I should still have the
equivalent of about twenty thousand a year English,
and I considered that Nancy could have a pretty good
time on that or less.

Anyhow, we had a stiff set of arguments up at
the Hurlbird mansion, which stands on a bluff over
the town. It may strike you, silent listener, as being
funny if you happen to be European. But moral
problems of that description and the giving of mil-
lions to institutions are immensely serious matters in
my country. Indeed, they are the staple topics for
consideration amongst the wealthy classes. We

haven't got peerages and social climbing to occupy us much, and decent people do not take interest in politics or elderly people in sport. So that there were real tears shed by both Miss Hurlbird and Miss Florence before I left that city.

I left it quite abruptly. Four hours after Edward's telegram came another from Leonora, saying: "Yes, do come. You could be so helpful." I simply told my attorney that there was the million and a half; that he could invest it as he liked, and that the purposes must be decided by the Misses Hurlbird. I was, anyhow, pretty well worn out by all the discussions. And, as I have never heard yet from the Misses Hurlbird, I rather think that Miss Hurlbird, either by revelations or by moral force, has persuaded Miss Florence that no memorial to their names shall be erected in the city of Waterbury, Conn. Miss Hurlbird wept dreadfully when she heard that I was going to stay with the Ashburnhams, but she did not make any comments. I was aware, at that date, that her niece had been seduced by that fellow Jimmy before I had married her—but I contrived to produce on her the impressions that I thought Florence had been a model wife. Why, at that date I still believed that Florence had been perfectly virtuous after her marriage to me. I had not figured it out that she could have played it so low down as to continue her intrigue with that fellow under my roof. Well, I was a fool. But I did not think much about Florence at that date. My mind was occupied with what was happening at Branshaw.

I had got it into my head that the telegrams had
something to do with Nancy. It struck me that she
might have shown signs of forming an attachment
for some undesirable fellow and that Leonora wanted
me to come back and marry her out of harm's way.
That was what was pretty firmly in my mind. And
it remained in my mind for nearly ten days after my
arrival at that beautiful old place. Neither Edward
nor Leonora made any motion to talk to me about anything other than the weather and the crops. Yet, although there were several young fellows about, I
could not see that any one in particular was distinguished by the girl's preference. She certainly appeared illish and nervous, except when she woke up
to talk gay nonsense to me. Oh, the pretty thing that
she was. . . .

I imagined that what must have happened was that
the undesirable young man had been forbidden the
place and that Nancy was fretting a little.

What had happened was just Hell. Leonora had
spoken to Nancy; Nancy had spoken to Edward; Edward had spoken to Leonora—and they had talked and
talked. And talked. You have to imagine horrible
pictures of gloom and half lights, and emotions running through silent nights—through whole nights.
You have to imagine my beautiful Nancy appearing
suddenly to Edward, rising up at the foot of his
bed, with her long hair falling, like a split cone of
shadow, in the glimmer of a night-light that burned
beside him. You have to imagine her, a silent, a no
doubt agonised figure, like a spectre, suddenly offer-

ing herself to him—to save his reason! And you have to imagine his frantic refusal—and talk. And talk! My God!

And yet, to me, living in the house, enveloped with the charm of the quiet and ordered living, with the silent, skilled servants whose mere laying out of my dress clothes was like a caress—to me who was hourly with them they appeared like tender, ordered and devoted people, smiling, absenting themselves at the proper intervals; driving me to meets—just good people! How the devil—how the devil do they do it?

At dinner one evening Leonora said—she had just opened a telegram :—

"Nancy will be going to India, to-morrow, to be with her father."

No one spoke. Nancy looked at her plate; Edward went on eating his pheasant. I felt very bad; I imagined that it would be up to me to propose to Nancy that evening. It appeared to me to be queer that they had not given me any warning of Nancy's departure. But I thought that that was only English manners—some sort of delicacy that I had not got the hang of. You must remember that at that moment I trusted in Edward and Leonora and in Nancy Rufford, and in the tranquillity of ancient haunts of peace, as I had trusted in my mother's love. And that evening Edward spoke to me.

What in the interval had happened had been this: Upon her return from Nauheim Leonora had completely broken down—because she knew she could

trust Edward. That seems odd but, if you know anything about breakdowns, you will know that, by the
ingenious torments that fate prepares for us, these
things come as soon as, a strain having relaxed, there
is nothing more to be done. It is after a husband's
long illness and death that a widow goes to pieces;
it is at the end of a long rowing contest that a crew
collapses and lies forward upon its oars. And that
was what happened to Leonora.

From certain tones in Edward's voice; from the
long, steady stare that he had given her from his
bloodshot eyes on rising from the dinner table in the
Nauheim hotel, she knew that, in the affair of the
poor girl, this was a case in which Edward's moral
scruples, or his social code, or his idea that it would
be playing it *too* low down, rendered Nancy perfectly
safe. The girl, she felt sure, was in no danger at
all from Edward. And, in that she was perfectly
right. The smash was to come from herself.

She relaxed; she broke; she drifted, at first quickly,
then with an increasing momentum, down the stream
of destiny. You may put it that, having been cut off
from the restraints of her religion, for the first time
in her life, she acted along the lines of her instinctive desires. I do not know whether to think that,
in that she was no longer herself; or that, having
let loose the bonds of her standards, her conventions
and her traditions, she was being, for the first time,
her own natural self. She was torn between her intense, maternal love for the girl and an intense jealousy of the woman who realises that the man she

loves has met what appears to be the final passion of his life. She was divided between an intense disgust for Edward's weakness in conceiving this passion, an intense pity for the miseries that he was enduring, and a feeling equally intense, but one that she hid from herself—a feeling of respect for Edward's determination to keep himself, in this particular affair, unspotted.

And the human heart is a very mysterious thing. It is impossible to say that Leonora, in acting as she then did, was not filled with a sort of hatred of Edward's final virtue. She wanted, I think, to despise him. He was, she realised, gone from her for good. Then let him suffer, let him agonise; let him, if possible, break and go to that Hell that is the abode of broken resolves. She might have taken a different line. It would have been so easy to send the girl away to stay with some friends; to have taken her away herself upon some pretext or other. That would not have cured things but it would have been the decent line . . . But, at that date, poor Leonora was incapable of taking any line whatever.

She pitied Edward frightfully at one time—and then she acted along the lines of pity; she loathed him at another and then she acted as her loathing dictated. She gasped, as a person dying of tuberculosis gasps for air. She craved madly for communication with some other human soul. And the human soul that she selected was that of the girl.

Perhaps Nancy was the only person that she could have talked to. With her necessity for reticences, with her coldness of manner, Leonora had singularly few intimates. She had none at all, with the exception of the Mrs. Colonel Whelen, who had advised her about the affair with La Dolciquita, and the one or two religious, who had guided her through life. The Colonel's wife was at that time in Madeira; the religious she now avoided. Her visitor's book had seven hundred names in it; there was not a soul that she could speak to. She was Mrs. Ashburnham of Branshaw Teleragh.

She was the great Mrs. Ashburnham of Branshaw and she lay all day upon her bed in her marvellous, light, airy bedroom with the chintzes and the Chippendale and the portraits of deceased Ashburnhams by Zoffany and Zucchero.* When there was a meet she would struggle up—supposing it were within driving distance—and let Edward drive her and the girl to the cross-roads or the country house. She would drive herself back alone; Edward would ride off with the girl. Ride Leonora could not, that season—her head was too bad. Each pace of her mare was an anguish.

But she drove with efficiency and precision; she smiled at the Gimmers and Ffoulkes and the Hedley Seatons. She threw with exactitude pennies to the boys who opened gates for her; she sat upright on the seat of the high dog-cart;*she waved her hands to Edward and Nancy as they rode off with the hounds and everyone could hear her clear, high voice, in the chilly weather, saying:

"Have a good time!"

Poor forlorn woman! . . .

There was, however, one spark of consolation. It came from the fact that Rodney Bayham, of Bayham, followed her always with his eyes. It had been three years since she had tried her abortive love-affair with him. Yet still, on the winter mornings he would ride up to her shafts and just say: "Good day," and look at her with eyes that were not imploring, but that seemed to say: "You see, I am still, as the Germans say, A. D.—at disposition."

It was a great consolation, not because she proposed ever to take him up again but because it showed her that there was in the world one faithful soul in riding breeches. And it showed her that she was not losing her looks.

And, indeed, she was not losing her looks. She was forty, but she was as clean run as on the day she had left the convent—as clear in outline, as clear coloured in the hair, as dark blue in the eyes. She thought that her looking-glass told her this; but there are always the doubts . . . Rodney Bayham's eyes took them away.

It is very singular that Leonora should not have aged at all. I suppose that there are some types of beauty and even of youth made for the embellishments that come with enduring sorrow. That is too elaborately put. I mean that Leonora, if everything had prospered, might have become too hard and, maybe, overbearing. As it was she was tuned down to appearing efficient—and yet sympathetic. That is the rarest of all blends. And yet I swear that Leonora, in her restrained way, gave the impression of being intensely sympathetic. When she listened to you she appeared also to be listening to some sound that was going on in the distance. But still, she listened to you and took in what you said, which, since the record of humanity is a record of sorrows, was, as a rule, something sad.

I think that she must have taken Nancy through many terrors of the night and many bad places of the day. And that would account for the girl's passionate love for the elder woman. For Nancy's love for Leonora was an admiration that is awakened in Catholics by their feeling for the Virgin Mary and for various of the saints. It is too little to say that the girl would have laid her life at Leonora's feet. Well, she laid there the offer of her virtue—and her reason. Those were sufficient instalments of her life. It would to-day be much better for Nancy Rufford if she were dead.

Perhaps all these reflections are a nuisance; but they crowd on me. I will try to tell the story.

You see—when she came back from Nauheim Leonora began to have her headaches—headaches lasting through whole days, during which she could speak no word and could bear to hear no sound. And, day after day, Nancy would sit with her, silent and motionless for hours, steeping handkerchiefs in vinegar and water, and thinking her own thoughts. It must have been very bad for her—and her meals alone with Edward must have been bad for her too—and beastly bad for Edward. Edward, of course, wav-

ered in his demeanour. What else could he do? At
times he would sit silent and dejected over his untouched food. He would utter nothing but monosyl-
lables when Nancy spoke to him. Then he was simply afraid of the girl falling in love with him. At
other times he would take a little wine; pull himself
together; attempt to chaff Nancy about a stake and
binder hedge* that her mare had checked at or talk
about the habits of the Chitralis. That was when he
was thinking that it was rough on the poor girl that
he should have become a dull companion. He realised that his talking to her in the park at Nauheim
had done her no harm.

But all that was doing a great deal of harm to
Nancy. It gradually opened her eyes to the fact that
Edward was a man with his ups and downs and not
an invariably gay uncle like a nice dog, a trustworthy
horse or a girl friend. She would find him in attitudes of frightful dejection, sunk into his armchair
in the study that was half a gun-room. She would
notice through the open door that his face was the
face of an old, dead man, when he had no one to talk
to. Gradually it forced itself upon her attention that
there were profound differences between the pair that
she regarded as her uncle and her aunt. It was a conviction that came very slowly.

It began with Edward's giving an oldish horse to
a young fellow called Selmes. Selmes' father had
been ruined by a fraudulent solicitor and the Selmes
family had had to sell their hunters. It was a case
that had excited a good deal of sympathy in that part

of the county. And Edward, meeting the young man, one day, unmounted and seeing him to be very unhappy had offered to give him an old Irish cob upon which he was riding. It was a silly sort of thing to do, really. The horse was worth from thirty to forty pounds and Edward might have known that the gift would upset his wife. But Edward just had to comfort that unhappy young man whose father he had known all his life. And what made it all the worse was that young Selmes could not afford to keep the horse even. Edward recollected this, immediately after he had made the offer and said quickly:

"Of course I mean that you should stable the horse at Branshaw until you have time to turn round or want to sell him and get a better."

Nancy went straight home and told all this to Leonora, who was lying down. She regarded it as a splendid instance of Edward's quick consideration for the feelings and the circumstances of the distressed. She thought it would cheer Leonora up—because it ought to cheer any woman up to know that she had such a splendid husband. That was the last girlish thought she ever had. For Leonora, whose headache had left her collected but miserably weak, turned upon her bed and uttered words that were amazing to the girl:

"I wish to God," she said, "that he was your husband, and not mine. We shall be ruined. We shall be ruined. Am I *never* to have a chance." And suddenly Leonora burst into a passion of tears. She pushed herself up from the pillows with one elbow and sat there—crying, crying, crying, with her face hidden in her hands and the tears falling through her fingers.

The girl flushed, stammered and whimpered as if she had been personally insulted.

"But if Uncle Edward . . ." she began.

"That man," said Leonora, with an extraordinary bitterness, "would give the shirt off his back and off mine—and off yours to any . . ." She could not finish the sentence.

At that moment she had been feeling an extraordinary hatred and contempt for her husband. All the morning and all the afternoon she had been lying there thinking that Edward and the girl were together—in the field and hacking it home at dusk. She had been digging her sharp nails into her palms.

The house had been very silent in the drooping winter weather. And then, after an eternity of torture, there had invaded it the sound of opening doors, of the girl's gay voice saying:

"Well, it was only under the mistletoe." . . . And there was Edward's gruff undertone. Then Nancy had come in, with feet that had hastened up the stairs and that tiptoed as they approached the open door of Leonora's room. Branshaw had a great big hall with oak floors and tiger skins. Round this hall there ran a gallery upon which Leonora's doorway gave. And even when she had the worst of her headaches she liked to have her door open—I suppose so that she might hear the approaching footsteps of ruin and disaster. At any rate she hated to be in a room with a shut door.

At that moment Leonora hated Edward with a hatred that was like hell, and she would have liked to bring her riding-whip down across the girl's face. What right had Nancy to be young and slender and dark, and gay at times, at times mournful? What right had she to be exactly the woman to make Leonora's husband happy? For Leonora knew that Nancy would have made Edward happy.

Yes, Leonora wished to bring her riding-whip down on Nancy's young face. She imagined the pleasure she would feel when the lash fell across those queer features; the pleasure she would feel at drawing the handle at the same moment toward her, so as to cut deep into the flesh and to leave a lasting wheal.

Well, she left a lasting wheal, and her words cut deeply into the girl's mind. . . .

They neither of them spoke about that again. A fortnight went by—a fortnight of deep rains, of heavy fields, of bad scent. Leonora's headaches seemed to have gone for good. She hunted once or twice, letting herself be piloted by Bayham, whilst Edward looked after the girl. Then, one evening, when those three were dining alone, Edward said, in the queer, deliberate, heavy tones that came out of him in those days (he was looking at the table):

"I have been thinking that Nancy ought to do more for her father. He is getting an old man. I have written to Colonel Rufford, suggesting that she should go to him."

Leonora called out:

"How dare you? How dare you?"

The girl put her hand over her heart and cried out: "Oh, my sweet Saviour, help me!" That was the queer way she thought within her mind, and the words forced themselves to her lips. Edward said nothing.

And that night, by a merciless trick of the devil that pays attention to this sweltering hell of ours, Nancy Rufford had a letter from her mother. It came whilst Leonora was talking to Edward, or Leonora would have intercepted it as she had intercepted others. It was an amazing and a horrible letter. . . .

I don't know what it contained. I just average out from its effect on Nancy that her mother, having eloped with some worthless sort of fellow, had done what is called "sinking lower and lower." Whether she was actually on the streets I do not know, but I rather think that she eked out a small allowance that she had from her husband by that means of livelihood. And I think that she stated as much in her letter to Nancy and upbraided the girl with living in luxury whilst her mother starved. And it must have been horrible in tone, for Mrs. Rufford was a cruel sort of woman at the best of times. It must have seemed to that poor girl, opening her letter, for distraction from another grief, up in her bedroom, like the laughter of a devil.

I just cannot bear to think of my poor dear girl at that moment. . . .

And, at the same time, Leonora was lashing, like a cold fiend, into the unfortunate Edward. Or, perhaps, he was not so unfortunate; because he had done what he knew to be the right thing, he may be deemed happy. I leave it to you. At any rate, he was sitting in his deep chair, and Leonora came into his room—for the first time in nine years. She said:

"This is the most atrocious thing you have done in your atrocious life." He never moved and he never looked at her. God knows what was in Leonora's mind exactly.

I like to think that, uppermost in it was concern and horror at the thought of the poor girl's going back to a father whose voice made her shriek in the night. And, indeed, that motive was very strong with Leonora. But I think there was also present the thought that she wanted to go on torturing Edward with the girl's presence. She was, at that time, capable of that.

Edward was sunk in his chair; there were in the room two candles, hidden by green glass shades. The green shades were reflected in the glasses of the bookcases that contained not books but guns with gleaming brown barrels and fishing rods in green baize overcovers. There was dimly to be seen, above a mantelpiece encumbered with spurs, hooves and bronze models of horses, a dark-brown picture of a white horse.

"If you think," Leonora said, "that I do not know that you are in love with the girl . . ." She began spiritedly, but she could not find any ending for the sentence. Edward did not stir; he never spoke. And then Leonora said:

"If you want me to divorce you I will. You can marry her then. She's in love with you."

He groaned at that, a little, Leonora said. Then she went away.

Heaven knows what happened in Leonora after that. She certainly does not herself know. She probably said a good deal more to Edward than I have been able to report; but that is all that she has told me and I am not going to make up speeches. To follow her psychological development of that moment I think we must allow that she upbraided him for a great deal of their past life, whilst Edward sat absolutely silent. And, indeed, in speaking of it afterwards, she has said several times: "I said a great deal more to him than I wanted to, just because he was so silent." She talked, in fact, in the endeavour to sting him into speech.

She must have said so much that, with the expression of her grievance, her mood changed. She went back to her own room in the gallery, and sat there for a long time thinking. And she thought herself into a mood of absolute unselfishness, of absolute self-contempt, too. She said to herself that she was no good; that she had failed in all her efforts—in her efforts to get Edward back as in her efforts to make him curb his expenditure. She imagined herself to be exhausted; she imagined herself to be done. Then a great fear came over her.

She thought that Edward, after what she had said to him, must have committed suicide. She went out on to the gallery and listened; there was no sound in all the house except the regular beat of the great clock in the hall. But, even in her debased condition, she was not the person to hang about. She acted. She went straight to Edward's room, opened the door, and looked in.

He was oiling the breach action of a gun. It was an unusual thing for him to do, at that time of night, in his evening clothes. It never occurred to her, nevertheless, that he was going to shoot himself with that implement. She knew that he was doing it just for occupation—to keep himself from thinking. He looked up when she opened the door, his face illuminated by the light cast upwards from the round orifices in the green candle shades.

She said:

"I didn't imagine that I should find Nancy here." She thought that she owed that to him. He answered then:

"I don't imagine that you did imagine it." Those were the only words he spoke that night. She went, like a lame duck, back through the long corridors; she stumbled over the familiar tiger skins in the dark hall. She could hardly drag one limb after the other. In the gallery she perceived that Nancy's door was half open and that there was a light in the girl's room. A sudden madness possessed her, a desire for action, a thirst for self-explanation.

Their rooms all gave on to the gallery; Leonora's to the east, the girl's next, then Edward's. The sight of those three open doors, side by side, gaping to receive whom the chances of the black night might bring, made Leonora shudder all over her body. She went into Nancy's room.

The girl was sitting perfectly still in an arm-chair, very upright, as she had been taught to sit at the convent. She appeared to be as calm as a church; her hair fell, black and like a pall, down over both her shoulders. The fire beside her was burning brightly; she must have just put coals on. She was in a white silk kimono that covered her to the feet. The clothes that she had taken off were exactly folded upon the proper seats. Her long hands were one upon each arm of the chair that had a pink and white chintz back.

Leonora told me these things. She seemed to think it extraordinary that the girl could have done such orderly things as fold up the clothes she had taken off upon such a night—when Edward had announced that he was going to send her to her father, and when, from her mother, she had received that letter. The letter, in its envelope, was in her right hand.

Leonora did not at first perceive it. She said: "What are you doing so late?" The girl answered: "Just thinking." They seemed to think in whispers and to speak below their breaths. Then Leonora's eyes fell on the envelope, and she recognised Mrs. Rufford's handwriting.

It was one of those moments when thinking was impossible, Leonora said. It was as if stones were being thrown at her from every direction and she could only run. She heard herself exclaim:

"Edward's dying—because of you. He's dying. He's worth more than either of us. . . ."

The girl looked past her at the panels of the half-closed door.

"My poor father," she said, "my poor father."

"You must stay here," Leonora answered fiercely. "You must stay here. I tell you you must stay here."

"I am going to Glasgow," Nancy answered. "I shall go to Glasgow to-morrow morning. My mother is in Glasgow."

It appears that it was in Glasgow that Mrs. Rufford pursued her disorderly life. She had selected that city, not because it was most profitable, but because it was the natal home of her husband to whom she desired to cause as much pain as possible.

"You must stay here," Leonora began, "to save Edward. He's dying for love of you."

The girl turned her calm eyes upon Leonora.

"I know it," she said. "And I am dying for love of him."

Leonora uttered an "Ah," that, in spite of herself, was an "Ah" of horror and of grief.

"That is why," the girl continued, "I am going to Glasgow—to take my mother away from there." She added, "To the ends of the earth," for, if the last months had made her nature that of a woman, her phrases were still romantically those of a school-girl. It was as if she had grown up so quickly that there had not been time to put her hair up. But she added: "We're no good—my mother and I."

Leonora said, with her fierce calmness:

"No. No. You're not no good. It's I that am no

good. You can't let that man go on to ruin for want of you. You must belong to him."

The girl, she said, smiled at her with a queer, far-away smile—as if she were a thousand years old, as if Leonora were a tiny child.

"I knew you would come to that," she said, very slowly. "But we are not worth it—Edward and I."

III

NANCY had, in fact, been thinking ever since Leonora had made that comment over the giving of the horse to young Selmes. She had been thinking and thinking, because she had had to sit for many days silent beside her aunt's bed. (She had always thought of Leonora as her aunt.) And she had had to sit thinking during many silent meals with Edward. And then, at times, with his bloodshot eyes and creased, heavy mouth, he would smile at her. And gradually the knowledge had come to her that Edward did not love Leonora and that Leonora hated Edward. Several things contributed to form and to harden this conviction.

She was allowed to read the papers in those days— or, rather, since Leonora was always on her bed and Edward breakfasted alone and went out early, over the estate, she was left alone with the papers. One day, in the paper, she saw the portrait of a woman she knew very well. Beneath it she read the words: "The Hon. Mrs. Brand, plaintiff in the remarkable divorce case reported on p. 8." Nancy hardly knew what a divorce case was. She had been so remarkably well brought up, and Roman Catholics do not practise divorce. I don't know how Leonora had done it exactly. I suppose she had always impressed it on Nancy's mind that nice women did not read these things, and that would have been enough to make Nancy skip those pages.

She read, at any rate, the account of the Brand divorce case—principally because she wanted to tell Leonora about it. She imagined that Leonora, when her headache left her, would like to know what was happening to Mrs. Brand, who lived at Christchurch, and whom they both liked very well. The case occupied three days, and the report that Nancy first came upon was that of the third day. Edward, however, kept the papers of the week, after his methodical fashion, in a rack in his gun-room, and when she had finished her breakfast Nancy went to that quiet apartment and had what she would have called a good read. It seemed to her to be a queer affair. She could not understand why one counsel should be so anxious to know all about the movements of Mr. Brand upon a certain day; she could not understand why a chart of the bedroom accommodation at Christchurch Old Hall should be produced in court. She did not even see why they should want to know that, upon a certain occasion, the drawing-room door was locked. It made her laugh; it appeared to be all so senseless that grown people should occupy themselves with such matters. It struck her, nevertheless, as odd that one of the counsel should cross-question Mr. Brand so insistently and so impertinently as to his feelings for Miss Lupton. Nancy knew Miss Lupton of Ringwood very well—a jolly girl, who rode a horse with two white fetlocks. Mr. Brand persisted that he did not love Miss Lupton. . . . Well, of course he did not love

Miss Lupton; he was a married man. You might as well think of Uncle Edward loving . . . loving anybody but Leonora. When people were married there was an end of loving. There were, no doubt, people who misbehaved—but they were poor people—or people not like those she knew.

So these matters presented themselves to Nancy's mind.

But later on in the case she found that Mr. Brand had to confess to a "guilty intimacy" with someone or other. Nancy imagined that he must have been telling someone his wife's secrets; she could not understand why that was a serious offence. Of course it was not very gentlemanly—it lessened her opinion of Mr. Brand. But, since she found that Mrs. Brand had condoned that offence, she imagined that they could not have been very serious secrets that Mr. Brand had told. And then, suddenly, it was forced on her conviction that Mr. Brand—the mild Mr. Brand that she had seen a month or two before their departure to Nauheim, playing "Blind Man's Buff" with his children and kissing his wife when he caught her—Mr. Brand and Mrs. Brand had been on the worst possible terms. That was incredible.

Yet there it was—in black and white. Mr. Brand drank; Mr. Brand had struck Mrs. Brand to the ground when he was drunk. Mr. Brand was adjudged, in two or three abrupt words, at the end of columns and columns of paper, to have been guilty of cruelty to his wife and to have committed adultery with Miss Lupton. The last words conveyed nothing to Nancy—

nothing real, that is to say. She knew that one was commanded not to commit adultery—but why, she thought, should one? It was probably something like catching salmon out of season—a thing one did not do. She gathered it had something to do with kissing, or holding someone in your arms. . . .

And yet the whole effect of that reading upon Nancy was mysterious, terrifying and evil. She felt a sickness—a sickness that grew as she read. Her heart beat painfully; she began to cry. She asked God how He could permit such things to be. And she was more certain that Edward did not love Leonora and that Leonora hated Edward. Perhaps, then, Edward loved someone else. It was unthinkable.

If he could love someone else than Leonora, her fierce, unknown heart suddenly spoke in her side, why could it not be herself? And he did not love her. . . . This had occurred about a month before she got the letter from her mother. She let the matter rest until the sick feeling went off; it did that in a day or two. Then, finding that Leonora's headaches had gone she suddenly told Leonora that Mrs. Brand had divorced her husband. She asked what, exactly, it all meant.

Leonora was lying on the sofa in the hall; she was feeling so weak that she could hardly find any words. She answered just:

"It means that Mr. Brand will be able to marry again."

Nancy said:

"But . . . but . . ." and then: "He will be able

to marry Miss Lupton." Leonora just moved a hand in assent. Her eyes were shut.

"Then . . ." Nancy began. Her blue eyes were full of horror: her brows were tight above them; the lines of pain about her mouth were very distinct. In her eyes the whole of that familiar, great hall had a changed aspect. The andirons with the brass flowers at the ends appeared unreal; the burning logs were just logs that were burning and not the comfortable symbols of an indestructible mode of life. The flame fluttered before the high fireback; the St. Bernard sighed in his sleep. Outside the winter rain fell and fell. And suddenly she thought that Edward might marry someone else; and she nearly screamed.

Leonora opened her eyes, lying sideways, with her face upon the black and gold pillow of the sofa that was drawn half across the great fireplace.

"I thought," Nancy said, "I never imagined. . . . Aren't marriages sacraments? Aren't they indissoluble? I thought you were married . . . and . . ." She was sobbing. "I thought you were married or not married as you are alive or dead."

"That," Leonora said, "is the law of the church. It is not the law of the land. . . ."

"Oh, yes," Nancy said, "the Brands are Protestants."

She felt a sudden safeness descend upon her, and for an hour or so her mind was at rest. It seemed to her idiotic not to have remembered Henry VIII and the basis upon which Protestantism rests. She almost laughed at herself.

The long afternoon wore on; the flames still fluttered when the maid made up the fire; the St. Bernard awoke and lolloped away towards the kitchen. And then Leonora opened her eyes and said almost coldly:

"And you? Don't you think you will get married?"

It was so unlike Leonora that, for the moment, the girl was frightened in the dusk. But then, again, it seemed a perfectly reasonable question.

"I don't know," she answered. "I don't know that anyone wants to marry me."

"Several people want to marry you," Leonora said.

"But I don't want to marry," Nancy answered. "I should like to go on living with you and Edward. I don't think I am in the way, or that I am really an expense. If I went you would have to have a companion. Or, perhaps, I ought to earn my living. . . ."

"I wasn't thinking of that," Leonora answered in the same dull tone. "You will have money enough from your father. But most people want to be married."

I believe that she then asked the girl if she would not like to marry me, and that Nancy answered that she would marry me if she were told to; but that she wanted to go on living there. She added:

"If I married anyone I should want him to be like Edward."

She was frightened out of her life. Leonora writhed on her couch and called out: "Oh, God! . . ."

Nancy ran for the maid; for tablets of aspirin; for wet handkerchiefs. It never occurred to her that Leonora's expression of agony was for anything else than physical pain.

You are to remember that all this happened a month before Leonora went into the girl's room at night. I have been casting back again; but I cannot help it. It is so difficult to keep all these people going. I tell you about Leonora and bring her up to date; then about Edward, who has fallen behind. And then the girl gets hopelessly left behind. I wish I could put it down in diary form. Thus: On the 1st of September they returned from Nauheim. Leonora at once took to her bed. By the 1st of October they were all going to meets together. Nancy had already observed very fully that Edward was strange in his manner. About the 6th of that month Edward gave the horse to young Selmes, and Nancy had cause to believe that her aunt did not love her uncle. On the 20th she read the account of the divorce case, which is reported in the papers of the 18th and the two following days. On the 23rd she had the conversation with her aunt in the hall—about marriage in general and about her own possible marriage. Her aunt's coming to her bedroom did not occur until the 12th of November. . . .

Thus she had three weeks for introspection—for introspection beneath gloomy skies, in that old house, rendered darker by the fact that it lay in a hollow crowned by fir trees with their black shadows. It was not a good situation for a girl. She began thinking about love, she who had never before considered it as anything other than a rather humorous, rather nonsensical matter. She remembered chance passages in chance books—things that had not really affected her at all at the time. She remembered someone's love

for the Princess Badrulbadour;* she remembered to
have heard that love was a flame, a thirst, a withering
up of the vitals—though she did not know what the
vitals were. She had a vague recollection that love
was said to render a hopeless lover's eyes hopeless;
she remembered a character in a book who was said
to have taken to drink through love; she remembered
that lovers' existences were said to be punctuated with
heavy sighs. Once she went to the little cottage piano
that was in a corner of the hall and began to play.
It was a tinkly, reedy instrument, for none of that
household had any turn for music. Nancy herself
could play a few simple songs, and she found herself
playing. She had been sitting on the window seat,
looking out on the fading day. Leonora had gone to
pay some calls; Edward was looking after some plant-
ing up in the new spinney. Thus she found herself
playing on the old piano. She did not know how she
came to be doing it. A silly, lilting, wavering tune
came from before her in the dusk—a tune in which
major notes with their cheerful insistence wavered
and melted into minor sounds, as, beneath a bridge
the high lights on dark waters melt and waver and dis-
appear into black depths. Well, it was a silly old
tune. . . .

It goes with the words—they are about a willow
tree, I think:

> Thou art to all lost loves the best,
> The only true plant found*

—That sort of thing. It is Herrick, I believe, and the
music was the reedy, irregular, lilting sound that goes

with Herrick. And it was dusk; the heavy, hewn, dark pillars that supported the gallery were like mourning presences; the fire had sunk to nothing—a mere glow amongst white ashes. . . . It was a sentimental sort of place and light and hour. . . .

And suddenly Nancy found that she was crying. She was crying quietly; she went on to cry with long convulsive sobs. It seemed to her that everything gay, everything charming, all light, all sweetness, had gone out of life. Unhappiness; unhappiness; unhappiness was all around her. She seemed to know no happy being and she herself was agonising. . . .

She remembered that Edward's eyes were hopeless; she was certain that he was drinking too much; at times he sighed deeply. He appeared as a man who was burning with inward flame; drying up in the soul with thirst; withering up in the vitals. Then, the torturing conviction came to her—the conviction that had visited her again and again—that Edward must love someone other than Leonora. With her little, pedagogic sectarianism she remembered that Catholics do not do this thing. But Edward was a Protestant. Then Edward loved somebody. . . .

And, after that thought, her eyes grew hopeless; she sighed as the old St. Bernard beside her did. At meals she would feel an intolerable desire to drink a glass of wine, and then another and then a third. Then she would find herself grow gay. . . . But in half an hour the gaiety went; she felt like a person who is burning up with an inward flame; desiccating at the soul with thirst; withering up in the vitals. One evening she went into Edward's gun-room—he had gone to a meeting of the National Reserve Committee. On the table beside his chair was a decanter of whiskey. She poured out a wine-glassful and drank it off.

Flame then really seemed to fill her body; her legs swelled; her face grew feverish. She dragged her tall height up to her room and lay in the dark. The bed reeled beneath her; she gave way to the thought that she was in Edward's arms; that he was kissing her on her face that burned; on her shoulders that burned, and on her neck that was on fire.

She never touched alcohol again. Not once after that did she have such thoughts. They died out of her mind; they left only a feeling of shame so insupportable that her brain could not take it in and they vanished. She imagined that her anguish at the thought of Edward's love for another person was solely sympathy for Leonora; she determined that the rest of her life must be spent in acting as Leonora's handmaiden—sweeping, tending, embroidering, like some Deborah,* some mediæval saint—I am not, unfortunately, up in the Catholic hagiology.* But I know that she pictured herself as some personage with a depressed, earnest face and tightly closed lips, in a clear white room, watering flowers or tending an embroidery frame. Or, she desired to go with Edward to Africa and to throw herself in the path of a charging lion so that Edward might be saved for Leonora at the cost of her life. Well, along with her sad thoughts she had her childish ones.

She knew nothing—nothing of life, except that one

must live sadly. That she now knew. What happened to her on the night when she received at once the blow that Edward wished her to go to her father in India and the blow of the letter from her mother was this. She called first upon her sweet Saviour— and she thought of Our Lord as her sweet Saviour!— that He might make it impossible that she should go to India. Then she realised from Edward's demeanour that he was determined that she should go to India. It must then be right that she should go. Edward was always right in his determinations. He was the Cid; he was Lohengrin; he was the Chevalier Bayard.

Nevertheless her mind mutinied and revolted. She could not leave that house. She imagined that he wished her gone that she might not witness his amours with another girl. Well, she was prepared to tell him that she was ready to witness his amours with another young girl. She would stay there—to comfort Leonora.

Then came the desperate shock of the letter from her mother. Her mother said, I believe, something like: "You have no right to go on living your life of prosperity and respect. You ought to be on the streets with me. How do you know that you are even Colonel Rufford's daughter?" She did not know what these words meant. She thought of her mother as sleeping beneath the arches whilst the snow fell. That was the impression conveyed to her mind by the words "on the streets." A platonic* sense of duty gave her the idea that she ought to go to comfort her mother—the mother that bore her, though she hardly knew what

the words meant. At the same time she knew that
her mother had left her father with another man—
therefore she pitied her father, and thought it terrible in herself that she trembled at the sound of her
father's voice. If her mother was that sort of woman
it was natural that her father should have had accesses*of madness in which he had struck herself to
the ground. And the voice of her conscience said to
her that her first duty was to her parents. It was in
accord with this awakened sense of duty that she un-
dressed with great care and meticulously folded the
clothes that she took off. Sometimes, but not very
often, she threw them helter-skelter about the room.

And that sense of duty was her prevailing mood
when Leonora, tall, clean-run, golden-haired, all in
black, appeared in her doorway, and told her that Edward was dying of love for her. She knew then with
her conscious mind what she had known within herself for months—that Edward was dying—actually
and physically dying—of love for her. It seemed to
her that for one short moment her spirit could say:
"*Domine, nunc dimittis.*" . . . Lord, now lettest thou
thy servant depart in peace." She imagined that she
could cheerfully go away to Glasgow and rescue her
fallen mother.

IV

A ND it seemed to her to be in tune with the mood, with the hour, and with the woman in front of her to say that she knew Edward was dying of love for her and that she was dying of love for Edward. For that fact had suddenly slipped into place and become real for her as the niched marker on a whist tablet slips round with the pressure of your thumb. That rubber at least was made.

And suddenly Leonora seemed to have become different and she seemed to have become different in her attitude towards Leonora. It was as if she, in her frail, white, silken kimono, sat beside her fire, but upon a throne. It was as if Leonora, in her close dress of black lace, with the gleaming white shoulders and the coiled yellow hair that the girl had always considered the most beautiful thing in the world—it was as if Leonora had become pinched, shrivelled, blue with cold, shivering, suppliant. Yet Leonora was commanding her. It was no good commanding her. She was going on the morrow to her mother who was in Glasgow.

Leonora went on saying that she must stay there to save Edward, who was dying of love for her. And, proud and happy in the thought that Edward loved her, and that she loved him, she did not even listen to what Leonora said. It appeared to her that it was

Leonora's business to save her husband's body; she, Nancy, possessed his soul—a precious thing that she would shield and bear away up in her arms—as if Leonora were a hungry dog, trying to spring up at a lamb that she was carrying. Yes, she felt as if Edward's love were a precious lamb that she were bearing away from a cruel and predatory beast. For, at that time, Leonora appeared to her as a cruel and predatory beast. Leonora, Leonora with her hunger, with her cruelty, had driven Edward to madness. He must be sheltered by his love for her and by her love —her love from a great distance and unspoken, enveloping him, surrounding him, upholding him; by her voice speaking from Glasgow, saying that she loved, that she adored, that she passed no moment without longing, loving, quivering at the thought of him.

Leonora said loudly, insistently, with a bitterly imperative tone:

"You must stay here; you must belong to Edward. I will divorce him."

The girl answered:

"The church does not allow of divorce. I cannot belong to your husband. I am going to Glasgow to rescue my mother."

The half-opened door opened noiselessly to the full. Edward was there. His devouring, doomed eyes were fixed on the girl's face; his shoulders slouched forward; he was undoubtedly half drunk and he had the whiskey decanter in one hand, a slanting candlestick in the other. He said, with a heavy ferocity, to Nancy:

"I forbid you to talk about these things. You are to stay here until I hear from your father. Then you will go to your father."

The two women, looking at each other, like beasts about to spring, hardly gave a glance to him. He leaned against the door-post. He said again:

"Nancy, I forbid you to talk about these things. I am the master of this house." And, at the sound of his voice, heavy, male, coming from a deep chest, in the night, with the blackness behind him, Nancy felt as if her spirit bowed before him, with folded hands. She felt that she would go to India, and that she desired never again to talk of these things.

Leonora said:

"You see that it is your duty to belong to him. He must not be allowed to go on drinking."

Nancy did not answer. Edward was gone; they heard him slipping and shambling on the polished black oak of the stairs. Nancy screamed when there came the sound of a heavy fall. Leonora said again:

"You see!"

The sounds went on from the hall below; the light of the candle Edward held flickered up between the hand rails of the gallery. Then they heard his voice:

"Give me Glasgow . . . Glasgow, in Scotland . . . I want the number of a man called White, of Simrock Park, Glasgow . . . Edward White, Simrock Park, Glasgow . . . ten minutes . . . at this time of night . . ." His voice was quite level, normal, and patient. Alcohol took him in the legs, not the speech. "I can wait," his voice came again. "Yes, I know they have a number. I have been in communication with them before."

"He is going to telephone to your mother," Leonora said. "He will make it all right for her." She got up and closed the door. She came back to the fire, and added bitterly: "He can always make it all right for everybody, except me—excepting me!"

The girl said nothing. She sat there in a blissful dream. She seemed to see her lover, sitting as he always sat, in a round-backed chair, in the dark hall— sitting low, with the receiver at his ear, talking in a gentle, slow voice, that he reserved for the telephone —and saving the world and her, in the black darkness. She moved her hand over the bareness of the base of her throat, to have the warmth of flesh upon it and upon her bosom.

She said nothing; Leonora went on talking. . . .

God knows what Leonora said. She repeated that the girl must belong to her husband. She said that she used that phrase because, though she might have a divorce, or even a dissolution of the marriage by the church, it would still be adultery that the girl and Edward would be committing. But she said that that was necessary; it was the price the girl must pay for the sin of having made Edward love her, for the sin of loving her husband. She talked on and on, beside the fire. The girl must become an adulteress; she had wronged Edward by being so beautiful, so gracious, so good. It was sinful to be so good. She must pay the price so as to save the man she had wronged.

In between her pauses the girl could hear the voice

of Edward, droning on, indistinguishably, with jerky pauses for replies. It made her glow with pride; the man she loved was working for her. He at least was resolved; was malely determined; knew the right thing. Leonora talked on with her eyes boring into Nancy's. The girl hardly looked at her and hardly heard her. After a long time Nancy said—after hours and hours:

"I shall go to India as soon as Edward hears from my father. I cannot talk about these things, because Edward does not wish it."

At that Leonora screamed out and wavered swiftly towards the closed door. And Nancy found that she was springing out of her chair with her white arms stretched wide. She was clasping the other woman to her breast; she was saying:

"Oh, my poor dear; oh, my poor dear." And they sat, crouching together in each other's arms, and crying and crying; and they lay down in the same bed, talking and talking, all through the night. And all through the night Edward could hear their voices through the wall. That was how it went. . . .

Next morning they were all three as if nothing had happened. Towards eleven Edward came to Nancy, who was arranging some Christmas roses in a silver bowl. He put a telegram beside her on the table. "You can uncode it for yourself," he said. Then, as he went out of the door, he said:

"You can tell your aunt I have cabled to Mr. Dowell to come over. He will make things easier till you leave."

The telegram, when it was uncoded, read, as far as I can remember:

"Will take Mrs. Rufford to Italy. Undertake to do this for certain. Am devotedly attached to Mrs. Rufford. Have no need of financial assistance. Did not know there was a daughter, and am much obliged to you for pointing out my duty.—White." It was something like that.

Then that household resumed its wonted course of days until my arrival.

V

IT is this part of the story that makes me saddest of all. For I ask myself unceasingly, my mind going round and round in a weary, baffled space of pain—what should these people have done? What, in the name of God, should they have done?

The end was perfectly plain to each of them—it was perfectly manifest at this stage that, if the girl did not, in Leonora's phrase, "belong to Edward," Edward must die, the girl must lose her reason because Edward died—and, that after a time, Leonora, who was the coldest and the strongest of the three, would console herself by marrying Rodney Bayham and have a quiet, comfortable, good time. That end, on that night, whilst Leonora sat in the girl's bedroom and Edward telephoned down below—that end was plainly manifest. The girl, plainly, was half-mad already; Edward was half dead; only Leonora, active, persistent, instinct with her cold passion of energy was "doing things." What then, should they have done? It worked out in the extinction of two very splendid personalities—for Edward and the girl *were* splendid personalities, in order that a third personality, more normal, should have, after a long period of trouble, a quiet, comfortable, good time.

I am writing this, now, I should say, a full eighteen

months after the words that end my last chapter.
Since writing the words "until my arrival," which I
see end that paragraph, I have seen again, for a
glimpse, from a swift train, Beaucaire, with the beautiful white tower, Tarascon with the square castles,
the great Rhone, the immense stretches of the Crau.
I have rushed through all Provence—and all Provence
no longer matters. It is no longer in the olive hills
that I shall find my Heaven; because there is only
Hell. . . .

Edward is dead; the girl is gone—oh, utterly gone;
Leonora is having her good time with Rodney Bayham, and I sit alone in Branshaw Teleragh. I have
been through Provence; I have seen Africa; I have
visited Asia to see, in Ceylon, in a darkened room, my
poor girl, sitting motionless, with her wonderful hair
about her, looking at me with eyes that did not see
me, and saying distinctly: *"Credo in unum Deum Omnipotentem.* . . . *Credo in unum Deum Omnipotentem."* Those are the only reasonable words she uttered; those are the only words, it appears, that she
ever will utter. I suppose that they are reasonable
words; it must be extraordinarily reasonable for her,
if she can say that she believes in an Omnipotent Deity.
Well, there it is. I am very tired of it all. . . .

For, I daresay, all this may sound romantic, but it is
tiring, tiring, tiring to have been in the midst of it; to
have taken the tickets; to have caught the trains; to
have chosen the cabins; to have consulted the purser
and the stewards as to diet for the quiescent patient
who did nothing but announce her belief in an Om-

nipotent Deity. That may sound romantic—but it is
just a record of fatigue.

I don't know why I should always be selected to be
serviceable. I don't resent it—but I have never been
the least good. Florence selected me for her own
purposes, and I was no good to her; Edward called
me to come and have a chat with him and I couldn't
stop him cutting his throat.

And then, one day eighteen months ago, I was
quietly writing in my room at Branshaw when Leonora came to me with a letter. It was a very pathetic
letter from Colonel Rufford about Nancy. Colonel
Rufford had left the army and had taken up the management of a tea-planting estate in Ceylon. His letter
was pathetic because it was so brief, so inarticulate
and so business-like. He had gone down to the boat
to meet his daughter and had found his daughter quite
mad. It appears that at Aden Nancy had seen in a
local paper the news of Edward's suicide. In the Red
Sea she had gone mad. She had remarked to Mrs.
Colonel Luton, who was chaperoning her, that she
believed in an Omnipotent Deity. She hadn't made any
fuss; her eyes were quite dry and glassy. Even when
she was mad Nancy could behave herself.

Colonel Rufford said the doctor did not anticipate
that there was any chance of his child's recovery. It
was, nevertheless, possible that, if she could see someone from Branshaw it might soothe her and it might
have a good effect. And he just simply wrote to Leonora: "Please come and see if you can do it."

I seem to have lost all sense of the pathetic; but still,

that simple, enormous request of the old colonel strikes me as pathetic. He was cursed by his atrocious temper; he had been cursed by a half-mad wife, who drank and went on the streets. His daughter was totally mad—and yet he believed in the goodness of human nature. He believed that Leonora would take the trouble to go all the way to Ceylon in order to soothe his daughter. Leonora wouldn't. Leonora didn't ever want to see Nancy again. I daresay that that, in the circumstances, was natural enough. At the same time she agreed, as it were, on public grounds, that someone soothing ought to go from Branshaw to Ceylon. She sent me and her old nurse, who had looked after Nancy from the time when the girl, a child of thirteen, had first come to Branshaw. So off I go, rushing through Provence, to catch the steamer at Marseilles. And I wasn't the least good when I got to Ceylon; and the nurse wasn't the least good. Nothing has been the least good.

The doctors said, at Kandy,* that if Nancy could be brought to England, the sea air, the change of climate, the voyage, and all the usual sort of things, might restore her reason. Of course, they haven't restored her reason. She is, I am aware, sitting in the hall, forty paces from where I am now writing. I don't want to be in the least romantic about it. She is very well dressed; she is quite quiet; she is very beautiful. The old nurse looks after her very efficiently.

Of course you have the makings of a situation here, but it is all very humdrum, as far as I am concerned.

I should marry Nancy if her reason were ever sufficiently restored to let her appreciate the meaning of the Anglican marriage service. But it is probable that her reason will never be sufficiently restored to let her appreciate the meaning of the Anglican marriage service. Therefore I cannot marry her, according to the law of the land.

So here I am very much where I started thirteen years ago. I am the attendant, not the husband, of a beautiful girl, who pays no attention to me. I am estranged from Leonora, who married Rodney Bayham in my absence and went to live at Bayham. Leonora rather dislikes me, because she has got it into her head that I disapprove of her marriage with Rodney Bayham. Well, I disapprove of her marriage. Possibly I am jealous.

Yes, no doubt I am jealous. In my fainter sort of way I seem to perceive myself following the lines of Edward Ashburnham. I suppose that I should really like to be a polygamist; with Nancy, and with Leonora, and with Maisie Maidan and possibly even with Florence. I am no doubt like every other man; only, probably because of my American origin I am fainter. At the same time I am able to assure you that I am a strictly respectable person. I have never done anything that the most anxious mother of a daughter or the most careful dean of a cathedral would object to. I have only followed, faintly, and in my unconscious desires, Edward Ashburnham. Well, it is all over. Not one of us has got what he really wanted. Leonora wanted Edward, and she has got Rodney Bayham, a pleasant enough sort of sheep. Florence wanted Branshaw, and it is I who have bought it from Leonora. I didn't really want it; what I wanted mostly was to cease being a nurse-attendant. Well, I am a nurse-attendant. Edward wanted Nancy Rufford and I have got her. Only she is mad. It is a queer and fantastic world. Why can't people have what they want? The things were all there to content everybody; yet everybody has the wrong thing. Perhaps you can make head or tail of it; it is beyond me.

Is there then any terrestrial paradise where, amidst the whispering of the olive-leaves, people can be with whom they like and have what they like and take their ease in shadows and in coolness? Or are all men's lives like the lives of us good people—like the lives of the Ashburnhams, of the Dowells, of the Ruffords —broken, tumultuous, agonised, and unromantic lives, periods punctuated by screams, by imbecilities, by deaths, by agonies? Who the devil knows?

For there was a great deal of imbecility about the closing scenes of the Ashburnham tragedy. Neither of those two women knew what they wanted. It was only Edward who took a perfectly clear line and he was drunk most of the time. But, drunk or sober, he stuck to what was demanded by convention and by the traditions of his house. Nancy Rufford had to be exported to India and Nancy Rufford hadn't to hear a word of love from him. She was exported to India and she never heard a word from Edward Ashburnham.

It was the conventional line; it was in tune with the tradition of Edward's house. I daresay it worked out for the greatest good of the body politic. Conventions and traditions I suppose work blindly but surely for the preservation of the normal type; for the extinction of proud, resolute and unusual individuals.

Edward was the normal man, but there was too much of the sentimentalist about him and society does not need too many sentimentalists. Nancy was a splendid creature but she had about her a touch of madness. Society does not need individuals with touches of madness about them. So Edward and Nancy found themselves steam-rolled out and Leonora survives, the perfectly normal type, married to a man who is rather like a rabbit. For Rodney Bayham is rather like a rabbit and I hear that Leonora is expected to have a baby in three months' time.

So those splendid and tumultuous creatures with their magnetism and their passions—those two that I really loved—have gone from this earth. It is no doubt best for them. What would Nancy have made of Edward if she had succeeded in living with him; what would Edward have made of her? For there was about Nancy a touch of cruelty—a touch of definite actual cruelty that made her desire to see people suffer. Yes, she desired to see Edward suffer. And, by God, she gave him hell.

She gave him an unimaginable hell. Those two women pursued that poor devil and flayed the skin off him as if they had done it with whips. I tell you his mind bled almost visibly. I seem to see him stand, naked to the waist, his forearms shielding his eyes, and flesh hanging from him in rags. I tell you that is no exaggeration of what I feel. It was as if Leonora and Nancy banded themselves together to do execution, for the sake of humanity, upon the body of a man who was at their disposal. They were like a couple of Sioux who had got hold of an Apache and had him well tied to a stake. I tell you there was no end to the tortures they inflicted upon him.

Night after night he would hear them talking; talking; maddened, sweating, seeking oblivion in drink, he would lie there and hear the voices going on and on. And day after day Leonora would come to him and would announce the results of their deliberations.

They were like judges debating over the sentence upon a criminal; they were like ghouls with an immobile corpse in a tomb beside them.

I don't think that Leonora was any more to blame than the girl—though Leonora was the more active of the two. Leonora, as I have said, was the perfectly normal woman. I mean to say that in normal circumstances her desires were those of the woman who is needed by society. She desired children, decorum, an establishment; she desired to avoid waste, she desired to keep up appearances. She was utterly and entirely normal even in her utterly undeniable beauty. But I don't mean to say that she acted perfectly normally in this perfectly abnormal situation. All the world was mad around her and she herself, agonised, took on the complexion of a mad woman; of a woman very wicked; of the villain of the piece. What would you have? Steel is a normal, hard, polished substance. But, if you put it in a hot fire it will become red, soft, and not to be handled. If you put it in a fire still more hot it will drip away. It was like that with Leonora. She was made for normal circumstances—for Mr. Rodney Bayham, who will keep a separate establishment, secretly, in Portsmouth, and make occasional trips to Paris and to Buda-Pesth.*

In the case of Edward and the girl Leonora broke and simply went all over the place. She adopted unfamiliar and therefore extraordinary and ungraceful attitudes of mind. At one moment she was all for revenge. After haranguing the girl for hours through the night she harangued for hours of the day the silent Edward. And Edward just once tripped up and that was his undoing. Perhaps he had had too much whiskey that afternoon.

She asked him perpetually what he wanted. What did he want? What did he want? And all he ever answered was: "I have told you." He meant that he wanted the girl to go to her father in India as soon as her father should cable that he was ready to receive her. But just once he tripped up. To Leonora's eternal question he answered that all he desired in life was that—that he could pick himself together again and go on with his daily occupations if—the girl being five thousand miles away, would continue to love him. He wanted nothing more. He prayed his God for nothing more. Well, he was a sentimentalist.

And the moment that she heard that Leonora determined that the girl should not go five thousand miles away and that she should not continue to love Edward. The way she worked it was this:

She continued to tell the girl that she must belong to Edward; she was going to get a divorce; she was going to get a dissolution of marriage from Rome. But she considered it to be her duty to warn the girl of the sort of monster that Edward was. She told the girl of La Dolciquita, of Mrs. Basil, of Maisie Maidan, of Florence. She spoke of the agonies that she had endured during her life with the man, who was violent, overbearing, vain, drunken, arrogant, and monstrously a prey to his sexual necessities. And, at hearing of the miseries her aunt had suffered—for Leonora once more had the aspect of an aunt to the girl—with the swift cruelty of youth and, with the swift solidarity that attaches woman to woman, the girl made her resolves. Her aunt said incessantly: "You must save Edward's life; you must save his life. All that he needs is a little period of satisfaction from you. Then he will tire of you as he has of the others. But you must save his life."

And, all the while, that wretched fellow knew, by a curious instinct that runs between human beings living together—exactly what was going on. And he remained dumb; he stretched out no finger to help himself. All that he required to keep himself a decent member of society was, that the girl, five thousand miles away, should continue to love him. They were putting a stopper upon that.

I have told you that the girl came one night to his room. And that was the real hell for him. That was the picture that never left his imagination—the girl, in the dim light, rising up at the foot of his bed. He said that it seemed to have a greenish sort of effect as if there were a greenish tinge in the shadows of the tall bedposts that framed her body. And she looked at him with her straight eyes of an unflinching cruelty and she said: "I am ready to belong to you—to save your life."

He answered: "I don't want it; I don't want it; I don't want it."

And he says that he didn't want it; that he would have hated himself; that it was unthinkable. And all the while he had the immense temptation to do the unthinkable thing, not from the physical desire but because of a mental certitude. He was certain that if she had once submitted to him she would remain his forever. He knew that.

She was thinking that her aunt had said he had desired her to love him from a distance of five thousand miles. She said: "I can never love you now I know the kind of man you are. I will belong to you to save your life. But I can never love you."

It was a fantastic display of cruelty. She didn't in the least know what it meant—to belong to a man. But, at that, Edward pulled himself together. He spoke in his normal tones; gruff, husky, overbearing, as he would have done to a servant or to a horse.

"Go back to your room," he said.   "Go back to your room and go to sleep.   This is all nonsense."

They were baffled, those two women.
And then I came on the scene.

VI

MY coming on the scene certainly calmed things down—for the whole fortnight that intervened between my arrival and the girl's departure. I don't mean to say that the endless talking did not go on at night or that Leonora did not send me out with the girl and, in the interval, give Edward a hell of a time. Having discovered what he wanted —that the girl should go five thousand miles away and love him steadfastly as people do in sentimental novels, she was determined to smash that aspiration. And she repeated to Edward in every possible tone that the girl did not love him; that the girl detested him for his brutality, his overbearingness, his drinking habits. She pointed out that Edward, in the girl's eyes, was already pledged three or four deep. He was pledged to Leonora herself, to Mrs. Basil and to the memories of Maisie Maidan and of Florence. Edward never said anything.

Did the girl love Edward, or didn't she? I don't know. At that time I daresay she didn't, though she certainly had done so before Leonora had got to work upon his reputation. She certainly had loved him for what I will call the public side of his record—for his good soldiering, for his saving lives at sea, for the excellent landlord that he was and the good sportsman. But it is quite possible that all those things

280

came to appear as nothing in her eyes when she discovered that he wasn't a good husband. For, though women, as I see them, have little or no feeling of responsibility towards a county or a country or a career—although they may be entirely lacking in any kind of communal solidarity—they have an immense and automatically working instinct that attaches them to the interest of womanhood. It is, of course, possible for any woman to cut out and to carry off any other woman's husband or lover. But I rather think that a woman will only do this if she has reason to believe that the other woman has given her husband a bad time. I am certain that if she thinks the man has been a brute to his wife she will, with her instinctive feeling for suffering femininity, "put him back," as the saying is. I don't attach any particular importance to these generalisations of mine. They may be right, they may be wrong; I am only an ageing American with very little knowledge of life. You may take my generalisations or leave them. But I am pretty certain that I am right in the case of Nancy Rufford—that she had loved Edward Ashburnham very deeply and tenderly.

It is nothing to the point that she let him have it good and strong as soon as she discovered that he had been unfaithful to Leonora and that his public services had cost more than Leonora thought they ought to have cost. Nancy would be bound to let him have it good and strong then. She would owe that to feminine public opinion; she would be driven to it by the instinct for self-preservation, since she might

well imagine that if Edward had been unfaithful to
Leonora, to Mrs. Basil and to the memories of the
other two he might be unfaithful to herself. And, no
doubt, she had her share of the sex instinct that makes
women be intolerably cruel to the beloved person.
Anyhow, I don't know whether, at this point, Nancy
Rufford loved Edward Ashburnham. I don't know
whether she even loved him when, on getting, at Aden,
the news of his suicide she went mad. Because that
may just as well have been for the sake of Leonora
as for the sake of Edward. Or it may have been
for the sake of both of them. I don't know. I know
nothing. I am very tired.

Leonora held passionately the doctrine that the girl
didn't love Edward. She wanted desperately to believe that. It was a doctrine as necessary to her existence as a belief in the personal immortality of the
soul. She said that it was impossible that Nancy could
have loved Edward after she had given the girl her
view of Edward's career and character. Edward, on
the other hand, believed maunderingly that some es-
sential attractiveness in himself must have made the
girl continue to go on loving him—to go on loving
him, as it were, in underneath her official aspect of
hatred. He thought she only pretended to hate him
in order to save her face and he thought that her quite
atrocious telegram from Brindisi was only another attempt to do that—to prove that she had feelings creditable to a member of the feminine commonweal. I
don't know. I leave it to you.

There is another point that worries me a good deal

in the aspects of this sad affair. Leonora says that, in desiring that the girl should go five thousand miles away and yet continue to love him, Edward was a monster of selfishness. He was desiring the ruin of a young life. Edward on the other hand put it to me that, supposing that the girl's love was a necessity to his existence, and, if he did nothing by word or by action to keep Nancy's love alive, he couldn't be called selfish. Leonora replied that showed he had an abominably selfish nature even though his actions might be perfectly correct. I can't make out which of them was right. I leave it to you.

It is, at any rate, certain that Edward's actions were perfectly—were monstrously, were cruelly—correct. He sat still and let Leonora take away his character, and let Leonora damn him to deepest hell, without stirring a finger. I daresay he was a fool; I don't see what object there was in letting the girl think worse of him than was necessary. Still there it is. And there it is also that all those three presented to the world the spectacle of being the best of good people. I assure you that during my stay for that fortnight in that fine old house, I never so much as noticed a single thing that could have affected that good opinion. And even when I look back, knowing the circumstances, I can't remember a single thing any of them said that could have betrayed them. I can't remember, right up to the dinner, when Leonora read out that telegram—not the tremor of an eyelash, not the shaking of a hand. It was just a pleasant country house-party.

And Leonora kept it up jolly well, for even longer than that—she kept it up as far as I was concerned until eight days after Edward's funeral. Immediately after that particular dinner—the dinner at which I received the announcement that Nancy was going to leave for India on the following day—I asked Leonora to let me have a word with her. She took me into her little sitting-room and I then said—I spare you the record of my emotions—that she was aware that I wished to marry Nancy; that she had seemed to favour my suit and that it appeared to be rather a waste of money upon tickets and rather a waste of time upon travel to let the girl go to India if Leonora thought that there was any chance of her marrying me.

And Leonora, I assure you, was the absolutely perfect British matron. She said that she quite favoured my suit; that she could not desire for the girl a better husband; but that she considered that the girl ought to see a little more of life before taking such an important step. Yes, Leonora used the words "taking such an important step." She was perfect. Actually, I think she would have liked the girl to marry me well enough but my programme included the buying of the Kershaws' house, about a mile and a half away upon the Fordingbridge road, and settling down there with the girl. That didn't at all suit Leonora. She didn't want to have the girl within a mile and a half of Edward for the rest of their lives. Still, I think she might have managed to let me know, in some periphrasis or other, that I might have the girl if I would take her to Philadelphia or Timbuctoo. I loved Nancy very much—and Leonora knew it.

However, I left it at that. I left it with the understanding that Nancy was going away to India on probation. It seemed to me a perfectly reasonable arrangement and I am a reasonable sort of man. I simply said that I should follow Nancy out to India after six months' time or so. Or, perhaps, after a year. Well, you see, I did follow Nancy out to India after a year. . . .

I must confess to having felt a little angry with Leonora for not having warned me earlier that the girl would be going. I took it as one of the queer, not very straight methods that Roman Catholics seem to adopt in dealing with matters of this world. I took it that Leonora had been afraid I should propose to the girl or, at any rate, have made considerably greater advances to her than I did, if I had known earlier that she was going away so soon. Perhaps Leonora was right; perhaps Roman Catholics, with their queer, shifty ways, are always right. They are dealing with the queer, shifty thing that is human nature. For it is quite possible that, if I had known Nancy was going away so soon, I should have tried making love to her. And that would have produced another complication. It may have been just as well.

It is queer the fantastic things that quite good people will do in order to keep up their appearance of calm poco-curantism.* For Edward Ashburnham and his wife called me half the world over in order to sit on the back seat of a dog-cart whilst Edward drove

the girl to the railway station from which she was to
take her departure to India. They wanted, I suppose,
to have a witness of the calmness of that function.
The girl's luggage had been already packed and sent
off before. Her berth on the steamer had been taken.
They had timed it all so exactly that it went like clock-
work. They had known the date upon which Colonel
Rufford would get Edward's letter and they had
known almost exactly the hour at which they would
receive his telegram asking his daughter to come to
him. It had all been quite beautifully and quite mer-
cilessly arranged, by Edward himself. They gave
Colonel Rufford, as a reason for telegraphing, the fact
that Mrs. Colonel Somebody or other would be travelling by that ship and that she would serve as an efficient chaperon for the girl. It was a most amazing
business, and I think that it would have been better
in the eyes of God if they had all attempted to gouge
out each other's eyes with carving knives. But they
were "good people."

After my interview with Leonora I went desultorily
into Edward's gun-room. I didn't know where the
girl was and I thought I might find her there. I suppose I had a vague idea of proposing to her in spite
of Leonora. So, I presume, I don't come of quite
such good people as the Ashburnhams. Edward was
lounging in his chair smoking a cigar and he said
nothing for quite five minutes. The candles glowed
in the green shades; the reflections were green in the
glasses of the book-cases that held guns and fishing-
rods. Over the mantel-piece was the brownish pic-

ture of the white horse. Those were the quietest moments that I have ever known. Then, suddenly, Edward looked me straight in the eyes and said:

"Look here, old man, I wish you would drive with Nancy and me to the station to-morrow."

I said that of course I would drive with him and Nancy to the station on the morrow. He lay there for a long time, looking along the line of his knees at the fluttering fire and then suddenly, in a perfectly calm voice, and without lifting his eyes, he said:

"I am so desperately in love with Nancy Rufford that I am dying of it."

Poor devil—he hadn't meant to speak of it. But I guess he just had to speak to somebody and I appeared to be like a woman or a solicitor. He talked all night.

Well, he carried out the programme to the last breath.

It was a very clear winter morning, with a good deal of frost in it. The sun was quite bright, the winding road between the heather and the bracken was very hard. I sat on the back seat of the dog-cart; Nancy was beside Edward. They talked about the way the cob went; Edward pointed out with the whip a cluster of deer upon a coombe three-quarters of a mile away. We passed the hounds in the level bit of road beside the high trees going into Fordingbridge and Edward pulled up the dog-cart so that Nancy might say good-bye to the huntsman and cap him a last sovereign. She had ridden with those hounds ever since she had been thirteen.

The train was five minutes late and they imagined that that was because it was market-day at Swindon or wherever the train came from. That was the sort of thing they talked about. The train came in; Edward found her a first-class carriage with an elderly woman in it. The girl entered the carriage, Edward closed the door and then she put out her hand to shake mine. There was upon those people's faces no expression of any kind whatever. The signal for the train's departure was a very bright red; that is about as passionate a statement as I can get into that scene. She was not looking her best; she had on a cap of brown fur that did not very well match her hair. She said:

"So long," to Edward.

Edward answered: "So long."

He swung round on his heel and, large, slouching, and walking with a heavy deliberate pace, he went out of the station. I followed him and got up beside him in the high dog-cart. It was the most horrible performance I have ever seen.

And, after that, a holy peace, like the peace of God which passes all understanding,* descended upon Branshaw Teleragh. Leonora went about her daily duties with a sort of triumphant smile—a very faint smile, but quite triumphant. I guess she had so long since given up any idea of getting her man back that it was enough for her to have got the girl out of the house and well cured of her infatuation. Once, in the hall, when Leonora was going out, Edward said, beneath his breath—but I just caught the words:

"Thou hast conquered, O pale Galilean."*

It was like his sentimentality to quote Swinburne.

But he was perfectly quiet and he had given up drinking. The only thing that he ever said to me after that drive to the station was:

"It's very odd. I think I ought to tell you, Dowell, that I haven't any feelings at all about the girl now it's all over. Don't you worry about me. I'm all right." A long time afterwards he said: "I guess it was only a flash in the pan." He began to look after the estates again; he took all that trouble over getting off the gardener's daughter who had murdered her baby. He shook hands smilingly with every farmer in the market-place. He addressed two political meetings; he hunted twice. Leonora made him a frightful scene about spending the two hundred pounds on getting the gardener's daughter acquitted. Everything went on as if the girl had never existed. It was very still weather.

Well, that is the end of the story. And, when I come to look at it I see that it is a happy ending with wedding bells and all. The villains—for obviously Edward and the girl were villains—have been punished by suicide and madness. The heroine—the perfectly normal, virtuous and slightly deceitful heroine —has become the happy wife of a perfectly normal, virtuous and slightly-deceitful husband. She will shortly become a mother of a perfectly normal, vir-

tuous, slightly-deceitful son or daughter. A happy
ending, that is what it works out at.

I cannot conceal from myself the fact that I now
dislike Leonora. Without doubt I am jealous of Rodney Bayham. But I don't know whether it is merely
a jealousy arising from the fact that I desired myself
to possess Leonora or whether it is because to her
were sacrificed the only two persons that I have ever
really loved—Edward Ashburnham and Nancy Rufford. In order to set her up in a modern mansion,
replete with every convenience and dominated by a
quite respectable and eminently economical master of
the house, it was necessary that Edward and Nancy
Rufford should become, for me at least, no more than
tragic shades.

I seem to see poor Edward, naked and reclining
amidst darkness, upon cold rocks, like one of the ancient Greek damned, in Tartarus*or wherever it was.

And as for Nancy . . . Well, yesterday at lunch she
said suddenly:

"Shuttlecocks!"*

And she repeated the word "shuttlecocks" three
times. I know what was passing in her mind, if she
can be said to have a mind, for Leonora has told me
that, once, the poor girl said she felt like a shuttlecock being tossed backwards and forwards between
the violent personalities of Edward and his wife. Leonora, she said, was always trying to deliver her over
to Edward, and Edward tacitly and silently forced
her back again. And the odd thing was that Edward
himself considered that those two women used *him*

like a shuttlecock. Or, rather, he said that they sent him backwards and forwards like a blooming parcel that someone didn't want to pay the postage on. And Leonora also imagined that Edward and Nancy picked her up and threw her down as suited their purely vagrant moods. So there you have the pretty picture. Mind, I am not preaching anything contrary to accepted morality. I am not advocating free love in this or any other case. Society must go on, I suppose, and society can only exist if the normal, if the virtuous, and the slightly-deceitful flourish, and if the passionate, the headstrong, and the too-truthful are condemned to suicide and to madness. But I guess that I myself, in my fainter way, come into the category of the passionate, of the headstrong, and the too-truthful. For I can't conceal from myself the fact that I loved Edward Ashburnham—and that I love him because he was just myself. If I had had the courage and the virility and possibly also the physique of Edward Ashburnham I should, I fancy, have done much what he did. He seems to me like a large elder brother who took me out on several excursions and did many dashing things whilst I just watched him robbing the orchards, from a distance. And, you see, I am just as much of a sentimentalist as he was. . . .

Yes, society must go on; it must breed, like rabbits. That is what we are here for. But then, I don't like society—much. I am that absurd figure, an American millionaire, who has bought one of the ancient haunts of English peace. I sit here, in Edward's gun-room, all day and all day in a house that is absolutely quiet.

No one visits me, for I visit no one. No one is interested in me, for I have no interests. In twenty minutes or so I shall walk down to the village, beneath my own oaks, alongside my own clumps of gorse, to get the American mail. My tenants, the village boys and the tradesmen will touch their hats to me. So life peters out. I shall return to dine and Nancy will sit opposite me with the old nurse standing behind her. Enigmatic, silent, utterly well-behaved as far as her knife and fork go, Nancy will stare in front of her with the blue eyes that have over them strained, stretched brows. Once, or perhaps twice, during the meal her knife and fork will be suspended in mid-air as if she were trying to think of something that she had forgotten. Then she will say that she believes in an Omnipotent Deity or she will utter the one word, "shuttlecocks," perhaps. It is very extraordinary to see the perfect flush of health on her cheeks, to see the lustre of her coiled black hair, the poise of the head upon the neck, the grace of the white hands— and to think that it all means nothing—that it is a picture without a meaning. Yes, it is queer.

But, at any rate, there is always Leonora to cheer you up; I don't want to sadden you. Her husband is quite an economical person of so normal a figure that he can get quite a large proportion of his clothes ready-made. That is the great desideratum of life, and that is the end of my story. The child is to be brought up as a Romanist.

It suddenly occurs to me that I have forgotten to

say how Edward met his death. You remember that
peace had descended upon the house; that Leonora
was quietly triumphant and that Edward said his love
for the girl had been merely a passing phase. Well,
one afternoon we were in the stables together, looking at a new kind of flooring that Edward was trying
in a loose-box.* Edward was talking with a good
deal of animation about the necessity of getting the
numbers of the Hampshire territorials* up to the
proper standard. He was quite sober, quite quiet, his
skin was clear-coloured; his hair was golden and perfectly brushed; the level brick-dust red of his complexion went clean up to the rims of his eyelids; his
eyes were porcelain blue and they regarded me frankly
and directly. His face was perfectly expressionless;
his voice was deep and rough. He stood well back
upon his legs and said:

"We ought to get them up to two thousand three
hundred and fifty."

A stable-boy brought him a telegram and went away.
He opened it negligently, regarded it without emotion, and, in complete silence, handed it to me. On
the pinkish paper in a sprawled handwriting I read:
"Safe Brindisi. Having rattling good time. Nancy."

Well, Edward was the English gentleman; but he
was also, to the last, a sentimentalist, whose mind
was compounded of indifferent poems and novels. He
just looked up to the roof of the stable, as if he were
looking to Heaven, and whispered something that I
did not catch.

Then he put two fingers into the waistcoat pocket

of his grey, frieze suit; they came out with a little neat pen-knife—quite a small pen-knife. He said to me:

"You might just take that wire to Leonora." And he looked at me with a direct, challenging, brow-beating glare. I guess he could see in my eyes that I didn't intend to hinder him. Why should I hinder him?

I didn't think he was wanted in the world, let his confounded tenants, his rifle-associations, his drunkards, reclaimed and unreclaimed, get on as they liked. Not all the hundreds and hundreds of them deserved that that poor devil should go on suffering for their sakes.

When he saw that I did not intend to interfere with him his eyes became soft and almost affectionate. He remarked:

"So long, old man, I must have a bit of a rest, you know."

I didn't know what to say. I wanted to say, "God bless you," for I also am a sentimentalist. But I thought that perhaps that would not be quite English good form, so I trotted off with the telegram to Leonora. She was quite pleased with it.

EXPLANATORY NOTES

At the time of *The Good Soldier*, Germany was a large empire extending from Russia to the western border of Alsace-Lorraine. It was composed of twenty-six states and divisions; over half its area comprised the kingdom of Prussia. At this time, India was of course part of the British Empire. The following notes reflect political divisions prior to the Great War.

1 *To Stella Ford*: the Dedicatory Letter was written especially for the second American edition (1927) and included in the second English edition (1928). Stella Bowen (1893–1947), Australian-born painter, was Ford's mistress 1919–27 and mother of his third child, Julia.

2 *Conrad*: Joseph Conrad (1857–1924), Polish-born English novelist; Ford's literary collaborator and intimate friend, especially from 1898 to 1909.

Cubists, Vorticists, Imagistes: practitioners of three pre-war avant-garde movements in the visual arts and/or literature. Cubism, developed by Picasso as early as 1907 and continuing into the 1920s, broke with the tradition of visual realism; it fragmented the planes and volumes of the three-dimensional object and recomposed them from several perspectives. Vorticism, led by Wyndham Lewis, flourished 1912–15; it attacked the sentimentality of Victorian art and celebrated violence, energy, and the machine in designs of geometric abstraction. Imagism, a revolt against romanticism by certain English and American poets led by Ezra Pound, flourished from about 1910 to 1917; it advocated direct presentation of the object, musical cadence rather than metrical regularity, and treatment of the image with hard, clean precision rather than symbolic intent. Ford said that, as early as the 1890s, he was following, in his own verse-writing, most of the tenets of Imagism.

tapageur: noisy, showy.

Jeunes: the Young; Ford's affectionate term for the youthful immediately pre-war generation of avant-garde writers.

Great Auk: non-flying sea-bird, with a large body and small wings; extinct since 1844.

Thrush: a short-lived poetry magazine. Although Ford published an essay in the *Thrush* in December 1909, he did not announce his determination to 'drop creative writing' until December 1914, in a magazine called *Poetry and Drama*.

Ezra . . . H. D.: Ezra Pound (1885–1972), American expatriate poet, critic, and translator. In 1909 Ford published nine of Pound's poems in the *English Review*; Pound and Ford soon became close and lifelong friends. *Eliot*: T. S. Eliot (1888–1965), American poet and critic who made his home in London; Stella Bowen had met Pound and Eliot before she met Ford. *Wyndham Lewis*: (Percy) Wyndham Lewis (1884–1957), British painter and writer. Ford published three essays of his in the *English Review*; Lewis published an opening portion of *The Good Soldier* in his magazine *Blast* in June 1914. *H. D.*: H[ilda] D[oolittle] (1886–1961), expatriate American Imagist poet. A friend of Ford's, she served as one of his amanuenses for *The Good Soldier*.

3 *translate it into French*: Ford began translating *The Good Soldier* during the Battle of the Somme in 1916; he apparently finished it in Paris in 1924. This translation was, however, never published. The first French translation to appear was by Jacques Papy (1953).

Maupassant: Guy de Maupassant (1850–1893), French realist short-story writer, and novelist deeply admired by Ford. He published *Fort Comme la Mort* (*Strong as Death*) in 1889.

John Rodker: (1894–1955) minor English poet, novelist, publisher, and translator from the French of such writers as Lautréamont, Romains, and Montherlant.

Mr. Lane: John Lane (1854–1926), publisher and founder, in 1887, of The Bodley Head.

5 *"Beati Immaculati"*: see Psalm 119. 1: 'Blessed are the undefiled in the way, who walk in the law of the Lord.' Commonly used in the liturgy; indeed, all Ford's uses of Catholic Latin would be familiar to those who, like his daughters, attended Catholic schools.

7 *Nice . . . Bordighera*: Nice, leading resort city on the French

Riviera. Bordighera, winter resort town on the northeastern coast of Italy.

Nauheim: Bad Nauheim, in the grand duchy of Hesse-Darmstadt, on the north-east slopes of the Taunus Mountains, near Frankfurt; a famous spa and holiday resort, it has several parks; its saline springs are particularly recommended for people with heart problems. Patients at spas follow strict, individualized cures prescribed by their specialists: the number of baths to be taken in the bathhouses (at Nauheim, usually two baths on successive days followed by a day off), the temperature of the bath, the amount of mineral water to be drunk (in sips), the food to be consumed, the amount of exercise. The Kur orchestra plays three times a day at given places and hours. A cure ticket admits one to the Trinkhalle (Pump Room) and to the Kurhaus with its music and reading rooms, concert hall, and wide terrace lit by thousands of lamps.

8 *Ashburnham*: Ford told about his loyalty to Charles I in *The Cinque Ports* (1900).

9 *Cranford*: allusion to Elizabeth Gaskell's novel (1853) about a quiet, old-fashioned, country village.

Chestnut and Walnut Streets: two streets in downtown Philadelphia near City Hall and fashionable Rittenhouse Square.

wampum: beads used by American Indians as money, decoration, or ceremonial pledges.

William Penn: (1644–1718) English Quaker leader who founded the state of Pennsylvania.

Fordingbridge: Hampshire market town.

10 *Homburg*: Bad Homburg, German spa town in the Taunus Mountains; famous for its mineral springs.

favours: ribbons worn as decorations at a party.

Trianon: small villa in the royal park at Versailles.

Hessian: pertaining to Hesse, grand duchy of south-west Germany, split by a narrow strip of Prussian territory.

Nirvana: supreme goal of Buddhist meditation; characterized by the extinction of desire and individuality.

11 *Wald*: forest.

12 *Swedish exercises*: system of therapeutic exercises.

13 *county family*: a family belonging to the gentry with an ancestral seat in a county.

14 *in saeculum saeculorum*: for ever and ever. (More commonly *in saeculo saeculorum* or *in saeculo saeculi*.) Standard in the liturgy.

17 *Peire Vidal*: (?–1200) Provençal troubadour. Ford's father, Francis Hueffer, discusses him at length in his book *The Troubadours: a History of Provençal Life and Literature in the Middle Ages* (1878).

mistral: violent cold dry wind in the south of France.

18 *Vassar*: exclusive women's college in Poughkeepsie, New York.

William the Silent (1533–84) Prince of Orange; led the revolt of the Netherlands against Spain.

Gustave the Loquacious: presumably Gustavus I Vasa (1496–1560), king of Sweden (1523–60), founder of the modern Swedish state.

Fantin Latour: (1836–1904) French painter, printmaker, and illustrator.

Flatiron: early New York skyscraper (1902), so called because of its wedge shape.

19 *crowstepped*: with step-like projections.

palazzi: Italian mansions, palaces.

modistes: milliners; dressmakers.

plages: beaches.

20 *Browning tea*: tea held to discuss the life and works of the English poet Robert Browning (1812–89).

Fourteenth Street: major thoroughfare in lower Manhattan.

Stuyvesant crowd: people who live near Stuyvesant Square in Manhattan; named for the last Dutch governor of New York, Peter Stuyvesant (1592–1672).

Franz Hals: (1580?–1666) Dutch portrait and genre painter.

Woovermans: family of seventeenth-century Dutch landscape painters.

Pre-Mycenaic: pertaining to Greek civilization of the Middle Bronze Age (about 2000–1550 BC).

Gnossos: or Knossos, city in ancient Crete excavated between 1900 and 1908; legendary site of the palace of King Minos.

Walter Pater: (1839–94) English essayist, critic, and aesthetician.

21 *chatelaine*: mistress of a château.

Troubadour: one of the poet–musicians who composed intricate romantic love lyrics between the eleventh and thirteenth centuries, chiefly in Provence.

22 *Holy Sepulchre*: church in Jerusalem built on the traditional site of Christ's crucifixion and burial.

Misses Hurlbird: Ford tells in *Return to Yesterday* how he met 'two adorably old-maidish maiden ladies from Stamford, Conn.' named Hurlbird in a Rhineland hydropathic establishment. The meeting occurred in November 1904, during Ford's severe nervous illness; two years later Ford and Elsie Hueffer visited the Hurlbirds in their American home.

Waterbury: Connecticut industrial town famous for its manufacture of clocks and watches.

23 *Democrat ... Republican*: members of the two chief US political parties, the former associated with social reform and the latter with business and financial interests. The Democrats elected only one president between 1860 and 1912.

24 *North Cape*: presumably the northernmost point of New Zealand's North Island, though there are other North Capes.

25 *New Forest*: Ford visited this large wooded area in Hampshire in the spring of 1904 seeking relief from his nervous breakdown.

29 *Leghorn hat*: straw hat.

Chapeau de Paille: *The Straw Hat*, by Flemish painter Peter Paul Rubens (1577–1640).

31 *Fourteenth Hussars*: light cavalry regiment.

32 *Martingales*: straps for checking or steadying the upward movement of horses' heads.

Chiffney: jockey Samuel Chiffney (1753?–1807), inventor of a horse's bit.

plater: an inferior racehorse.

Burlington Arcade: covered passageway in London's Piccadilly; famous for its small shops.

33 *Gadarene swine*: see Matt. 8: 28–32.

35 *Assizes*: sessions of the High Court of Justice, held periodically in English counties.

36 *Wiesbaden*: German town and spa in the Prussian province of Hesse-Nassau near Mainz and the Rhine.

Bonner Hussaren: hussars of Bonn, Germany.

Lelöffel: Ford and Violet Hunt knew a polo-playing German lieutenant named Count Lelöffel in Nauheim in 1910.

38 *plastron*: man's starched shirt front.

39 *corsage*: the bodice of a woman's dress.

41 *round table*: allusion to King Arthur's Knights of the Round Table. In *Rossetti* (1902), Ford quotes the painter's comment on the demise of the Pre-Raphaelite Brotherhood: 'So now the whole Round Table is dissolved.'

42 *Fachingen water*: a German mineral spring water.

43 *Grand Duke*: it was the Grand Duke of Hesse-Darmstadt whom Ford and Violet Hunt met in Nauheim and who expected to be asked out to dinner. 'Nassau Schwerin' is probably a fictitious title.

bonne bouche: tidbit; special treat.

44 *traps*: luggage.

45 *Kummel*: cumin-flavoured German liqueur.

Æsculapius: Greek god of medicine. Those healed at his temples would offer a sacrifice—usually a cock—to him.

46 *M——*: Marburg, ancient German university town in the Prussian province of Hesse-Nassau and site, in 1529, of a theological conference between Luther and Zwingli on the subject of Transubstantiation.

47 *St. Elizabeth of Hungary*: (1207–31) princess canonized for her ministrations to the sick and her extreme generosity; she built a hospice for the poor in Marburg.

Lahn: tributary of the Rhine.

pour le bon motif: for valid reasons.

Baedeker: famous series of nineteenth-century German guide-books; first English edition in 1861.

Ludwig the Courageous: Dowell means Philip the Magnanimous, Landgrave of Hesse (1504–67). A zealous protector of German Protestants, he called the Marburg Conference in 1529. Later, he pressured Luther into permitting him to enter a bigamous marriage. Philip had a son and a grandson named Ludwig; both became landgraves of Hessian states.

48   *muffs:* people awkard at athletics.

Armenians: followers of a seventeenth-century progressive theo-logical movement reacting against Calvinism and based on the ideas of Dutch theologian Jacobus Arminius (1560–1609); *Erastians:* upholders of state supremacy in ecclesiastical affairs; named for the Swiss theologian Thomas Erastus (1524–83).

49   *Mrs. Markham:* pseudonym of Mrs Elizabeth Penrose (1780–1837), author of popular histories for schoolchildren.

Schloss: castle.

History of the Popes . . . Table Talk: History of the Popes: history of the papacy by Leopold von Ranke (1795–1886), known as the father of modern historiography. *Renaissance:* series of essays (1875–86) on the Italian Renaissance by English biographer, poet, and essayist John Addington Symonds (1840–93). *Rise of the Dutch Republic:* a classic work (1856) by the American histor-ian John Lothrop Motley (1814–77); it celebrates the triumph of Protestantism and political freedom over Catholic despot-ism. *Table Talk:* Luther's observations on human affairs, col-lected by his friends and published in 1566.

50   *stomachers:* ornamental chest coverings worn by women under the lacing of the bodice.

meadow-sweet: a white-flowered plant.

51   *Hessen:* Hesse.

droschka: low four-wheeled open carriage.

52   *Pennsylvania Duitsch:* people living mostly in eastern Pennsyl-vania who retain the traditions of their eighteenth-century German ancestors.

trinkgeld: gratuity.

firebacks: decorated cast-iron plates in the backs of open fire-places.

the Reformer: Martin Luther (1483–1546), biblical scholar and founder of the Reformation in Germany. His doctrine of justification by faith rather than works led to the rise of the Protestant Church.

53 *the Protest*: the Articles of Marburg enunciated fundamental principles common to the Lutheran and Reformed Churches. In 1910 Ford took Violet Hunt to the Schloss and showed her the document.

Bucer ... Zwingli: Martin Bucer (1491–1551), German Protestant reformer who mediated differences between the adherents of Luther and Zwingli. Huldrych Zwingli (1484–1531), important Swiss religious reformer who had doctrinal differences with Luther.

57 *"thank'ee-marms"*: holes or bumps in the road that cause travellers to bounce up and down.

Free City: three cities, Bremen, Hamburg, and Lübeck, were sovereign states within the German Empire.

Spa: town in north-east Belgium famous for its mineral springs, reputedly the oldest in Europe.

60 *Kursaal*: public building at a German health resort, provided for the use of visitors.

61 *Chitral*: state in the extreme north-west of colonial India and site of a British outpost.

65 *Linlithgowshire*: county in south-east Scotland.

pipped: annoyed.

66 *Circe*: sorceress in Greek mythology who turned men into animals.

67 *General Trochu*: (1815–96) governor of Paris who failed to keep the Prussian army from conquering the city during the Franco-Prussian War.

70 *Scarlet Woman*: according to Protestant controversialists, the Catholic Church.

Friends' Meeting House in Arch Street: the oldest Quaker meeting house still in use in Philadelphia, and the largest in the world.

71 *Nonconformist*: member of a Protestant sect dissenting from the Anglican Church.

72 *degraded*: lowered in rank.

79 *pellitory*: low bushy plant, growing upon or at the foot of walls.

82 "*Requiem ... aeternam erit*": Dowell wrongly inserts 'per', and deliberately stops before the last word, 'justus'. The complete translation is: 'Eternal rest give to them, O Lord; and let perpetual light shine upon them. The just shall be in everlasting remembrance.' From the mass for the dead.

83 *northern light*: aurora borealis, a luminous atmospheric phenomenon best seen in Arctic regions.

86 *Reiseverkehrsbureau*: tourist office.

87 *Schreibzimmer*: writing room.

93 *Rialto*: Renaissance bridge over the Grand Canal in Venice.

Strathpeffer: Scottish village and spa whose sulphurous springs attracted sufferers from anaemia, rheumatism, etc.

Ledbury: Herefordshire market town.

95 *General Braddock*: Edward Braddock (1695–1755), unsuccessful British commander in North America in the early stages of the French and Indian War (1755–63).

96 "*Pocahontas*": named for American Indian princess (1595–1617), who died on a visit to England. Ford and his wife returned to England from New York in 1906 aboard the *Minnetonka*, named for the home of the mythical Indian princess Minnehaha.

97 *Rye Station*: reference to Rye, a residential suburb of New York City, with its trolley-cars and commuter trains.

101 *Sandy Hook*: a bay and narrow peninsula in New Jersey passed by ships on their way out to sea.

103 *cinque cento*: sixteenth century.

106 *Hoboken*: port city in north-eastern New Jersey on the Hudson river, facing Manhattan.

110 *D.S.O.*: Distinguished Service Order, awarded to officers for meritorious service in war, but not necessarily in the enemy's presence.

111 *V.C.*: Victoria Cross, awarded to any member of the British

armed forces for a signal act of valour performed in the presence of the enemy.

Lohengrin: hero of German legend who comes to the aid of a lady in distress but leaves her when she breaks her promise never to ask his origins.

Chevalier Bayard: Pierre Terrail (1473–1524), French soldier known to his contemporaries as 'the fearless and blameless knight'.

112 *the Cid*: popular name of Rodrigo, Dias de Bivar (1043–99), Spanish military leader and national hero.

124 *au mieux*: on excellent terms, intimate.

127 *prussic acid*: the solution in water of hydrocyanic acid, an extremely poisonous volatile liquid.

128 *"Zum Befehl, Durchlaucht"*: 'very good, Serene Highness'.

130 *Rakocsy march*: by Hungarian composer Franz Liszt (1811–86).

140 *Bowery*: neighbourhood in lower Manhattan, known as a refuge for drunks and derelicts.

141 *affaissement*: collapse.

146 *Mænad*: nymph attendant on the Greek god Dionysus.

Corpus Christi: Roman Catholic festival in honour of the Eucharist.

Roehampton: socially select girls' public school.

saturnalia: scene of wild revelry. In his book on Provence, Ford tells about convent schools in Tarascon where such celebrations were permitted.

149 *Fort William*: town in western Scotland.

Forest: the New Forest.

156 *jalousies*: blinds or shutters with adjustable horizontal slats.

guy: one who is odd in appearance or dress.

old Mother Sideacher: perhaps from a game involving Old Mother Witch. (Witches may be like elves, who traditionally shoot arrows into people's sides causing stitches.)

159 *chaise*: light open carriage.

espaliers: fruit trees or plants trained to grow flat against a building or support.

fives: a game in which a ball is struck by the hand against the front wall of a three-sided court.

161 *Sandhurst*: Royal Military College where cadets train to become regular army officers.

Froissart: Jean Froissart (?1333–1400), Flemish historian whose *Chronicles* are the classic history of feudal France, Britain, and Spain from 1325 to 1400.

Lord's: Britain's foremost cricket ground, in St John's Wood, London.

172 *Romanist*: disparaging term for Roman Catholic.

180 *big bank failure of 1907*: the rich man's panic of October 1907; preceded by speculative excesses and followed by many bank failures.

183 *Dreyfus*: Franco-Jewish officer wrongly accused and convicted of treason in 1894; most famous trial in modern French history.

187 *give her the keys of the street*: throw her out.

189 *Town*: London.

190 *Eau de Melisse*: medicinal herbal tea.

192 *fireships*: ships carrying combustibles among the enemy's ships to set them on fire.

193 *menus plaisirs*: little luxuries.

194 *jointure*: an estate settled on a wife.

"*blued*": squandered.

196 *Simla*: town in Punjab, India; under colonial rule, it was the summer home of the viceroy and the social centre of the British population.

198 *brevet*: military commission giving an officer nominally higher rank than that for which he is paid.

South African War: also called the Boer War, 1899–1902. War between Great Britain and the two Boer Republics, the Transvaal and the Orange Free State; the most expensive war for Britain between the Napoleonic Wars and the Great War.

199 *veldt*: South African grassland.

spruit: small, often dry, tributary stream in South Africa.

203 *punkah*: Anglo-Indian term for a large hanging fan.

ex's: expenses.

205 *pest-house*: hospital for people with contagious diseases.

sent in his papers: resigned his military commission.

208 *maundering*: doting.

215 *lâcher prise*: let go.

216 *ad majorem Dei gloriam*: for the greater glory of God. Official motto of the Society of Jesus (Jesuits).

236 *Zoffany ... Zucchero*: John Zoffany (1733–1810), British portrait painter and founding member of the Royal Academy. Frederigo Zucchero (1543–1609), Italian painter. In 1576 he was in England and painted a portrait of Elizabeth I. Many other English portraits once attributed to him are now ascribed to others.

dog-cart: light two-wheeled carriage.

239 *stake and binder hedge*: a dead hedge held in by stakes as an obstacle for horses to jump over, especially in fox hunting.

251 *Christchurch*: Hampshire seaside town.

Ringwood: ancient town on the border of the New Forest.

257 *Princess Badrulbadour*: the beloved of the hero of the Arabian Nights tale of Aladdin and the wonderful lamp.

The only true plant found: from 'To the Willow-Tree', by Robert Herrick (1591–1674).

259 *Deborah*: Dowell is mistaken here. The biblical Deborah was not a handmaiden at all, but a Hebrew judge who led the Israelites to victory over their Canaanite oppressors.

hagiology: literature that treats of the lives of the saints.

260 *platonic*: theoretical.

261 *accesses*: fits.

Domine, nunc dimittis ... : Luke 2: 29. Used in evening prayer.

269 *Crau*: generally arid plain in the south of France.

Credo in unum Deum Omnipotentem: Nancy omits the word 'Patrem' after Deum. 'I believe in one God, the Father Almighty.' From the Apostles' Creed.

271 *Kandy*: commercial centre in central Ceylon.

276 *Buda-Pesth*: Budapest, city on the River Danube and capital of the kingdom of Hungary.

285 *poco-curantism*: indifference.

288 *the peace of God which passes all understanding*: Phil. 4: 7.

289 "*Thou hast conquered, O pale Galilean*": from 'Hymn to Proserpine', (line 25), by Algernon Charles Swinburne (1837–1909), Pre-Raphaelite poet and friend of Ford's grandfather, Ford Madox Brown.

290 *Tartarus*: in Greek mythology, the deepest part of Hades; the place of punishment for the wicked.

"*Shuttlecocks!*": persons bandied about by external forces; refers to the piece of cork fitted with a crown of feathers and used in the game of battledore and shuttlecock. In his *Henry James* (1914), Ford notes appreciatively James's application of the term to the young heroine of his novel *What Maisie Knew*.

293 *loose-box*: stall in which a horse can move about freely.

territorials: local volunteer army reserve troops.